# Not To Us

# Also By Katherine Clare Owen

## *Seeing Julia*

# Not To Us

*~A Novel~*

## Katherine Clare Owen

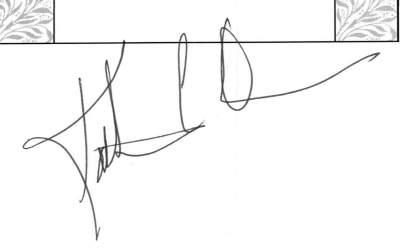

*The Writing Works Group*
Visit our website: www.thewritingworksgroup.com

Book Jacket Design by: *The Writing Works Group*
Photo image: Yuri Arcurs Aarhus, Denmark #47034

Book Design by *The Writing Works Group*
Special Font: Wallflowers & Alana Pro by Laura Worthington
Text Fonts: Adobe Garamond Pro, AR Decode, Palatino Linotype

Printed in the United States of America

*To Michael, my one and only wish.*

# ❦ Not To Us ❦

# CHAPTER ONE

## Surreal Things

There are all kinds of ways for a relationship to be tested, even broken, some, irrevocably; it's the endings we're unprepared for. My life has become a roller coaster ride mixed with equal amounts of pure joy and exposed fear; and, sometimes, this unfathomable incredulity. This arrives in spurts, like adrenalin or injected heroin; well, how I imagine injected heroin would feel. That's when I consider that change—change, and its inevitably—is coming. And, I can't stop it. Then, the incredulity comes again. Is this really happening to me? Yes. Incredulity arrives unannounced and jump-starts my failing broken self.

Up until now, I've had the audacity to consider my life perfection. I married my college sweetheart, Bobby Bradford. I've borne three gorgeous kids with him. I live in a grand house on Bainbridge Island and indulge in an editorial career for a successful New York publisher. Respected, beloved, that's me. Everything in my life rang true and perfect, until the day at the Four Seasons, three weeks ago. After that day, I look at what I once thought of as my perfect life and discover the foundation is literally breaking down, disintegrating all around me with each passing day.

I'm watching the B-action movie of my life. I'm the damsel in distress caught onboard the runaway amusement park ride careening out of control, going faster and faster. I can't control the action any more than I can write the script. Let alone, direct it.

And, I'm the heroine already slated for trouble. *Or worse.*

It's been three weeks of bad movie scenes—my life careening out of control in absolute silence. I don't say anything. I don't react to what I know to be true. I just go through the motions with my ever-predictable life script, fighting the ever-growing panic, and acknowledge I'm going to have to do something to save myself. Soon.

*Besieged.* I sit in the office chair opposite of Dr. Michael Shaw, anticipating a reprieve from more bad news. I've had enough bad news for a lifetime already in just the past three weeks. I play at normal in the starring role as Ellen Kay Bradford—the one I've played for over eighteen years.

I'm giving Michael one of my winning, former-University-of-Washington-cheerleader smiles and watch its predictable impact play across his golden features with his captivating return smile.

We banter pleasantries back and forth in his medical office for the first five minutes about the kids, Robert, Carrie, what the plans might be for Thanksgiving and Christmas and back to the kids again. They're fine. Great. Fine. Great.

Finally, he takes a deep breath and closes his eyes for a brief moment and then opens them again and just looks at me. "The biopsy shows malignant cells. You have cancer, Ellie," he says in this let's-look-at-the-bright-side, manly voice, though I hear it tremble. "Stage two, aggressive, treatable, but we need to move fast." His words cascade down on top of me like unexpected rainfall. I actually start to shake as his diagnosis begins to resonate with the working parts of my brain. *This isn't happening.* This can't be happening. I try to form my brightest smile, but I can't make my face work.

This isn't happening. *Not to us.*

I'm getting my bad news mixed up. I'm not making any sense. I'm just sitting here, looking at him, trying to find some sort of silver lining in all of this. This unravelling of my life. This fucking roller coaster ride. This god-damn ride I want to get off of now. God damn it. I sit silent. Searching for perfect control, I finally form a smile for him. I'm waiting, waiting for the punch line.

"This is a joke; right? You just didn't tell me I have cancer, because, frankly, if we're being honest, Michael." My voice wavers. I try to smile again, but can't quite make it work. "I've got enough shit going on right now."

"No."

I can't find any solace in his tone. I shift in my chair and just look at him. We've known each other for almost twenty years, since the days at the University of Washington when all four of us had been sophomores in college. I've seen him naked a half dozen times, in those innocent moments, when we had all gone camping together, drank too much, and let strip poker go a little too far. He is my best friend Carrie's husband. He is best friends with my husband, Robert. My friend even.

And, yet, in this moment, all I can think of is that there is worse news than this—worse news that I will eventually have to tell *him*. My resolve gives way. My eyes betray me first and fill with tears, not for myself, but for Michael.

"Ellie, it's going to be okay," he says, misinterpreting my tears.

"Not really," I say. *Breathe.* "There are worse things going on."

His handsome face immediately changes to anguish. *He knows.*

"When did you find out?" Michael asks in a distant voice.

"Three weeks ago." I clasp my hands together. "You?"

"Three months ago." He gives me a wry smile as he gets up from his chair, promising to be right back. "Come on, Ellie," he says when he returns. "Let's get out of here."

~ঞ্জ~

Sitting in Michael's car, an ostentatious, black Lexus SUV, ensconced in the riches of onyx leather, all my senses are quietly being assaulted by the smell of his cologne. I covertly glance over at him. Even in profile, he is handsome, *always has been* goes the errant thought in my head. It's too bad I married Robert Bradford; Michael Shaw would have been better for me.

"Where are we going?"

"I haven't thought that far, yet," he says with a flash of his white smile.

Again, I feel this attraction for him. What the hell is wrong with me? This man is my husband's best friend. He is my best friend's husband. He is the godfather to my sixteen-year-old son. And now, he is my surgeon. It's apparent on this rainy day in October that, perhaps, I should have gotten a different surgeon, a different opinion. I certainly didn't like what this doctor, this friend of mine, had to say, but Dr. Michael Shaw is the best. And, Carrie had insisted.

*Carrie.* I love Carrie. She's been my best friend, since our freshman year in college. It's hard to believe that she and Robert have become involved. I wrestle with all of these competing thoughts, while sitting in Michael's car, consciously acknowledging that I like his cologne and his profile. Maybe, Robert and Carrie's liaison was as simple and innocent as this. Maybe, one day, Robert told Carrie that she had cancer and their love affair had started on such a simple premise.

Cancer. I have cancer. No, that's where the similarities between Carrie and me end. I have cancer; she doesn't. I'm crying, again. Michael reaches over and takes my hand in his.

"Ellie, it's going to be okay," he says.

The gentleness in his voice is my undoing and I slide across the seat to be next to him. "Really, Dr. Shaw? You think so?"

I give him a weepy smile. I should be devastated right now, but there is this overwhelming feeling of longing at Michael's touch. I should be scared out of my mind, but Michael makes me feel wanted, safe.

An hour later, I stand looking out at a view of Lake Washington from the Woodmark Hotel at Carillon Point. Somehow, I know that Michael's logic follows that being on *the Eastside* is far enough away from the doings of downtown Seattle and Bainbridge Island and our intertwined lives there. It seems risky to me, but I am too out of sorts to question his reasoning beyond a studied stare out the window, waiting for Robert or Carrie to suddenly come into my view, floating somehow on the white caps of this giant blue lake and accuse us. We haven't done anything, but I'm prepared to accept my fate as a sinner this day.

Room service delivers the food and drink Michael ordered: a bottle of champagne, strawberries, a pot of coffee, a pot of tea, two slices of cheesecake and two orders of French fries and gourmet burgers. I lift the lid on one of the burgers and give Michael a quizzical glance. He shrugs. "I didn't know what you would be in the mood for, but I do know what you like." He smiles at me then, in that hesitant, shy boy way of his.

I take a knife and delicately cut the burger in half and take a tentative bite from one. He watches me with studied fascination and I grin back at him.

"It's good." I set the burger back on the china plate, feeling self-conscious as he continues to gaze at me. "How long?"

"They've been going at it since the Grand Canyon trip."

"God. I had no idea. I hated that trip."

"Me, too." He has this half smile and shakes his head. I look at him, numb with disbelief and uncertainty. "Carrie and I had been fighting about going on that trip for weeks and then, when we got there…well, I should have seen it, what was happening, but I just couldn't make myself look at what was really going on between them." He gives me this sly smile as he picks up the other half of the burger and takes a bite.

The Grand Canyon trip had been Carrie's idea. Robert was keen to take our kids and Carrie was keen to take Elaina. I was keen to do none of it. There was nothing about the Grand Canyon trip that had appealed to me. I wanted to go to the beach, but Robert and Carrie sided together against the protests of Michael and me and we ended up going to the Grand Canyon and staying on a houseboat at Lake Powell instead of going to San Diego and the beach. It rained much of the time—some unusual weather that no one could have predicted. We'd spent the majority of our time inside; complaining about the rain since we lived on the outskirts of Seattle. Rain is a standard event eight months out of the year here. Only Robert and Carrie had found the fun on that trip and to learn now from Michael what that fun had entailed just crushes me.

I can't breathe. I stand up and go back over to the window gasping for breath. I look intently out the window at the white caps of the lake and try to find the equilibrium in my life.

"Are you all right?" Michael asks, as he comes up beside me.

"No," I say. "I'm fucking dying and my husband is fucking around with your wife."

"You're not dying," Michael says with a sigh. "I won't let that happen. The other part is true and I'm afraid there's not much I've been able to do about it."

He puts his arm around me and I find myself turning into him. It has been a long time since Robert has held me this way, longer than the fourteen months since the Grand Canyon trip the summer before last. Michael's arms feel different—warmer, safer still. I breathe in his masculine scent.

For a moment, I try to forget we're both married. I lose myself being in his arms and pretend I don't have cancer.

The kiss between us plunders away almost twenty years of time. We're sophomores, again, in that moment, kissing each other for the first time. I am Ellie Miles, again, the UW cheerleader and Michael Shaw is the Huskies' star wide receiver. Robert Bradford and Carrie Weathers are strangely absent from this apparition. This kiss obliterates the reality that we have been in each other's weddings; married our college sweethearts; that he was at the christening of each of my three children; that I was in the delivery room with him and Carrie when their daughter Elaina was born. All of that is lost, when we kiss each other. It's as if twenty years of shared memories between families and friends never happened.

He carries me to the bed and begins to undress me. And, I let him. I'm heartbroken by what Robert and Carrie have done and I know that Michael is, too, and yet, here we are, embarking down the same path and I can't stop it from happening because I want it to, have wanted it, *wanted him*, for longer than I can remember.

"Michael," I say now. *Why do I always have to destroy the moment?*

"Ellie," He says my name with reverence.

"Michael...I...have cancer." The shock of this news overwhelms me and I cling to him, now, willing it to not be true.

"I know, Ellie, and I'm going to save you."

Michael kisses me again. Some hold inside of me releases and all I can see is him.

Our shared past disappears. The future seems like this bright light up ahead of us, beckoning us both.

For years, I've watched this man eat cheesecake. His slender surgeon hands delicately grasp the fork and he eats cheesecake one bite at a time. I timed him once. He and Carrie had come over to our house for dinner to celebrate Robert's newly-formed partnership status at the law firm about seven years ago. It worked out to an average bite every two and half minutes. It took him thirty-seven minutes to take the last bite of his cheesecake that night. I share this story now, as we lie in each other's arms with the sun sliding towards the horizon.

"You watched me eat cheesecake?" Michael asks.

"I love the way you eat cheesecake."

He leans over and takes a bite and then feeds me one. "This changes everything, you know," he says.

"Does it?"

"Ellie, I want to be with you. I'm leaving Carrie; I've already secured an apartment downtown."

"Why didn't we go there today?" Insecurity takes a firm hold.

"I didn't want this to look like a planned seduction." He grins above me now.

"It wasn't planned?" I ask, trying to be nonchalant, as if, committing infidelity is something I do every day. A flash of Robert and Carrie together comes to mind, causing me to shake.

"I didn't know how up to playing around you would be," he says slowly. "I had to deliver the news that you have cancer. I'm referring you to another surgeon, now that we're now involved."

"Is that so? Are we just playing around?" My voice trembles.

Michael pins me beneath him. "Ellie, I'm right here. I'm not going anywhere. I've wanted this…*you*…for a long time."

"So, why now?" I search his face for answers; guilt takes over.

"Because, now, you need someone more than ever. Someone who loves you more," he says.

I'm sitting in my own silver Mercedes SUV waiting for my two sons, Nicholas and Mathew, feeling the after effects of sex with another man other than my husband and the news that I have breast cancer—all in the same day. *Can things get any more surreal?* My cell phone rings. *It's Carrie.* Yes. They can get even more surreal.

"Hey," I answer.

"Hey, Ells. How are you?" Carrie's voice sounds guarded and distant. Something I had begun to notice in the last three weeks, now, that I was in the loop on her affair with Robert. "I'm good." I glance at myself in the rearview mirror and see myself smiling.

How is this possible between breast cancer and what I now know to be true about Robert and Carrie? I think of Michael. I've missed something Carrie has said.

"I've got to go." I end the call as Carrie's talking in mid-sentence. She calls me back and I power my cell phone off. I am all powerful now and laugh out loud in the car's waiting silence.

My favorite time of the evening is here. Dinner is over—a somewhat harried affair, since I live with mostly boys ages thirty-eight, sixteen, and thirteen and only one five-year-old girl. As the guys talk sports, I am fast becoming ignored. We are in the beginning of basketball season and my adorable eldest son, Nicholas, a replica of his father with dark wavy brown hair and grey eyes, is playing on the junior varsity high school basketball team.

Bainbridge Island is a small community. Elaina Shaw, Carrie and Michael's daughter, is a junior in high school just like my son. I am aware that Nicholas has developed something beyond friendship with Michael and Carrie's daughter. I am not supposed to be aware of it, but I, most definitely, am. I watch Nick as he slyly takes his cell phone off the charger and heads to his room, knowing he's intent on calling Elaina. I smile, as he moves past me with this innocent, nonchalant look, but I am not fooled.

Mathew lags behind. He vies for dad's attention, while Robert moves away from him with concentrated determination toward his home office, calling out that he needs to finish up a brief in preparation for his day in court tomorrow. At the dining room table, my five-year-old, Emily, is busy drawing a picture of a cat. She looks up and gives me an inquisitive look, then goes back to her artwork. I clear the rest of the table and load the dishwasher humming to myself, enjoying the façade of normalcy. I'm taking it all in, as if to etch it into my memory. In my fantasy of how things will be, I envision the four of them functioning just fine without me.

We could easily put the additional household chores that I perform each day on to Mrs. Sanchez, increase her responsibilities along with her salary. I am easily replaced. I determine all of this in a swift moment of clarity, as I make subtle observations of my little family tonight.

Then, more troubling thoughts flash at me. I think of Carrie and Robert and of Carrie being a stepmother to *my children*. Neither of these thoughts put me into a good place. I begin to lose it. The earlier tranquility dissolves and panic sets in. *I have cancer. I'm scared. I'm alone. I'm replaceable.*

My cell phone rings. It's Michael.

"I'm on my way home. I wanted to make sure you're okay. Have you told him?"

"No."

"You should." I hear the hesitation in Michael's voice. It makes me uneasy. "Ellie, I feel bad about earlier. We should have waited."

"Why?" I sound desperate.

Of course, Michael doesn't know what I've been going through tonight, seeing my home life go on without me, if breast cancer takes my life.

"It's not that I wanted to wait, it's just that you have so much deal with right now. It's not fair for me to…tell you…to show you how I feel."

"How do you *feel?*"

"I feel like I'm finally with the love of my life," he says gently.

I'm taken aback by what he's said. I wipe away the tears gathering at my lashes. "Michael, I…"

Mathew comes into the kitchen. He gives me a questioning

look. "Who are you talking to, Mom? Are you *crying?*"

"Can't talk right now," I say with hesitation. "But I did *hear* what you said and I…"

"Can't talk right now," Michael echoes.

"Right." I sigh. "Mathew's here. I should go."

"I'll call you tomorrow, during the day around 11:00 or so. I've got a call into Josh Liston. He's the best surgeon, besides me," Michael says with a hesitant laugh. "Ellie, you're not alone in this. I'm right here."

"I know."

"You're not going to tell him; are you?"

"Not tonight. I've got to go. Thanks…thanks for calling me."

"Ellie…I have more to say," Michael says.

"Me, too." I end the call, lock the phone, and look over at my middle child. This combination of joy over Michael, fear over cancer, and misery over Robert and Carrie takes over. *How can I feel all of these emotions at the same time?*

"Mom, are you okay?" I see the sudden look of concern in Mathew's eyes. He is the sweetest child, even now, when he pulls away from me more all the time.

"I'm fine, honey. Everything's fine. Do you want some ice cream?" I open the freezer door and hide behind Viking's finest and wipe my eyes again.

"I'm not a baby anymore, Mom. Something's wrong. Why won't you tell me?"

"There's nothing wrong, Mathew. Everything's fine." I close the freezer door and give him a ready smile. I'm just making it up as I go at this point.

"That's what you always say. Is it because of Carrie? Is that it? There's something going on between Dad and Carrie isn't there?"

He is an exact replica of me with blonde hair and intense blue eyes. Right now, his nose is crinkled at the bridge as he stares at me. I see disappointment in his features, too, and hold my breath as I gaze at him. How does he know these things? How could he have seen this, when I didn't even see what was going on?

"What do you mean?" I ask him, carefully, now.

"It's nothing." His face becomes indifferent.

Robert has taught him so well. My son is well on his way to treating all women with this…apathy, me included. I feel my failure of him and start to cry.

"I know what's going on with your father and Carrie," I say through my tears. I see the surprised look come across Mathew's face as I cross the kitchen and stalk towards Robert's office, dabbing at my face as I go. Mathew follows me; I start to check myself and wonder if this is the best way to approach this, but I'm done pretending that everything is okay.

"I need to talk to you," I say to Robert.

"Babe, I've got to get this brief done." Robert barely glances up from his laptop to look at me. I stare at him in frustration.

"Bobby, it's important," I say with an edge to my voice.

"Ellie, I've got to get this brief done."

"Right." I look at my husband for a full minute and take in his handsome face. His dark brown hair and steel-grey eyes have always been what I love best about him, but as he looks away from me, I feel this sudden hatred for him that I have never felt before. Rage builds inside of me, too. Instead of saying anything more, I just turn and race out of the room up the stairs.

"Mom!" Mathew yells after me. I turn at the top of the stairs and look at my son. "Are you okay?" He climbs the stairs two at a time and comes to stand next to me.

"I'm fine." I pull him into my arms even though he is now taller than me by a good three inches and hug him tight. "I love you Mathew. Never forget that." Mathew hesitates as if he has more to say, but he goes to his room telling me he has homework to do.

14

Robert noisily climbs the stairs and enters our master bedroom. It's after eleven and I lie awake in the dark. He takes his time in the bathroom and eventually slides into bed next to me.

Hot tears slide down my face in the darkness. When did the love between us die? When did we become complete strangers? We started out so well together and now it's all gone. The loss of us washes over me in fresh waves of sorrow and regret. I'm sure Robert felt the loss of us, too, at some point, although he has Carrie now. He's moved on and probably doesn't even miss us. Maybe, he doesn't even see us, anymore. My bitterness is sudden and profound. And, I hold my breath to keep from crying out.

"What did you want to talk to me about?" Robert asks now, reaching out to me.

I let my breath out slowly. "It's not important."

"I'm sorry, Ells…it's been hard lately. There's a lot of pressure at work…to keep the billings up. You know how it is." I have heard this excuse so many times I give him the expected answer. He reaches for me, again, but I turn away from him. "Come on, Ellie."

If I didn't know what I know about him and Carrie and if I hadn't been with Michael earlier in the day, I would give in. Tonight, I pull away from him. Ten seconds later, I slide out of bed and head to the guest room and lock the door behind me.

"Ellie!" Robert calls out in anger on the other side of the door. "You *can't* be serious."

At his noisy reaction, I jerk open the door and pull him inside and shut it. My own fury surges. "Let me tell you how *serious* I am, Bobby. I know about Carrie, you son of a bitch! *I know.* I saw you together three weeks ago at the Four Seasons. *I know.* Okay? Please stop treating me like some fool that doesn't have a clue as to what's going on."

Robert sinks into the chair by the bed. He puts his head in his hands. "I'm sorry," he says in a weary voice.

"Since the Grand Canyon trip? Was I that bad of a wife for you, Bobby? Was it so hard for you to love me? Then, it had be *Carrie*?"

"It just happened."

"Yeah, it's so easy. It just *happens*." I think of Michael and what we did this afternoon. Guilt overtakes me. I think of my marriage to Bobby—eighteen years of life together. Bobby and me. All gone, just like that.

"I'll end it. I'll end it, now. I'll tell her it's over. I don't want to lose you, Ellie."

I look at him with a twisted smile and my eyes fill with tears. "Don't end it. I have breast cancer. Who knows how this will all turn out?" I turn away from him and go back to our master bedroom and crawl into bed. He comes in a few minutes later and slides in next to me and presses his body to mine. At first, I can't figure out what the sound is—this muffled, broken sound—until I realize it's Bobby, crying. I turn to him in surprise. "What's wrong?"

"I…don't…want…to…lose…you…Ellie."

I take him in my arms and hold him to my chest as he sobs, unsure of what else I can do. I stroke his face and tell him over and over that everything is going to be okay. I've always been able to lie really well; and, sometimes, even I believe the things I say.

# CHAPTER TWO

## Reaching Back

I have to convince Robert to act normal. Be normal for the kids the next morning I tell him. I make breakfast, as I always do, going through a dozen eggs, having mastered the art of scrambled eggs, cooked just so and sprinkled with four different blends of shredded cheese. I serve them up on three plates and scrape the remaining in the pan on a saucer. I tend to eat at the counter these smaller portions that Robert used to tease me about, birdlike, he'd say. Now, he doesn't tease me anymore. I stop for a moment and wonder when that changed, then fill three glasses with orange juice and set them on the table.

The boys and Emily race into the kitchen with only fifteen minutes left before they have to be out at the end of our long drive for the school bus and Emily's carpool ride. I promise to pick them up after school at the designated time of 4:30 P.M. after basketball practice, while Emily is playing at a friend's house.

Robert comes in looking exhausted and weary in his navy blue Armani suit. His hair is not quite right and I walk over and pat a few wayward strands back into place. He reaches for me and buries his head into my neck. The kids' chatter suddenly stops at this display of affection for me from their father. I whisper to Robert to act normal, once again, and move away from him. Robert wants to stay home with me and I'm insistent that he go to the office.

"I want to be with you," he has said repeatedly this morning.

I tell him "No, I have work to do." This is true. I have been putting off an editing job for the publisher that I work for remotely out of New York. I am a week behind on the promised manuscript and I have yet to put my blue pencil to in any form.

Mine is a nice-to-do job. At least, that is what Robert has always said. Except for today, when he incessantly whines about staying home with me and continues to harp on me for even thinking about working today since so much has happened.

He is undone, overwrought. I am sympathetic, but firm. On this day, he reminds me of how he used to be before we had kids, centered on me, not himself. Those were heady days, those two years before we embarked down the road of parenthood. I had just graduated from the University of Washington and landed my first editorial job and was also trying to write full time. On some days, when Robert was still in law school, he would skip class and we would spend all day at the house in each other's arms.

I could see that this was what he wanted to do today. For a moment, I wish that the thing with Carrie had never happened. For a single moment, I want to go back in time and start over.

We discovered this thing about our marriage ten years ago. As is often true with life, the patterns emerge. Friends marry, have children or don't, get divorced or don't…all this angst and turmoil seemed to take place at about the ten-year mark with all of our friends. Our boys were six and three and it seemed everyone we knew was going through a divorce with the exception of us and Michael and Carrie Shaw with their then six-year-old daughter, Elaina.

"Not to us," we'd said.

We were so blissfully happy, then. I felt guilty that our lives were so complete. We watched the split between so many of our friends and felt this instant trepidation. It was as if the failing of a relation-ship were a contagion, flu or a cold.

"Not to us," Robert said. He'd given me a secret smile and stared at me, longingly, over the heads of our two children, as they played on the family room floor. It seemed we had discovered the magic for keeping the relationship alive, to keep it going. I was unsure what it was, but I knew it had to be some kind of unexplainable thing.

"Not to us," I said back to him.

But, I do wonder, now. My capability for optimism is less sure then Robert's. My own parent's divorce was proof of that. Of course, they waited until I was eighteen before splitting up. As if, somehow at eighteen instead of, say, fifteen, it made some sort of difference and left a dissimilar impression entirely. It didn't.

I had vowed to be unlike my mother, yet, here I am trudging down the same path. Infidelity. Is it so easy? I look over at Robert and try to understand this. I think of Michael and our liaison just twenty hours ago. Yes, infidelity is so easy; it seems.

Emily and the boys race down the long drive to their respective rides to school bus. I watch from the window feeling the vague touch of their hasty kisses on my face, where they just kissed me right before they fled down the drive. Robert stands next to me and stares out the window.

"Ellie," he says. I turn to look at him. "I'm so sorry. I love you so much." His grey eyes fill with tears. I touch his face and wipe away the tears.

"Bobby," I say. "I just don't know if we can make this work."

This grown man before me cries harder. He is broken on so many levels; I don't know what to do for him. I should be angry with this man. He has broken my heart and yet, I find myself in his arms holding him, comforting him, assuring him that everything will be okay. *I have no proof of this! What am I saying? Why am I saying it?*

Robert calls the office in a subdued tone and tells his assistant he won't be in today. There go my plans for escaping. In my mind, I have already packed my suitcase and left the home that we have built here and lived in the last sixteen years. Now, Robert looks at me and follows me from room to room. I'm never going to get any work done. His cell phone rings and I watch Carrie's familiar number come up.

"Answer it," I say.

He shakes his head and powers off the phone. "No."

I shrug and go upstairs to each of the children's rooms, retrieving forgotten clothing off their floors. Robert follows behind me back down the stairs with an amazed look on his face, as he watches me fill the washer with the measured amounts of liquid detergent and fabric softener. I turn around and he pulls me to him and kisses me tenderly.

"I love you so much, Ellie." I haven't heard him say that in months, not even on our anniversary in July. I look at him and search his face looking for some sign of the man that I have always loved. His eyes are bloodshot and his face is streaked with old tears. I touch his face and then I kiss him and close my eyes. His lips remind me of the man that he has always been—my Bobby Bradford. We are back in time, in college, when our love was fresh and new and wonderful. For a minute, in this laundry room, it feels the same. He holds me now and I feel him wanting me. I feel this overpowering desire. I am all powerful. My body of its own volition heads up the stairs with this man. We are undressing one another in a frenzy and barely make it to the bed as we crave each other.

Why hasn't it been like this for so many years? I wonder how often he has been with Carrie and I ask him this now in the throes of our own passion. He stops and looks at me, stunned by my question.

"What?" Bobby asks in a wounded voice. His erection withers away. He searches my face while I pull away from him.

I get up and walk into bathroom and start the shower. Why am I the bad guy here? He's the one who cheated. What I did yesterday has now become an aberration of my imagination, although I glance at the clock and begin to anticipate Michael's call.

*I have cancer. I can do whatever the hell I want.*

You should go to work I tell him through the streaking wetness of the glass shower door. He wipes himself off and proceeds to get dressed. Ten minutes later, I hear the front door slam, while I dress.

Now, we're back to where we've been. I'm sure he has already reached Carrie on his cell phone.

Downstairs, I pour myself another cup of coffee and congratulate myself on further fucking up my life. I'm such a wonder. My self-loathing is at an all-time high. I begin to cry.

My crying is so loud and painful that I do not hear Bobby re-enter the kitchen, until he is standing in front of me with a wilted bouquet of pink Gerber daisies and a price tag on the cellophane indicating the Safeway flower market. He holds two mochas in the other hand. He is dressed in a pair of sweats and a purple University of Washington Huskies football t-shirt.

"These are for you, Ells." He holds out the flowers and I take them from him and sniff their mixed fragrance.

"They're great."

"Why are you crying?" Bobby could always undo me with that tender voice.

"I'm such a bitch."

"Nah, you're great, Ellie. I'm the one who has so much to be sorry for." He sets the coffees down and takes me in his arms. "I'm sorry, Ellie. And, I will make it up to you."

The familiarity of his touch is my final fallback position. I'm powerless. We take the coffees with us upstairs and finish what we started less than an hour before.

Afterwards, I lie in his arms and wish that he still felt like he belonged to me, but all I can see in my mind is Carrie's face. Carrie has always been beautiful and my features are so ordinary in comparison. And, even as Robert traces them with his fingers and kisses my eyelids and my cheekbones and my breasts, I still wish for Carrie's striking looks in every way. I have, in the back of my mind, always questioned why Robert Bradford chose me over Carrie. Why after their first and only date; he chose me. I ask him, now. This time he is ready for my questions about Carrie and for my questions about me.

"Why me?" I ask. How many years had I wondered? *Eighteen.*

"Because you smile like you have a secret," Robert says, now. "When you smile, that is. For some reason, you haven't been smiling and I know now that's what I miss, most of all. So, Ellie, I want to spend the rest of my life seeing you smile and being the reason for it."

He kisses me tenderly and I intertwine my legs with his. This has always felt so right; and yet, I find myself thinking of Michael—his face, his body, his kiss.

I close my eyes and pretend it is yesterday. For a moment, I forget that I have cancer and that everything has changed, including me.

It is a week of next mornings. I have packed and unpacked my suitcase a dozen times. It is never the right time to leave.

Robert and I have made love every day since that first day of reconciliation. Michael has called every day at exactly 11:00 in the morning and I have answered every day, except that first day when I was with Robert when he called. I couldn't reach the cell in time. The truth? I didn't exactly know what I was going to say.

For the last seven mornings, Michael and I have only spoken. Today is a going to be different. We are going to do more than talk on the phone. I am taking the ferry from Bainbridge Island to

Seattle. We have eight hours of uninterrupted time ahead of us at the apartment that he has set up in downtown Seattle just off the waterfront.

This morning as soon as everyone's gone, I duck into the master closet and find my biggest suitcase and start packing up my clothes. Consciously, I've made my decision. I need to leave. I'm not sure why. I'm not sure for how long. I just know that I need to go. That if I don't, I'll completely lose myself in this house, where, no matter where I look, I'm completely alone and changed.

I can no longer pretend to want what Robert and I have had. Maybe, it's the threat of cancer. If I die from cancer, is this the life I would have chosen? If I don't die from cancer, would I still choose this life?

Maybe, it *is* Michael. Whatever *this* is…this unrest within me… this change that has shifted my view of the world, now makes me question everything. *Is this what I want?* That is the first question.

I sweep my make-up off the dresser into an open bag. I throw in perfume, lingerie and bath salts. I empty my side of the medicine cabinet. By the time I'm done, even *I* can sense my absence in this room. I wonder if Robert will, too. Well, based on the last seven days, I am sure that he will, in fact, notice.

Thinking about this dissolves my determination to leave in the first place, so I try not to dwell on that. *When did my life get so complicated?*

I have been to see Dr. Josh Liston and the lumpectomy of my left breast is scheduled for tomorrow. Michael was able to get my case put to the front of the line and Dr. Liston was happy to help out his friend. I know Dr. Liston was confused about my relationship with Michael.

I know that he does wonder where my husband, Robert, is in all of this. I have kept Robert out of the plans regarding my cancer. I'm not sure why. Except that in my way of thinking, somehow, my cancer is responsible for bringing him back to me and that in itself is wreaking havoc on all other aspects of my life. I have put Robert off from asking too many questions about my cancer treatment by telling him that my appointment with Dr. Liston was not for another two weeks. I've told Robert there is little to be concerned about and that we would find out more then. Of course, by then, I would have had the surgery. Since it seemed like a fairly straight-forward procedure, I didn't tell Robert about it.

I have so many secrets and have told so many lies; it's difficult to keep them all straight. I've barely told Michael. I haven't seen him since…since that first day.

Today, after I drive off the ferry, I almost turn the car back towards Bainbridge Island at least six times. What am I doing going to Michael's apartment? What am I thinking getting involved with him at this crucial time of my life? But somehow, Michael seems to be the only one in my life who makes sense, who truly cares about me and loves me, despite cancer. Not because of it, which seems to be Bobby's reasoning. So, what happens to Bobby and me, when I don't have it anymore, huh? I do wonder.

My cell phone rings. Carrie's name flashes on the screen.

"Ellie," she says in a shaken voice when I answer. "I just heard."

"From who?" I ask in sudden irritation.

Robert and I agreed to keep this on the down low for the kids' sake. I know Michael would know better than to say anything to her.

"Well, the office manager, Liz Banner, is from Bainbridge. She called me, wondering why you're seeing Dr. Liston. Why are you doing that? Michael is the best for this kind of thing."

"This kind of thing. You mean *cancer*?"

I really hate it when people talk all around cancer without invoking the word and my tone is impatient and full of derision.

"I'm aware of Michael's extraordinary…surgical skills," I say.

I blush and glimpse my face in the car's rear-view mirror in just thinking of Michael's hands all over my body from that one and only day we were together, more than a week ago. My uncertainty resolves at taking the next exit. Now, I'm determined to get to his apartment as fast as I can.

"Carrie, I'm going to be okay," I say with reassurance. I feel reassured by what I say and I can hear my former best friend crying through the phone taking solace in what I say. The fact is I sense her life falling apart across the phone lines and I feel sorry for her.

"Ells, I love you. You know that."

I *do* know this, which makes it harder still to fathom why this girl that I have known and loved for almost twenty years would royally fuck me over. My anger is instantaneous and I strike out at her now without thinking it through.

"I guess you love Robert more though, right; Carrie? You've been fucking around with him for more than a year, so I guess you made your choice. Live with that, friend, and don't call me anymore."

"Michael left me," she says in a broken voice.

"Yeah, I know that, too."

I hang up the phone and I don't answer when her name flashes across the cell screen, thirty seconds later. Right now, I have both Robert and Michael in my life, apparently, making me their first priority. Carrie, normally, always the winner, seems to have lost this round to me.

I'm glad that I have packed at least a week's worth of clothing in my suitcase. I feel liberated as I pull into the underground garage of Michael's condominium and find him standing there, waiting for me.

*Hello world. I have cancer and it may lead me to the best part of my life.* I smile at Michael as he comes over to me and retrieves my suitcase from the trunk.

"Are you moving in?" I hear wistfulness in his voice.

"I'm not sure. For an hour, for a day, for a week, for a year, for a decade, for eternity. What do you think we should do? How much time do we have?"

"Forever," he says. He kisses me. It feels like I've come home.

"Your wife just called," I say in a nonchalant tone. I follow him on to the elevator with all of my bags.

"She's not having a good day. She'll be served divorce papers within a few hours."

I only nod, although I feel uneasy. "Are you sure?" I ask.

"I'm sure." Michael looks at me with a desire that I have never seen on a man's face before. I am taken aback and it shows in my faltering step as we step off the elevator. "Don't be scared, Ellie. You're all I want—you're all I have ever wanted." He puts his arm around me and we head into his apartment.

I fight the sudden urge to leave and feel this strange foreboding. Now, I'm anxious, as if I'm trying to keep my balance on the unstable earth beneath my feet.

*I've told too many lies. I hold too many secrets. Who can I really trust? Who can trust me when I don't even trust myself?*

# CHAPTER THREE

 *Day 89*

The alarm goes off on the opposite night stand, farthest away from me. It buzzes incessantly. I try unsuccessfully to stretch my body and good arm across the made-up side of the bed to turn it off. Finally, I jump out of the bed and go around and pull the clock radio, plug and all, from the wall in rapid fury.

"Damn you, Robert!" I scream into the empty room.

I look at my haggard self in the mirror. My blonde locks are going every which way. I look like Cinderella on a really bad hair day. My torn t-shirt drapes wearily off my shoulders. Robert's t-shirt—the one I've kept because the scent reminds me of him. Even in this moment, when I should hate him the most, I still seek comfort in the smell of his clothing.

"Damn you," I whisper to the empty bedroom. I wearily crawl back into the bed and pull the covers over my face.

"Momma?" I open my eyes and peek out from my contrived fortress of bed sheets and the duvet at my five-year-old daughter-going-on-twenty, who stands in the doorway. "Momma, you have to wake up and take me to school."

Emily, another blond replica of me, stands with her hands on her hips in a mismatched red and white outfit—a plaid skirt and a polka-dot shirt. The colors were fine, the patterns not so much.

I don't have the heart or strength to tell her this right now. I sigh.

"Mathew and Nicholas are eating breakfast. I'm just checking on you. You do remember that you need to take me to school; right Momma?" She comes over to me and shakes my shoulder as I struggle to keep my eyes open. The bottle of wine that I managed to drink all by myself last night doesn't shake loose of me, now.

"I'm up, Em," I say in a shaky voice.

"No, you're not. You're lying down, Momma. You *need* to get up."

"Send Mattie up. Tell him, I need him to do the lunches today."

"He's already done the lunches, Mother."

I sit up with a quick humph and slide my feet from underneath the warm covers down across the cold carpet in one swift movement. Emily hands me my bathrobe. I put it on and follow her, listless, down the stairs.

My house is in disarray. Everything is out of place. My house reflects myself. I am in disarray. In silence, I curse Robert as I make my way down the stairs and into the kitchen. Mathew is busy trying to fill the coffee maker with ground coffee in the water section.

"Mathew, I got it." I move over to him and brush my lips across his forehead. My thirteen-year-old gives me a wistful smile and I try to smile back, but fail.

"Morning, Mom. I've packed the lunches." My middle child proudly shows me three paper sacks filled with lunch items for himself and his two siblings.

"Thank you, sweetie." I glance over at my sullen, sixteen-year-old son, Nicholas. "Good morning, Nicky."

"Is it?" He looks over at me with barely veiled disdain, taking in my much disheveled appearance. "Exactly, *when* are you going to get it together, Mom? It's been three months."

"Two months, twenty-nine days," I answer. "Tomorrow's the day." There are audible sighs of relief from all three of my children.

I smile over at Nicholas with a smile that I didn't know I could manage. He grins back at me, now. My first-born is still my baby. "Love you, Nicky," I say now.

"Love you too, Ellen Kay Bradford." I laugh at his impertinence—my son, the charmer. He got this from me, not his father, Robert. "I've got a basketball game tonight, Mom, at 4:30 P.M. Will you come?"

I haven't been out socially, well, for eighty-nine days. I can feel my oldest child staring at me, projecting his will on me, waiting for my reply. I resist the urge to stammer an automatic *no*, as I've done for almost three months, now.

"I'll be there," I say, before the word *no* transfers from my brain to my lips. I give him another weary smile and he beams back at me.

"Great, Mom. I'll see you at the game at *4:30* P.M. I made varsity. It's no big deal."

It is, in fact, a big deal. Huge for Nick and I know this. I already start berating myself to keep my promise to him and make this different than the other eighty-nine days that have passed us by, in which, I have miserably failed my children and myself, at every turn.

"Nicky, I'll be there. I...will...be...there." I pull him to me and give him a brief hug, before he awkwardly pulls away from me. Emily is grabbing me at my waist and Mathew hovers nearby. "Shall we go watch your big brother play basketball tonight?"

I receive excited nods from my two younger children and realize how much my mental absence has affected them all. I feel bad. I blame Robert and Carrie. The sudden anguish must appear on my face as all three of my children each come closer to me, as if to hang on to me, in case, I might just fade away.

"I'll be there," I whisper.

The moment ends. The living room clock chimes eight o'clock signaling arrival of the school bus in less than three minutes. The boys grab their backpacks and lunch sacks. Emily and I watch them race up the long driveway to catch the bus. It's just us girls, now, my daughter and me. I openly sigh, while my daughter gives me an intense, appraising stare.

"Were you going to change?" Emily finally asks.

I look down at my open tattered bathrobe, a gift from Robert on our third anniversary, and my Huskies football t-shirt faded to a light purple from too many washings, and a pair of ugly boxer briefs of Robert's and little else.

I had, in too many days to count now, slid into the car in this very outfit. I get the distinct impression from her today that was not going to happen, nor would be acceptable to her.

"I'll change," I say with an edge of defensiveness.

I race up the stairs and clumsily pull on skinny jeans and a white angora sweater, brush my hair and clip it back in a ponytail, and line my lips with plum-shaded gloss. Studying my face in the mirror, I scrutinize the emaciated forlorn woman staring back at me. I start adding a little foundation, blush, eye shadow and mascara. I try to remember the last time that I actually got dressed and put on make-up. I touch my long blonde hair and finger-fix the tendrils on each side into place and spray a little hair spray to keep it there.

I should be glad I have my hair. It seemed like the cancer had taken everything else: my normally attractive looks, the sheen of my hair, my boundless energy, my normally somewhat positive outlook on life, my best friend Carrie, my husband Robert, and even Michael. Oh, I didn't want to think about all of that. Truth be told: Robert and Carrie's actions took most of that stuff away, not the cancer. Michael, well, that was another story. I don't want to think about him today either. I take one final glance in the mirror and start toward the door, only to find Emily standing there, regarding me with the uninhibited enthusiasm only kindergartners possess.

"You look beautiful, Momma," she says, breathless.

How does this child know how to give away such gifts? Tears fill my eyes. I wipe them away, trying to regain my composure. I finally look over at her. "Thanks, Em," I manage to choke out.

I have succeeded in getting the long promised manuscript edited for my boss. I glance at my many blue pencil markings with satisfaction. I stuff it into the Fed Ex envelope and mark the address for my employer in New York City.

I make the unusual foray into town and mail it off. I'm three weeks late in editing this manuscript and I have to hope I still have a job. When I call my office to let them know the tracking number, I have to take in the praise that is given and deflect the questions regarding my health. "Yes the radiation treatments are done. Everything is fine. I'm fine. We just have to wait and see. Yes, I'll have a follow-up in the next few weeks and we will see if there is any more cancer. Yes, I'm great. Just have to wait and see. Robert is fine. I guess. He's fine. He…he's fine. The kids are great. Okay, just send me the next one," I say with manufactured cheerfulness. My energy wanes the longer this conversation goes on. My office does not know about the blow-up of my life just eighty-nine days ago.

I pull into Safeway and practice my automatic responses to the invariable social questions that will come up, as I head into this grocery store where much of the Bainbridge Island community shops. I have not been here for eighty-nine days. I have not been anywhere except my doctor appointments in downtown Seattle and Swedish Hospital for ultrasounds, radiation and consultations. I am put to the test right away with Marjorie Bingham.

"Ellie!" Marjorie exclaims. She pushes past two other shoppers' carts to reach me. "You look fantastic! I can't believe it."

An unwelcome wasp, she's practically vibrating with unchecked fervor as she alights upon me. I haven't said anything, yet. Marjorie is not my favorite person. If I could only choose a few people that

I wanted to see on a desert island where I had a limited choice of friends and companions, Marjorie wouldn't make that list.

Carrie and I used to make fun of Marjorie. Her shallow tendencies had always grated on us both. I think of this now and I'm sad. I really do miss Carrie. Tears threaten to spill over as I try to find the right words to respond to Marjorie Bingham.

"Oh, Ellie. I'm so sorry about everything. It's great to see you."

"I'm doing great. The kids are great. Everyone's great. Cancer's all, but gone. Just doing check-ups, now," I say in a hushed, please-don't-ask-me-any-more-questions voice.

"And you kept your hair," Marjorie gushes. She touches my hair like people do when you are eight months pregnant, when your stomach is sticking out as if there's a basketball under your shirt and people assume your personal space is now theirs and they touch your stomach as if it is art on display. Marjorie fingers my blonde locks this same way. I have to prevent myself from physically stepping back from her, so I don't appear bad-mannered, even though, clearly, she is being impolite by doing this to me. I can feel the tears reform behind my eyes with her invasion. I am just about undone. I move my cart away from her as a form of a subtle goodbye.

"I've got to get on with this. We've eaten pizza every night for the last three months. I'm here for my children." I form a weak smile, move away from her, leaving her standing there with her mouth open, still trying to form her next words for me.

Cancer is hard. There are many things the doctors don't tell you. Such as, after you have a lumpectomy that you can't really raise your arm for weeks at a time, which means vacuuming is an excruciating challenge and makes even getting dressed awkward and somewhat unmanageable. Try doing the housework by yourself during the day, while your children are at school with your one good arm. It takes the majority of the day.

That's wasn't the hard part, though. The hard part was eighty-nine days ago, when Robert moved out after learning that I was involved with Michael. And, Michael, who became uninvolved with me because he learned that I was still sleeping with Robert, because I had cancer and well, it had just happened, but apparently, these reasons were not enough for Michael. I haven't talked to either one of them for eighty-nine days, which explains my current distraught, worn-down state and the general upheaval of my home and existence.

Yeah, cancer's hard, but well, when your whole world comes crashing down in so many different directions, all at once. Cancer is the least of my problems.

Dr. Josh Liston has been great, except for the omission of the minor details of how long my recovery from this little procedure would take. He had recommended *radiation only* because he said the margins looked good and *we* got it all. *We* got it all. *We* did that. As if, I was, somehow, a part of a team. I was grateful for that.

In fairness, I was grateful to Michael for pulling strings to get me in and take care of this so quickly. I was ungrateful to Michael because of his adverse reaction to the whole thing with Robert. I thought he would understand, but he didn't. He said that he didn't want to see me anymore because clearly I didn't know what I wanted.

"Is that so?" I'd asked. "If Carrie hadn't fucked around with my husband, you would have seen your way to me?"

My question took him by surprise. Michael had this troubled look and didn't really answer me.

We were all four of us, a mess. Imagine the loss between just the four of us. We had done *everything* together for eighteen years—weddings, anniversaries, vacations, bowling nights, dinner parties, birthday parties, summer barbecues, even work promotions.

*Everything.*

I lost my husband, my best friend Carrie, and Michael. Michael lost his wife, his best friend Robert, and me. Carrie lost her husband and me, her best friend. Robert lost his best friend Michael and me, if I even counted.

I'm not sure that Robert felt that bad about losing me; once he found out I was involved with Michael. Robert, out of all of us, seems to be doing just fine.

*The rest of us? Well, we're a mess.*

I signed the divorce papers two weeks ago, which is why I've been drinking an entire bottle of wine each night for the last fortnight. You know, to celebrate my newly single status in my unkempt house, with my somnolent children, who just want their mom to mentally return back to the homestead. I believe my children are alarmed and tired out by my ghostly presence. I've done little else, except sleep, drink wine at night, and drive the SUV when one of them tells me where to take them.

I stand in line at the check-out counter, awaiting my turn, and then, absently load the groceries on the conveyor belt. We are out of everything, so I have a lot to buy. I give the clerk my card and she runs it through with an exasperated sigh.

"Declined," she says in a biting tone.

"What?" The conveyor belt stops. The clerk looks over at me, expectant. "Run it, again," I command in a tired voice.

"Declined," she says. Her loud voice carries two check stands over where another four people can hear her. "The total is $198.42. Do you have any cash?" She speaks to me as if I am an imbecile.

Automatically, I dump out my wallet and count out five twenty-dollar bills. I find twenty-two cents in change and hand it all over. I'm standing there, in a frozen state of mind, wishing that I had never gotten out of bed. The tears well up in my eyes and I'm about to tell her that I have *cancer*, which isn't exactly true anymore, but

I am ready to use this excuse with her, to embarrass her into sympathy for me. Without reason, I hate this rude oversized, twenty-something-year-old, who stands before me with her uncombed straggly black hair, pock-marked face, and scornful expression.

"Here," says a too-familiar voice.

My rescuer shoves a crisp one-hundred-dollar bill into the outstretched hand of this Satan of a person. I turn with gratitude and find myself staring into the sympathetic vivid green eyes of my former best friend, Carrie Shaw. The entire community of Bainbridge Island seems poised to hear how I'll react and respond in this crucial moment. I move, willingly, as if in a play and perfectly deliver my lines.

"Thank you."

Wow. It's been almost four months, since I've seen this woman who systematically tore my life apart, worse than cancer ever could have done, and all I can say is *thank you* because I live by decorum and manners and saying *fuck you* openly in a grocery store, especially, Safeway, is just not done.

The impudent Safeway checker packs up my groceries, keys in the cash return on her register. The change gets sent automatically down the change maker machine. I stare at it for a moment and then look over at the cashier.

"Keep it. Save it up for a dermatology visit, hon."

I hear Carrie's familiar laugh from behind me. Blindly, I give my former best friend a tight smile and head out to my car at a frantic pace.

I'm reeling. I have just seen Carrie. I have been assailed by an employee of Safeway. Could my life take any bigger of a turn? I guess I now need to visit the bank and find out what the hell was going on with the bank account. I surely couldn't call Robert. I'm sure Carrie was already on the phone to him reporting my faux pas.

I am thinking all of this as I slowly load up the groceries in the back of my SUV with one hand. I still can barely use my left arm. It has been more than twelve weeks—twelve weeks since the surgery. Dr. Liston has assured me that this is normal. Normal for whom? I want to know.

"Ellie," Carrie calls my name as I struggle with the last bag.

"I'll pay you back," I say, glancing over at her.

She stands next to me, resplendent in a tailored pair of black linen pants that show not one wrinkle and a white silk blouse that enhances her perfect cleavage just so. Her long auburn hair is swept up from her face in a diamond clasp that I recognize and know to be real. Her green eyes sparkle and her make-up is perfect.

Carrie Shaw looks like a million bucks standing there. I dissolve to five and dime status, no better than Monopoly money. I am worth *nothing* and look the part, too.

"You look great," she says. "How are you feeling?"

"I'm great," I say sharply. Carrie gives me the once-over. I lift my head in defiance at her scrutiny. "All cured. No side effects," I say wryly. "Kept my hair and everything. Thanks for asking." I give her one of my brilliant smiles—one of my cheerleader smiles of the old days that are automatic. Yeah team!

Carrie laughs. "God, I miss you." She touches my left arm and I cannot move it because I will be in pain, which Dr. Liston has said, again and again, is normal. I give a little shrug instead.

"I miss you, too." I apparently have said this aloud and she stares at me, waiting for me to share even more. *I can't do this.*

I close the back of the SUV. "I have to get going. Go to the bank and figure out what is going on with the account."

She nods in silent contemplation. A shadow crosses her face. "Robert isn't depositing money in that account any more. I thought you knew that? Maybe, the alimony and child support haven't kicked in, yet?"

I realize that she is trying to help me figure this out, but I am not appreciative in this moment. I'm angry because she's done this to me. And, I have *no one*. And, she has *Bobby*.

"I've got to go," I say in this barely audible voice.

"We're getting married."

It's as if a physical blow has landed into my chest. I struggle to take in air and hide my face behind my long hair as I confront a parade of emotions beginning with excruciating pain and ending with utter bewilderment. I find an inanimate object just past her face and just silently nod. "Robert wanted to wait, but I want to get on with things. Build a life together, you know?"

I cannot speak. Her words have left me powerless, helpless in the Safeway parking lot. I may never be able to go grocery shopping again. The havoc that this little foray for groceries has cost me is just too much. I cannot bear this kind of pain, so much worse than cancer. But, I just stand here and stare at her. Finally, I glance at my watch. It's eleven in the morning.

"I have to go," I finally say. "Nicholas has a game today. He's playing varsity."

"Oh, yes. We're going to try and make that." Carrie gives me this beautiful, defiant look.

"Please, don't," I say in this wan, faraway voice. "I have to be there for him. Go another time when I can't...be there." My eyes fill with tears. "Congratulations, Carrie. I hope you two will be very happy."

I have attained guaranteed angel status in heaven with these words. I'm ready to go to heaven, right now. Truly, I would welcome death this very minute after this conversation. I numbly get into my car. The tears start to flow freely as soon as I reach the first stop light.

"Fuck!" I scream in my car after I have ascertained that no one on Bainbridge Island can possibly see or hear me. Shaking, I take the road toward home to my empty house and vacant life.

Hours later, I've returned from the mother ship, Gene Juarez Hair Salon and Spa, in downtown Seattle. The receptionist was sympathetic as soon as she caught sight of my tear-streaked face. I was ushered back to Raul, where he shampooed, colored, cut, and styled my hair. My body from my head to my toes was cured: scrubbed, clipped and painted. One of the assistants was kind enough to rush over to Nordstrom's and came back with a complete outfit, including lingerie and shoes for my son's basketball game. Apparently, I needed it all.

Luckily, my American Express sailed through, when the bill for $876.53 came up on the cash register. Thank God for the small stuff, too, huh? Hopefully, I can hang onto my editor's job, so I can eventually pay for all of this.

I drive off the ferry in a rush to pick up Emily from all-day Kindergarten. I casually wave at a few neighbors who recognize me as I race off.

I glance down at all my finery: new designer jeans, a light blue angora sweater that apparently sets off my eyes and summer skin tone, and a white leather jacket with rabbit fur that I never would have bought for myself. The strappy sandals with four inch heels in a shiny black patent leather show off my pedicure of red-painted toenails. The shoes are all the rage, according to my stylist.

"Even in January?" I'd asked.

She'd given me a withering look. "Especially in January. After what you've been through, Ellie, you can wear them in any season." Several members of the Gene Juarez staff now know my life story. All are on my side. People on my side of things is just what I need to show up to the basketball game where I'm sure to find Robert and Carrie—the happy, newly-engaged, soon-to-be-married couple. I have to look my best. The Gene Juarez staff threw in my make-up session for free. God is on my side today. I stare at myself in the car mirror. I look like a *million and one bucks*. I'm determined to look better than Carrie Shaw soon to be Carrie Bradford by at least a dollar in the looks and style department.

Late. I swing into the parking lot of Wilkes Elementary and spy Emily standing on the sidewalk, looking forlorn. I park the car and do the unthinkable: I get out. Parents are not allowed to leave their cars, trained to keep the traffic moving, but I just park in defiance and deference and physically walk over to my youngest child.

I'm not sure she recognizes me at first. She looks past me for another minute.

"Have you seen my mother? She looks like a bag lady?" Emily asks with a laugh.

I sweep her up with my good arm and kiss her. "Hey baby. Come on. Let's go home and get you changed. We have to be at the Nick's game in just over an hour."

"Mom, you look . . . amazing," Emily says. I help her into her car seat, while the whistles from the parking staff start blowing all around us because I'm holding up the line. I give Emily my biggest smile and just ignore them.

"Thanks, Em."

"I mean it, Mom. You look so beautiful, like Giselle or something."

This is high praise. *Enchanted* is Emily's favorite movie and Amy Adams as Giselle is my daughter's current crush. I slide into the driver's seat and grin back at her in the mirror. I'll have to write a personal note to Gene Juarez's staff for this moment alone.

# CHAPTER FOUR

## Let The Game Begin

*P*erhaps, I have overdone it with the Gene Juarez day spa visit. Or, it's my newly-single divorcee status wreaking its own brand of terror on the community of married women in the Bainbridge High School gymnasium. The reconnaissance of me is either open or covert, where these females, once comrades, regard me full of disdain and defensive posture or pretend not to. It's unnerving, but I hold my head high and stride toward the home team bleachers with a contrived yeah-team smile and do my best to control the trembling. All of us release audible sighs, as Emily, Mathew and I settle into the stands. Nicholas is already over to us. "You came," he says in wonder.

"I said I would."

He shakes his head. "Yeah, but I didn't believe you." Nick grins up at me. "You...Mom, you look great." I blush at his compliment.

"Go get 'em, Nicky." He gives me another elated smile as he heads off to warm-up with his team.

Mathew touches my leg. I look over at him in surprise. "Mom, I'm...you do look great," he says. I nod, grin over at him, and lightly move my left shoulder, connecting with his.

"Thanks, Mattie."

"You're going to be okay, right?" Mathew asks. He glances at sideways, looking worried.

In that moment, I realize how much my children have been frightened by this whole cancer ordeal. Personally, I always believed Michael. I always knew I was going to be okay, but it's suddenly clear to me I've been less open at delivering this reassurance to my children.

They've just seen the disintegration of my life with their father. I feel bad for not recognizing their fear about losing me. Truth be told, I've lost more of myself in the divorce from Robert and in the loss of Michael. I haven't focused on my children at all. I grimace at this realization and vow to change that beginning now.

"We're going to be okay," I pronounce for the group.

Emily takes my hand and squeezes it. I squeeze hers back. Smiles light up the faces of my children with this declaration. I just wish I'd said it weeks ago.

Elaina Shaw, Michael and Carrie's sixteen-year-old daughter, comes into the gymnasium. She speaks briefly to my son. I see the undeniable hints of first love between them and watch as a mother and feel a tinge of sadness. How special that first love is. I wish I didn't have the burden of experience that brings along the inevitable recognition that it will not last.

Nicholas says something to Elaina that makes her laugh and I see the joy and elation on her face as she stares up at my oldest son. He says something else to her and then, she glances up at me and waves. I wave back. Then, I have to look away or I might start to cry.

Oh. This is going to be one of those memorable, painful nights.

I've already gone through so much today. I'm not sure I can take it. I concentrate on the growing crowd.

There's the familiar rumble of footsteps on the bleachers. I look up to see Elaina coming towards us.

"Hi Ellie. You look fantastic." She hugs me close.

"Nick's so glad you're here. I can't begin to tell you how much it means to him," she says.

Elaina has called me, *Ellie*, forever. I grin over at her.

I've known her since the day she was born. I love this girl. She has auburn hair, just like her mother, and incredible blue eyes. She is sweet, loyal, vivacious, and wonderful. There isn't a better match than Elaina Shaw for my Nicky.

"It's great to see *you*, E. You look fantastic, yourself." I grin at her and give her a hug leading with my good side as she settles into the seat right next to me with Emily and Mathew on my other side.

"Mind if I sit with you guys? I think my mom is coming with… Robert, well, to watch Nick play. Dad, too."

*Michael is coming? Oh God.* I automatically smile, but my mind races with this news. I try to concentrate on the player warm-ups and note that Nick keeps glancing over at us. I'm getting concerned for his ability to concentrate on the game. I'm getting concerned for my own ability to concentrate on the game as my heart rate accelerates at the idea of seeing Michael.

It seems all of the Bainbridge community is attuned to my social life problems. There isn't a face in the room over thirty that doesn't glance my way, when Robert and Carrie walk into the gymnasium. It must be the official coming-out for them. I guess all have been invited to openly assess my reaction to this particular coupling. I provide a yeah-team smile for my gaping fans.

"Daddy's here," Emily says in a wistful tone. I sense her alliances being tested.

"Go ahead and sit with him and Carrie, if you want. You too, Mathew. I'm fine here." I give them my best everything-is-going-to-be-okay smile.

"Are you sure?" Mathew asks in his most loyal voice.

"I'm absolutely sure. I know you miss him. Go be with him," I say. "I'll catch up to you after the game."

Mathew and Emily scramble from their seats and settle in next to Robert and Carrie. I raise my hand in a semi-wave.

Robert waves back with an uncertain look. Then, he rewards me with a smile. He might not love me, right now, but the man will always love his children. All of Bainbridge Island seems to breathe a heavy sigh of relief at my benevolence. I recline further in my seat, slowly remove my white leather jacket, and wince at the pain this action causes. Elaina sees this, grabs the other sleeve, and helps me off with the jacket.

"You are so cool," Elaina says to me under her breath. I give her a quizzical stare. "Nick says it's been pretty rough for you."

"Well, I'm not made of stone," I say with a slight laugh.

Elaina takes my hand and holds it in hers. "You're the bravest woman I've ever known."

I dig my nails into the palm of my free hand to keep from reacting to Elaina's kind words because I'm almost ready to cry again.

Nicholas comes back over to us. "Mom, are you okay?" He inclines his head in the direction of Robert and Carrie and his siblings.

"Nicky, I'm fine. Babe, you need to focus on the game and quit worrying about me. I'm great, *really*, I am."

"She's great, Nick. Elaina and I will sit with her," Michael says.

The familiar cadence and thrumming of his deep voice is almost my undoing. It feels as if I'm being transported away from this loud crazy place just upon hearing it. A peculiar feeling of serenity settles over me. I look up at him as he sits right next to me. His right thigh rests against mine and I catch my breath at his touch. *Michael.*

"Hey," I say. I take in his blue eyes and his golden hair and clasp my hands together, so I don't physically reach out to touch him. He smiles at me, as if he knows what I want to do. I watch in stunned amazement as the crinkles at the corner of his eyes come alive as he smiles down on me. I experience a flashback to college and the first day I met Michael Shaw and experience the same roiling sensation in seeing him again.

I'm fully aware the entire gymnasium is watching us, watching whatever this is between us unfold before them. "Hi," I say. Then, I bite my lower lip to still its trembling. A nervous habit left over from my college freshman days.

"Hi." He flashes me that white smile of his, blinding me with it. "You look fantastic, Ellen Kay." My pulse races even faster as he uses my full given name.

Elaina is watching our exchange with unbridled enthusiasm, her wide grin giving her away. "Dad," she says with a laugh. "Nick wants us to come over after the game. Can we do that?"

With this announcement, I falter. The forces are rising up against me faster than I can possibly keep up. I'm at a loss as to what to say, at this point. Nick has arranged a social event at our house. What's the state of our downstairs at home? I don't recall actually putting the groceries away from this morning, before I made my absolutely necessary escape to the Gene Juarez Spa. I can't recall the status of the kitchen, the dining room or the living room, at this point. I'm incoherent, dealing with the panic of entertaining at our house and seeing Michael all in the same evening.

"Is that all right, Ellie?" Michael asks me in this silky voice.

"You're both welcome to come over, but you'll have to forgive me the mess, in advance," I murmur. "I can't actually remember what I got done today."

Michael looks at me with this barely veiled, brazen look. The memory roars through me of how his lips feel on my body from our one and only time together. I close my eyes to suppress it, then open them again, and discover Michael watching me. He smiles wide as if he knows what I was just thinking about. "Are you okay?"

"Yes," I say with little conviction.

"Are you *sure*?" Michael teases.

"No." He and Elaina both laugh at my answer. I smile, shake my head, and take an unsteady breath.

I smile again and try to mask my uncertainty and better control my breathing. *In and out. Even breaths. Just breathe.*

Elaina leans against me like she's my daughter, while Michael touches my thigh with his from the other side. Nick scores one of the first baskets and we all cheer him on. I watch four quarters of basketball in a daze. I'm completely out of sorts, even as Nick's team wins the game. Final score? Who knows?

Michael towers over me, now, standing up to stretch. I grab my jacket and he helps me put it on. It's awkward for me, since I still favor my left arm. He gives me a strange look.

Elaina runs off to talk to Nick before he heads into the locker room. "We'll see you guys at the house," she calls back to us.

"She has a car," Michael offers with sideways glance at me.

"You gave your sixteen-year-old daughter *a car*?" I can't keep the incredulity out of my voice. He gives me a helpless look.

"Carrie's idea," he says. "With the divorce and all of that..."

"Of course."

Emily has come back to us and throws her arms around Michael's leg. "Hi Michael! It's great to see you! It's been a loooooong time."

Leave it to Emily to point out the obvious without any sense of social consideration as to why it has been such a long time, since we've seen Michael.

"Hey, Em!" Michael easily picks her up and carries her along as we make our way down the bleachers to the gymnasium floor.

I glance over and realize Robert and Carrie are walking toward us with Mathew. I hesitate. This is a little more than I can take today, but, Michael pulls me along gripping my right arm.

Mathew runs run over to me. "Hey Mom. Did you see that final shot Nick took? It was amazing!" My peace-making child tries to dispel the awkwardness.

"I saw it; couldn't believe it," I say with forced enthusiasm.

Mathew laughs and goes to put his arm around my left shoulder, but when I cringe, he drops back. "Sorry, Mom."

"It's okay, babe."

"I'm taller than she is," Mathew says.

Michael nods, but he giving me this odd look again, while he still holds on to Emily, who has her arm wrapped around his neck.

All of the straggling Bainbridge community watches with baited breath as the fearsome foursome meet on the gymnasium floor. Robert seems unsure of how to proceed. I sense his hesitation. Robert is normally good at confrontations, but I think he sees the lines of support in my favor, as my youngest children and Michael rally around me.

Elaina and Nick make a quick turn in our direction as well. I've decided to ignore Carrie completely. She has really outdone herself today and I can't take anymore. I do hand her a check written out for a $100 without comment. She takes it from me and I barely glance in her direction.

I look directly at Robert, now. He has done this to me and my look tells him this.

"Ellie, I'm sorry about the fiasco at Safeway," Robert says. "I put $10,000 in the checking account, until we get things figured out."

"Okay," I say. Michael studies my face and I blush under his scrutiny and recalling the Safeway fiasco as Bobby put it. This is my final humiliation, well, not quite; my darling daughter has the last word on that.

"Carrie wants me to be the *flower girl*, when she and Daddy get married," Emily says.

Michael looks stunned at this news. I feel bad I didn't warn him. Elaina is apparently taken by surprise, as well.

"What?" Elaina asks as she and Nick walk up to us.

"Nice touch, *really*, Carrie, Robert. You two just continue to amaze us all," I say with uncontrollable rage.

I turn and race toward the open gymnasium doors. I cannot make it to the SUV fast enough. My hands are shaking as I try and open the car door, but I've set off the car alarm instead. I stare in stunned amazement at my car as it makes this hideous screeching sound and flashes its lights. I start kicking the front tire with my strappy shoe. Pain shoots up my toes, but I just keep going.

Minutes later, Michael grabs the keys from me, undoes the lock, and gets the alarm to stop. He starts the car and I give up kicking the tire. In a daze, I watch Michael put a sobbing Emily in the backseat and strap her into her car seat. Elaina and Nick stand there watching me, while Mathew gets in the backseat from the other side. I observe it all from this faraway place.

"Come on, I'll drive you home," Michael says to me. "Nick, can you take my car to your house?" He throws the keys towards Nick. "Nice game, buddy."

"Thanks, Michael," Nick says. He turns to me because I'm just standing there, unmoving, it seems. "Mom, it's going to be okay." He touches my left arm and I cry out.

"See you at home, Nicky," I say with a wan contrived smile. "Nice game, babe."

"Thanks, Mom. Sure you're okay?"

"I'm fine." I smile again, going for a reassuring state as I promised myself I would do earlier for my kids. "Be careful on the roads."

"We will. I'm always careful," he says with a grin.

I watch him and Elaina traverse across the parking lot toward Michael's car and Elaina's. Hers is a sporty white Jetta. It seems a little small and I shake my head and worry for a moment that Elaina even has a car, but then, I see them laugh and gesture to one another about who is going to follow who to the house; and I can't help, but smile a little, just watching the two of them together.

The captain of our little ship, Dr. Michael Shaw, gives us a lifeline with his reassurance and solidarity. He calmly puts the car in gear and drives us away from the speculative crowd.

I appreciate Michael's understanding about sharing in companionable silence for a few minutes, while I attempt to get it together for the sake of my kids. Weary by the turn of events of the day, I hold my head in my good hand for a few minutes striving for some semblance of control. Eventually I look up, blink back the tears, and glance into the back seat at Emily and Mathew.

"Hey you two, everything's okay. No worries; all right? We'll go home and have some dinner and celebrate Nick's great game. Party on at the Bradford's." They both try to smile. "Hey, Em, there's no problem with you being the flower girl; okay? Daddy should have just told everyone sooner, so we weren't all so surprised, but, everything's fine."

"Okay," she says wiping at her face and eyes. "Are you *sure?*"

"I'm sure. It's great, very exciting, baby," I say again. Mathew gives me an uncertain look and I smile wider. "Right Michael?"

"It's great, Em," Michael says. He looks up her in the rear-view mirror and smiles. "Best flower girl there will ever be," he says.

I covertly glance in his direction and smile, but now he's looking at me with concern. "I need to talk to you," he says quietly. I just nod over at him in the darkness.

My house is a disaster. There are countless pizza boxes from the eighty-nine days of exile that the little family passed-over by Robert Bradford has endured. Elaina and Nick have taken it upon themselves to help me pick up. I try to ignore the obvious dire circumstances that must stand out so clearly for Michael and Elaina Shaw on how the Bradford family has been coping these past few months. The dust in the living room floats in the air. My housekeeping abilities have been limited. I had to let Mrs. Sanchez go, since my financial situation became unclear until the divorce was final. My financial situation is still unclear. Sad, but true. I really need to get a grip. I vow to do this tomorrow.

I watch Michael subtly count the number of discarded wine bottles. There are over thirty. I know this, too. He watches me as I do everything one-handed. His frown increases in depth from a surface one to a regular furrow. "Sorry about this," I keep repeating over and over as we make our way through the house.

Nick and Elaina volunteer to go out and pick up pizzas, per Michael's suggestion. My children are mute on the fact that they have had pizza every night for three months. I give the youngest ones some orange juice and pull out cheese and crackers and a veggie tray. Again, Michael is watching me do all of this one-handed.

"I need to talk to you," he says again. Once the kids are settled in front of some G-rated movie in the family room, he firmly pulls me along to the home office and closes the door behind us.

"What's wrong?"

Michael doesn't waste any time. He comes over to me and undoes the front two buttons of my shirt and pulls it over my head. In the light of the office lamp, he examines and runs his fingers along my underarm and lumpectomy scar.

"Does it hurt that much? You don't use your left arm very much," Michael says. He gets this vexed look.

"Yes, it still hurts. Dr. Liston said it was normal. I see him next week to do another round of x-rays to make sure it's all gone."

"You just did radiation?"

"Yes, radiation. No chemo."

"It shouldn't hurt like that, anymore," Michael says. "I wonder if he cut through additional tendons."

My heart pounds fast. Fear grips me at the somber look I see on his face. "Michael, what are you afraid of?"

Without answering, he helps me put my shirt back on. He pulls it over my head and secures the two buttons for me.

"I want you to come with me to the office tomorrow. We'll just do some quick x-rays and I'll talk to Josh."

"Michael…"

"Ellie…" He pulls me into his arms. His embrace feels so right and I hold on to him for few seconds. I've missed him. "God, Ellie. I'm sorry. I never should have…I won't let you go, again."

"Michael. No. I can't do this."

I struggle out of his arms and step back from him. I clasp my arms around my chest as if I can protect my heart from him by this gesture alone. He starts to move toward me and I hold my good hand to stop him from getting closer. "Don't."

"Yes," he says, grabbing my hand and putting it to his lips. His tender kiss of my hand rushes through all of me; the sensation feels electric. "Look, I'm sorry. I don't deserve you, but I love you, Ellie. I've always loved you."

I lift my head in defiance. "I don't believe you."

"I'll spend the rest of my life convincing you, then."

He pulls me to him. I'm too weary, too exhausted, too undone to resist him. My body betrays me and goes willingly into his arms. The rapid beating of his heart near my face and fresh sage scent of his cologne is intoxicating.

Our lips meet. His arms wrap around me. I sigh.

How I've missed this man. He moves in closer. I'm draped all along his body and he's kissing my neck, my face, and then my lips.

"Don't do this to me, Michael," I say without conviction.

"I love you, Ellen Kay. I can't believe I just wasted eighty-nine days not being with you."

The fact that he knew the exact count of the number of days it has been, since the big blow-up between all of us is enough for me. When he says this, I smile beneath his lips and he smiles back, pulling me even closer. I'm at a loss for words and he doesn't seem to need any.

We've forgotten the outside world completely. We've forgotten that we have four children milling around the house and now they're looking for us. A rapid knock at the door has us both stepping away from each other, guilty, just as Nick, then Elaina, followed closely by Mathew and Emily, come through the door.

"What's going on?" Emily asks.

"Your Mom and I are just working some things out," Michael says with a wide grin.

Elaina and Nick look at each other, then back at the two of us. They both smile.

"Working things out?" Elaina asks, now, in her most angelic voice.

I hang my head in shame. I have no morals left. Michael laughs and I look up at him, trying to give him a warning look.

"Okay," Michael says to the group. "Look, everything has been a little unsettling these past few months, but now, everything is starting to come together. Elaina, your mom is marrying Robert."

His only child nods at him. "And, that's great," Michael says gently. "Because Ellie and I…"

He looks over at me with this tender expression, grabs my right hand, and pulls me to him.

"Ellie and I love each other and so…we're all going to be to-gether as a big family because sometimes, that's just how things work out. Things always work out like they're supposed to."

"Does that mean you're going to be my daddy?" Emily asks. She has her hands on her hips in her usual, intimidating-Emily stance as she stares down Michael.

"Well…your Daddy will always be your daddy, Em. I'll be…" Michael looks over at me. This whole scene has gotten way ahead of us, as we all stand there in the semi-darkness of the office.

"Michael…" I give him another we-shouldn't-do-this look.

"What? We need to take time to get to know each other before we take the next step?" He rakes his hand through his hair.

"Ellie, I've known you for more than eighteen years," he teases. "What? You need to play the field to make sure I'm the one? Let me save you the trouble." He wraps his arms around and kisses me, much to the apparent surprise of the children and myself.

I hear giggles from Emily, as Michael lifts his head from mine. "Do it again! Do it again!" Emily says with a laugh.

"Okay, the pizza is getting cold and frankly, I don't think I can watch anymore," Nick says in feigned disgust. Then, he winks at me.

He and Elaina, both grinning, head out toward the kitchen holding hands. Mathew and Emily follow, while Michael takes my right hand and pulls me along behind him. I walk along after him in a daze, wondering what we just committed ourselves to.

You can eat pizza ninety nights in a row and survive. My children and I have proven this. It sounds as if this has also been proven at Michael's place as well.

Elaina and Nick have worked out some elaborate plan. Nick borrows Michael's car and follows Elaina with her car over to Carrie and Robert's new residence so they can spend more time alone together. Michael has not announced his plans for leaving. I have left the front door unlocked for Nick's return and cleaned up the downstairs to the best of my abilities.

A little while ago, I sent Emily off to get her pajamas on, knowing she's worn out by the range of emotions and activities of this night. Now, I climb the stairs to monitor her progress for bed and find Michael languishing across her bed and reading her a story. Emily is under the covers with her favorite stuffed bunny with a satisfied, contented smile on her face. I can't even look at Michael without giving myself away. The man is beyond distraction.

Mathew is also getting ready for bed. I say good night to him. He calls good night to Michael and gives me a secret smile.

Thrown off balance by Michael's presence, I stand in the hallway, uncertain. I contemplate going back downstairs and opening a bottle of wine, but feel the fatigue from the many events of this day. Michael finds me in the hallway. "I should go," he says.

"Don't go."

These are not planned words by me. Without thinking, I pull

him along to the master bedroom. I've changed everything: the mattress, the bedding, the linen. I babble on about what I've done during one of my limited days of divine energy in the past few months, while a wide smile spreads across his face. "I want you to stay, Michael. I want your face to be the first thing I see." It's the most honest I've been about my feelings in months. I smile back at him, now. So, we begin this thing we started twenty years and ninety-seven days before.

# Chapter Five

 *Day 90*

I wake up to Emily tapping the side of my face. "Mommy, Michael's making all of us pancakes this morning. I let him in and he has coffee for you and everything. He's making pancakes and eggs and even bacon." Her joy is infectious; I can't help but smile, wondering how Michael snuck out of the bedroom, let alone the house.

"Wow, that's great, Em. Special day; huh? " She crawls up in bed with me.

"Momma, you're not mad at me; are you? That Carrie wants me to be a flower girl when she marries Daddy? How does that work, since he's married to you?" Her little nose crinkles; I reach out and touch it.

"I'm not mad at you, Em. Sometimes, mommies and daddies don't stay together. They don't stay married, but they're still friends because they share their family. That's what ours is like. I think it's great that you're going to be a flower girl. It's going to be so special, Em."

She puts her head down on my chest and I stroke it with my left arm, which is still hard to do because the pain is still there. I grimace when I feel it, and then look up to find Michael standing in the doorway carrying a breakfast tray just watching me.

"See, Michael? I kept her in bed, just like you told me to!"

"You did great, Emily. There's breakfast downstairs for you and your brothers." Emily hurries out of the room with an excited shout still carrying her favorite stuffed bunny with her.

"Good morning." Michael gives me a sly smile, brings the tray over, and sits down on the bed beside me.

"Good morning." My shyness comes unbidden. I'm mesmerized by this man and his generosity and beholden to this amazing sensation between us. "How did you manage to get outside?"

"I went and got coffee and Emily was kind enough to let me back in. No sense getting her confused, right now. I think Robert and Carrie are busy enough doing that." I nod.

"Thank you, Michael. It…it means everything to me."

"You mean everything to me, Ellen Kay." Then, he shows me just how much.

The nurse at Dr. Liston's office draws blood from my arm. I have already given a lot of blood this morning and I am, somewhat, disconcerted as to why we're doing it again.

"More tests," the nurse says in a non-committal, unhelpful voice.

Michael has gone on to his medical office. I'm to meet him there, when I'm finished here.

I'm still reeling a bit from the earlier conversation with Dr. Liston, who is now as worried as Michael about the fact that my left arm is still sore so many weeks after this simple lumpectomy was performed.

I've already reconciled that the lumpectomy may have been simple, but not enough. And, now it appears that the x-rays they've done this morning might show something else, though no one has taken the time to tell me what that means. I know it means something, but no one is willing to tell me what exactly. I'm tired, now.

Waiting is not my strongest virtue. My mother used to say this. Today, I would welcome a visit from my mother, who resides in a retirement community in the land of the sun. Even though my life has gotten beyond complicated and all she would do is ask me too many questions about it, today, I would welcome her high-pitched voice and raised eyebrows, while I'd inevitably use the word, fuck, too often in a sentence. I miss my mom this day. I could use the company and the distraction.

The nurse comes back and tells me that I can get dressed. I do this in about three minutes flat, now anxious to leave this claustrophobic space where my mind has too much time to wallow with fear and the unknown. The nurse returns and escorts me to Dr. Liston's office; I'm surprised to see Michael. I smile at him, grateful for his presence and slide into the chair next to him opposite Dr. Josh Liston.

"So?" I say with a soft tone. "What's going on?"

"We've been going over your charts and the x-rays, Ellie," Dr. Liston says. His face is somewhat bleak and I'm taken aback by it.

In the next ten seconds, Michael is taking my hand and I look at him for a moment, trying to discern what's happening from the look on his face, but all he does is give me this measured reassuring smile. But there's something in his eyes that I see before he looks away. In the next instant, I realize what it is, *fear*.

"Tell me," I say.

"Well, the lumpectomy looked promising. The margins looked good; an indication we got all the cancerous cells," Dr. Liston says. "However, the latest films indicate the possibility of something. We need to go back and take a look. With that procedure, we'll remove any cancerous-looking cells, ensure the margins are clear and do more radiation and add chemotherapy to the regimen as well. We need to go back in and take a look at the lymph nodes. But, there's…more." He takes a deep breath and gets this wan smile.

"Ellie, you're pregnant. We just picked this up in one of the routine tests we did this morning."

"*What*? How is that possible? Robert had a vas…" I turn to Michael. "How is this possible? I thought you were…? Dr. Liston, can I have a moment with Michael, please?" I ask in this faraway voice. My heart pounds away in my chest.

The room goes silent, when Dr. Liston leaves. The only thing I hear is Michael's jagged breathing. I'm dry-eyed and there is no explanation for that. Normally, I cry at everything—sad movies, love stories, anything to do with Lassie or Golden Retrievers, *babies*.

"Michael, is this *possible*?"

"I don't know," he says in an unsteady voice. "Carrie…could never conceive with me. That's why we used a sperm donor for Elaina. But, Ellie, you have to have the chemo. You can't keep this baby."

"What? No. Michael. No. We have to keep this baby. It's a miracle." These competing emotions of joy and fear run through me at an accelerated rate.

"Ellie. This is your life we're talking about. We have to do *everything* to fight the cancer. This baby is a complication we don't need. Can't you see that?"

I'm surprised by his dire tone. He's emphatic already as if we're not even going to discuss this, so different from Robert where we always talked everything through.

"Michael, this baby is a miracle. Can't you see that?" I watch his face. It remains impassive and unmoving at my words. Anger begins to stir inside of me. I'm pregnant. I'm having a baby. It's a miracle. It's a sign of what path I need to take. Why can't he see that? Why doesn't' he understand what this baby could mean? To me? To us? I move away from him as he reaches for me.

"Ellie, we have to stay focused on treating your cancer."

"No," I say from the other side of the room, folding my arms across my chest. I lift my head in defiance and stare at him.

Dr. Josh Liston returns and takes his formidable position behind his desk. I retake my chair. Michael remains standing.

"First things first," I say only to Josh. "You want to go back and look at the margins around the lumpectomy and the lymph nodes."

"Yes."

"Okay, when can we do that? And, I'll just do a local, no general anesthesia." Michael is out of his chair saying *no,* as I finish.

"*Yes,*" I say. "Michael, we have to keep all our options open and do what's best for this baby—*our baby.*" I give Dr. Liston a wide smile. He nods in this helpless, charming way. I smile back at him.

"I'll get you scheduled first thing for Friday morning. We'll do it as an outpatient procedure and no general."

"Great, thank you, Dr. Liston," I say.

"I'm scrubbing in, Josh," Michael says from beside me. I can sense his tension just sitting next to him. I'm tempted to look over at him, but know he might mess with my resolve about all of this. I'm reeling from all the implications sounding brave, but feeling scared and elated all at the same time. My hormones seem to have taken off like a bottle rocket, since I learned I was pregnant ten minutes ago.

"Do you really think that's a good idea, Michael?" Josh asks.

"Probably not, but, I'm doing it anyway."

"Okay." I hear the audible sigh of frustration from Josh Liston.

It matches the mood of all three of us, perfectly, for very different reasons.

It is after six at night on Wednesday. I'm back at Michael's medical office, where he is drawing my blood himself. Elaina is with Emily and Mathew at my house. Nick will be coming home from basketball practice in the next half hour with pizza for all of them. Day ninety at the Bradford house for pizza. We must be setting some kind of world record. Emily is busy telling me about her day as I hold the cell phone to my right ear while Michael draws blood from my left.

"So, what did you do when got the word, *giraffe,* right, Em?" She tells me that she took a bow and sat down. I am laughing, now. Michael is looking at me with a half smile. "Hey, baby, I have to go. Michael is helping me with some tests. We'll be home soon. I love you." I hang up the cell phone and look at him.

"The most precocious child I know," I say. Michael can only nod at me.

After a few minutes, he sighs and gives me a studied look. "Okay, we're all done. I had Stephanie wait around, so she can take these directly to the lab. I've asked them to a put a rush on them."

"What kind of tests are we doing?"

"Just the standard genetic stuff, Ells," Michael says with a shrug.

"As in paternity?"

"No. These are just the ones for genetic markers that we would normally do. Some of them are little early. I can test for paternity if you want me to."

"Well, unless you can tell me for certain that a vasectomy can fail after almost five years; there's no point."

"Highly unlikely, but possible."

"This baby is yours, I can feel it," I say. "God, one time with you; and you knock me up."

"Ellie," Michael says in exasperation.

We have gone round and round about this baby already. He looks troubled, as if, this, alone, will change my mind.

I remain steadfast and resolute about keeping this baby. He shakes his head, picks up the blood samples, and leaves the room without another word to me.

I'm disappointed with his response. He is obviously unhappy with mine.

Last night's love making session and the melding of our future seem like long time ago. Today, our newfound relationship is already being tested in ways I couldn't have imagined even yesterday.

I'm putting on my jacket when he returns. "Let's go home," he says. Just like that with his engaging smile he builds a bridge back to me. I smile up at him, move in closer and with my good arm pull him to me and kiss him.

"I like the sound of that," I say with a little laugh.

A half hour late, we're sitting in his Lexus, Seattle side, waiting for the ferry back to Bainbridge. "What are you doing this weekend?" Michael asks. He looks over at me with this thoughtful expression on his face and slowly smiles.

"I don't know," I say slowly, and then grin. "Are you asking me out?"

"I'm asking you out," he says with a laugh. "I have a surprise for you, so don't make any other plans."

"I don't like surprises. You *know* this," I say, getting a little anxious at the secretive smile on his face, but Michael seems intent on ignoring this known fact about me.

"It's a good surprise," he says.

"We'll see," I say with a tight smile.

Once on the ferry, we elect to stay in his SUV. I watch the gorgeous blue waves of Puget Sound rush past, while Michael watches me. A few minutes later, I slide over to his side of the car and lean back against his chest while his arms close around me.

He brushes my hair aside and begins kissing my neck. I can't help but respond to him.

A secret mission forms in my mind to learn more about his surprise. I climb onto his lap and maneuver myself between him and the steering wheel.

"Are you going to tell me the surprise?" I ask after few seductive moments. I lift my head from his lips and stare intently at his handsome face and smile.

"Are you trying to seduce me, Ellen Kay? I'm not telling you the surprise even if you do have your way with me on this ferry ride,"

Michael says with a laugh. "You'll have to wait and see."

"Oh, we'll *see*," I say.

The surrealist connotations that my life has taken do not escape me. On Friday, with just a local anesthetic, Dr. Josh Liston and Michael re-open the scarred incision at my left breast and take a look at the margins and explore my lymph nodes. I give in to the fear of it all, unable to take my mind off of things. My life circumstances parade before me. I'm pregnant. I haven't even begun to deal with that fact yet. The myriad of tests that Michael ordered show that this baby is fine—no genetic abnormalities have shown up, yet. This baby is due to be born in early July. I'm divorced from Robert. I've lost the friendship with Carrie in all of this. I'm in love with Michael.

I look over at him now. His eyes are this intense cerulean blue mirroring mine at a cosmic level. His golden brows furrow as he concentrates on the process of looking for any and all cancer in my body. He looks over at me, sensing me watching him, and I know he smiles at me behind his surgical mask.

"It's going to be okay," I say in my most magical voice, the one I normally reserve for my children's bumps and bruises.

The fear in his eyes extinguish just a little bit and I know he so wants to believe me. I want to believe me, too. Josh looks over at both of us. I see the light come into his brown eyes and know he smiles behind his mask, too.

"How are you doing, Ellie?"

"I'm okay," I say.

"You're officially the bravest woman I've ever met," Josh says with a laugh. His sincerity causes my eyes to fill with tears, my throats gets tight, and all I can do is smile in answer.

I'm in recovery after a two-hour surgery where the margins of my lumpectomy have been reviewed, surgically incised, and are now being tested and analyzed. The tissue samples taken have been rushed to the lab and even more blood work has been done and taken there. I've been moved to the head of the line because my doctors wished it so. I do feel, as if I have been summarily run over by a fast moving train. In reviewing the procedure that just transpired in my mind, I conclude I'm beyond brave, too. The nurse comes in, waving paperwork that requires my signature concurring she's carefully reviewed my at-home care.

"What day is it?"

"It's January 22nd," the nurse says back to me. I stop signing my name.

"It can't be."

"It is Mrs. Bradford." With a strangled cry, I finish my signature and write the date.

"It's my daughter's sixth birthday," I say to the alarmed nurse.

"Oh."

"I forgot."

"Ooooooooohhhh," she responds.

No words can describe this onslaught of failure. Failure.

*Mommy failure.* It's Emily's birthday. She's six-years-old today and I've missed it.

I start to cry. I barely said hello to her this morning. I was cranky because I couldn't have any coffee or anything to eat and Michael was a little late in picking me up to go to the hospital, so we had to rush to catch the ferry to Seattle. Elaina and Nick took care of getting Emily to school. I remember talking to the two of them as we hurried out the door. But Mathew? I can't even recall really seeing my middle son this morning, let alone remember what he was wearing. And Emily? The birthday girl? Whose outfit for *her birthday* day is always paramount; this big event we plan for. I don't even know what she wore to school today for her big day. I don't even remember kissing her good-bye.

*Failure.* It settles in.

For her sixth birthday, Emily wants a castle cake—white, pink and purple with four spires and flags and fairies.

I vaguely recall committing to all of this for her over a month ago. She wants pink and white balloons, *everywhere*. Her description of how the house should look. And anything, but pizza, could be served. Just a castle party, that's all. Here I am in the middle of the day, *her day*, only now remembering that my only daughter was born six years ago today in this very hospital.

Granted, I could use the excuse that my cancer may be back. That it may have, in fact, never have been gone. But, it isn't my day; it's Emily's day. Perhaps, I could somehow blame this all on Robert and Carrie, too. They should have remembered. I am, after all, fighting breast cancer, but, I'm Emily's mother. I should have remembered more than anyone else.

I grab my cell phone and call the Red Balloon Company and beg them to help me. I tell them I need thirty balloons—ten white, ten light pink and ten dark pink; and I need them in an hour.

Next, I call the Town & Country Market on Bainbridge. I tell the baker my dilemma. This is a crisis," I say. "She's turning six, but going on twenty. What can you do for me?"

We come up with a plan. They'll stack two sheet cakes together, add four ice cream cones for spires, and decorate with purple, pink and white icing. Dorothy, in the bakery, takes pity on me, when I tell her I'm calling from Swedish Hospital recovering from an outpatient procedure. Somehow, I start telling her that this is my second surgery related to breast cancer.

She promises to have the cake done in an hour and a half which should be just about perfect.

"I need fairies, flags, candles and ice cream, too," I say.

She promises to have everything ready as she hands me off to the delicatessen, where I order a family size tray of lasagna and a large ready-made green salad and two loaves of garlic bread. Everything will be ready. All I'll have to do is re-heat it. I resort to the *I'm in the recovery room* story, but I'm already being assured that Dorothy is already over at the deli filling them in.

By the time Dr. Michael Shaw enters the room; I am halfway dressed in my jeans and shoes, trying to remove my hospital gown.

"Ellie, what are you doing?" Michael has this alarmed look when he sees me.

"It's Emily's *birthday*, Michael. I forgot. We all forgot. So, this day just stopped being about me."

"Ellie…"

"Michael, can you have them give me another dose of local anesthetic? I've got a lot to do and I've got to get out of here."

He gives me a long steady look and then he smiles. "I guess there's no arguing with you…and, since I drove you here, I guess we're leaving," he says more to himself than to me. "Would you like to know how the surgery turned out?"

"Only if it's good news," I say with a dismissive wave.

It's awkward, but I attempt to take off the hospital gown, but soon realize I need Michael's help in even attempting to put on the sports bra my chest is all bandaged up. I give him my best, we-are-leaving-don't-argue-with-me look. With reluctance, he begins helping me with the sports bra hooks in the front, but takes his time redoing the ace bandage hooks around my bandages which cover the incisions. I give him an impatient exasperated look.

"It's good news," Michael says with a smile, tracing my jaw line. "The margins are perfect. The lymph nodes are clear." He kisses me and I willingly succumb to his ministrations for a few precious moments. "We'll need to talk about the radiation and chemo with Josh," he says with a stern doctor-knows-best tone.

"Next week," I say with a sigh. "I promise. I'll be willing to talk all about it. But right now, Michael, this day, *today*, is only about Emily."

I give him my biggest smile. Then reach for him and gently trace his lips and kiss him one last time.

"Okay," he says, looking bemused. "It's Em's day."
"Yeah, team!" I say with a laugh.

# CHAPTER SIX

 *Emily's Day*

The employees of Town & Country Market have outdone themselves for me. I have just become their most loyal shopper, vowing to go out of my way by two miles, so that I never have to shop at Safeway on the Island again. Michael's car is loaded up with balloons; a magical, pink, and purple castle cake; vanilla ice cream with chocolate swirls, lasagne, bread, and salad. We couldn't fit another thing in it, even if we wanted to. We have a half hour to get this stuff into the house before Emily arrives home from an after-school play date.

I'm busy trying to wrap Emily's gifts—a humongous Dream Barbie castle with a new Barbie—that we spent all of five minutes buying in downtown Seattle. The task is difficult because my left side is bandaged around my arm and rib cage. I secretly believe that this is some conspiracy on Michael's part. When Elaina and Nick walk in the door, Elaina volunteers to finish wrapping Emily's gift for me.

Michael, Nick, and Mathew put out the white linen table cloth on the dining room table and stage the cake in the middle of it. Balloons hang throughout the downstairs. Elaina lights candles everywhere as the afternoon. I climb the stairs to change into a nice pair of crème colored wool pants and light pink sweater.

Michael comes in and asks if I need help. I try to smile.

The truth is I'm exhausted and I haven't quite figured out how I'm going to dress myself with the newly bandaged arrangement that the nurses put together, when they gave me that final shot of local anesthetic.

I try to step out of my jeans with an awkward show of balance, but Michael is already there helping me. He holds me steady as I step into the wool slacks. He undoes the ace bandage that holds my arm to my chest. He carefully takes off my t-shirt and pulls the pink sweater over my head and starts to re-secure the ace bandage.

"Can't we just leave it off for tonight for the party?"

"*No.* I wanted you to stay overnight at the hospital. Be happy with the ace bandage," he says in a slightly threatening, with a not-much-of-a-bedside-manner tone. "How are you feeling? On a scale of one to ten with the pain—with ten being severe, how do you feel?"

I haven't really thought about the pain. I've lived with it for a while, now. "It's okay."

"Number?" Michael holds on to me, waiting for an answer.

"Two. It's not that bad." He nods, satisfied, and puts his arm around my right side and kisses my forehead. "You are a fantastic woman, you know that; right, Ellie?"

I shake my head. "I forgot her birthday." The tears come right away. It's already been a very long day.

"Emily won't even care when she walks into this house and sees what you've done." Michael leans down and kisses me. I feel his love and warmth in that kiss and I kiss him back. I cannot fully explain what kissing him does to me. It is like a startling promise, kissing Michael. I think it is because I feel we instinctively fit together and he never reminds me of Robert. He is just Michael. Has always been Michael; and we just fit.

"Thank you."

"Ellen Kay," he says, stroking my face with his exquisite surgical hands. "I love you."

"I love you, too," I whisper back.

"Tomorrow," he says with hesitation, then gives me this intense look. "You're mine for the entire day. I've already got Elaina and Nick watching Emily and Mathew. You're *mine* for the day."

"Michael...no surprises," I say. He puts his fingers to my lips, effectively silencing my protest.

"Trust me. This surprise you'll love." He gently takes me in his arms again and holds me to him.

"You make it impossible to say *no*," I complain, kissing his hand.

"Do I?" His feigned surprise makes me laugh.

"How good are you with putting on make-up?" I ask.

"Not so good. I think, I'll draw the line here and send Elaina up."

Elaina has finished retouching my make-up for me and even brushed my hair. I probably could have done all of this myself, but I'm exhausted from being at the hospital so early and the stress of the surgery, too. I give her a wan smile and stare at her beautiful face and amazing green eyes so much like her mother's, while she applies the last touches of foundation to my face.

"Thanks for doing this," I say. Elaina rewards me with a big smile; it reminds me of Carrie. I have this overwhelming sense of loss because I really do miss Carrie.

"Ellie," she says slowly and gives me an uncertain look. "How did everything go today?"

This intense look comes across her face. It dawns on me how much of a strain my health concerns have put on all those around me.

"It went well. I'm going to be fine."

Her eyes fill with tears as she lets out a sigh. I reach for her with my right hand and touch her face, catching a stray tear.

"Really. *Truly.* I'm going to be fine. Your dad believes this too, you know."

Elaina nods. The tears still trail down her face. "I love you, Ellie." She puts her arms around me and I try to hug her back, though the ace bandage makes this nearly impossible.

"I love you, too, Elaina."

"Would it be all right if I call my mom? She's been worried about you all day."

I nod, too overcome to speak. The thing is I miss Carrie. I miss Robert, too, even if we are divorced. We have all been friends above everything else and not having them in my life has been hard.

"Let them know it would be great if they could come by for Emily's birthday. Tell them that we all forgot and we are making it up to her tonight," I say.

"Ellie." I sense her hesitation and look up to see her as she catches her lower lip and looks at me more uncertain. "They went to Vegas for the weekend," she says quietly.

"Oh."

It's perfectly clear why they would have gone to Vegas. I turn away before Elaina can see me cry. It's not that I care. It's just I cannot believe that after being married to Robert for so many years that he has not even called me to tell me this is what he was planning to do with Carrie. It's too much. And, I'm pregnant. It begins to settle in with me now that all of this is just a bit too much to take in. In the awkward silence with Elaina, I tell myself that anyone would fall apart at this juncture. I lean over the sink to keep the tears from streaking my newly applied make-up, fully aware that Elaina watches me.

"I'm sorry," she stammers.

I nod from the sink still intent on salvaging my made-up face.

"It's just…well, I'm tired, you know? And, where does that leave

Emily being their flower girl?"

I dab a tissue at my face and contrive to laugh through the tears. "Give me your cell phone."

With a clear lack of enthusiasm, Elaina hands me her cell phone. I dial Carrie's cell phone number by heart.

"Elaina," Carrie says at once.

"It's not Elaina. It's Ellie."

"Ellie." Carrie's voice falters for a split second. "How are you?"

"I'm okay. I just got home from the hospital. We're having Em's birthday party tonight. Will you two be able to make it?" I give Elaina a conspiring look as she stands there, as if we're in on this solidarity together. She tries to smile.

"Well, no...we're...out of town. It's Emily's birthday, tonight?" I hear the vagueness in Carrie's response.

"Put Robert on the phone." I hear the rustling of the phone being passed; wink at Elaina, whose smile just gets wider.

"Ellie?" Robert's deep voice comes across the phone line.

"Bobby, I'm so sorry. I completely forgot to call and remind you about Emily's birthday. We're having her party tonight. You know how she wanted the castle party theme. She's so excited." I lie, as if I have any idea how my daughter is feeling today, since I've barely seen her. I hear a heavy sigh from Robert as I say this.

"Ellie, we're out of town."

"Out of town? Where, out of town?"

"We're in Vegas." Robert sighs again.

"Oh. Since when do you like to gamble?"

"We're not gambling," he says.

"You're not? Well, Robert Nicholas Bradford, I think you might be. Well, good luck with all of that. You might want to call in a few hours and wish your only daughter a happy sixth birthday."

"Ellie! You should have told us sooner," Robert says.

His attitude immediately ignites my temper. I should just let it go, but, I unleash my fury on him for all of this.

"I know…the thing is Bobby; I was in the hospital most of the day having surgery to re-check for cancer, so I'm sorry that I've been so remiss in reminding you about Em's sixth birthday." I sigh. "And, what about having Emily as the flower girl in your wedding? Carrie all but promised her this. I guess Emily will just have to learn to live with the disappointment of that, too."

"God damn it, Ellie. Why are you doing this to me?"

"I have *cancer*, Bobby." I hear him such in his breath. "I'm just not *myself*, but you two enjoy yourselves in Vegas. God, those are going to be some happy wonderful memories for the two of you. Your mother is just going to *love* that." I hang up the cell phone, while my ex-husband is shouting in mid-sentence and innocently hand the phone back to Elaina. "You might not want to answer that for a few minutes. Bobby's pretty riled up," I say airily and force myself to smile. Part of me already regrets lashing out at Bobby like that.

Elaina nods as she pockets the cell phone back in her jeans. It's already ringing.

"Ellie, you are so awesome."

My smile fades. "Not really. Everything's just so mixed up right now; you know?" My voice trembles.

"I know."

"Hey, can you do me favor and go make sure they've got everything ready? I'll be down in a minute." Her cell phone starts ringing again. "Maybe have Em call him back. She should be here in the next couple of minutes." I put my arm around her and give her a hug. "Thanks for the make-over," I manage to say.

"You're sure you're okay?" Elaina asks.

"Never better," I say, watching her leave with a sense of relief.

I give myself five minutes to experience the pain of losing Bobby forever, of going through a major surgery with just a local anesthetic, and for being a bad mother in forgetting Emily's birthday all together. None of these things are reconcilable, even with Michael's miraculous love. I let the tears flow by bending my head over the sink and manage to avoid streaking my face. With a few eye drops, no one will ever know about my crying jag. I reapply a little blush and finger fix my hair and stare at the face in the mirror. *I am Ellie Bradford, no more. Who am I, now?*

Fifteen minutes later, I walk back downstairs and discover Emily twirling around the room in surprise, completely enthralled with her castle party theme.

"Momma! Did you do all of this?" My daughter runs at me. I half duck from her to avoid the onslaught of pain. Emily stops about three feet from me. She eyes the bulkiness of my pink sweater and must spy the heavy ace bandage underneath wrapped tightly around my arm and chest that peaks out from my collar bone. "Momma!"

Emily bursts into tears. I realize, yet again, the profound impact my cancer has been having upon my family and feel this building anguish. "Baby, I'm okay," I say.

"No, you're *not*!" Emily cries even harder and clutches my good arm.

I look up and find Michael watching us with this look of disquiet. In fact, everyone has gathered around and is watching the two of us now. I see the stress and fear in the faces of Elaina, Nick and Mathew. All of them.

"Okay, I can see that we're going to have to get into the gritty details of this, *now,*" I say with a half-hearted laugh.

I half carry Emily with me as she still clings to me and sit with her in one of the cozy chairs by the fireplace. I give Michael a quizzical look and he gives me this imperceptible nod.

"So, Dr. Liston and Michael took another look at my…well, right here." I point to my upper chest and shoulder with my free arm. "They were looking for the bad cells that could make me sick, but the good news is that they didn't find any." I take a deep breath and look around at all of them. "Isn't that great? So, now all we have to do is have some x-rays taken of that area to make sure the bad cells don't come back. Michael doesn't think they will. Do you, Michael?" I look directly at him with a please-do-this-for-me expression.

"Nooooo," he says slowly. "We got it all and everything looks good. Your mom is going…to be fine." Michael struggles to enunciate these last words. I'm sure he is stepping beyond the bounds of what a surgeon normally promises. I detect his hesitation and reticence to do so. I give him my brightest smile.

"Yeah team!" I say with as much enthusiasm as I can manage.

Michael starts to laugh and the tension leaves the rest of them all at once. It's obvious that these children, no matter how old they are, take their cues from Michael and me.

In an instant, I'm surrounded by everyone. They take turns giving me a hug or touching me in some way. Michael is last. He kisses the top of my head as all the kids remain watching the two of us.

I lift my head and look at him. "Thanks," I whisper to him.

It is the middle of the night and I awaken to darkness with searing, burning pain—the after effects of surgery. The local anesthetic has clearly worn off and now my whole upper left side is aflame. I shift my body; uncomfortable, trying to raise myself unsuccessfully to a sitting position, just as Michael rises from the chair beside the bed in the semi-darkness.

"Are you okay?"

"What are you *doing* here?" I whisper. I'd told him good-bye hours ago.

"Ellie, someone needs to take care of you," he says.

"What about the kids?"

"I think…the kids have a better sense of what is going on

between us than you do," he says with a slight smile.

He helps me up and I go into the bathroom for a few minutes. The pain is intense. I whisper the word fuck a few dozen times as if this will provide some sort of relief and barely avoid crying out, knowing Michael will hear me. After a five-minute respite, he comes into the bathroom giving me the once-over. "How do you feel, now? How's your pain?"

"Right now?" I stall. Michael gives me an exasperated look. I try to prevent myself from physically recoiling, knowing the pain will get worse if I move at all. "It's about a nine, I think." I'm helpless now to admit or fabricate anything else.

"Okay."

He leaves without a word and returns a few minutes later with a glass of water and two white pills.

I take the pills and chase them down with the water. The pills start to work after another ten minutes of standing there in the semi-darkness. Excruciating pain seems to tame to almost bearable. We're both enveloped in this companionable silence, too physically exhausted and too emotionally spent, to do more than gaze at each other.

"Thanks," I finally say with a weary smile.

"May I?" Michael gestures with his hands, indicating he wants to take a look at my incision. I nod, too overcome with a mixture of pain and helplessness. He undoes the white men's dress shirt I'm wearing and the front hooks of the sports bra. He takes a clinical look at my incision in my breast and my underarm. I can barely lift my arm as he examines me. He pulls the bra edges back together and deftly hooks them again. The pressure on my wound is almost unbearable and I catch my lower lip to keep from crying out. He buttons up the white shirt, again. "Sorry," he says with a frown.

"How does it look?" I ask, trying to sound uninterested.

"It looks fantastic because I'm a very skilled surgeon."

"You mean Josh."

"No. I did the surgery. Josh assisted me today."

"Dr. Shaw," I say in a raspy voice. "Are you giving me special treatment?"

"God, I hope so," he murmurs.

Michael catches my chin with his finger and kisses me.

# CHAPTER SEVEN

 *Will You?*

It is the next morning and I have not slept well for a variety of reasons that I prefer to forget. I look over at Michael and watch him sleep. This is a new experience. I try to remember the last time that I watched Robert's face this way, but I really can't remember. Robert was falling away from me, long before Carrie moved in on him to end it; I'm no longer sad about this. This admission surprises me. How is it possible to have someone in your life for so long—someone you're married to, you've lived with, and have children with and yet, it suddenly ends and you no longer feel the loss? Is it possible it was never mine in the first place? Is it possible I am found in being with Michael? I think that is my answer, at least, for today.

I stare at Michael. His chest moves up and down in an even rhythm. The love for him surges through all of me. It's still early. The house with us and three other children is wonderfully quiet. It's an extraordinary experience: this silence and just watching Michael sleep. After a few minutes, I move in closer to his body and he puts his arm around me.

"Ellie," he says softly with his eyes still closed. "Are you okay?"

"Yes, Michael." I smile as I say his name.

"I'll get up in a few minutes and go out and get coffee."

"Okay," I say.

His generosity to protect the emotions of my children overwhelms me. He moves nearer to me now. The love for him just emanates from me now like a light bursting from inside of me. I do love this man. It really is that simple.

We're sitting in Michael's car in front of the most extraordinary beach house property I've ever seen on Bainbridge. The house is about two hundred feet from the sandy beach and Puget Sound. A long gravel driveway with numerous towering Cedar trees gracing each side of it lead visitors to this welcoming home. It's magnificent.

"What do you think?" Michael asks. "Do you remember this place?"

"Yeah, I remember it," I say softly. I look over at him. "I love it. I always have. What was it fifteen years ago that the Mackey's had a Halloween party, here?" David and Helene Mackey have since divorced and left the Island. I sigh to myself.

"Would you like to go inside?"

"Can we? I'd love to. I wonder what's been done to the place."

"I got the key from a friend of mine. It's empty. The owner's away most of the time. I thought you might like to see it." Michael shares an abbreviated story about knowing the owner. Then, he smiles at me in that secret way of his and hands me the key. I gingerly get out of the car, being careful with my left side as I undo the seat belt and slide out.

We've had a great morning. The fiasco of forgetting Emily's birthday is behind us and in combination with our wonderful evening with all of the kids last night all but forgotten possibly even by me. The pleasant morning we just shared with all of them has practically erased my guilt of mother failure. If it wasn't for the dull aching pain in my upper torso that even pain killers have not been able to reach today, I'd be in a virtual state of bliss, right now.

As it is, I've hidden my discomfort from Michael all morning. I paste a wide smile on my face now and try to damp down the throbbing pain by holding my arm tight to my chest. *Oh, the webs we weave and the truths we hide.*

Our life together seems to get more multifaceted with each passing day. But, for now, I just want to take a moment away from our complex reality and embrace an extraordinary one with the chance to go inside and see this beach house that I've always coveted. I think Michael knows this. He seems unable to contain his excitement and his smile only deepens, as we enter this private and perfect oasis.

"They redid the whole interior," Michael offers.

I turn the key and push open the front door. He follows behind me.

I gasp in wonder at the simple brightness—pale yellows and light crèmes set off with pure white wood trim and navy blue accents in the foyer and the living room. The beach-house color scheme along with the cozy dark navy sofa and chairs make the place so inviting. Michael flips a switch and the gas fireplace comes to life. It's done in river rock with an all-white, painted wood mantel and hearth. I run my hand along the smooth surface and smile over at him.

"Want to see the kitchen?"

"Yes."

I follow Michael out to the kitchen and practically moan with envy at the Viking gas stove and matching refrigerator in gleaming stainless steel. "Love the white cabinets and the earth-tone granite counter tops. It's perfect. I would have done it this way, too."

Forgetting my sore left side for a moment, I run my hand along the smooth cool surface of the counter tops and touch the red knobs of the gourmet Viking stove.

"It's great." My voice is less than enthusiastic.

Michael gives me a quizzical look. "You okay?"

"Sure." I give him a contrived wide smile. "This looks great. I love the way this looks. They really pulled warmth into the room with the gold tones and the light colors and the touches of navy blue—a true beach house theme."

We walk through the lower floor of the house. I hold on to Michael's hand and try to temper my emotions which have climaxed with excitement and growing dismay.

"You like it?"

"I do," I say, subdued.

"What's wrong?"

"I love it," I say with a shrug. "It's perfect. It'd be great if this place were for sale." I try to hide my feelings of disappointment behind a weak smile.

"You would move?"

"In a heartbeat. Look how private it is and the view and the waterfront. The house is beyond..." My voice trails off.

"Old," Michael muses.

"No! It's lived in and treasured," I say to him with a hesitant laugh. I start to climb the stairs, holding on to the banister with my good hand. "Hey, there are more bedrooms than I thought," I call out, racing ahead of him now. With a quick survey, I've counted six bedrooms. At the end of the hall, we stand in the middle of the master bedroom.

"It's a little small," Michael says with a touch of deprecation as we step inside.

"Hmmm...I love it." I touch the white lace duvet. "Whoever decorated the place kept things simple and understated. They have great taste." I smile over at him as we look around. "It has its own charm. The master bath is fabulous, too. Wow, it's like the house is..." My voice trails off and I look up at him, overcome with shyness all at once.

"What Ellie?" Michael looks at me with a bemused smile.

"It's like it's already…ours," I say wistfully.

Michael takes a deep breath; then grins over at me. "It is."

"What?" I ask in a faraway voice.

"I bought this place two months ago."

"How is that even possible? We weren't even speaking two months ago?" I ask in irritation.

"Well, that was only a matter of time. I had three months to get my act together and win you back."

"It was never you, Michael. It was *me*," I say with sadness.

"No. It's never been just you, Ellie. It's always should have been you and me. Once I allowed myself to believe in that, I was intent on buying this house for you…for our family. I just didn't know the significance of six bedrooms at the time." He pulls me to him and brushes my stomach with his hand and gets this thoughtful look. "Ellen Kay, will you marry me?"

How could I have not known that this would be what he would ask of me? I'm still in shock that I'm pregnant and haven't ventured further into where that might lead us. I look up at him now in true surprise. This was not what I'd been expecting because I thought we were in agreement about not rushing into anything. I tell him this now.

"Michael…" A rush of words form in my head, but nothing comes out.

"I know it's crazy. I know that we should wait, but, Ellie, you're pregnant with my child. I want to marry you and it's honorable and everything, but, that's not why I want to marry you."

"Well, why then?"

"Because I want a life with you and I want that life to start right now—this very minute. So, Ellen Kay, will you marry me?" His blue eyes do not leave my face and he stares into mine, openly conveying his wishes.

"Yes," I say without thinking. Michael Shaw seems to be connected to me at a soul level.

*Why would I even wonder if this the right thing to do?*

"I thought you might say yes," he says with a mischievous grin.

"What?" Now, I feel this panic invade me as if I've been trapped in some way.

"I told the kids that you would probably say yes."

"You *told* the kids?" I'm having second and third thoughts, now. "Exactly, what did you tell them?"

"I told them that we love each other and that we wanted to be a family and that I wanted to make it official."

"You do know that Nick and Elaina are not exactly brother and sister. Just how are you going to address those little details in the grand scheme of this house?"

"Well," he says with a wicked smile. "It's a smaller house, not quite on the grand scale of yours. I think it will be to our advantage and Nick and Elaina will figure out, too late, that it's not to theirs."

"Uh-huh. Oh…Michael…this is too much."

I move away from him, take the stairs two at time, and find refuge in the living room by warming my hands in front of the fire. "God, I love this house," I say with a tinge of regret. I whirl around, realizing he knows this. "Was this part of your seduction all along? Get me into this house? Knowing full well that I would find it impossible to say *no* to you?"

"You want me for my house?" Michael teases me now.

"That didn't come out right," I say. "I love the house. I have to have this house. You … you are *trouble*, Dr. Shaw." I give him an exasperated look.

"Come out to the beach," Michael says.

His seductive tone is impossible to resist. I watch him go.

He opens the French door to the backyard and begins to make his way down the gravel path that leads to the shoreline.

I follow him, mindless, reeling from the events and revelations of the past few minutes. I love the house. I love the patio. I love the yard. I love the landscape. I love the trees. There's a sandy beach right there. The waves lap in this methodical rhythm.

*Damn him. Why is he doing this to me? I love this place.*

It would be different enough to embrace and the same enough to feel right at home. The kids would love it. We could be a family right on this sandy shore on the very first day. I can already imagine the nights we could cook out on the beach and roast marshmallows or dig in the wet sand for clams. Oh, he's making this so hard to turn down. I glare at him as I make my way down to the sandy beach, where he stands, watching the waves gently lap the shore. He glances sideways at me.

"What?" He asks in that innocent voice of his. "What's wrong, Ellie? It's too perfect; isn't it?"

"Yes, that's it exactly."

I stare at him. A shaft of sunlight breaks through the clouds and shines down on his golden head, illuminating his remarkable face. He smiles at me.

We're in this strange dance. Unplanned. Unforeseen. I've changed partners after an almost lifetime, but I can't even remember Robert's face any longer. All I see is Michael's. Is it just me? Or, does Michael experience the same thing. I don't miss Robert because I have found a better way to complete my life with Michael.

"Do you miss her?" My hands move out in front of me, imploring him to tell me the truth because I have to know.

"I don't."

His honesty brings a weird connection between us that passes through us both at once. I see this incredulous expression cross his features when it happens. I smile wider, witnessing this magic.

"I don't miss him, either. It's strange; isn't it? Why do you think that is?"

"Because you've always been standing right in front of me," he says. "And now that I can touch you any time I want; I'm not lonely anymore. I'm complete with only you, Ellen Kay."

I am the master of words. I am editor. The writer.

Yet, it is Michael who has said the words that perfectly describe what I feel. Blame it on the cancer; blame it on the pregnancy, but now I start to cry. This man moves me to tears with his words.

"Well, I can't say *no* to you, now."

"No, you can't." Michael pulls me into his arms and kisses me.

I feel this cloak of happiness form around us as the shaft of sunlight envelops us both. This is the magic of Michael and me.

Then, I have this flitting unspeakable thought: *How long can it last?*

# Chapter Eight

 Good & Bad

hings have been moving at a kaleidoscope pace. Things change, but with the slightest movement, they change again. Good and bad. The good. I have healed from my surgery in that my incisions have healed up, but my pain remains. The bad. My doctors are vexed by this turn of events. My left side is still too sore to fully use. The bad.

Finally, both doctors, Josh and Michael, we have long dispensed with the formalities, have decided to go back to square one. They openly admit that they cannot explain why I still have pain on my left side.

So, today, I'm getting an MRI scan that will x-ray my entire upper torso. I have asked if this harmful to the baby and I have been assured the baby will be fine. I did notice that it was only Michael who said this to me. I must confess that I didn't completely trust his answer. He was less and less committed to this baby—our baby—because of my continual battle in wrestling cancer. The bad.

There is a mystique—a godliness to doctors. I have noticed this more and more. Doctors really do believe that they perform miracles every day, but my doctor, *my doctor,* did not seem to recognize the miracle that we had made together, beyond medicine. This was wreaking havoc on both of us. Doctors were definitely different than lawyers, at least the lawyer I had been married to for eighteen years, who has since married my best friend. Robert and Carrie being married was the least of my problems these days. I would have to call their marriage: the good.

Michael and I have been busy moving and combining our things into the beach house at a glacial pace. The good.

We are supposed to marry in three weekends at the beach house on the 21st of February. Emily will finally get to be a flower girl, while Elaina will be my only bridesmaid and my two sons will be groomsmen for Michael. We have a judge coming from Seattle, who is an old friend of Michael's from our college days. The cake has been ordered as well as the flowers. My dress is a beautiful crème colored sleeveless number that flows like spun sugar around me. Michael's black tuxedo is hanging in the quaint master bedroom of the beach house already. Elaina has already placed crème colored candles in candelabras throughout the house. The caterer has already created the menu with a nice Pacific Northwest cuisine theme to serve sixty.

It will be an intimate elegant beach party for our closest friends. After much debate, we've included Robert and Carrie on the guest list.

My mother is coming and so is my father, much to my complete surprise. Somehow, I know that an Ellie-is-your-only-daughter-and-she-had-or-may-still-have-cancer-and-we-all-need-to-be-there-for-her discussion has ensued with my mother doing all of that talking to my father. My secret conclusion: it was about time my dad stepped back into my life after a twenty-year absence with only the placation of birthday cards and infrequent phone calls. Yeah team! The good.

Now, I lay in this white tube ticking off these good and bad things and fight the claustrophobic feeling and the anxiety that ensues about staying still for more than half hour. Why is it that no matter who you marry there comes this little inkling of doubt on whether this is the right thing to do or not?

This has come about with even Michael and me because of this baby. It is ironic that the very thing that probably caused us to move faster toward this juncture of impending nuptials is the very thing that threatens to undo all of these illustrious plans between us. The bad.

At least, we finally got everything out in the open yesterday. We were at my house working with the movers on what to move to the beach house and what to leave behind. Michael and I had a rare private moment in the master bedroom. The movers were outside arranging bedroom furniture from the kid's rooms and the master bedroom into their gigantic moving truck.

The kids were negotiating deals with their friends for some of the stuff they'd discovered in the garage they no longer wanted. Not wanting to dampen their entrepreneurial enthusiasm; I gladly sent them off with their various treasures.

Frankly, it gave Michael and I a half day of *alone time*, which we hadn't been able to have since, well, since this whole new idea of getting married and moving to the beach house had taken root a mere two weeks ago. So, during that *alone time*, Michael brought up the fact that I'm now more than sixteen weeks along and we really need to talk about this.

"Talk about what?" I had to ask.

Well, this apparently upset him enough to come across like a complete jerk when he said, "We're talking about your *life*, Ellie, and you insist on putting this baby ahead of you. I didn't sign up for that."

Well, that was bad.

"Michael," I said. "You said I was going to be just fine. Are you going back on that promise, now?"

I had never seen him cry. The big, burly movers returned to our master bedroom and warily witnessed this tall golden god of a man's breakdown just as I did.

"I can't promise you that anymore, Ellie! That's what I've been trying to *tell* you. You should be fine. You're not fine. Ellie, I want to marry you, but I want you to be *here*."

This god-like man wept in front of me and the two big, burly, must-like-football-and-eat-hot-dogs-on-Sundays kind of men. Michael cried and he didn't stop. The bad.

"Okay," I finally said in desperation. "Okay. I hear what you're saying. You cannot promise me that everything is going to be okay. Okay. I will get the MRI tomorrow and then we will see what it says, what it tells us. If it's bad, then Michael, you and I, *together*, we'll decide what to do. Okay? We'll decide together what we have to do. I want to be here, too, Michael. I want to be here with *you*." The good.

"Ellie," he said in this heartbreaking voice, "Ellie, I love you."

"I know this to be true," I said. The good.

Referred pain. Reflective pain where the pain or problem is somewhere else in the body, but is felt in a *referred place*. This is what I have. The joke is played out on all of us as they—the radiologist, Michael, and Josh—discover, all at the same time, the tumor in my other breast which has been causing all this angst and havoc. I can tell by the grim look on all their faces that this is not a good thing. The bad.

How much more bad news can there be? Oh. I shouldn't even ask that. I shouldn't even think that thought. Based on my promise of yesterday, I have no doubt that this pregnancy will not even come up on a list of priorities. I can already tell this by the determined look on Michael's face. The topic of our baby is already closed and not even open for debate.

If I were able to salvage or save five things, what would they be? I ask myself this in this listless state.

My answer: me; myself and I—my two breasts.

My sense of humor has not completely left me. I smile to myself.

Why am I not more scared? I do not know. If I look at any one of their faces for too long though as they study the x-ray scans, I begin to get scared. They are talking as if I am not here. Maybe, I'm not. The bad.

"Jesus," Josh Liston is saying now. "I can't believe this. She had a mammogram six months for both right and left. It didn't even show up. It's aggressive. We'll need to call in Tom. We'll do a *double mas* with a complete reconstruct. I'll schedule the OR. We'll biopsy it this afternoon just to make sure we know what we're dealing with, but based on the growth level. Jesus. God damn it!"

Michael is not even talking. Josh is talking. The radiologist, Ben Thompson, is nodding. He points out the shadow on the right side of the screen and does a quick measurement from one of the films. "One point three centimeters in less than six months. This is not a nice cancer."

"Are any of them nice?" I ask, coming up behind them to look at the films for myself. I have interrupted a boy's group session. They automatically turn to me and begin to realize that I've been standing here the whole time, completely forgotten. All three of them hang their heads for a moment.

"Ellie," Josh says, breaking the silence. "We have to do a double mastectomy. We're going to call in Tom to do the reconstructive surgery. We'll do radiation, chemo—the works." His voice breaks at this point.

I can see that Dr. Josh Liston is out of options and possibly promises. The bad.

I struggle for composure, somehow sensing I need to provide it for all of us. I smile at my team.

"Well," I say with as much valor as I can emanate. "I guess I better meet with *Tom*, pronto, because I have always felt that these..." I point to my perfect "C" cup breasts. "These are my best feature, so he's going to have to promise perfection."

I give these three miracle workers my best smile. I know I have succeeded in making them forget, momentarily, how dire our current situation is because, as a team, all three of them smile at me. My only regret is that my Oscar-worthy performance is not caught on film of any kind. We only have x-ray machines in the room all around us, no cameras.

"Well, when do we do this biopsy?" I say in this false bravado voice.

"Thirty minutes," Michael answers for the group.

One of the nurses comes in with one of those toasty blankets to keep a patient warm and she leads me to a chair and drapes it over me. I have spa treatment status at the hospital, now, because of my team—Michael, Josh, Ben and soon to be, Tom. My status as a special client is now complete. I do thank the nurse. If she could just bring me a cup of tea like they do in real spa, I could actually forget that I'm sitting in a radiologist's suite surrounded by x-ray machines and films with my name on them with nothing good in the news. My bravado starts to wear off. About to cry, I head to the bathroom in my blue paper slippers and cotton hospital gown, turn the water on full blast and let the tears stream down my face. The bad.

Dr. Thomas Giordani is Italian, which immediately endures me to him because he seems sympathetic to my most womanly fears. He is a friend of Michael's. *Who isn't a friend of Michael's in this hospital?* He is invited to our wedding. I didn't even know this, until we start talking about it. I give him the lowdown on all of our wedding plans. His face becomes a bit of a mask of feigned interest and dull enthusiasm as I talk. I can tell that he's uncomfortable and faraway.

"Ellie," he finally says. "You're planning on getting married in three weeks?"

"Well, yes. You got the invitation."

"Ellie, what does your dress look like?"

"It's gorgeous. This sexy, sleeveless number..." I have not obviously thought about the ramifications of a *double mas*, as Josh called it, and breast reconstruction and what it will mean. I do now. Dr. Thomas Giordani, *Tom,* since he will now be a part of my growing team is looking at me with this kind of dismay and obvious sympathy. "I won't be able to wear it."

"No."

"I guess I better talk to Michael."

Tom nods. "I think so."

"So, will you be able to make similar bodacious tah tahs for me?" I ask, trying to put a good spin on things. I'm not sure where all this optimism is coming from. It's like I saved it up from my first thirty-eight years and am using it up now in these past few precious weeks.

"Yes," Tom says with an easy laugh. "Ellie, you're going to be okay, you know?"

"Easy for the plastic surgeon to say," I tease. I like Tom. I trust him.

"Monday, then."

"Monday, it is," I say back to him as he leaves the room. "If you see Michael, can you send him my way?"

"You got it." Tom winks at me as he leaves.

"We have a problem," I say to Michael as soon he comes into the patient room where they have me waiting for the biopsy. We've been here for hours. I would very much like to go home, but I refrain from complaining because I notice my husband-to-be is barely hanging in there.

"Just one?" Michael asks with a faint smile.

He has this wave of stress that continues across his features. His smile is forced. I can feel him breaking apart right in front of me. I take his hand and hold it in mine.

"Well, I'm choosing *just one* to focus on, right now," I say with a laugh. "I really want to wear that wedding dress. It's just such a fabulous dress and I know how much you're going to enjoy it… later."

"So, you're saying you want to get married this weekend."

"I believe that is what I'm saying. If, you're up for it." I watch him sigh and take a deep breath. He tries to smile.

"I guess I'm going to have to remind you I'm one that asked you in the first place and couldn't wait." Michael takes my hand and presses his lips to it.

"Still can't wait, though?" I ask a little uneasy, now.

"Still can't wait."

"Okay," I say.

"Okay."

"We could still host a party for all those flying in. I would still like to see my dad, my mom, and your parents. You only marry your soul mate once."

His blue eyes light up at this last part. I note a little bit of his stress ebb away from his face.

"We could get married twice. Different dress," Michael says.

"Long sleeve, high neck showing very little cleavage number?" He nods. "It's going to cost you," I say with a wicked grin.

"Don't care."

He kisses me, now. "I love you, Ellen Kay."

"I love you, Michael." He presses his lips to my hand.

This has been the longest day. The biopsy is finally done and only confirms that the cancer is malignant. No surprise there. I wish I hadn't had to hang around for two additional hours to find out something that deep down everyone already knew, but there is always process and procedures to follow.

Michael is driving us back off the ferry. We take an unfamiliar route.

I forget that it was only yesterday that we moved the last of our furniture to the beach house. I didn't even stop to enjoy and embrace the last night I spent in the old house—the home I had shared with Robert for sixteen years.

This melancholy steels over me. Damn it. Why am I ready to cry over something that is long gone, long past? Maybe, because it is something I was sure about and the future up ahead now seems uncertain and ever changing.

"What do you want to tell the kids?" Michael asks.

"Well, let's tell them we're getting married on Saturday," I say absently while staring out the window.

"That's *tomorrow*."

"It is? Oh, God. I thought it was Thursday." I stop for a moment. "Okay," I say and nod my head. "Well, I would rather get married tomorrow, so we have Saturday night to, you know…consummate this thing between us. That way I can eat something, anything I want, past midnight. Tomorrow works."

Michael is laughing. "Ellie, you constantly amaze me, you know that?"

"I do? Constantly?" I carefully lean over and playfully stroke his face.

"Constantly," he says.

"Michael," I say with so much emotion it is hard to speak. "You amaze me, too."

So, telling the kids has not gone as well as we had expected it to go. They're on edge and suspicious as to why all of a sudden the date for the wedding has been moved up by three weekends. They're not buying the we-are-anxious-to-get-married-and-just-want-to-be-all-together shtick.

My little biopsy incision begins to ache. Michael looks over at me. "What's the number?"

"Seven." I get up from the cozy chair in the family room and go to our fabulous white and gold granite kitchen for a glass of water. He follows me and hands me two white pills.

Emily is watching us the entire time. "What is *wrong* with you, mother?" Apparently, Emily has spokesman status for the entire brood of children, now. Mathew, Nicholas, and even Elaina are looking at her with true admiration. Emily stands there in that all-too-familiar stance, hands on her hips, and asks the question they've all been afraid to ask.

"Momma's sick," I say in my best and lightest tone. "They found more bad cells and I have to have a big surgery on Monday to take care of all that, so we wanted to get married and have all of you get dressed up and celebrate being in this house…together…this weekend." I pause, looking for the right words to tell this story. "Because…well, after Monday, we may be having pizza every night for a few more weeks." I try to smile at them all with this news. "We're still going to have the other big wedding celebration. This one tomorrow will be just for us."

"I don't get it," Emily says. Her frustration is unmistakable and every child in the room, even the two about to turn seventeen, seems to await my answer. The room holds its collective breath.

I look over at Michael and wanly smile. "Well, I want to wear my most fabulous wedding dress and I won't be able to wear that at the big party in the next few weeks," I say slowly. "I'll have to wear a different dress."

Elaina starts to cry. She just starts *crying*.

My six-year-old gives her a funny look, trying desperately to understand or read her mind. I see in Emily's face the question: What does Elaina know that I don't know?

Then, Elaina comes over to me. I enfold her in my arms even though my upper chest hurts like hell from all the procedures that I've had done in the last few hours.

"Ellie!" She cries out.

"Elaina, it's going to be okay," I say in my most soothing voice. "It *really* is."

"How do you know?"

"I believe that. Your dad believes that." Michael comes to stands beside me. He touches his daughter's arm with his. She lifts her head from my chest and stares at both of us.

"Elaina, it's going to be okay. I promise," Michael says.

I look over at him. He hasn't been able to do much promising the last few hours, let alone the last few days. I smile at him, now.

"Mother!" Emily says, all at once, in front of our little group. "Do you have *cancer?*"

*Is it possible that we've never said the word around her? Around any of them?* Both my sons' heads whip around looking at my mouth to see what I will actually utter.

"I do," I say. "I...do...have...cancer, but the big surgery on Monday will take care of all of that and I won't have it anymore. I'm going to be fine." I am not lying. I truly believe this.

My conviction must show on my face because they all come toward me and we do this family hug kind of thing. I can feel the emotion and power of their love. It radiates from all of them. I look over at Michael and I know he senses it, too. There is this look of wonder on his face. I reach out to him and hold his hand and give him one of my these-are-the-moments-we-will-always-have looks and smile for him alone.

The bedrooms are situated fairly and far enough apart, everyone is sleeping where they are supposed to be. I tell Michael that we really need to have the Elaina and Nicholas conversation between us; and then, with them, too, sometime soon. He agrees, but says not tonight. I agree. It is late Friday night. We are both awake and lying there in the dark together. "I put a lot of pressure on Tom for perfection for the bodacious tah tahs," I say finally. We have not spoken of my double mastectomy and immediate breast reconstruction surgery scheduled for Monday. Not one word. For a procedure that Michael performs with the surgical team at least once a week, he is reluctant to talk about it. He laughs in the dark at the bodacious tah tahs comment though and reaches for me, now. I am instantly on fire at his touch, in a good way. "Thank God for pain killers."

"Yeah," he says back to me. "Thank God for those."

"I'm not usually this high maintenance, you know."

"You're not high maintenance even now," he whispers.

"I love you, Michael. We'll make another."

"We will," he says back to me.

His tears mingle with mine. I know he's crying because of the sacrifice that he acknowledges I'm making in giving up this child, but I don't think he realizes I'm crying because I just want three things—him, the kids, and me, myself and I. My sense of humor is still intact. Okay, really eight things if I list off the kids separately and count my breasts. Well, really, nine things, if I'm being honest, since I continue to hope for the miracle baby inside, too.

Nine things. Only nine, less than ten. That's it. I won't ask for more.

# CHAPTER NINE

## Wedding Day

An unusual delicious aroma wafts its way from the kitchen downstairs. It's a tantalizing mixture of bacon and coffee. I open my eyes and contemplate the idea of getting up, tempted by the enticing smell of fresh coffee, and even the bacon. Now, I feel Emily, whose little legs are spread wide between us, Michael and me. We cling to our respective edges, trying not to fall out of the king-size bed as my daughter takes over. Her arms are flipped out over her head like the broad bony wings of a large bird and her sharp elbows are near both our defenseless faces. Emily is a dangerous creature in sleep, which is why she isn't normally allowed to sleep with me. Late last night, she came wandering in, crying from a bad dream and before I'd had a chance to redirect her back to her bed, Michael turned on the bedside lamp, opened the covers, and allowed her to crawl right in.

I gave him a wary look. "Are you okay with this?"

"Yeah. She's mine, too, Ellie. She's just scared." He stroked the side of Emily's face and she just burrowed further into the covers between us.

"Thanks, Michael," Emily said still half-asleep, instantly cured of her fears.

"She's a wild thing in bed," I said in warning. "She'll probably give one of us a black eye with her elbows before the night is out."

Michael had just laughed and turned out the light. A few minutes went by; Emily already snored softly.

"As wild as you?" Michael whispered in the dark.

"Almost." I giggled. Then, he'd snaked his hand across Emily and held mine.

*Coffee. Bacon.* The delectable scent dizzies my senses and confuses me. I open my eyes and look around. Emily is still sleeping. Michael is still there, too. Who's making coffee and bacon? Neither Nicholas nor Mathew is allowed to use the stove. Nick caused a small kitchen fire about a year ago and there is a ban in place for both of them because of this. And, after the mishap with the coffee maker a few months ago, I'd banned the privilege of unsupervised cooking of any kind for all my children.

I look over at Michael as I slide out of bed. He opens his eyes. "Who's here?" I ask. "Because my kids aren't allowed to cook. Does Elaina?"

"I don't know," he says in answer to all my questions.

He sits up in bed. His bare chest immediately bewitches me and I mischievously smile over at him.

"Well, good morning to you," I say when he passes me; his hard-on evident through his boxers makes me smile wider.

"Give me five minutes," he says. Curious, I follow him into the bathroom.

"Exactly, what do you plan to do with Emily, since she is in our bed? This is another reason why I didn't want to invite her into it," I whisper in my I'm-not-getting-my-way voice.

Michael comes over to me and holds me in his arms, bends down, and kisses me.

"I'll meet you in the sixth bedroom," he says with meaning. I smile in answer.

I hurriedly brush my teeth for our upcoming rendezvous. This house is like some kind of miracle, I muse, languishing on the gold duvet waiting for him. After a few more elongated minutes, Michael comes in. He immediately shuts and locks the door.

"Carrie's here," he says, bemused.

"Carrie?" I half-smile; uncertain. What's Carrie doing at the house?

"She's making breakfast for everyone. Nick and Elaina are helping." He shrugs and then gets a wide smile. "Let's not talk about Carrie, right now."

And, so we don't.

Michael's lovemaking is inexplicable, life-altering. I can't really explain it. He is gentle in his touch. I'm trying to remember if this is because I have had numerous surgical procedures or if he is always this way. His touch makes every cell of my body react. Respond. It is my undoing. I cannot control myself after a certain point. I have to answer in kind to his touch with some of my own because my body at some point must dance to this music. I think he knows this because there is a point after we come together when he gets this bemused look upon his face. Today, I say a silent prayer to God for this man and pain killers. I popped a few of those, while waiting for him. The aching pain across my chest has all, but gone away. "What?" I ask in this playful way when I see his thoughtful look as we languish in each other's arms a half later. I don't really expect him to answer, but he does.

"Ellie," he says, now. "I'll always be here. I'll never leave you." I believe him in the moment when he says this, but then, this senseless uncertainty drifts over me.

"Michael, I'll always be here, too, and I'll never leave you," I say with this sudden urgency, smothering the other irrational thought before it can take hold.

Carrie is in my kitchen, well, Michael's kitchen and now mine.

She has poured me a cup of coffee with cream, just the way I like it. It has been months since we have shared a cup of coffee together, so long ago, I can't even remember that particular day.

She sets a plate of scrambled eggs and bacon in front of me. I sit at the wide granite counter top bar across from her as she works away in our kitchen. Nick and Elaina sit at the kitchen table eating breakfast. Michael has come in fully dressed in Levi's and a UW Huskies' t-shirt, carrying Emily who is still in her Little Mermaid pajamas. He sets her down at the table and Carrie hands him a plate of food for her. My husband-to-be slides into a bar chair next to me, while Carrie sets a plate of food resembling my breakfast in front of him.

*It's a surreal scene.* "So," I finally say. "What's the agenda for today?"

"You need to be ready by two in the afternoon," Michael says with a mysterious smile. "Everything else is taken care of." He gives Carrie a meaningful look.

"Yep, everything else is taken care of," Carrie says, now.

I'm at a loss. I just cannot put this puzzle together. "So, what... we're all friends, now?" I have this queer, unsettled feeling and I know it's apparent in my voice.

Everyone stops eating to look at me and appears spellbound in who is going to respond first to my question. It's Carrie.

"We have always been friends," she says. "And now, well, now... we are friends more than ever before because I love you both." She struggles with her words and I sense she's about to cry. I discern her suffering and watch her from this faraway place and wonder what she's been suffering from. "I don't want to *lose* you, Ellie."

*Geez!* She's crying in front of my children and her own. All these children warily contemplate this scene as it unfolds.

I move quickly. I silently thank God again for painkillers.

With determination, I pull my former best friend along with me through the French doors of the home office. Through my peripheral vision, I see Nick, Elaina, Emily, and Mathew, and even Michael, gaping at Carrie and me through the glass doors.

"Okay," I say a little out of breath. We stand apart from each other, while I still hold on to her hand. "Carrie, get a grip. They're all watching."

Carrie looks at me in anguish with tears streaming down her face. "Oh, Ellie," she says. "I can't lose you. I can't. I just couldn't take it."

"I'm not going anywhere," I say with disdain. I reach out and touch her hand. "Hey, I'm going to be *fine*." My action unleashes her and she hugs me tight. I'm taken aback by her heartfelt sentiment. "Carrie," I finally say. "That hurts like hell."

"Oh, God, I'm sorry." She steps away from me and openly stares at my chest, as if she can see right through the white button-down blouse I'm wearing.

"They're still there," I say dryly.

"Oh," she says. "Well, I know how much your bodacious tah tahs mean to you and since it is your best feature, I just…"

I start to laugh, a slight laugh, at first, and then, full-on laughter grips me. Then, Carrie laughs.

It's twenty-one years ago, when we first became friends at college. I'm the lost, broken, and homesick freshman; and she is *Carrie*, the bubbly, alive and courageous freshman roommate I've just met. I think of all of this and abruptly stop laughing and just stare at her, transfixed, now. "I miss you. I miss you so much, Carrie." My words are involuntarily stolen from me and I realize their truth as I utter them.

"I've missed you, too," Carrie says. "I thought I would have everything I want. Everything I need, but Ellie, I…"

"You can't live without me?"

"I can't," she says.

I glimpse her remorse, just now, just for a moment. Carrie starts to cry, again. I glance over through the glass French doors and see the assortment of our family standing there, even Robert's arrived.

"Well, okay." I take a deep breath and drape my somewhat good left arm around her shoulders. "You won't have to. I promise. I'm not going anywhere."

"You're the best liar in the world," she says now. "Don't say it, unless you *mean* it."

"I *mean* it. I'm not going anywhere. I *will* be okay."

"And, what about the bodacious tah tahs?" Carrie asks.

"Tom Giordani has promised new perfection—even *better*—bodacious tah tahs," I say with a slight smile.

"He's the best," she murmurs. "That's great. Okay." She takes a deep breath and wipes away at her tear-streaked face. "Ellen Kay, I'm sorry. I'm just so sorry."

"Sorry? Sorry that you led me to the best part of my life? There's no need to be sorry for that, Carrie."

She looks at me with those green eyes of hers in this state of wonder and awe as if God has come down and bestowed sainthood upon me. She smiles as if she knows that secret.

"What?" I ask, suddenly defensive.

"You are so amazing, so extraordinary, Ellen Kay."

I smile. There are no words that I can come up with in that moment. My smile falters and I can feel the tears welling up in my own eyes. My bravado fades. "I've missed you, too," I say in this weakened state. "And, frankly, I could use a best friend, right now. It's really not fair to burden Michael…to saturate him with all this *need*, all this worry, right now."

"Michael can handle it. He's got enough strength for all of us. Ellie, he loves you so much."

I stare at Carrie, open-mouthed. Her words are like a gift—a blessing. I feel this release from guilt and anguish. There's been this implicit barrier between Michael and me. In that moment, I realize it's *me* and these feelings I harbor over Carrie, causing me this uncertainty. Somehow, in choosing me, Michael has gotten the lesser prize. Add to that, my battle with cancer and I'm no prize at all. Apparently, I've spoken of these insecurities out loud. Carrie gapes at me in disbelief.

"He *loves* you. He's *always* loved you. It's why...it's why I finally reached out to Robert. I just couldn't take it anymore. I could never be *you*."

"What?" I ask in bewilderment.

"Ellie, he has always loved you. Always." Her tone is so matter of fact, so believable. "It's always been you. I knew this before I even married him that he was in love with you, but you were married to Robert, by then." Carrie shrugs and gives me a twisted smile. "I think we both thought, if we got married that somehow the love would just grow between us and in some ways, it did. In others... well, I could never be *you*."

I've heard too much. I can't take it anymore. I move to the sofa in the room and sit down with a profound shudder. Carrie comes to sit beside me and takes my hand. She apologizes for upsetting me. She thanks me for listening to her, even though, at this point, I can barely hear her. I'm so far away in another place, her voice is like a whisper to my ears and the words make no sense. Michael has always loved me? And, she has known this? For like, ever? I don't understand. I can't understand this.

"What about Robert?" I ask anxiously. "Do you *love* him?"

"I do." It's the way that she says this. Carrie, who never really shares her feelings, is being truthful. Her voice resonates with this sincerity. It's so solemn and enlightened.

"I love him," she says now. Her beautiful face lights up in a way I have never seen before. It is a new face. It is in her eyes and her features—a face of wonder, delight and contentment.

"You're happy?" I ask, still uncertain. I cannot help myself. I have to know.

"I am." She smiles.

"So am I." Emphatic; I say this in a you-will-not-be-taking-him-from-me kind of way.

"I know." The benevolence in her voice is not lost on me.

We have made it through this hell, these past months, without talking, without sharing our lives, with nothing, but disappointment and rage between us. It's been hard, heartbreaking, and sad. It's been like walking across fire, but now, I am on the other side and she is with me. We are together, again. We sit in silence for a few minutes, savoring the forgiveness between us.

Then, Carrie gives me a sideways glance and finally smiles. "I know, Ellie. I know you're pregnant."

I nod and look over at her in anguish. "I don't get to keep it."

"Because Michael says so?"

"Because *they all* say so."

"Who's your oncologist, Ellie?"

I look at her in surprise. "Ben is my radiologist. They want to do chemo, I guess, I'll get an oncologist, then."

"Uh huh. It's such a boys club." We sit in stalled silence, lost in our own thoughts. Then, Carrie stands and pulls her cell from her pocket. "I'm calling Lisa, right now." I stare at her a moment and realize she's wearing an old blue sweater of mine from college.

"That sweater's mine, you know."

"Yeah, I know." She stares at me. "I was missing you. Sometimes, I wear your stuff that I've kept, to be close to you." She smiles and I watch her as she holds the cell phone.

"Lisa, it's Carrie. Hey…God, Lisa, I need your help. My best friend, Ellie, I told you about her. Well, she's scheduled for a *double mas* with immediate reconstruction on Monday." I watch Carrie's face; she gets this vexed look on it. "Yeah," she says. "Look, Lisa, she's pregnant and they want her to terminate, but I think you should talk to her first. I mean the boys have this all worked out. Yeah, Liston, Shaw, Giordani, Thompson…"

Carrie stops talking and I can hear this profound long string of swear words through the phone. I smile as I listen.

"Yeah, I know," Carrie says, after the tirade stops. "Look, Ellie's marrying Michael today. Why don't you come? They'll all be here. We can have a little pow-wow—a little gender mix-up at the reception." Carrie laughs at something this Lisa says.

This conflicted feeling washes over me, a filmy cloud of uncertainty. These things that Carrie is talking about sound incongruent to Michael's wishes, but I'm too intrigued by the confidence in her voice and the enchanting sound of this Lisa's voice on the other end of Carrie's cell phone.

"Yes, absolutely, she should come," I say with spontaneity to Carrie and to this Lisa on the phone, ignoring the uneasiness that assails me as soon as the words are out of my mouth.

# CHAPTER TEN

 *No Words*

It's another surreal moment. I'm standing in my new-to-me master bedroom staring into the gilded mirror at my sumptuous sleeveless white Vera Wang wedding gown. It's twenty minutes after one in the afternoon and I am marrying Michael in another forty. I've been bathed, buffed and polished. My Gene Juarez saviors were engaged for all of this, per Carrie, who has reached guardian angel status at this point. All I want to do is sit down. I bite my lip and wonder what the consequences for doing so might be.

Robert Bradford strides in. Now, he stands, transfixed, staring at me.

"Bobby, what are you doing here?"

We have not really spoken. He has had assignments from Carrie that involved squiring Michael away from the house for the majority of the morning.

I've been left in the dark about most everything. The Gene Juarez entourage just left. I think they even put colored lip gloss on Emily. I'm helpless and control nothing, at this point. Somebody really needs to come up with a way for a bride to sit down. Standing for forty minutes, before going down the aisle, is a bit much.

"So? What? Are you supposed to do, stand there, until they call you?" He looks completely perplexed. It makes me laugh.

"I guess so," I say.

"Well, that's crazy." Bobby comes over and undoes the pearl buttons on the back of my dress, unzips it, and helps me step out of it. I have these thigh-high, white nylons with an intricate lace pattern of lilies on them and this crème colored bustier, matching panties; and that's it. "Wow, Ellie, you look so beautiful."

"Bobby Bradford, knock it off. Just help me hang this thing up. I can't reach my arms that high. What are you doing here, anyway?" He takes the wedding gown from me and puts it on the silk hanger and hangs it on the hook on the wall.

"Well, since you made up with Carrie...I just wanted to thank you for that."

"I just want you to be happy." We say this together at the same time and both start to laugh.

"Look, Ellie. These past few months have been..." Robert Bradford has no words for me. This is highly unusual. The man is articulate to a fault.

I just grin over at him. "The best and worst of your life?"

"Yes."

"Bobby, we're going to be okay." I pat his left hand, innocently touching his new gold band.

"Ellie...are *you* going to be okay?" There are tears in his eyes and his sentiment slays me right there. There are all kinds of love in this world and I still love this man, not like Michael, but I still love Bobby and I can see that he still loves me. Oh, this day, it's almost more than I can take. I grab his hand and squeeze it.

"I'm going to be fine," I say with a laugh.

He comes towards me and pulls me into his arms and kisses my forehead. "Ellen Kay, you are amazing."

*How many times will I hear this? Will I ever believe it to be true?*

Carrie comes in. The look of insecurity and consternation on her face speaks volume as she surveys me in my lingerie and Bobby in his tuxedo still hugging me. It appears we have a long way to go towards completely trusting one another again. I give her a wry smile.

"I just wanted to sit down." I move out of Bobby's arms, across the room, and slide into a chair. Carrie drapes a quilt over me.

"I brought you some tea," Carrie says as she carries over this cup of steaming liquid.

"What have you done with my best friend Carrie? You don't have to get me any other gifts. The tea is perfect," I add, when I see tears in her eyes. Robert goes over to Carrie and puts his arm around her and kisses her.

"She's going to be fine. She told me so and the woman cannot lie." I laugh and almost spill the tea. Carrie gives me a secret smile. The fact that Robert has never figured out that I can lie like a tarot card reader is hilarious.

Michael chooses this moment to come into our intimate little setting.

"What are *you* doing here?" Carrie and I ask at the same time.

"It's *my* house," Michael says. He looks only at me. He's stunning in his black tuxedo with a silver tie and silk vest and formal white tuxedo shirt. "Soon, to be yours and mine," he adds with an uncertain laugh.

"Thank God for Armani, pain killers, and you, today," I say only to him. "You look amazing." This weird look of disquiet crosses his face. The word, amazing, has been overused so much lately. I grimace and try for another. "Stunning, handsome, prince-like, wondrous…" I stammer now, unable to stop. Michael shakes his head and laughs.

"You're killing me with your prose, Ells. You better have your vows written down. You look nervous. You're not even dressed!" He kneels beside me. "Second thoughts?"

"No."

I look around him at Carrie and Robert, who stand there unsure of what they should be doing. I smile.

"Can you give us a minute?" I ask. "You'll stand up for us; won't you?" I see the gleam in Michael's eyes and know this is one of the things we were going to talk about.

"Yeah," Carrie says in this hoarse voice. "You've got ten minutes, Dr. Shaw. And then, I'll be returning to put Ellie *back* into her dress."

"Okay," Michael says without looking at either of them. He only looks only at me.

Michael is unsure. I discern his hesitation as I watch my future husband pace the floor from my vantage point where I still recline in the chair next to the blazing fire.

"Ellie, I...I'm getting ready and I'm thinking of you and I'm thinking of all that you've been through. Well, I start to think that maybe, I've been pushing you too much. That this," he gestures wide with his left arm. "All of this is too much. I want this so much, but I don't want any of it, if you don't want the same thing. So, Ellie, if you don't want to do this, well, it's okay. We don't have to do this."

I'm stunned by what he's just said. For a moment, I want to give in to the hurt that his words cause, but the anguish in his face stops me. Now, I see his vulnerability for what this really is. He loves me enough to let me go. If that is what I would choose, he would do it. His sentiment is so moving I want to cry, but the Gene Juarez entourage flashes through my mind and vanity prevails.

I take a deep breath and let it out. "Michael, there is nothing and no one in this world that I love more than you. You are my life, now. I don't want anything else, but you." He looks over at me for a long time. Then, he comes to kneel beside my chair.

"Okay," he says simply.

He reaches into his pocket and slides this gigantic diamond ring on my left ring finger. I stare at it unable to speak.

It is gorgeous, sparkly, and huge. I turn my hand this way and that, watching it catch the light. The week before, we decided to go with simple gold wedding bands for each other. I'm speechless at the platinum brilliant diamond ring that sparkles on my left hand.

"Michael, I thought we agreed to keep it simple."

"I changed my mind," he said. "You deserve everything, Ellie. I want the world to know that I know that."

"Show off," I whisper.

"You want me to take it back?" He starts to slide it off my finger. I pull my hand away.

"No. I'm keeping it. It's gorgeous. God knows, I deserve it for putting up with you." My pretentious complaint causes him to laugh. "I assume you traded in the keep-it-simple wedding bands to match this ring?"

"Something like that. Emily has the wedding rings."

"Oh, God, Michael, no." I groan. "She loses everything."

"I think she can handle it, Ellen Kay."

He kisses me, then and I put my arms around his neck and pull him to me. "I love you, Michael."

"I love you, too," he says with a dazzling smile.

Just as we break away from this thoughtful embrace, Carrie strides back into the room. She's wearing this beautiful, long, silver, sleeveless dress that she stole from my closet earlier in the day. We decided to do the *matchy matchy* thing with her daughter as much as we could. Elaina is also dressed in a beautiful silver silk dress with spaghetti straps, but it's a little less revealing than Carrie's.

"Your friend, Samuel Davidson, just got here, Michael. You better go tell him where he needs to be. He's looking for the marriage license and stuff."

"Okay," Michael says, while still looking at me. "I'll see you in fifteen minutes, Ellen Kay. Don't be late." He kisses my left hand.

"I won't." He pulls me up and brushes my lips with his. "See you in fifteen," I call out and hear his laugh down the hall.

I've written my vows down. I did this late last week when I couldn't sleep one night. I already know that they are inadequate for what I'm feeling about Michael, how he makes me feel. They're just words and I realize this as I reread them now. Me. The writer. The editor. I am at a loss for words about Michael. I don't know how to say what I feel. I experience this building terror, so powerful, my body shakes.

Carrie gives me a curious look as she takes my wedding gown from the hanger and coaxes me into stepping in it. "Careful... Careful...," she says over and over. In a last minute effort, she has removed my strappy white sparkly sandals from my feet. My perfectly painted light-pink toe nails flash up at me.

The panic takes over. I start babbling. "I don't know what to say. I wrote down my vows, but it's not going to be enough. It's not going to come out right."

"Ellie, it's going to be fine." She zips up the back of my dress and re-does the pearl buttons. I wave my hands in agitation. Ellie." Carries steps around in front of me, surveying her work and grasps my arms. "The look on your face says it all."

"The look on my face?"

"Trust me. Your vows will be fine. Your words will be more than enough." She retrieves the veil and puts it on top of my head. The Gene Juarez crew styled my hair in a loose chignon at the back of my neck and she attaches the veil to it and pulls a few tendrils forward. "There, you're perfect."

"You look so beautiful," I say. My eyes fill with tears.

"Thanks, Ellie...there are no words to describe you, friend." Carrie beams at me. "Now, get a grip. Don't cry. You'll ruin all that make-up from the Gene Juarez trio."

I gaze at Carrie. She is so striking. Her auburn hair swirls around her delicate porcelain shoulders. Her make-up is flawless. Her lips the perfect color of rose. Her green eyes sparkle. She wears a flashy diamond on her left hand that Robert must have given her for her own nuptials in Vegas a few weeks before. Mostly, though, what I notice is how happy she is. It's there in her movements, in her voice inflections, and in her eyes. We have come full circle. I know that we both feel it. I grab her hand and hold it in mine.

"Thank you for everything, Carrie," I say. Her smile deepens. "Don't cry."

Elaina and Emily walk in, dressed in all their silver and pink finery, respectively, with all the flower bouquets. I can smell the fragrance from the mixture of white and pink lilies and roses from across the room.

"Momma," Emily says in pure joy. "You look so beautiful! Even better than Giselle."

I flash my daughter a bright smile, while I tuck my note card with my vows inside my bouquet. "Let's go," I say to this group of gorgeous girls.

The sun has come out. I take it as a sign as I stand before Michael and his friend, Samuel, who is marrying us. My dress swirls around me in the light breeze. We stand at the edge of the lawn under an arch that has miraculously appeared like so many other things that some angel has planned for me this day. I suspect it is more than one angel, perhaps a coalition comprised of Michael, Robert, and Carrie. I'm overjoyed, heady with nerves and indescribable bliss. Michael is looking at me now with this intense love, as he has been for the last twenty minutes. Samuel tells the crowd that we have prepared our own vows.

Michael goes first. "Ellen Kay, you are my soul mate. I love you as if you are the air I breathe. As you stand here in front of me, I can only thank God that now I can touch you any time I want because I'm complete with only you, Ellen Kay."

His words cause my eyes to fill with tears. He has said these similar words to me before in this very place, just weeks before. I should have known that he would know exactly what to say—what vow to make to me today. I smile at him, but my mind becomes this blank slate and the minutes stretch on. I'm not paying attention any longer. I've drifted someplace else entirely.

"Your vows, Ellie," Samuel says to me. Michael smiles at me. I've taken too long.

"Oh." I whip out my piece of paper from the flowers. Michael is watching me. His steady gaze is making me even more nervous. I cannot read the words on the page. I stare at them for a minute.

The breeze picks up. I look over at the white sandy beach and the blue sapphire water and feel momentarily lost in all of this.

"Ellie," Michael's steady voice brings me back. "It's okay."

His words have a calming effect. I'm transported back and find myself standing in front of him. I see only him. It no longer matters that more than a hundred people have shown up today for this *just us* affair that has turned into some sort of spiritual renewal for everyone here. All that matters is him and me. I nod at him now. A slow smile spreads across my face. I let go of the paper and watch it fly away across the sand.

"There are no words to adequately describe what you mean to me," I say in this beguiling voice. "I put my life in your hands because you complete me. We may be tested. There will be obstacles put in our way. Cancer may try to take me, but I will stay, here with you because you're all I want, all I need, all I see. I love you, Michael."

Michael is crying. Samuel is crying.

I turn because I hear more tearful cries behind me from this unexpected crowd of people that are gathered on our lawn in this rare display of sunshine on Bainbridge Island on this seventh day of February. People are wiping tears from their eyes. Bobby Bradford is *crying*, so is Carrie.

It is Emily Bradford who breaks the moment, probably, because it needs to be broken. There is too much emotion. Although I suspect she has grown bored in dutifully just standing there waiting for us to finish. "So, when do we get cake? When are you going to kiss her, Michael?" Emily tries to whisper, but the crowd moves at her words and little snippets of contained laughter wend their way toward us. I smile over at Emily and then back at Michael, who smiles only at me.

"Em, just a few more minutes, okay?" Michael says to her.

Emily nods and grins at both of us. "Okay," she says. "Go on." She waves her little hand in the air.

"Do we have the rings?" Samuel asks with a laugh. Emily brings the heart-shaped pillow up to us and gallantly displays the rings in her little hand, then retakes her place next to Elaina.

We exchange rings among the laughter. Finally, Samuel pronounces us man and wife before the enthusiastic, celebratory crowd, whose emotions seemed to have been on a roller coaster ride as much as our own as restless sighs reverberate throughout. "You may kiss your bride, Michael," Samuel says.

I don't know what I was expecting. I thought we would have this simple kiss, since Emily is trying to hurry this along, but Michael chooses this moment to begin our lives together with this never-ending kiss. It is a possessive, I-am-only-going-to-love-you kind of kiss. I kiss him back in kind. Then, with Emily loudly saying, "It really is time for cake." We draw apart.

"I love you, Ellen Kay," Michael whispers.

"I love you, Michael Thomas," I say.

It is magical all around us. I bask in the amazing light, but then shiver with an unexpected gust of wind whipping up from the water and swiftly wonder; *how long it will last?*

# CHAPTER ELEVEN

 *Options*

There are too many miracles in this day. My mother and father are here. Michael's parents are here. Upon learning the wedding date had been moved up, the Town & Country Market catered the entire thing and managed to feed the one hundred and ten people who have just shown up. Everyone I have ever cared about is here, including my wonderful boss, Harriet Windstrom, from my publishing firm in New York City. It is truly unbelievable. There are wedding gifts overflowing the table on the patio. The four-tier white wedding cake that someone ordered at the last minute has managed to feed the entire crowd and there's still more cake for tomorrow. The cake is still a work of art decorated with shaved white chocolate and strings of white pearls on each layer. The photographer that also miraculously arrived, on short notice, has taken formal and candid shots of all of us. I don't think I have stopped smiling, since I walked down the aisle to Michael.

It is four thirty in the afternoon, now. Some of the crowd has dispersed or left. There is a charming white tent with a dance floor set up on one side of flowing green lawn. I have taken a few too many turns on the dance floor with Michael, Robert, and my dad. I am now truly exhausted and this aching pain throbs in protest along my chest wall. I mixed a few glasses of champagne with a set of my pain killers. I was hoping I wouldn't need them. The pain from yesterday's biopsy has been bothering me. I had to slip away to take a few more. I haven't given a thought to my pregnancy at all. I can't think about it. It makes me sad and I don't want to be sad today.

My groom is busy talking to Josh, Ben and Tom, whose wives all hover together to one side of these men. Doctor's wives, they all hang out together. This makes me a little uneasy, as if this is something I will have to learn to do. I watch from a distance with a dose of trepidation and envy. Will I ever fit in to that kind of crowd?

Carrie is coming over to me. She is arm-in-arm with a beautiful, tall brunette with this charming smile that lights up her face and dark brown eyes, who looks like a real life version of Angelina Jolie's Lara Croft with the long dark hair, slender and tall, with an airy self-confidence that unmistakably conveys no one dares mess with her. *I like her instantly.*

"Ellie, I want to introduce you to Lisa. Dr. Lisa Chatham, this is my best friend, Ellie. Ellie Shaw."

My new name sounds strange. I think my surprise at Carrie's casual use of it shows on my face. Dr. Lisa Chatham is grinning at me.

"Just call me, Ellie. It's nice to meet you, Dr. Chatham."

"Ellie, it's great to meet *you*. Call me, Lisa." I glance over at Michael across the way who's giving me a curious look. He says something to his group of friends and they all turn at once to stare at the three of us.

"I see the boys club is already on the alert," Carrie says.

"What is your specialty, Lisa?" I ask. I suspect I already know what her specialty is. This little warning bell goes off in my head. Somehow, I already know that our first test of marriage has just arrived with this extraordinary woman, Dr. Lisa Chatham.

"I'm an oncologist as well as a gynecologist."

"Wow that must keep you busy." I can barely breathe.

"Carrie has filled me in on your health status, Ellie," Lisa says. I look at Lisa and then at Carrie who just nods.

"I have breast cancer. There's a double mas with complete reconstructive surgery scheduled for Monday morning," I say with bravado. "I'm sixteen weeks pregnant due in July. That's my *status*."

"Yeah, well, let's talk about that," Lisa says. "I assume your surgeon has told you all the side effects with a double mastectomy and is intent on terminating your pregnancy? They've proposed radiation, chemo—the works, right?" Her tone is deprecating and to the point. She mimics words that I have just recently heard from Josh and Ben and Tom and Michael. The implication of her words twists across my face in a way that I haven't allowed myself to feel. I'm sure my desolation shows.

"I've been promised a new perfect set of bodacious tah tahs," I say in this soft, wistful voice. Carrie and Lisa exchange half-smiles. Lisa shakes her head and then laughs. I can't laugh. I'm stricken with this weird sense of isolation. *Is this really happening to me? Is this what I want?* I glance around Carrie and Lisa and discover Michael making his way over to me along with Ben, Josh and Tom.

"Well, I'd like to talk to your doctor before you proceed with these surgeries, Ellie," Lisa says in this serious, no-one-dares-fuck-with-me tone.

"Great, you can meet them all." I gasp for air. "Because here they all come."

Carrie steps forward, as if to shield both Lisa and me from the male-dominated doctors' entourage that descends upon us. She makes the introductions of Dr. Lisa Chatham, oncologist and gynecologist to Dr. Michael Shaw, surgeon and my new husband; Dr. Benjamin Thompson, radiologist; Dr. Joshua Liston, surgeon; and Dr. Thomas Giordani, plastic surgeon.

There are no words spoken after introductions for a few minutes. The tension is evident. As if to add another element to this fine group of doctors, Lisa turns and her face lights up as this tall, dark handsome cliché of a man walks up and puts his arm around her.

"This is my husband, Dr. Stephen Chatham, he specializes in oncology and gynecology as well," Lisa says, introducing Stephen to all the doctors she's just met. I suspect that she knows of them all, at least, because she doesn't miss a single name or their specialty.

"So, Carrie has filled me in on Ellie's health condition. I understand you have her scheduled for a *double mas* with complete reconstruction on Monday," Lisa says.

"Yes," Michael says. He looks defiant as he stares down Lisa and Stephen Chatham. Then, he turns and looks over at me with this pleading look as if to say help-me-out-here.

"I think we should talk about options before we get to the let's-just-cut-her-up-and-replace-it-all-with-silicone-stage," Lisa says in an even tone. I hear the intake of shuddering breaths that runs through the group in a single instant, as if we're witnessing how spontaneous combustion really works.

Everyone talks at once. All these doctors' voices get louder and louder trying to make themselves heard. Carrie is speechless, although I don't think she is too surprised at this turn of events. She has been around doctors more than me. I've only known Michael. I've only been a doctor's wife for two and a half hours. I was a lawyer's wife for eighteen years. It's different. I must admit. The lack of decorum, the need to get points across, the need to be right is the same, just the process in which one conveys one's thoughts is different; no one takes turns for argument here.

I step away from the turmoil of these miracle workers, if that is what they are. Lisa's words—before-we-get-to-the-let's-just-cut-her-up-stage-and-replace-it-all-with-silicone—resonate with me in a peculiar way. I cannot get the cadence of her voice or her choice of words out of my mind. Lisa, Stephen, and Carrie move toward me and away from my *team*. "What options?" I ask above the noise.

"What options?" I ask again.

I can hear the hope and desperation in my own voice. Michael must hear me, too. He stops talking and there's a look I've never seen on his face before. Betrayal. It travels across his features in the guise of disappointment. *In me.* Apparently, as the patient, I'm not even allowed to ask what options I might have.

The party is over. It is dusk, now. The children are inside. The Chatham's have left. The newly-married Bradford's are the only remaining guests. Even my mother and father have been squired away, by some kind neighbor—I cannot recall who—back to their respective hotels intent on catching early-morning flights from Sea-Tac Airport back to their homes.

Emily is already in bed. "Being a flower girl makes me tired," she said to me, a half hour ago. I told her I understood because being a bride has been pretty exhausting, too.

Elaina is packing her suitcase. She is going with Robert and Carrie. Nick is sullen and sad to see her leave. Carrie and I have had a quick conversation regarding this young love between them. She and I are on the same page. We agree that it is the best thing for Elaina to go home with them tonight. Our two lovebirds do not agree with us.

Michael is out on the patio, sulking. He has been sulking for the past three hours. I notice a freshly opened bottle of champagne is next to him. I can only sigh.

It has been agreed to by all my doctors, by *my team*, we will meet at Josh's medical office tomorrow afternoon, Sunday, to go through all the films with the Doctors Chatham, but that is all we have agreed upon.

The tension on my team is almost more than I can take, but I have convinced them all, including Michael, that I would like the Doctors Chatham to see my films and review my prognosis before we just cut me up on Monday. Michael openly winced when I said it this way, but he loved me enough to agree.

I'm not sure he loves me as much as he did when we said *I do* in front of the one hundred and ten people this afternoon, but we shall see soon enough. We were supposed to go to a hotel for the night, but I have begged off on this option. I'm just too tired, too wrung out. I just want to wake up in our home, tomorrow, I told him earlier. Michael agreed, well, he nodded in complete silence and moved off to the patio, at that point, to brood alone. I hold on to this: we have something we agree upon.

"Ellie," Carrie says simply. She gives me a hug. I try and take strength from it, now. She pulls me into the pantry of my new-to-me kitchen and closes the door. I'm still in my wedding dress. She's still wearing the sexy silver number. "He gets this way. You *know* that. He's just worried about you and it's clouding his judgment and his normally open mind. It's your wedding night, try not to worry. He'll come around."

I can only nod. This disconcerting thought that she knows him much better than I do weighs me down. I have to quell the fear and turmoil I'm feeling at Michael's behavior and this overriding thought: Do I really *know* him? I blink back a tear and try to smile.

"Carrie, thank you for everything you did today. I cannot even begin to tell you what it means to me. Everything you've done for us, for me."

"Ellie, everything's going to be okay." I nod, again. "Everybody wants the same thing. Everybody wants you well."

"Yeah," I say. "I just want to be here."

"You *will* be here."

Carrie hugs me and I hug her back and ignore the pain that courses through me. The physical pain is so much less than this heartbreak that has overtaken me in Michael's reaction to the Doctors Chatham questions about my cancer treatment. His reaction hurts me more.

Carrie opens the pantry door. We discover Michael and Robert standing there talking quietly. Robert smiles at us. Michael does not. Elaina and Nick soon appear and take in the subdued atmosphere. To break the tension, I go over and give Elaina a hug.

"We'll see you tomorrow, Elaina. You look so beautiful. Thank you for being a part of this... special day." I hug her tight.

"Thanks, Ellie." She hugs me again, pulls back and searches my face. I give her a forced, bright smile, hoping to reassure her that everything is okay. She looks at me for a long minute and nods. "You're the best thing to ever happen to Dad," she whispers.

"We'll see you tomorrow." I move over to put my good arm around Nicholas. I kiss the side of his face, tweak his cheek, trying to perk up his glum expression at Elaina's leaving.

"Daddy, what's wrong? You look...is there something wrong?" Elaina asks as she steps over to Michael and he hugs her.

"Everything's fine, baby. Just tired, that's all," Michael says.

He doesn't look at me. I feel his coldness toward me all the way across the room. Nick and I, arm-in-arm, follow the newly-married Bradford's and Elaina to our front door. We say our final good nights to them and Nick and I close the front door together.

"Mom, you really looked so beautiful today, still do," Nick says.

We make our way back through the family room and into the kitchen, arm-in-arm. I watch Nick give Michael a secret smile across the room and see my new husband's faint nod of acknowledgment at my oldest son's compliment of me.

Nick kisses the side of my face and announces he's going to bed.

"Good night, Nicky," I call out. Michael says nothing.

Now, I cannot get out of this dress by myself, but I'm out of people to ask, so I steal back down the stairs to try and find Michael. He's sitting in the formal living room in the dark. We barely use this room and I wonder why he has chosen this one to brood in. I turn on the light, flooding the room with it. "Can you help me with this zipper? You have to undo the pearl buttons first, then the zipper."

He stands up and I turn around, facing away from him. I'm standing there waiting for him to undo my bondage from this dress…waiting…waiting. I finally turn around to see what's keeping him from undoing the dress and he isn't even there.

I'm fuming, now, completely pissed off. I turn off all the lights downstairs and check the locks at the front door and the French doors at the patio. I discover an open bottle of champagne and grab myself a fresh flute and slowly pour the liquid into it and take a long drink. Before long, I've finished the glass. I pour myself another and finish that one, too.

Swaying on my feet, I stand at the French door that leads to the back patio and look out at the view of the water. It shimmers in the moon light. *How did I get here?* I stand here in my beautiful crème-colored Vera Wang gown and wish for a magical answer. I just want to hear what the Doctors Chatham have to say. I just want to explore the options, if there are any. The truth is simple. I don't want to die, but I want this baby and Michael.

I hear Michael come into the room and defiantly raise my third glass of champagne to my lips and swallow. In the dark, I hear him as he fills his own glass. Then, he comes over and stands beside me.

"I was waiting for you upstairs."

"Well, I was *waiting* down here," I say to him in irritation. I take another long drink of champagne. "I'm standing here, waiting for you to unzip my dress and you're not even *here*."

"You shouldn't be drinking, Ellen Kay."

"I shouldn't be doing a lot of things. It seems."

I finish my glass of champagne and move away from him toward the kitchen and set the empty flute on the counter.

He follows me. I can feel his sorrow and his apology; his feelings emanate from him to me. We're connected. I feel his pain and he feels mine. I climb up the darkened stairs and hear his heavy footsteps behind me. We have to make this right. We cannot start off the first night of our marriage on this unsteady foundation. The champagne softens the edges of me. My anger at him from earlier begins to dissipate. Desperation takes its place. *I want to live. I really do. I want to be with him. I really do.*

One by one, I stop and check in the doorways of my three sleeping children. I cover up Emily with the blanket that has been pushed down at the end of her bed; adjust the Mathew's sheet so his gangly long arm is now covered; turn off the light that Nick has left on and retrieve the book from his hands that he must have reading. Michael follows me into every room. I can feel his anger for me disappear.

I walk down the long hallway to our master bedroom and he still trails behind me. He stops long enough to close and lock the bedroom door. I turn at the sound of the turning lock. He gives me a hesitant smile. It is time for me to speak. It is time for me to tell him, to remind him, again, why we are doing all of this.

"I have six wishes that are all I want and need," I say. "You, Nick, Elaina, Mathew, Emily, and me." He gives me this uncertain smile, now, and his blue eyes fill with fresh tears.

"I would like these bodacious tah tahs as opposed to imitation silicone. I know it's vain, but it is two of my extra wishes. I would like this unborn child, too, but I'm not willing to make a trade for any of these wishes for the others."

"And, if you only have one wish, what would it be?" Michael asks. The desperation in his voice surprises me.

"I wish for you. *You*. Michael. Just as you wish for me because that is what soul mates do." So, I have to make it harder, more meaningful, because words are everything to me and I believe they need to be said. "There are no words to adequately describe what you mean to me," I say in this broken hearted voice. "I put my life in your hands because you complete me. I know that we may be tested and that there will be obstacles put in our way. That cancer will try to take me, but I will stay, here with you, because you're all I want, all I need, all I see. I love you, Michael."

My god-like husband looks troubled. "Ellie," he says to me, now. "I just want you to be here, so I can touch you any time I want. That's all I want. I'll do whatever it takes to make sure that happens. I cannot live without you. I can't. I won't…be able to.

He has trumped me again with his words. The man is too perfect. I tell him this. He shakes his head and tells me no.

"I've been waiting all day to make love to you in this dress," he says, leaning over me to undo the pearl buttons. "That's why I didn't want to help you take it off." He smiles sheepishly.

"Michael," I say as we fall to the bed in our magnificent wedding clothes. "Why didn't you just say so? We could have been here and done this, hours ago."

It is almost dawn. We've gotten three hours of sleep. Michael sleeps right next to me. My legs are intertwined with his. His right arm curls underneath and around my waist and the other rests on my bare stomach. And it is then, that I feel this fluttering sensation in my abdomen. It takes me a full minute to realize what it is. It happens again.

Michael's hand moves across following the movement. I turn and from the light of the moon that streams in our room from the large windows I see he's awake. I don't even have to ask if he felt the movement. I can tell by the look of wonder on his face that he has.

This is one of those life-affirming moments and we have just captured it together. He moves in closer to me, now. I lift my head and look at him.

"Do you want to know what it is?" Michael asks.

We've done every test under the sun allowable for this baby. I've had an amniocentesis, too. Yet, with all the testing that Michael has ordered done or had my own gynecologist do, I've not asked any questions. The girl who doesn't like surprises has not asked the gender of this baby. To do so, would make it mean too much and letting go will be hard enough. But, Michael knows. I see this as I stare at him now in the semi-darkness of this early morning. I just nod.

"It's a boy, Ellie." His voice breaks as he says this to me.

A son would mean everything to Michael. I can tell just by his saying it out loud, the circumstances for this child have just changed. The pendulum just swung in the opposite direction. And, as if to prove that point, our unborn child flutters across my stomach again and, somehow, Michael feels it beneath his fingers, just as I do.

"Nine wishes, Michael. You, the kids, this baby, and me myself and I." I point to each breast as I say, myself and I." I look over at him a little fearful and try to smile. "Seven for certain, if I don't get to keep my breasts, but nine if we get it all. Surely, we can have it all. We've waited long enough." I move in closer to him.

"Nine's a good number," he finally says.

His love shines on me in the darkness. I reach out and hold on to him as if he might slip away from me.

# CHAPTER TWELVE

*Sunday*

Our first morning as a married couple begins with breakfast in bed served by my three children. The morning rushes by as we spend the majority of it packing the kids for a ten day stay at Robert and Carrie's. The plan is to drop off the kids for this early afternoon because of my impending surgery tomorrow. Robert and Carrie are taking them all bowling for the day. She and I exchange conspiring glances at this plan. Nick and Elaina are not enthusiastic about bowling, but even Robert Bradford is putting on a good show about how fun it is going to be for all of them. I laugh as my ex-husband carries on about this. Carrie and he exchange these knowing glances. They're about to feel the full impact of four kids, instead of just Elaina. I hand Carrie the schedule I've typed up and she has this dazed look as she reads through it.

"All *this*?" Carrie asks.

"It'll be fine. The kids are great about calling. Thanks for doing this," I say. I glance over at Nick and give him a knowing wink. He comes over to me and puts his arm around my shoulder. The pain shoots through a little, but I do my best to hide it.

"Mom, don't worry about anything. I've got it handled. Just take care of yourself. Be nice to your doctors," Nick says with a laugh as Michael comes up to us.

"She's always nice to me," Michael says, trying to laugh. "She's going to be fine, Nick." Michael looks only at me when he says this. "I'm going to make sure of it."

I kiss and hug each child goodbye one more time as all four of them give me these long searching looks and put on my former-UW-Cheerleader-yeah-team-smile for them and kiss them all one last time before we leave. "We'll call you tonight," I say from the car as Michael drives us away toward the ferry dock to Seattle.

Our car ride is mostly silent. I'm lost in thought about only yesterday and these cascading emotions of uncertainty and elation that we've been through, since we said "I do" less than twenty-four hours ago. Michael clinches his jaw the only outward indication that he's stressed, though he keeps his eyes on the road looking straight ahead. On the ferry, we doze in each other's arms, exhausted from the events of yesterday, and that stress of what may lie ahead. He looks over at me with this pensive look as he starts the SUV, then concentrates on negotiating the narrow lane and the cars ahead of us before taking the familiar route to Swedish Hospital.

"Michael," I finally say, breaking the long silence between us. "We want the same things—you and I. Let's just hear what the Doctors Chatham have to say. I just want to know all my options."

"Ellie." He looks straight ahead. "Okay," he says after a while.

"Ben saw it on a mammogram review six months ago—left breast, one point two centimeters in size. The biopsy tests confirm it's malignant. A lumpectomy is performed on October 7th by Josh. The margins look good. The lymph nodes are clear," Michael says. He looks over at Josh Liston for help.

Josh picks up the threads of the story, now, with the Doctors Chatham's listening intently without comment. "We continued with regular check-ups to see if there were any more symptoms or occurrences. Ellie tells me she is still experiencing pain. I remember thinking, well, maybe we cut more lymph muscles than we intended. I wrote a note in the chart to further explore this…"

He stops and gives out a copy of my chart to everyone. I can clearly see his handwriting regarding this. "We do radiation treatments as part of the treatment with the lumpectomy. That goes well. All follow-up films show no signs of cancer in the left breast." I hear the way Josh is talking. His words are carefully chosen. I look at him curiously. The Doctors Chatham are looking at him this way, as well.

"Ellie's pregnant during radiation," Lisa states in this flat, all-knowing voice. Did you know that?"

"No," Josh says.

"*I* didn't even know I was pregnant. Believe me, I didn't even think that was possible," I say in defense of Josh. Michael won't even look at me, now.

Michael clears his throat and says, "So, I see Ellie in January at her son's basketball game and I'm noticing how she is favoring her left arm—her left side. She barely uses it. I haven't seen her for three months, so I'm surprised by this. She should be feeling and doing so much better. So, Josh, Ben and I start looking at her films. We do a resection and check the margins. They're perfectly clear. Everything looks good, clear, even her latest films of her left breast look good after the second surgery when we look at the margins," Michael says in this low voice. "We can't figure it out."

"We decide to go back to square one. Do an upper torso scan with an MRI. We just can't figure out what we're missing," Josh adds.

"Referred pain," Lisa murmurs. She has already figured it out. Granted, she knows that I have a tumor in my right breast, but I get this uneasy feeling. I can tell that my male team of doctors is waiting to exhale, at this point. "And, she's pregnant and you do an MRI," Lisa says.

"Yes…we knew after the battery of tests that she was pregnant, but our focus still remained on Ellie and saving her life," Josh says.

"It was *my call*," Michael says, now. He has tormented look on his face and this remorseful tone. "I told Josh and Ben that we should proceed with the MRI. We couldn't figure out what was going on with Ellie. We were missing something. I didn't want… We were missing something. I didn't want to lose her because we were *missing something*."

"As soon as we see the films, we see the tumor. One point three centimeters. I pull the mammograms from six months ago and it isn't even there. Fast growing," Ben says.

"Biopsy indicates malignancy," Josh says. "We are all in agreement that we need to do a double mastectomy with an immediate breast reconstruction. And, that's when we call in Tom," Josh says for all of them.

My Italian doctor has been waiting patiently. He gives Lisa and Stephen Chatham a wide smile. "I met with Ellie this past Friday. I saw the films. I'm in agreement with Josh, Michael, and Ben that a double mastectomy is the way to go. I've talked with Ellie at length about the procedure and have assured her that we will try and match that perfection. It's standard operating procedure," Tom says to the Doctors Chatham.

"Yes, I guess that would be one way of putting it," Stephen Chatham answers, before Lisa can respond. He's touching her shoulder in this affectionate way. I think they have some sort of system worked out on who does the talking and when.

"Ellie," Stephen turns his grey gaze to me.

Stephen Chatham has this George Clooney thing going on, a taller version; I'm completely disarmed in his presence.

"How do you feel about the double mastectomy surgery and the immediate breast reconstruction by Tom?" Stephen asks.

*How do I feel about that?* I haven't allowed myself to even go there. I realize this as I sit here and feel all of their eyes upon me.

"What else can I do? I don't have a choice," I say. "I want to live. I want Michael. I want my kids. I want me, myself and I."

I try to smile my brightest smile, but it fails. I realize too late that I have spoken my wishes aloud. My smile fades.

"I would like to keep my bodacious tah tahs. I would like to have this baby, but I cannot make a trade of either of those things for the others. I want it all. I guess I'm asking for too much."

I *am* asking for too much. I can see it in the eyes of my team of doctors, but the eyes of the Doctors Chatham are elsewhere—they are looking at each other, now.

"Ellie," Lisa says with a rewarding smile as if she knows a secret. "Stephen and I like to take things one at time. Our philosophy is a little bit different than other specialists. We don't like cancer to dictate the terms for how we proceed. You have an aggressive cancer. You have an excellent team of doctors' intent on eradicating your cancer, but the question remains how do you feel about a double mastectomy and breast reconstruction?"

I don't answer for a few minutes. I sit up straighter and clasp my hands together and try to smile and then look only at Lisa. "I would prefer to keep my breasts and my baby," I finally say. I hear Michael shudder beside me. The Doctors Chatham both raise their heads at the same time and look over at him.

"Okay, let's just slow this down a bit," Lisa says in this soothing tone. "The lumpectomy was the right choice for the left side. The margins are clear; the lymph nodes, too; and even when you went back in and did the resection—everything looked good. So, why not take the same approach on the right side?"

It is Michael who speaks. "Because, if we *miss* it, if we let one cell get by us, I have to live with that and *she won't*." The pain is evident in his voice. He's overwrought and at the breaking point.

"Dr. Shaw," Lisa says gently, now. "You are *too close* to this case."

Michael doesn't answer. He gets up from his chair, goes over, and begins looking at the films of my breasts. I'm not sure if he actually sees them. His shoulders shake every so often. He might be crying and I'm not sure he cares.

"This case is *my wife*," he says in this broken voice after a few minutes.

My body moves of its own volition over to him. "Babe, it's going to be okay," I say to him. I link my arm through his and we stare at the films together. I give him a few minutes with our backs turned away from his colleagues to get it together. I stroke his arm with my right hand. "Everyone in this room is here to help us." I see him nod imperceptibly and only at me.

"How about this?" Stephen asks in the ensuing silence. "Do the lumpectomy on Monday and see if the lymph nodes are involved. If they're clear, we move on to chemotherapy. If they're not clear, we come back and re-visit the option of a double mas with immediate reconstruction."

"How does chemotherapy work with our baby?" I ask.

"Chemotherapy is a better option than radiation, Ellie, for the baby and probably you," Lisa says.

I'm stunned. I think it shows. I glance at Michael and he looks grief-stricken. I can see that he has already taken the blame for everything that has transpired, every wrong turn or decision that's been made. I cannot ask him to help me make this one.

"I need to talk to Michael alone for a few minutes."

I take his hand and pull him along out of the room. We make our way into the darkened hallway to Josh's office. I turn on the light and push him into Josh's office chair. I go back and close the door, then sit on the edge of the desk in front of him. He holds his head in his hands and will not look at me. I kick off my strappy sandals. He raises his head to see why I'm doing this. I settle myself down on top of him in the office chair effectively pushing him back. He stares at me, completely undone and broken, while I wipe away the trace of tears from his face.

"Have I told you, today, how much I love being your wife?"

He gives me a half smile. "Not today."

"Well, it's been twenty-four hours—a whole day. I must tell you it's been a heady experience being your wife. I will *never* give that up," I say this with such conviction he almost smiles.

"It's the ring; isn't it? I knew it was over the top," he says in this weary voice.

"Not the ring."

"It's my charismatic personality, especially last night, when I was drinking champagne and completely ignoring you."

"Not that either," I say. "It's this." I lean down and touch his lips with mine. "I like the I-can-touch-you-any-time-I-want idea. I'm taking it for my own."

"It's pretty good, huh?" Michael asks his lips against mine.

A few minutes go by and he sighs. "Ellie, I can't be your husband and your surgeon, too. Lisa is right about that. I'm too close to the patient."

"Well, you're not divorcing me, now. I'm never going to let you go," I say with a laugh.

"Michael, I want all nine things," I say to him, now. "I want you. I want the kids. I want our baby. I want me, myself and I. It's a big list of wishes, but I want them all."

There is long silence between us. I watch his face as he wrestles with competing thoughts—those of a surgeon and those of a husband. He looks at me and finally smiles.

"So do I," Michael says.

# Chapter Thirteen

 *Tuesday*

It's Tuesday. Monday is over. My bodacious tah tahs are still here, ensconced in a sports bra. A lumpectomy on my right breast was performed yesterday: the margins good, the lymph nodes clear. We know all of this because the lab results were completed in record time. Michael called in favors from just about every department at Swedish from the OR to the lab to the surgical staff to radiology. I'm at home, somewhat lounging on the sofa in the family room, reading a manuscript with my blue pencil poised in mid-air hand ready to correct the text presented in front of me. But my concentration wanes because the whirlwind of my life seems to be catching up to me.

Michael insisted on staying home with me, so he's in the kitchen making each of us a cup of tea. I glance up and see him watching me. He has been doing this all day, watching me. I have an ultrasound at the Doctors Chatham's office in a few hours and I start chemotherapy on Thursday.

The Doctors Chatham do not mess around. They already have an aggressive plan all laid out for me. We will be going over that plan after the ultrasound this afternoon, we, as in, my husband and me, with both Lisa and Stephen. I'm wearing one of Michael's dress shirts and a pair of comfy sweats. I'm sure that it's all mental, but my pain level is not that bad. Michael remains skeptical about this and asks me again what it is.

"Three," I say. "It's not that bad." He gets this incredulous look on his face. "Josh is pretty awesome. Not you, of course, but…" Michael shakes his head at me. I see his hesitant smile. "You know I love you; right?" I tease him. "There's no doubt in your mind about that is there?" He sets my cup of tea down on the travertine and kneels in front of me and puts his head in my lap.

"No doubt," he says now.

I stroke his golden head of hair going gently back and forth. He closes his eyes. I realize how tired he must be. We've been going full speed with no letdown for weeks.

"Why don't you take a little nap? We've got an hour before we need to catch the ferry."

"Okay," He moves to the sofa next to me and lies down with his head in my lap again. I raise my manuscript above him so I can see his face. "Just remember, I can touch you any time I want," he says to me with this wicked grin.

"Oh, that's right," I say to him, now. I watch him close his eyes and can only smile.

The Doctors Chatham's medical office is like a spa. There's no other way to describe it. Oncology and gynecology must be lucrative because the place is decorated with the nicest designer furniture and just the right amount of subtle lighting overhead to instantly make a patient feel at ease and almost forget they're at a medical clinic.

As we're escorted along through the Chatham's medical office, Michael and I see that each patient room is decked out as well when we exchange glances. The nurses call them *suites*. The nurses, themselves, are dressed in these sportswear-like outfits, as if they were dressed by a personal shopper at Nordstrom. Michael slows down with each step he takes. His face gets grimmer and more astonished as we walk down the hallway. The opulence and over-the-top design of this medical office is definitely weighing upon him.

The *Nordstrom* nurses have offered him a cup of tea and he has declined. I did, too, but not for the same reason, I think. I just didn't want it. I think Michael just wanted to be able to say *no*. Disbelief crosses his features. I think that he's having second thoughts and probably thirds about our decision electing to go with the lumpectomy and forgo the double mastectomy and reconstruction—standard operating procedure—*really*, since we stepped inside this surreal place. He's a surgeon, first and foremost, and to unnecessarily leave surgical work undone and live on a wing and a prayer, well, he is struggling with that. I can see it. I think he knows that I can see it. The spa-atmosphere of this medical office is not helping.

Both Doctors Chatham enter the room. They're wearing matching white surgical coats. I can see Lisa's designer dress beneath and she is wearing black strappy sandals like the ones that my Gene Juarez fans retrieved for me from Nordstrom. Stephen is wearing a white dress shirt and red tie and dark trousers. They look impeccable—a beautiful couple in their medical office spa. Michael is looking more and more uncomfortable and lost. I take his hand in mine, as we sit in these comfy chairs across from this dynamic medical duo.

"Ellie, how are you feeling?" Lisa asks.

"I feel good. *Really*. Michael keeps asking what my pain level is and it's been a steady three at its highest point." I give my new husband an affectionate smile.

"That's great." Lisa grabs a remote from this glass coffee table that is staged between the four of us. "Let's take a look at what we have." With a push of the button, the lights in the suite dim and a screen comes down and a film of my chest comes up on the screen. Within thirty minutes, we have visited both the before and after x-rays of my left and right breasts. The films look good and cancer-free, even Michael has verbally agreed to this.

He seems to take a special interest in the film of my right breast and asks Lisa to go back to it. He gets up from the chair and goes closer to take a look.

"It looks great. I'm really pleased," he murmurs after a few more minutes of study. "Josh did a great job."

"He did. The films look great," Stephen says. With some unknown signal, the lights come back up and Michael comes back and sits down next to me. His face appears more relaxed; I breathe a silent sigh of relief. He is obviously pleased with the post-op films.

"So, let's move on to the ultrasound, take a look at your baby, and then we'll talk about the next steps based on that," Lisa says now.

I get this uneasy feeling, like there is something being left out, something that hasn't been said. Lisa hits another button and a sportswear nurse comes in and takes my hand and gently leads me to another room where I am encouraged to change into this spa-like robe. It is heated up like a warm blanket like the ones I have gotten at the hospital before. The sportswear nurse comes back after a few minutes and brings me back into the room where Lisa, Stephen and Michael wait for me. The nurse leads me over to a twin-size bed that sits up three times as high as normal and she helps me up on to it.

Another woman enters the room. She is petite in size with cropped golden brown hair spiked everywhere. Her green eyes seem to sparkle when she greets me. She gets this huge smile as she walks over to me.

"Hi, Mrs. Shaw. I'm Melanie. I'll be working with Doctors Chatham and your husband, Dr. Shaw, to do the ultrasound. Just let me know if you need anything or if you are uncomfortable in any way."

I'm mesmerized by the lilting, relaxing nature of this woman.

She is so nice and so gentle that I involuntary sigh as she helps me lay back.

"Okay," I say.

"Your lumpectomy was Monday, right?" I nod at her.

She puts the gel on my abdomen and I am surprised that it is the perfect temperature—not too hot and not too cold. I tell her this and she just smiles. I keep waiting for Lisa, Stephen and Michael to make their way over to me. I glance over at Michael and raise my finger motioning him over. He gives me a weird look as he and the doctors remain seated where we all sat before.

The lights dim, again, after Melanie tells the doctors that she is ready. A screen comes up behind Lisa and Stephen and this sixty-inch high definition television displays the image of our baby. It's incredible. Michael is already up and looking closer at the image. Melanie's voice is soft as it comes over the ceiling speakers from the small microphone from the headset she is wearing as she takes measurements and points out various aspects of what we are looking at.

"Ellie, according to your recollection—the first day of your last menstrual period was September 25th which puts your due date at July 2nd," Melanie says in this lyrical voice. I'm slowly nodding trying to do this math. Melanie prints out a pregnancy calculator and hands it to me. I stare at the dates.

"Let's do some measurements, Mel," Lisa calls out from the front of the room where the three of them are now gathered. "How many radiation treatments did you go through, Ellie?"

"Three weeks for five days a week; once a day. Ben did larger doses of radiation." Lisa and Stephen exchange this weird look. Concern races across their features; then it's gone.

"And when was that?"

"Josh did the lumpectomy on Monday, October 7th and they did radiation that Wednesday, October 9th through the first part of November, once per day, five days a week.

"What are the measurements, Mel?" Lisa asks quietly.

My pulse gets faster and more erratic at her serious tone.

"We're halfway through week twenty. The measurements are right on for that date," Melanie says quietly.

I'm half sitting up, ignoring the pain that this is causing me. "That can't be right," I say in a panic. "I thought I was in week eighteen." I'm the first to admit that I haven't been paying attention to my pregnancy. I've only seen the gynecologist once. We've been so focused on my breast cancer treatments that I haven't been very good at keeping track of everything with this pregnancy. "I need my purse, the check book. I keep track of it there."

Within a minute, Melanie hands me one. Michael has turned back from the television screen and stares at me steadily now as he walks over.

My hands shake. I can't think. The numbers blur before my eyes. Melanie squeezes my hand as she retrieves my purse and hands it to me. I grab the check book and look at the calendar. There is the date for the beginning of my last period circled for September— the 25th with the word 'light' written across it. I track it this way for my gynecologist as I have a tendency, like now, to forget the dates.

Melanie prints off some nifty due date calculator and I'm staring at it—sex with Michael on Thursday, October 2nd, and sex with Robert Bradford the next seven consecutive days after that and, then, my surgery on the 7th and radiation therapy the 9th through the first part of November, twice a day.

Our baby has been exposed to it all and I'm farther along than I thought. If we're going to make any decisions about this baby, they'll have to be made in the next day or two.

Lisa and Stephen are reviewing all the genetic testing has been sent over from my previous gynecologist, as I leave the suite.

I'm getting changed again and feeling more unsteady and overwhelmed by the minute.

Once dressed, I sink down into the side chair for a moment and try to get my perspective back.

The sportswear nurse comes back for me. I give her a weak smile and ask her if I can have a minute. I lean back in the chair and close my eyes. *It's just too much.*

I wanted this baby, but if it's not Michael's—and that is what is weighing heavily on me, now. Can a vasectomy fail? Is Bobby the father? And, if the radiation has harmed this baby, which from what I've already read really scares me; we really need to talk about all of this.

There's a soft knock and the door opens. Lisa enters, closes the door, and sits in the physician chair opposite me.

"What's going on, Ellie?"

I give her a twisted smile. "Can a vasectomy fail?"

"Yes. That's why there's a follow-up. Usually, at three months, even earlier, sometimes later, to ensure the procedure worked. Why?"

"Bobby had a vasectomy in July. I thought it was weird after all this time of cajoling him to get it done; he finally agrees to go in. I stayed on the pill for a few more months and then after that… It's not like we were having sex every day, but he and Carrie probably were…" I sigh trying to catch my breath. I can feel my face getting hot.

How to explain this musical chairs life shift between the four of us to anyone else. "I don't know what Carrie has told you. We were best friends since college, then we had a falling out over Bobby, but now I'm with Michael."

"She told me."

"Okay, well." I smile bitterly now. "I may have royally screwed up and I'm going to blame it directly on the cancer. Michael and I were together only once, physically, on the 2nd of October," I say slowly. "Then, I was back together with Bobby because, well, once I told him I knew about Carrie and that I had breast cancer, it seemed to make him sympathetic so…" A single tear begins to roll down my face and I brush at it impatiently. "I'm so tired of *crying.*"

Lisa grabs my hand and takes my pulse. I cannot tell, if she is really interested in determining my heart rate or trying to comfort me by holding my hand.

"I think you're just plain tired," Lisa says. "Getting married is stressful, having cancer is stressful, being pregnant is stressful; the combination of all three, daunting."

"Daunting, that's my life, right now," I say with half-smile. "I love Michael. I've loved him for a long time, but this baby..." I try to decipher what I'm really trying to say. "It's been a point of contention between us since this whole cancer thing started, but if it isn't his, more than anything, I want to be here with him."

"You want a paternity test."

I look at her in surprise. "I do. What's involved with that?"

"Well, there was an amniocentesis done. Michael ordered it."

"I thought he didn't test for paternity?"

"He may not have specifically ordered it, but it would come up with the genetic markers for that," Lisa says now.

"So, what do we need to do?"

"Well, we need to order this additional part of the test to be done with the lab. Come on, let's go talk to Michael. He's waiting for you, Ellie." Her words soothe me on some level. I slowly take in air. My chest feels less tight. Maybe it's the pain killers, but maybe it's Lisa, her non-judgmental attitude, her unwavering support of me. I feel like she's a lifelong friend, even though I've only known her for a few days.

"Lisa," I say. "Thank you."

"Ellie, just know you can talk to me at any time; okay? About anything," she says with a meaningful look.

"Thank you." We walk out into the hallway together. I take in the spa atmosphere once again and shake my head and half-smile. "Where's Michael? Having some tea or something?" I ask with a hint of humor. I half expect to find Michael in a spa robe drinking green tea.

"Nah, I think he's drinking cognac with Stephen in our private office," Lisa says with a laugh.

"This is quite a set-up you have here, Lisa."

"Pregnancy and cancer and gynecological issues of any kind are all very difficult to begin with—this is supposed to be a refuge for all that."

"A refuge," I say. "That's exactly what it feels like."

Lisa gives me a reassuring smile.

I trail behind her, trying to shake this sudden uneasy feeling that comes over me. I straighten my shoulders back, as if by doing so, I can right the tilt in the axis my little world seems to be making.

We discover Michael and Stephen having a friendly conversation about basketball and sipping cognac just as Lisa had said. Lisa is the smooth operator in telling them both that we want to get a complete profile from the amniocentesis, including paternity. She easily explains that these are my wishes without saying anything more. Michael gives me a measured look, downs the rest of the cognac, and follows Lisa to the laboratory without a word or glance in my direction. I get more on edge while Michael provides his DNA for testing in the lab, but successfully hide it from the Doctors Chatham.

A half hour later, we say goodbye to Stephen and Lisa and make our way back to the ferry and home to Bainbridge. Michael keeps giving me these quizzical glances as we make our way off the ferry and head toward the beach house.

We haven't had more than a superficial conversation about anything, beyond what to have for dinner, and agreeing to check-in on the kids sometime this evening, and what my pain level is, since we left the Chatham's medical office.

Michael stops at the Town & Country Market. I stay in the car and he returns in fifteen minutes with two bags of groceries. I take my cell phone out and discover two voice mail messages, but just don't have the energy to play them. I should have already checked in with my children, but I can't do that either. I'm suddenly exhausted.

Ten minutes later, we're driving down the gravel drive toward home. Our beach house welcomes us in a dark window kind of way, as if we have been gone too long and this is our chastisement for being so late, but the house involuntarily makes me smile as soon as I see it. Gingerly, I get out of the car and follow Michael as he carries the groceries inside.

"What's the number?" Michael asks again as he heads to the kitchen.

I have to stop and think about what I would classify the number to be. My right upper torso feels like it is on fire. *And I'm just noticing this?* "An eight, I think," I say to him now.

Michael disappears for a few moments and comes back with a cold glass of water, two white pills, and watches me take them. His hand brushes my face in this casual way and I move in to feel his touch even more. He enfolds me into his arms and holds me for a long while. All his gestures and actions tell me that everything is going to be okay, but he doesn't say anything more, neither do I.

I've changed into my pajamas—a black silk camisole with some funky matching pants in black and white. I slip on my best silk black robe and come back downstairs. Intent on sitting in the family room and working on editing a manuscript I'm behind on. Michael watches television. It's some kind of romantic comedy where the laughter fills in at all the strategic parts. He turns it off after a few minutes and sips at his cognac appearing in deep thought.

We have had nothing, but this surface conversation, since we came home, ate dinner, and went our separate ways.

I sense we are at the end of that scene right now.

"Don't you think we should talk about this," he finally says with a heavy sigh.

I put down my manuscript. *Yes, apparently, we are going to talk about this.* "Michael."

"It doesn't matter to me, Ellie. Just like Elaina, I *will* be the father to this child."

I release the breath that I've been holding since he first spoke. I do not want to have this conversation. Our roles are suddenly reversed. Now, he wants this baby and I'm unsure. Regardless, he wants to bend my will to his.

"It *matters to me*," I say. "All of it matters. I had radiation therapy, which may have inadvertently affected this baby. I have days instead of weeks to think about what I want to do and so, I want to know all the facts before I decide."

"*You* decide!" Michael leaps from the sofa and comes over to me and takes my hands. "You meant *we* decide."

I stare at him; resolute and unbending. I cannot really explain what is happening to me and why, all of a sudden, I doubt everything, including him. "Of course," I say in this soothing tone. I can lie like no one else and I'm doing it now. I catch my lower lip to keep it from trembling, but he's watching my face.

"Ellie," he says in this wounded tone. "You're lying to me." I attempt to pull away from him, but I can't because I have had too many surgical procedures to move quickly and freely. He holds on to my forearms. "Ellen Kay," he whispers. "Don't do this to us."

"Michael," I say in this pleading voice. "I have all these...doubts. I don't know what to do anymore."

"Trust me," he says. "Believe me. *We*, you and I, together will figure this out."

I look into his eyes then because I so want to believe him, to *trust him*. I want to believe that somehow we will make the right decision, but I have all these reservations now and this inexplicable fear. "It's too much...it's too many wishes," I say with foreboding.

My cell phone rings interrupting the tense moment. I suddenly remember the two voice mail messages from earlier that I've never played. For some reason, I start to feel cold and anxious. Michael lets go of me, retrieves my ringing phone from the kitchen counter, and answers the call.

"Robert," Michael says after a moment. "No, we just got home a little over an hour ago." Michael looks over at me with a reassuring look, but then it falters. He's silent for a few minutes, listening to what Bobby has to say. His face turns pale and he turns away from me.

My mind starts reeling in this slow motion kind of way. I struggle to breathe. Pain rages through me and I register its high level on some distant plane as if it's happening to someone else.

"Where?" Michael asks. "Okay. We're on our way. No. We'll catch the ferry. Give us an hour." Within seconds, his voice changes to this clinician way of speaking, no emotion whatsoever. "No, not right now. We'll call you from the ferry and she can talk to them then."

I'm standing now, shaking, and distantly feel my breath leave my body in one silent whoosh. I don't even know what's happened yet, but I can feel the shock and grief of it settle over me, like an unwanted cloak I may never be able to remove.

I race up the stairs, tear off my robe and pajamas. Frantic, I pull on jeans and one of Michael's dress shirts. I push my feet into ankle boots, and gingerly put on the white jacket. Part of me is disgusted with the idea of taking up precious time for this wardrobe change because, on some level, I'm perceptive enough to know that time's already run out. Another part of me is taken up with the idea of getting it just right as if I, somehow, have the power to change whatever lies ahead by what I'm wearing, including time.

It's true; my mind has already begun the slow descent into disbelief. It races with this one pervasive thought: this can't be happening, not to us.

I go back downstairs. The house feels like a silent tomb as if it too is holding its proverbial breath, awaiting the answers to the questions I cannot even begin to ask. I grab my purse and cell phone.

Michael waits for me by the front door. He's just standing there in a t-shirt and blue jeans with his hands buried deep into the pockets of his brown leather jacket.

I look at him. His face is a mask of indifference, a surgeon's face, prepared to tell the patient the bad news.

"Don't tell me, yet," I say in a low voice.

Michael nods at me and just watches the tears stream down my face. My mind shuts down, preparing for something so bad; I can't even face it yet.

The silence from Michael only confirms it for me. I'm losing one of my wishes.

# Chapter Fourteen

 *Messages*

The ferry ride from Bainbridge Island to Seattle takes thirty-five minutes. My cell phone serves as some kind of lifeline and I hold it in my hand and just stare at the voice mail symbol with the number two beside it. I could play the messages and probably know more of what is happening, but now I'm afraid to hear them. Michael is restless. He seems to struggle with the news that I don't yet know.

"I'll be right back," he finally says to me. He gets out of the car and heads toward the water side of the ferry. He keeps his head down as he moves along the row of parked cars. I only realize he's crying, when he wipes the sleeve of his leather jacket across his face. It isn't raining. There is no other reasonable explanation for this.

Five minutes go by in this oppressive silence. With trembling hands, I press the speakerphone symbol and play the messages on my cell phone. It's from Robert. He's crying and I close my eyes as I hear the sound of his broken voice.

"Ellie," Bobby says. "Call me as soon as you get this message."

The second message is from Robert as well. "Ellie. Ellie, where are you? We're at Swedish Hospital. Ellie, have Michael call me. Have him call back as soon as he can." My heart rate quickens because Robert doesn't hold back bad news. He likes to say it and get it over with. It's so bad that he cannot even say it on the message.

I scan the ferry deck looking for Michael, but I don't see him. I close the cell phone and drop it in my pocket and open the car door. The pain in my right breast and underarm knifes through me as I scramble from the car.

"Michael!" I still can't see him and now it's getting dark. They have shut off half the lights on the car deck to probably save money, always trying to save money. "Michael!"

The wind whips me around and carries my voice away with it. I'm frantic, searching for him now. I've move past the last row of cars and see the open deck up ahead. There is a large orange plastic netting fence that runs across the front of the steel deck as if to hold back all the cars should they pitch forward for some reason.

I'm just about to turn and go, when I see Michael sitting at end of the deck hanging on to this gangly oversized rope as if it were his own lifeline. His head is between his knees with his one arm circled around the rope and the other around his legs. He looks like a for-lorn child gripping this fence. I hear his sobbing as I move closer.

The lights come on overhead, signaling that we are close to our destination, surprising us both. "Michael." I gently touch his arm.

"We have to go. Come on, baby. I'll drive."

He lifts his head and looks at me. His face is streaked with tears. My pulse races as I discern his fight with the bad news that I still don't even know.

"Come on, baby, I'll take you back to the car."

Instinctive, now, I know that it's Elaina—something has hap-pened to Elaina. I gasp for breath, but somehow, manage to help my six-foot four husband to his feet and get him back to the car. My surgical incisions all, but forgotten as a different kind of pain rips across me now. I drive the SUV now. Michael just stares straight ahead and every once in a while, he wipes a tear from his face, unembarrassed, it seems, at this open display of emotion. I compartmentalize my fear, refusing to feel it as we make our way through downtown Seattle. Fifteen minutes later, I pull into Swedish Hospital and park in Michael's designated parking space. His medical office is right by the hospital and he has parking privileges here. Somehow, I already know this, even though I can only recall being at this parking spot one time, the first day we were together, the second day of October, when this whole journey between us began.

Any other day I would think of this and it would be a spiritual experience but, today it is an empty sentiment. I can't feel anything, as my mind prepares for the grief and sadness that awaits us inside.

I help Michael from the car and he absently takes my arm. The searing pain rips through me again and it's obvious he's forgotten my surgery as well as he leans into me for support.

I look up at him then; he meets my glance for only a moment and then turns his head away. "I love you, Michael."

"I love you, too, Ellie," He doesn't turn back to me when he says this.

We ride the elevator in silence each supporting the other by linking our arms together. I welcome the physical pain I feel, hoping that it will take away the other one. *Elaina.* I envision her beautiful face and those green eyes so clearly. I smile thinking of her long auburn hair swinging back and forth in her signature ponytail. How beautiful she looked three days ago in her bridesmaid dress for our wedding. I'm lost in the memories of this beautiful child and don't even realize that the elevator doors have opened, until I look up and see the crowd of crying teenagers gathered there. Michael and I step out.

"Oh, Mrs. Bradford, I'm so sorry," one of the girls from Nick's class says to me as we pass. News of my nuptials and name change has not reached the teen crowd of Bainbridge High School.

I am somewhat stunned to see this many of Nick and Elaina's classmates in one place. I move numbly forward with Michael, scanning the crowd, searching for Robert and Carrie, my children, and Elaina.

I trail behind Michael to the nurses' station. We are on the floor for the ER. I'm trying to control my panic as I look around for Robert or Carrie yet, or my children or Elaina, but still can't find them. Michael pulls me along past the nurses' station. He stands outside of Trauma One for a moment. He just stands there.

"Michael? Where's Bobby?" I ask in this faraway voice.

"I don't…know." Michael looks over at me with so much pain in his blue eyes that I catch my breath.

"Dr. Shaw, your daughter is this way. We put her in Trauma Two." A blonde nurse with the name tag, Katrina, has come over to us and is motioning us this way. "Are you a family member?" Nurse Katrina asks of me.

"She's my *wife*," Michael says. He puts his arm protectively around me and we follow behind Nurse Katrina through the double doors marked Trauma Two.

I'm not at all prepared for what awaits me on the other side of those doors. There is a gurney and this body lies upon it with so many tubes going every which way from the arms, the chest, and the throat. Then, I see her auburn hair. It's all I recognize. Elaina's face is covered in blood and her beautiful eyes are closed and the machines are whirring all around. There is no one else in the room, except for a nurse who stands near the monitor.

I recognize the designer jeans Elaina's wearing. I bought them for her on a quick shopping spree to Seattle, right after Michael and I decided to get married. It's the same shopping trip where we picked out Elaina's dress as well as Emily's and even my wedding gown.

My mind races, my thoughts incongruent, unfinished. I can't believe what I'm seeing. The monitor displays her respiration pattern, heart rate, and blood pressure, but I can't reconcile the girl lying in this hospital bed to Elaina Shaw. Michael goes over to her and takes her hand in his and begins talking to her.

I come up alongside him and touch her hand, too. I'm surprised how cool to the touch it feels. For some reason, I was convinced our touch would cause her eyes to open, but she doesn't stir at all. A heavy stillness envelops the room. The only sound is the whirring of life-support machines and the unsteady breathing of both Michael and me.

I don't know how long we've been here, but when I look up, Robert is there. He takes Elaina's other hand. He doesn't look at me. His face is streaked with old tears, but fresh ones begin to fall. He looks over at Michael and I watch in dazed fascination as they exchange this fleeting look. Michael shakes his head from side-to-side and Robert begins to cry harder.

I'm dry-eyed, watching this scene unfold in this surreal stupor. *Nicky must be so sad.*

"Bobby, where's Nicky?" I ask.

It is Robert's face that I remember even now, when I ask the question: "Where is Nicky? My Nicky?"

Robert's face crumbles, when I say our son's name. The look of devastation on his face is like nothing I've ever seen before.

I drop Elaina's hand and step away from her. I hold my arms out in front of me, as if by doing so; I can stop what is happening here. This invisible runaway train comes crashing into me, taking away my life, as I know it to be.

"No," I whisper. "No. No. No. No. No." I'm a master of words and can only say *no*.

No words can describe this pain. And, I soon discover; there's nothing in this world that will take it away either.

Nicholas Robert Bradford was sixteen years, eight months and eight days old, when he died on the 10th of February—a Tuesday. I hadn't seen him since that Sunday—the day after I married Michael and we had dropped all of my children off at Carrie and Robert's to go bowling. I spend a lot of my time trying to remember just how much of him I saw that day. All I can remember is his wide smile, when he saw Elaina as he scrambled from the car and gave her this big hug for all of us to see. I take comfort in that memory now, knowing that he was with Elaina when he died. He was happy because he was with her. On some unknown level, deep inside, *I live, knowing that.*

One of my wishes has died and I don't even bargain with God anymore for the others. There are no words to describe this pain. I can't function. I don't feel anything beyond extreme sadness.

Nicky's funeral was much like our wedding just days before, only four times as many people came and most of them were under the age of eighteen and all of them were crying. The service had to be held at the Bainbridge High School because there were so many people that wanted to come and pay their last respects to my son; there wasn't a church on the Island big enough to hold them all. I was somewhat appalled that his funeral was held there, but I was swept up into the planning by Lisa Chatham, who seems to have stepped into the role as my new best friend, since Carrie and Michael spend all their time at the hospital in vigilance over Elaina.

Elaina. Elaina, who has yet to regain consciousness to even learn of Nick's death. The doctors are unsure, if she will ever recover, but my surgeon husband Michael and my best friend Carrie are praying for a miracle, expecting one, in fact.

*Is it less painful when you have more time to say goodbye?* Nick is ripped from us in a single instant and we never get to see him alive again. The pain is so great and the loss of him even greater.

We have spent the last month with Elaina at her bedside. She never regains consciousness. I've spoken to her for endless hours about Nicky and somehow I know she hears me. I think that is why she leaves us, finally.

Michael goes home for a much needed rest, while I stay. His vigilance for his daughter ends for just a few hours and when he leaves, she dies. I'm prepared for Elaina's death when it comes. Michael is not.

I believe in heaven and I see both of them there. I could never reconcile the Elaina in that hospital bed with the Elaina that I knew and loved. I am hoping by believing in heaven that they are now together as they should be. Carrie knows. We've talked about it. It's why we can agree to have their cremated ashes side-by-side in matching silver urns. We take turns with the urns holding the remains of our children at each of our homes, but always together. We have decided to wait to find just the right place to spread their ashes, when Michael is ready, when Michael is talking again. When he can talk about Nick and Elaina, we will decide what to do with the ashes of our two beautiful children.

How beautiful young love is, even in death. There is another funeral at Bainbridge High School. The mourners are the same. The tears are the same. The sadness is the same. We have Elaina cremated in her silver dress that she wore to my wedding because Carrie and I agree that she loved that dress.

She was so beautiful in life; it's hard to believe that she's gone. I just expect her to come walking in to the funeral in that exquisite silver gown and begin dancing for all of us. This is how I remember her. Of course, her first question would be: *Where's Nick?*

I think of this as we stand together at her service and her urn is slowly showered with all these pink roses by all these mourners. Emily stands between Michael and me holding both our hands. Mathew is on my right holding my hand, suddenly taller, sadder.

Nick's death has been hard on Mathew; and now with Elaina, too. It is too much for all of us.

Michael.

*Michael.*

He isn't even here. I try to talk to him, but he does not hear me. I realize, now, that there are all kinds of ways for a relationship to be tested, to be broken. Irrevocable? I don't know. He stands in front of me, but he doesn't touch me anymore.

Stephen and Lisa Chatham stand with us at the funeral for Elaina while Carrie and Robert stand across on the other side. After it is over, the Chatham's follow us in their car to the beach house, where there is a smaller gathering of mourners.

Someone is serving all this food that has miraculously appeared from the Town & Country Market. We have become the adopted family.

I stand uncomfortable in this black maternity dress in a daze of sorts, not even knowing where the dress that I'm wearing has come from. I don't remember getting dressed this morning. I don't remember anything about the day, except the pink roses and Elaina's portrait—a single picture taken of her at our wedding where she is smiling at the camera like she has a secret. Her life-size portrait is now in front of me on a wooden easel that someone has brought back from the service. I'm staring at it. Yes, she has a secret and his name is Nicholas Robert Bradford. I know this. It makes me smile. It is an unnatural reaction from me in this past month of sadness.

"Momma." Emily hovers near me and looks up at me. "You're smiling."

"She's thinking of Nicky." I point to the portrait. Emily scrutinizes it for a minute and then nods.

"She is!" Emily hugs me tight. "Momma, your tummy is getting big."

"Too many pop tarts," I say in this strained voice.

We have not told the children about this baby. We have not told the children because Michael and I have barely spoken in the past month.

He has spent all his time at the hospital. He was either working at his medical office or at Elaina's bedside.

I've been working through manuscripts with a newfound zeal for editing other people's words. I've tried to put our life back together, taking care of Emily and Mathew, but struggle to make sense of it all.

We have had pizza every night because all I seem to know how to do is drive to the pizzeria and pick it up or dial the number and have it delivered. The pizzeria knows me when I call; they no longer say how sorry they are about Nick and Elaina.

My pain for all of this comes unbidden. I have to make my way outside to be alone. I have to hold myself together with my arms wrapped around me to deal with this sudden onslaught of heartbreak, this grief. I am usually alone when this happens to me. Today, there are people *everywhere*. I stumble to our detached three-car garage, to find a place to hide and bear this pain alone. I wrench open the door to Michael's SUV and slip inside.

The grief takes me where it wants me to go. I cannot stop crying. Something has been released inside of me and I cannot stop. Two of my wishes have died and I cannot count the others anymore. None of this makes any sense. I was fighting for my life because of cancer, but, instead, I have lost two of my children. I cannot reconcile this outcome.

After a long while, the tears diminish, but they still trail slowly down my face and I feel them wend their way down my bare arms. I'm too weak to even lift my head. I know that I've been gone too long. The driver's door opens and I turn my head long enough to see Michael's profile.

"Ellie," he says from faraway. "Baby, everyone's looking for you."

"Can't...take...it...anymore." I force myself to say them.

It's the most we've been able to say in a month to each other.

I start to cry, again. I feel his arms around me. He pulls me closer into his arms.

"Ellen Kay."

"Michael," I say in this heartbroken voice. "Two of my wishes have died."

"I know, baby," he says back to me.

I look over at him and see the sadness etched into his face as if it is a permanent scar.

Dr. Lisa Chatham is having a fit. She's beside herself. Michael and I come back into the house arm-in-arm and there she is all, but freaking out. "Time's up," she says. Forcefully, she pulls Michael and me along to the office and shuts the door with a finality that surprises us both. "Look, I know that this has been...I know this is hard. I cannot even begin to understand it, but Ellie; we have to start your chemotherapy. We can avoid radiation therapy, but we cannot ignore your chemotherapy treatment any longer."

"You haven't been getting *chemo*?" Michael asks in this incredulous voice.

My lies have finally been found out. I've given Michael the impression I was working with Lisa this entire time on my chemotherapy treatment because I didn't want to have this argument.

"I haven't been getting chemo." This defiance slips over me and it is the most profound feeling that I have had in the past month. My breathing gets erratic. This rage runs through me. "*You* haven't been here. The kids needed me. I didn't see the point of getting chemo, right now."

"God damn it, Ellie! It's your life; we're talking about here."

"No. I don't want to do anything to endanger this baby. I'm not getting chemo!"

"Ellie, there are drug therapies we can use that will not harm your baby. If you would keep your appointments with me, you would have learned this," Lisa says in exasperation.

"Lisa, I can't do it. I don't have…any more wishes." Fresh tears well up and begin to spill over.

"Let me talk to her," Michael says now.

"You never…never talk to me, anymore, Michael. You're never…even here."

"Five minutes," Lisa warns us, as she leaves.

I turn to Michael. My accusations evident by the way I look at him. He steps back.

"I'm sorry, Ellie. I'm so sorry. I haven't been here for you. I've let you down."

I cannot say anything. I just stare at him while this pain travels through me. I wrap my arms around my chest and step back away from him.

"I can't…take…it…anymore." I angrily wipe away the tears from my face. "First Nicky; now, Elaina. I can't take it. It's too much…it's too much loss to bear, Michael."

Michael comes to stand in front of me now. Close enough to reach out and touch me, but he doesn't. He just stands there, as I warily watch him. Finally, he raises his hand and touches my face. He trails his fingertips across my lips. I see his sad smile. I haven't seen him smile in so long; I involuntarily tremble as I stare at him.

"Ellen Kay, you're my soul mate. I love you as if you are the air I breathe. You make me complete. As you stand here in front of me, I can only thank God that now I can touch you any time I want. I'm whole again, because of you, Ellie."

His words sound hollow.

*Where has the magic between us gone?*

I reach out my hand and touch his face. He closes his eyes and sways in front of me.

"There are no words to adequately describe what you mean to me," I say.

He opens his eyes. His sadness is so profound; this incredible fear comes over me as I witness it.

"I put my life in your hands because you complete me," I say. "I know that we may be tested and that there will be obstacles put in our way. That cancer will try to take me, but I will stay, here with you…Michael. I want to be *here* with *you*."

He pulls me into his arms and kisses me then. I kiss him back, but I'm astonished at his tears. His grief is tangible between us.

"It's going to be okay, Michael."

He buries his head into my collar bone, but doesn't answer. This ominous feeling just about pulls me under.

# CHAPTER FIFTEEN

## The Worst Day

G rief is like cancer. It ebbs and flows within you. Then, it changes and transforms you. Forever. Grief. Cancer. Both force you to face your worst fear—death.

Grief and cancer. Both undermine your optimism of life. You finally *see* the cup is really just half full, even if you believed otherwise your whole life. Both teach you to believe that bad things can happen to people, whether they're good or bad or rich or poor or young or old, alike. Grief and cancer *corner the market* for all. Grief and cancer take all comers. Both rule. *Do they always win?* I begin to wonder.

My grief over Nick and Elaina lies dormant for hours, sometimes days at a time. After Michael and I declare ourselves, yet, again; I feel renewed. It's as if I have the upper hand with grief. I begin to believe that I will get through this, whatever *this* is. I believe I've been to the deepest abyss of grief and re-surfaced with Michael at my side. I believe that.

It is the end of the third week of March. Nick has been dead for six weeks and Elaina for two. The normalcy in our household has never found its equilibrium though. And, I'm beginning to notice this, even through my own hazy state of barely functioning.

This morning, I covertly watch Michael as he gets up and out of our bed at 5:30 a.m. He puts on his running gear in a methodical ten minutes of repetitive steps and quietly eases out the bedroom door. He thinks I'm still asleep, but I've been waiting for him to wake up and perform this new routine of his that he's embraced since Elaina's death. As soon as he leaves, I pull on my own clothes—jeans, blouse, shoes and coat. I leave behind a note on the kitchen counter for Mathew and Emily that tells them I went for a run and I'll be back soon.

My mind lectures me now: *I should not being doing this.* His retreating form is already far down our pristine gravel drive. I slip into my SUV and follow him slowly out to the road. I'm not sure why I'm doing this, except that grief and the threat of cancer have warped my mind and there is *something.* Something, I discern. It's the way Michael looks at me now. There's this sadness surrounding him, but there's something else; I can't explain. I'm trying to figure out what that something is and so I'm following him.

He has chosen to run along the main road, so I hang back. I'm far enough away that I cannot really tell what color his sweatshirt really is from this distance, even though I know it's navy blue. I watch him as he runs; his golden head hangs down as if he's afraid to look up ahead.

And, then, I see the something I'm certain that I'm not supposed to see. It's *Carrie.* She's parked by the side of the road in her white Mercedes sedan. I know it's hers.

Michael stops running and gets in the passenger side and closes the door. I press down on the gas pedal and tail Carrie's car as it weaves its way down the winding road. A few miles down from our beach house, her car pulls off at the state park.

I park my car at the edge of the parking lot in the shadows and just stare into Carrie's car. The parking lot is deserted and they just sit there in the car—two shadows about a foot apart. My heart rate beats fast and I watch them in shock. I can't reconcile what I'm witnessing with what I believe to be true about my life, about me and Michael. Yet, the evidence of their liaison is right here in front of me only three hundred feet away.

This is so like Carrie. I have known the woman my entire adult life. I *know* Carrie. When she's scared or frightened, she always turns to a man, *always*. It seems innocent enough to an outsider observing, who didn't know Carrie, but I do. I know what Carrie needs. I know what Carrie wants. Perhaps, it's never been about Bobby, perhaps it was about what Bobby and I had together. Carrie—the most attractive one, still looking and searching for what I might have: love, devotion, security. I know Carrie well enough to understand that she would see what I had with Michael and would want him back, to make him her own, again. *Michael.* Michael might believe that Carrie's just interested in sharing their grief and sadness over Elaina, but I know Carrie would *need* more. Carrie would *take* more.

I'm standing outside of my SUV, now. I don't know how I got here. I wildly look around for a place to hide, but there isn't one. *And, why should I hide?* I step toward Carrie's car. My legs just take me there. While my mind lectures: *this is a bad idea.*

I don't know what I expected to see. I thought I would see my husband fighting this vixen off, declaring his love for me, but as I draw closer, a part of me registers more shock as I discover the two shadows have merged together. I don't realize this until it's too late, when I'm standing at the passenger window and watch Michael kiss Carrie.

A high-pitched scream invades the stillness, as if there's a wounded animal crying out in pain. It takes a full minute to realize it's me. I tremble violently and can't seem to stop.

Michael is in front of me, now, touching my face trying to capture the tears that fall. "Don't touch me!" I back away from him.

He shakes uncontrollably and I cry out again when I see the incredible remorse and panic in his face.

"Ellie! I'm sorry. She just wanted to talk about Elaina and then she started crying and...nothing happened."

I'm looking at him, incredulous, taking in the state of his appearance. He has this pink flush across his neck and on his face that he tends to get in the heat of our lovemaking. His running jacket is askew. His lips are swollen, as if Carrie bit them in her haste. But, I do what I know will prove him wrong before he realizes why I'm doing it. He puts his arms around me and I grab him and feel his erection with my free right hand and then, push him away so violently he stumbles backward towards Carrie's car.

"You son of a bitch! God damn you, Michael!"

I run back to my car. He's too stunned by what has just transpired to follow me right away. I've already started the engine, when he appears at my driver's door and tries to stop me from going. I just press on the gas pedal and drive away from him. Looking back in my rearview mirror, I see him running to catch up to me, but he just gets farther and farther away from me.

Within minutes, I'm back at the house; I leave the car in the drive and race inside. I grab my passport, retrieve cash and credit cards from the office, empty my side of the closet, and push it all inside my suitcase. "God damn it," I mutter over and over. I find my cell phone cord and grab the laptop and a pile of manuscripts. The tears stream down my face and I wipe at them in frustration.

I stand there a few moments, trying to decide what to do. I cannot think.

"Nicky!" I race to his room. "Nick, I need you to watch Mathew and Emily. I have to go someplace. I'll call, when I can. Nick! Where are you?" I check the bathroom, expecting to find my oldest son there. It's empty. I stand in his room, looking at his made bed. "Nick."

My minds catches up to me again as I suddenly remember where Nick is. There is a part of me that collapses to the floor and remains there, weeping over my dead son. Another part of me leaves the room and finishes retrieving my belongings. I drag the suitcase down to the living room and add the two urns on the fireplace mantel to my treasured collection of stuff and zip it up. I carry everything out to the SUV and load it up.

I have reached the breaking point. I sit in the car with the engine running for a minute and acknowledge this.

It is too much and I have lost another one of my wishes, really, *four more*: Michael, me, myself and I. It's true. I have to leave before something happens to my two remaining children, my last two wishes. I cannot even think about the unborn one I carry.

"Bobby," I say as he answers his cell phone. "I need you to take care of Mathew and Emily." I careen down the gravel drive as I try to get the words out.

"Ellie, what's wrong?" Bobby Bradford asks in sudden alarm.

"*Everything*, Bobby. Just come to the house and get the kids off to school. You'll have to pack up their stuff. I'll call later tonight."

"Ellen Kay, what the hell is going on with you? Tell me." I hear the pleading in his voice, but I cannot break his heart. I decide to let Michael and Carrie tell him that story.

"I can't," I whisper, as I end the call.

It's as if God is helping me out today. God knows; he owes me.

I make the ferry just before it pulls away from the dock. They're lecturing me about being late, but they take my money anyway and let me on board.

The traffic in downtown Seattle is cooperative, heavy, but moving. I haven't solidified my plans, but I head to the airport because some part of my mind tells me to go there.

I long for a destination that doesn't have cancer, grief, or death.

I toy with the idea of Paris. Robert and I had always talked about going there, but we never did. I'm looking down at my suitcase and then back up at the departure board. "Where shall we go?"

I ask Nick and Elaina. Their cremated remains are tucked inside my suitcase. "Maybe, Paris. Let's not decide, right now. Let's get to New York and decide then."

My ability to lie has come in handy. I fabricate this complete story about meeting my son, Marco and his girlfriend in Italy. I tell the ticket agent how excited I am, being able to surprise them this way. "It's all so last minute," I say. "It's just wonderful!" After a few minutes of exultation, she hands my one way ticket to New York. She offers to book me through to Rome, but I tell her that I might want to stop in Paris as well and I'm just not sure of my plans. I dazzle her with one of my best, former-UW-cheerleader-yeah-team smiles. Even I *believe* what I'm saying.

She checks in my single suitcase and I have this sudden fear that I will lose Nick and Elaina's remains in baggage claim, but I can't chance taking the bag through security. I'm pretty sure cremated remains are not allowable items for a carry-on. Cremated remains would, somehow, be seen as a worse offense than six ounces of hair gel or a large tube of toothpaste to the TSA. Reluctantly, I watch my suitcase move along the conveyor belt to the hidden abyss of the airport's baggage system and say a silent prayer that I'll see it and them in New York on the other side.

When the chime for 10,000 feet goes off, I let out a deep breath. It is, then, only then, that I pick up the mobile air phone and swipe my credit card through and call Mathew's cell phone. It goes straight to voice mail because, of course, he is at school now.

"Mathew," I say as his greeting ends. "It's Mom. I just want you to know how much I love you. I'm sorry I'm not there, right now, to tell you this in person." I wipe at my face. "Just know that I love you. Tell your sister, too. I'll call you soon. I love you, Mattie. I love you, Em. Play this for her, too." I finish in a rush, too afraid that I will start crying too hard to make any sense. I hang up the phone with one hand and numbly swipe away at my tear-streaked face with the other.

My seat mate in first class stares at me. He is this handsome, dark-haired stranger with these enigmatic grey-blue eyes. He can't be more than thirty and wears this grey, crew-neck t-shirt, some kind of nondescript worn brown leather jacket with a pair of Seven Jeans.

I recognize the brand, Seven Jeans, because Nick has a pair just like them. *Had.* Had a pair. No. He still has them. Well, I have them. This thought of Nick and his Seven Jeans sets me back and I have to close my eyes and let the wave of grief pass. I have to wait until it gone before I open my eyes again. And, there is this stranger still staring at me, watching me. I give him my best impersonation of Dr. Lisa Chatham's please-don't-fuck-with-me look.

"Very good," he says. "That should work well for you in New York." His smile dazzles me now and I cannot look away.

"Right. Okay. Thanks," I finally say in this glacial voice and force myself to look away.

I reach for my laptop and try to ignore him, but I can feel him watching me and everything I do. After an indeterminable wait for the laptop to power up, I click on Outlook and begin typing e-mail messages to my team with the exception of Michael and Carrie.

I start with Robert. I'm unsure why this is.

> Bobby,
>
> I'm sorry about this morning. I'm sorry that I'm leaving you with this mess. Just promise me that you will take care of the kids for me. I'm worried about both of them. Mathew is struggling. I don't want him to think that he has to become Nick for us. You know what I mean. Emily will act like "Miss Independent" but she will still want to be in your arms, if she has a bad dream. Enchanted is still

her favorite movie. I think she likes the happiness that Giselle emulates. In any case, just do this for me. Be there for both of them, until I figure things out. Thank you, Bobby. I love you. E

Lisa and Stephen,

I'm sure that you have figured out that I will not be making my appointment today. I know it was our first one and all…well; my circumstances have taken a different course. I want to thank both of you from the bottom of my heart for being there for me as part of my team and as my good friends. These past few months have been so hard, but your support and love is what has made them bearable. I treasure our friendship and your wisdom, just know that. I will be in touch when my journey becomes more certain.

I love you both, E

Harriet, I'm still working away on the manuscripts. I may be in your neighborhood. Where can we meet? E

I pause at this last message. What am I doing? If I involve my boss, I'll give away my location. I move the message to the drafts folder. I cautiously look over at Mr.-Handsome-Seat-Mate-in-First-Class and discover him still watching me.

"Did you want to send those? They have Internet access on the flight," he says. "I could…I could show you how to do it." His voice is so silky and soothing, all I can do is nod.

He takes the jack from the phone and plugs it into my laptop with another flash of his bright smile. I swipe through my credit card and the connection is made in a matter of ninety seconds. My outbox empties and the messages are gone within seconds. New e-mail messages come in. They are all from Michael.

"Looks like those download to your C drive. Did you want to stay connected and send something back?"

"No. Absolutely not."

"That sounds like a definite *no*," he says with a laugh.

"It is." He undoes the connection and reinserts the connector into the phone. "Thank you," I murmur.

"Court. Court Chandler." He puts his hand out and I weakly shake it.

"Elaina Miles," I say swiftly.

My ability to lie stays with me and I inadvertently smile, as I secretly acknowledge this. I'm a new person. I've become someone else. I'm half this sixteen-year-old girl, Elaina Shaw, and half my thirty-eight year old self, Ellie Miles, from twenty years ago, before Robert, before Michael.

"Oh," Court says. "I thought your name was Ellie."

"It's a nickname for Elaina," I say. "I prefer Elaina, but some people call me Ellie." I do this little shoulder shrug thing and turn back to my laptop. Within my peripheral vision, I see him nod and lean back in his seat.

This conversation with this helpful stranger is over. I'm some-what relieved. I cannot afford to get too involved with another human being.

I have to seek anonymity and too many more of Mr. Court Chandler's probing questions could prove to be my undoing with this goal. I take a look out the window and try to breathe. Then, I click on the e-mail from Michael. I go in the order they were sent, starting with the first one this morning.

> Ellie,
> You're not standing in front of me and I'm lost
> without you. I came home and you were gone.

Robert came and took the kids to school. I'm hoping that you will be back before they get home—that is what I promised them. We need to talk this through, Ellie, I love you; let me explain. Michael

Michael, you messed up. I'm not standing in front of you, probably will never stand in front of you again. You've broken my heart. E

Ellen Kay,
As I wrote in another email, Robert has already been here. He told me that you called him very upset and crying. I know I did that. I'm so sorry. He is going to pick up the kids from school. I am at a loss. I need to talk to you. Please don't do this. Come home. Michael

Michael,
Let Robert have the kids. They need to be with their father. I don't know what you need. Carrie? I'm not coming back. E

My hands start to tremble. I stop for a moment and stare out the airplane window at the vast blue sky and puffy white clouds, taking steady breaths in and out, and attempt to find some sense of equilibrium somewhere inside of me.

I lean back against the headrest and close my eyes for a few moments. *Breathe. In and out. This can't be happening. It just can't.*

Then, I open my eyes and click on another e-mail because on some twisted level, I'm beholden to the torment that rages inside. I have to *feel* it all.

Ellie,

You are the love of my life, just know that. I screwed up. Carrie has been so sad and I thought if I just went to meet her this morning, we could talk through her feelings of loss over Elaina. I didn't realize how unhappy she was, until we parked at the park and she started telling me how much she misses Elaina. It was hard, Ellie. She is so broken. I was just trying to comfort her and then, she...well. Nothing happened. I'm going to lose you because of this. Ellie, please come home. Michael

Michael,

I don't believe you. If I was the love of your life, you wouldn't have done this to me. I hope you and Carrie will be very happy together. No, I don't. I think you must deserve each other. I don't think you will ever be happy. E

Ellie,

Lisa just called the house. I know you missed your first chemo therapy appointment. Ellen Kay, you have to have these treatments. You can't mess around with this anymore. Please, Ellie, come back for the treatment. I promise I won't pressure you about anything else, but please, Ellie, come home. Michael

Michael, don't tell me what to do. You did this to us. It doesn't matter anymore. I've lost four more wishes. You, me, myself and I. Don't write to me anymore. It's too sad for me to read and I have nothing more to say. E

I attach the connector back into my laptop and run my credit card through for the third time and press send. There are already more messages in my inbox as the outbox empties the ones I have just replied to. There are four new messages from Michael and two from Carrie and two from Robert and two from Lisa.

"No!" I say in frustration. "God damn it!"

Court Chandler undoes the connector for me. He takes my laptop and closes Outlook for me and powers off the laptop. "You can look at these later," he says in this gentle voice.

He hands me back the laptop. Tears start pooling on the plastic case, but all I can do is sit here with the laptop on my knees and cry. Eventually, he takes the laptop back and wipes it off with his jacket sleeve and puts it in the front pocket of my seat. I'm sobbing now, unable to stop. He lifts the armrest up, slides over to me, and pulls me into his arms, while I just cry into his shirt.

We've caught the attention of the first flight attendant who comes over to ask in a cheerful voice if everything is all right. I hear Court Chandler reply that we need a pillow, a blanket, and a glass of water. I'm confused by all of these requests.

The flight attendant comes back in a few moments apparently fulfilling them all. I keep my eyes closed because my humiliation is rising with each passing second as I rest in the arms of this stranger. I have already ruined his shirt. I take a quick look and see the black mascara stains up close streaked across the grey of his t-shirt. He tucks a blanket in around me and wedges a pillow behind my neck. I hear him unlatch the food tray and hazard a guess that a glass of ice water has arrived, too.

"Elaina," he says. It takes a second time with his saying *my name* for me to open my eyes. "Elaina. Drink the water. You *do not* want to get dehydrated." The way he says this, it is as if dehydration is a fate far worse than cancer. It makes me laugh. He's looking at me strangely, now. He hands me the water. I obediently drink it down.

It is a small plastic glass of water. It is a gift from the gods according to Court Chandler.

"You're very strange," I say now.

*Bitchy. Unappreciative.* That's me. Well, I have cancer, a broken heart, a dead son, a dead step-daughter. Take your pick. I've lost too many wishes, including Michael and me.

A few minutes later, I'm recovered enough that contrition runs through me. As Elaina, now, I smile at him—this benevolent, for-mer-UW-Cheerleader-yeah-team-smile.

He holds his breath when he sees it. He shakes his head from side-to-side and looks disconcerted. I'm aware of the effect that my smile has on people. I've known this for years. It's almost as effective and powerful as my ability to lie.

"You know if you keep smiling like that, I'm going to have to stop talking to you," Court says.

I sense his uneasiness. He gets this anxious look. This only encourages me. I'm Elaina, the incorrigible, and I continue to smile at him, while I wipe away tears. "I'm married," he says in a voice that seems to indicate regret.

I nod. Then, my smile falters.

"Me, too," I whisper.

# Chapter Sixteen

## Untenable

e've deplaned and relax in the Flagship Lounge for American Airlines Gold passengers. Mr. Court Chandler is a coveted member. I sip a glass of ice water, but gaze longingly at his glass of red wine. He sees this and orders me a glass of his expensive Cabernet. I'm wearing this oversized long coat, so Mr. Court Chandler has no idea that I'm pregnant, a little over six months pregnant, if one were counting, if one were thinking of that, if one had the capacity left to care at all, about that. I've hidden it well, but I can feel myself wavering as I begin to lose the illusion of Elaina Miles that I've fabricated for this man and myself.

"Elaina," he says to me now. "If that is your name," Court murmurs. "I mean I call you that, but you don't respond half the time." I look over at him with my mouth formed in an *oh* kind of surprise. The lies begin to catch up to me as keeping the façade up begins to wear me down.

"You can call me Ellie, if you want," I say in this generous voice.

"It appears everyone does." Court stares at me over the rim of his wine glass. "Who's Michael?"

"You read my e-mail." I'm not mad. I'm not anything. I just look at him warily, trying to figure him out.

"It was right *there*." He gestures his hand towards the laptop bag that is propped up next to my suitcase, the one Court graciously retrieved for me from baggage claim. "So, who is he?"

"He's my…he was the best thing that ever happened to me." I give him my most withering, I-don't-want-to-have-this-conversation look.

Court just laughs. "Come on, Ellie. You can do better than that. I've *seen* it."

Court Chandler is this very engaging man. His dark brown hair is a little long and has this wave to it that just makes you want to reach out and touch it. His eyes are this impossible grey-blue. He surprises me at every turn with his wit and charm. We've talked politics, the stock market, and even high tech. He owns his own company, but he downplays what it is. I think I'm supposed to recognize him and he's amused that I don't.

"I bet you don't even shop at Costco," I teased him earlier.

"Too much quantity for the two of us," he said with a shrug.

"Who are you, Mr. Court Chandler?" I asked with a smile. He just smiled back at me.

Pretty swanky, he had said when I told him I lived on Bainbridge Island. I'd shrugged my shoulders again, hoping that I was casual enough that he would move on to a less sensitive topic. I was getting careless, now, sharing too much of myself with this stranger from Seattle.

"Hey, did you know the two teenagers that died in that car accident, a few months ago?" Court asks now in connection to our Bainbridge Island conversation from a few minutes before. "That happened on Bainbridge. It was all over the papers in Seattle. So sad."

My small amount of happiness that I've found for the day seeps out of me completely. I give him this measured look, take a deep breath, and finish my wine in a single long swallow. I look away from his probing gaze

I haven't answered his question. *Did I know them? I loved them. I still love them.*

I stare at my suitcase. Nick and Elaina's ashes are still inside. I know this because earlier I ran my hand inside the bag and felt for the two metal urns, making sure they were there.

"Ellie, what's wrong?" Court asks now.

I try to smile. "I need to go. Thank you, Court, for…everything. Your kindness is…extraordinary." I stand up and hastily grab my purse, the suitcase, the laptop and move toward the swinging doors.

"Ellie." He says from behind me, but I don't turn around.

Once I'm out in the terminal, I begin to make more plans. I just don't have the energy to get on a plane to Paris tonight. It's only five in the afternoon in Seattle, but it's eight in the evening here. I feel myself getting more tired as I place one foot in front of the other.

Anxious now, I hail a taxi. New York City is swarming with taxis, so it is only a matter of minutes, before I am ensconced in one with my Pakistani driver whose name tag reads: Georges. He asks where I want to go in heavy accented English.

*Where do I want to go?* "Home, Seattle." He looks at me with an incredulous are-you-crazy-lady? stare. *Why yes, I am.* "Gramercy Park," I say now. I stayed there once. When I came to meet with Harriet a few years back, I stayed at Gramercy Park. It is only a few blocks away from Harriet's office and my place of employment. For some reason, choosing some place I'm familiar with reassures me. Michael wouldn't recall the name of that hotel. Two years ago, he was less involved in the day-to-day machinations of my life.

My heartbreak surfaces with this thought. This crushing pain catches up to me. The utter stress of the day and traveling exacts its toll on me as well. I lean back in cab and close my eyes. My life seems over. It seems over. The tears fall as Georges drives me across town to Gramercy Park and I give into the grief of it all.

179

The front desk staff at the Gramercy takes pity on me. Miraculously, they find a suite in this fully-booked hotel. I'm overwhelmed and grateful to the bell hop, Johnnie, who helps me with my luggage and the laptop. Within in fifteen minutes, I'm standing in my hotel suite by myself. With reverence, I open my suitcase and take out the two urns and set them down on the modern wooden office desk. In my haste, I've packed an eclectic array of clothes and hang them up in the closet with this pretense that I'll be staying for days, even though I do not have any plans to do so.

I power up my cell phone and plug it in to the adapter. The number "5" flashes next to the voice mail symbol. My hand shakes at the memory of checking messages, recalling Bobby's from six weeks ago.

I lay the phone down and walk over to the closet surveying my wardrobe. There are dresses there that I don't remember packing, let alone buying. These must be gifts from Carrie or Lisa. I grab a blue crepe one and hang it up on the bathroom hook.

*Carrie.* Just thinking her name makes me cry. Why? I wonder. Why does she hurt me so? Over and over, she hurts me. Why?

I've taken a bath, put on make-up and gotten dressed. The blue dress I'm wearing is this kind of ballooned mini-skirt number. Something I wouldn't normally wear, but it hides the baby bump well and, at this point, that is all I care about. I brush my hair and leave it hanging down my back. I still have my hair. Cancer has not taken that yet. I cannot make myself think about the chemo therapy. Is that the other reason it was so easy to run away?

I survey myself in the mirror. This chic, sophisticated woman with blue eyes and long blonde hair stares back at me. I finish the look with a dark red lipstick.

I stare at my cell phone for five whole minutes, before I decide that calling right now will just unravel my plans. With deference, I turn it on silent, grab my room key card, and make my way to the elevators. Once on, I press the down button for the lounge on the first floor.

Elaina Miles is going out because Ellie Shaw, most certainly, would stay in.

I sidle up to the magnificent wooden bar without being too conspicuous and sit at the end that is free of patrons. I've already decided what to order on my way down in the elevator. One drink. That's it. So, I want to make it a good one. Something I can drink slowly and savor for at least an hour. I'm Elaina Miles, not Ellie Shaw. Elaina Miles is not pregnant and doesn't have cancer. I can order and drink whatever I want. This is the bargain I've made with myself. One drink. That's it.

"Hello," says this twenty-something bartender. "Would you like a table?"

"No, thank you. This is great. This is perfect."

"What can I get you?" He gives me that appraising, interested male look. This only makes me smile wider. This is what I need. This is what Elaina Miles wants.

"I was thinking of a martini…something, well; my friend once made me a Crème Brulee Martini. Would you know how to make that?" He gives me this incredulous look and laughs.

"Half and half, Frangellico, vanilla vodka, Cointreau?"

"That's it." I give him my best, yeah team smile. He returns it.

With a dramatic flourish, he pours a little Frangellico on a plate and rims the glass with it and then dips the edges in raw brown sugar. My smile gets deeper because this is exactly how I'd made them for a Thanksgiving dinner, a few years ago.

Within three minutes, he combines all the ingredients with ice and masterfully shakes the martini shaker and pours it out in front of me with an exacting, entertaining flair. He smiles at me.

"Perfect. It's great." I wipe away the froth of cream and brown sugar from my lips, while he stares at me in this fascinated, still attracted way. What is with these men I've encountered today? Am I giving out some kind of signal? Maybe, Elaina Miles is?

"What's your name?" The bartender of twenty-something asks. I glance around, realizing I'm his only patron at the bar now and the tables behind me are mostly empty, at the moment.

"Elaina. Elaina Miles." I nod as I tell this lie and then shake his outstretched hand. I smile again and then ask him his name.

"Dan," he says. His brown eyes are this warm caramel color. He studies me closely as he pours a glass of ice water and sets it down in front of me. He's tall, muscular, and interested. He grins at me slowly, as I sip my drink seeming to take it all in stride. I stare back with interest as well. We talk about his job. He attends NYU, taking courses in English Literature. I tell him about my editing job. He's even more interested now. He's a writer. "So am I," I tell him in a silky voice. I tell this lie and realize I need to make it true. My ability to plan for a future makes me feel better. I take another swig of my martini and smile at Dan over the rim of my glass. A cocktail server is trying to get his attention from the other end of the bar and he moves off with this reluctant shrug, while I return an interested look of my own.

The alcohol courses through me faster than pain killers ever could. Dan returns within minutes and hands me a dinner menu. I give him a quizzical look; he moves off, again, when another cocktail server waves for his attention. His charming smile reminds me of Mr. Court Chandler. I feel this brief twinge of guilt for being so unkind to Mr. Chandler in the end, leaving so abruptly after all he did for me this day.

My mind goes on. If he hadn't brought up the two dead teenagers on Bainbridge Island, well, maybe it was best he brought that up because things were heading into an untenable direction.

I smile as I think of the word untenable. I *like* the word *untenable*—baseless, without sound reasoning or judgment and groundless. Yes. Untenable. Things were getting untenable between us—very untenable, indeed.

My mind drifts even farther as the alcohol catches up to me. I haven't eaten today. I sway a bit and grip the granite edge of the bar with my hands. Perhaps the half and half can serve as food in my system. Perhaps not. I contemplate Elaina Miles' next move.

"There you are," says this voice from behind me. I turn and meet the grey-blue eyes of Mr. Court Chandler. He slides on to the bar stool right next to mine.

"What are you doing here?" *Untenable. This is untenable. That's what this is.*

"I wanted to make sure you were okay, Ellie Shaw, mother of Nicholas Bradford and wife of Dr. Michael Shaw, father of Elaina Shaw." Court holds up his Blackberry. His cell phone screen displays the newspaper article showing Elaina's mangled car. The headline, alone, makes me shudder: *Teenage Sweethearts Tragedy in Worst Car Accident on Island.*

My lies unravel right in front of me. "Don't do this," I plead, looking away from Mr. Court Chandler. Dan comes over prepared to do his duty as my first knight. Chivalry is not dead. I try to smile.

"Is there anything you need, Elaina Miles?" I hear the automatic protectiveness for me in my twenty-something Dan-the-bartender's voice.

I slowly shake my head and give him an everything-is-okay-kind of look. Dan looks warily at my bar mate.

"What can I get you?" Dan asks.

"Whatever she's having," Court says with a disconcerted grin.

"Are you *sure*? It's kind of a girl's drink." I don't hide this trace of irritation at the man next to me. It begins to beat steadily within me; it comes across in my tone.

The truth is I'm unprepared for Court Chandler and his endless questions. My distress only encourages Court. He repeats his request to Dan, who with a reluctant shrug moves off to make *my drink* for this latest patron.

"How did you…how did you find me?" I wonder if he is just highly intelligent? Or, is my trail so obvious and wide open that even Michael will eventually make his way here?

"Not going to say," Court answers. He takes a sip of the identical drink of mine that Dan sets in front of him and smiles over at me.

"Crème Brulee Martinis? Say it isn't so," Court pronounces. "My wife loves these."

"She does?" I ask in surprise. Court nods at me.

For some reason, this makes me laugh. I feel this release deep inside of me of some of the grief I hold.

My lies have all, but spun out with this man. He knows my secrets, well, most of them. My baby moves in a sluggish way inside of me. This twinge of guilt replaces the grief. I swig the last of my martini. "What's her name?"

He laughs, then answers more subdued. "Her name is Eve."

My smile fades. "Are you sure your name isn't Adam?"

"I'm not sure of anything anymore," Court says. He looks anguished and tormented.

Unthinking, I reach up and touch his face. "Me neither," I say.

A half hour late, Dan grudgingly makes us a shaker of Crème Brulee Martinis and charges them to my room. My protector gives me one last pleading look, then, hands me the sugar-rimmed glasses, while Court takes the ice-cold shaker from him.

"Let me know if you need anything, Ms. Miles," Dan says with a trace of dejection, as we walk away from the bar.

"I will. I promise."

I give him a benevolent smile and turn away before I can feel too guilty about leaving the bar with Court, but not before I see this injured look on the twenty-something-year-old bartender's face. What is with these men today?

Now, Court and I share the elevator up to the 19th floor. I hold my room key card in my hand. He tells me that he's going to check into a room in this hotel, too. I can only nod.

We are silent, resigned but, beholden to this thing between us. We're emboldened enough to take the next step, riding the elevator together because of this thrilling sexual tension that's been apparent, since we first sat together on the American Airlines flight, just seven hours before.

I'm not scared. I'm not accountable. My baby bump assures me that this thing will end soon enough. I'm not worried. I don't experience guilt. I file it away in this secret place inside of me, remembering it all. Remembering how easy it all is…this infidelity thing. It's *easy*.

It makes me less upset at Michael. I think of Carrie and her beauty and her wanton ways and her need for validation, intellectually, emotionally, and sexually, *all the time*. Michael didn't have a chance. He's helpless prey in her spider's web. Carrie is the spider.

Am I Carrie, now? I sway with the movement of the elevator. I close my eyes and try to think. I could never be Carrie. No one can. That's the thing. Always. I could *never* be Carrie. I could never *be* Carrie. I could never be *Carrie*. I can feel the tears sting behind my eyes. *I can never be* Carrie. Now, I can't even be *Ellie*.

"What's your room number?" Mr. Court Chandler asks. I open my eyes and stare at him.

"1923," I say, knowing that I'm taking action that I may not be able to take back. "Nineteen, twenty-three," I say again as if I'm announcing the year.

I'm at ease because my pregnant state, upon his discovery, will turn this right around. I'm so confident that I give him my best, former-UW-cheerleader-yeah-team smile, as we walk down the hallway together. I hand him my room key card and he swishes it through the lock, one-handed, and we enter my hotel suite. I carry the martini glasses and set them down with a flourish. Court shakes the martini mixer behind me. The rimmed sugar glasses sparkle, as he pours the martini mixture into each one. I'm still doing all right, even as he hands me a glass and gives me a meaningful seductive look.

I clink my glass with his and just smile. He glances around the suite with interest. And, I know exactly when his eyes come to rest on the two polished silver urns that sit on the desk. The urns are engraved with their names, their birth dates, and the dates of their deaths in this beautiful script writing. Court leans down to read the captions seemingly unable to actually pick them up. I go over to help him out.

I pick up Elaina's first. "Elaina Marie Shaw was born August 3rd, 1993 and died March 10th of this year," I say, overcome with emotion. I set Elaina's urn down carefully and reach for the other. "Nicholas Robert Bradford was born June 2nd, 1993 and died February 10th. Elaina and Nicholas—two angels on Earth and now, two angels together in heaven—my son, Michael's daughter. I couldn't leave them, so I brought them with me."

There's nothing more to say. I take a drink from my martini glass and stare at Court.

"I'm sorry, Ellie. I'm so sorry."

"Yes. I'm sorry, too." I finish the glass in one long swallow and set it down. I'm swaying on my feet.

The game is up. The play is finished. I have to stop this thing. "You should go," I say.

"I should go." Court looks at me and tries to smile. "I should... most definitely...go."

"Yes. This is an untenable situation."

"Untenable," Court says to me. "Baseless, without sound judgment, weak, questionable, without grounds...untenable." His voice is melodic. I smile at him. It only seems to encourage him.

This infidelity thing…is so *easy*.

He sets down his martini glass. His hands reach for me and he pulls me in his arms. His kiss is tentative at first; and then, it is *everywhere*. He has unleashed something inside of me and I'm kissing him back because Elaina Miles wants to. We make our way over to the king-size bed. His hands and lips are everywhere setting me on fire wherever they touch me. Until, they rest in one place, on my baby bump and all his actions stop. I open my eyes to stare at him. He sits up and stares back at me with too many questions and this sudden dawning of understanding in his eyes.

"Ellie, you're pregnant," Court says this, as if it is the most wondrous thing.

I'm undone by his tone. He is an angel, here to save me from drowning.

"I am."

"And, when were you going to tell me this?" He asks with this crooked smile. Mr. Court Chandler is unflappable, calm, and composed.

"I was working up to it." I give him an uncertain smile, captured by his amazing touch and the way he looks at me now. All the pain of the day seems to fade away in his presence.

"What else haven't you told me," he asks now. "Because I'm pretty sure there's more. What causes a beautiful *pregnant* woman to get on a plane and fly from one end of the country to the other side in a single day with the cremated remains of her children in her suitcase? Why does this goddess lie about her name and who she is? Why would someone do that? Unless, things are so bad, so awful at home that she can't take it anymore? What can be worse than losing your children?" Court asks. Then, with sudden clarity, he says, "What did Michael *do*? What happened, Ellie? What did he do to you?"

Mr. Court Chandler is bringing me down. The combination of alcohol, no food, and the sadness that is my life catches up to me.

"Do we have to have this conversation? Can't we just drink the martinis?"

"No."

"It's so easy…this untenable situation. Infidelity is so easy, don't you think, Court?"

"No, it's not something I normally engage in." I hear the misery in his voice and look over at him, scrutinizing him, weighing my ability to trust him.

"What's Eve like?" I ask.

"She's beautiful, intelligent, and independent. She doesn't want kids," he says with desolation.

"And, you do." He can only nod. "Maybe, she'll change her mind. You can buy my empty house on Bainbridge Island, get a Golden Retriever, and then, she'll want kids. Your paradise will be complete." I sound disillusioned even to myself. I try to smile, but fail.

"What's Michael like?"

His question catches me off guard. I'm at a loss to describe Michael. I shake my head and finally sigh. "He's beautiful, intelligent. Michael's…everything. He loves me even on my worst day."

"What's been the worst day?" Court asks.

"It should be February 10th," I say slowly. I look up at him. "But…It's probably today."

This acknowledgement troubles me. I'm sure it shows.

"What happened today, Ellie?" Court asks the question in such a thoughtful way that I'm compelled to answer.

"I found him kissing Carrie, his ex-wife."

Words have left me. I can't talk anymore. I slide off the bed and cross over to the drapes at the window, push them aside, and stare out into the dark night. I'm unable to see anything, nothing at all. "Carrie is everything. You know? She's beautiful and sexy. She gets what she wants," I say in this bitter tone.

"She wanted Bobby and she got him. She loses Elaina and she

188

wants Michael back, so she takes him, *my life*, takes *him*. Takes him away from me."

"Who's Carrie?"

"She was my best friend."

"Geez, are you sure they were together? I mean, are you sure?"

I turn back from the window. I'm dry-eyed. Tears have left me. I feel this sudden burst of anger.

"I *saw* them together. He was kissing her…he…yes! Yes! I'm sure." The pain engulfs me as I re-live the scene of Michael and Carrie from earlier today.

"I can't believe this has happened. We were so happy. We were… He loved me so much. But, I knew, deep down, I knew something wasn't right. He hasn't been the same since Nick died and then… Elaina. He doesn't touch me anymore. I can't explain it, but I think I knew; and then, today. Today, I followed him and I saw them together and…" Words finally fail me. I cross the room and take a swig of the martini. Court is there. He takes the glass from my trembling hands.

"You shouldn't be drinking," he says.

I shrug and walk back to the darkened window, unseeing of anything. All this talking of Michael and what happened brings about all this all this heart wrenching sadness. I feel outside of myself, vulnerable, and out of sorts. I stare at Court's reflection in the window.

"Is your real name Courtney?" I turn back toward him.

He gives me a wry smile. "I usually go by that, but my PR firm is trying to make me seem older."

"How *old* are you?"

"I'm almost thirty." He sounds so defensive; it makes me laugh. The comedy of our situation overtakes me for a few minutes. I just laugh. Then, I stop.

"Why are you here? Why did you find me?"

"I didn't like the way things ended at the airport."

He walks over to me. "I...I don't do this kind of thing, but you...you are so incredible, Ellie." Court traces my collar bone with his finger and I involuntarily shudder at his tender touch. "I had to see you, again, to determine if this is real or not."

"You're married to Eve," I say for both of us.

"You're married to Michael," he says back to me.

"Not for long. This is untenable."

"Untenable, but real," Court says. He leans over me and then kisses my neck and then the connection between us starts up again. "Not possible," he murmurs and then kisses me.

"Impossible," I say against his lips. I hear his quiet laughter. He has unhinged me from sadness. He has unchained me from the heartbreak. I am undone because of him from both of these things. In this moment, I believe he can cure cancer, too.

This infidelity thing is too easy. It is the good and the bad.

We have come to our senses at the same time; we both pull away from each other. "It's not too late for either of us," I say now. "Is Eve a good person?" I stare at him, imploring him to answer.

"Yes," he says with a smile. I hear his reluctance and regret.

"And you...you are a good person and... so am I. Michael is... Michael is a good person, too." The truth of my words hits me full force. I get up from the bed where we've been kissing and exploring each other; we've come so close to consummating this thing between us, half undressed, half in half out, we share this jagged breathing between us. He's touched me everywhere and I've done the same. Yet, we stopped all at once, at the same time.

I stagger over to the chair by the fireplace and sit down. Court comes over and kneels in front of me, staring up at my face, his bare chest heaving up and down, his erection evident through his boxers. I catch my breath, staring at this magnificent man, this rescuer of me this day. His hand reaches out and catches the trail of the fresh tears that run down my face. His touch is exquisite. *He would never hurt me.* This thought assails me, cutting through the web of heartbroken misery and grief that sequesters me like a permanent prison.

"Ellie, you're so miraculous." Court brushes his lips with mine. Slowly he gets up. I watch him as he pulls on his jeans, his t-shirt, and then his jacket. In one swift motion, he picks up the two martini glasses and the metal shaker. "I'll take these back to Dan."

"Court," I say. "Thank you."

"Ellie." I look up in surprise because I hear this heartbreak in his voice. "I don't think… I can see you, again."

"Why?" I ask with a faint smile, even though I already know the answer.

"Because we can't…just *be* friends."

"I know." He seems to feel my sadness from across the room. He comes back over and sets down the bar ware. "Thank you for being…my friend, Courtney Chandler," I say just as he pulls me up from the chair and into his arms.

"Sure." His kiss is so final and so passionate that I feel light-headed, when he pulls away. "Goodbye Ellie Shaw."

I watch him leave. He flashes me his crooked smile one more time and then the door clicks behind him.

I let out a slow breath and with it go the final remnants of today's brief fleeting moments of happiness with Mr. Courtney Chandler.

# CHAPTER SEVENTEEN

## If Nothing Happened

*I* lay on the rumpled bed in my hotel suite for an interminable amount of time. The Boze clock radio on the hotel night stand flashes 10:00 p.m. Mr. Court Chandler left over an hour ago and I haven't moved. Now, I check the menu for room service and order a steak and salad and a slice of cheesecake. Within a half hour, the food is delivered to my room. Food makes me feel better. I leave the cheesecake untouched because it reminds me of Michael. I can only stare at it now. The headache lessons from my martini binge. I change from the blue mini dress and slip into a long hot bath. Then, I put on a white silk camisole and black yoga pants. I pull the clasp out of my hair and leave it down. I'm now officially out of things to do. I've entered that I-should-be-tired-but-I'm-not-phase and glance at the clock. It's almost midnight.

My cell phone rings. I go over to it and stare at the screen. *Michael.* He is five plane hours away and thousands of miles further than that from me.

I pick up the cell phone and slide my finger across the screen bar to answer. "Michael." My voice sounds strange and faraway.

"Ellie."

I close my eyes as he says my name in that special way of his. I can feel his love for me as if he has reached out and touched my face. In that moment, the brief interlude with Mr. Court Chandler all but fades and is replenished by Michael's voice alone.

"Michael, I'm so...far...away." I start crying. "I'm in New York."

"I know," he says. "I just got here. The plane just landed. Where are you, Ellie?"

It is the love in his voice and the apparent release from the spell of Mr. Court Chandler, all at once, that have me undone, now. I cannot lie. That, alone, gives me pause. I am willing to only speak the truth and I do not completely understand it. The experience with Mr. Court Chandler has done something to me. Something has been resolved within me. It has shown me another side of my-self—another side of Michael, inadvertently. I try to tell him this now, but my words come out garbled and confused.

"Michael, I need you," I finally say. "I'm staying at Gramercy Park."

I hear him say the name of the hotel to someone else; I assume it's his cab driver. "I'm almost there, Ellen Kay," Michael promises. I can hear the remorse in his tone. "I'll be there as soon as I can."

Call ended comes up on my phone. I stare at it for a long time. He sounded so close; I'm suddenly afraid. I think of Mr. Court Chandler and where that particular encounter was leading.

I'm at the precipice and I've lost so much: the people I love, and me, myself and I. I have to find a way to keep from losing anyone else.

It is 9:15 p.m. in Seattle. I finally pick up my cell phone and call Robert.

"Ellie?" Robert's tense voice answers on the first ring.

"Bobby."

"Where have you been, Ells? What's going on? Michael is out of his mind. He got on a plane to New York this afternoon after he tracked down your American Express charges. Emily is beside herself and Mathew won't even talk to me. What happened?"

In what all he has just said, I ascertain that Bobby Bradford has not been apprised of the role that his current wife has had in all of this.

"Bobby, I'm sorry. Michael and I...had a misunderstanding. I know he's on his way. We'll work it out. Put Emily on. Let me talk to her." I hear the background noise of my youngest child's voice. She is asking him to read her *Winnie the Pooh*. We have regressed by three years in a single day.

"Momma. Is that you?" She sounds wary; I cringe.

"Hey Emily. How are you, Em? How was school?'

"School was fine," she says in this firm little voice back to me. "Where are you, Momma? Daddy is worried; Michael, too. Where are you?"

"I'm sorry, baby. Mommy had to leave. I had to be alone to think some things through, but I'm going to be home soon."

I spend another ten minutes telling Emily about my day. She wants to know all about the plane ride, what New York City is like. I make up a bit of a story about seeing my editor, but she is having none of it.

"Michael is sad, Momma. So *sad*. He said you needed a break. That you were too sad. Why Momma? I like Michael. He's the best. I don't why you had to leave. Are you mad at him? Mother?"

"I know, baby. Sometimes, grown-ups don't agree. And, it just takes time and we have to talk things through. You know, we'll work it out."

"Uh-huh. Well, I guess," she sighs. "I'm going to have Daddy read me a story. He promised."

"Okay, Em. I'll see you...soon. Go give the phone to Mathew. I love you, Emily."

"I love you, too, Momma." I hear Mathew say that he doesn't want to talk to me, but Emily, being Emily convinces him. There's shuffling noises as the phone is handed off to Mathew from his little sister.

"Mom," says my sullen middle child.

It doesn't matter that Nick is no longer with us. Mathew will always be my middle child, probably even more so.

"Mattie, I'm sorry. I...look, Michael and I had a misunderstanding and I...I'm sorry that I probably worried you today. I'm sure your Dad has been great. Just know that I love you and I'll be home soon."

"Is everything all right with you and Michael, Mom?"

"We're working things out." I wipe the tears away that stream down my face and try to keep an even tone, but I think he knows I'm crying. "It's been hard, you know. I promise. I'll be home soon. Mathew, I love you so much."

"Mom," he says. "You have to get the chemo. You have to promise as soon as you get home that you'll get the chemo." How does he know this? Before I can blame Michael for telling him about this, he starts talking again. "Lisa called. She's very upset that you left. She told me that we have to find you and you need the chemo now."

"Mathew, everything is fine, really. I'll be home soon. I don't want you to worry."

"Promise me, Mom."

"I promise." I have carefully chosen my words. I have promised him something, but I'm not sure what that is, yet.

"I love you, Mom."

"I love you, Mathew. Things are going to be okay. I'll be home soon. Love you Mattie. Can you find Carrie and give her the phone?"

After a few minutes more, I hear the shuffling of the phone and then I hear my former best friend's voice say my name. The sound of her voice sets me off and I'm furious all at once.

"Tell me," I say. "Tell me what happened."

I hear the sound of a door closing and I hear Carrie start to cry. "Tell me!"

"It was…while we were at the hospital with Elaina. We…got a hotel room. We were tired and just wanted to sleep. I…I just wanted her back. I just wanted what we had back. I just needed him. I needed to know if we could get it back. I'm sorry."

I hear her crying and listen to it from this faraway place. Something deep inside of me gives way. Michael lied to me when he said that nothing had happened. I cannot speak.

"He wanted it, too, Ellie. He was hurting and he kissed me and it just happened…we both agree it's wrong. We're ending it," Carrie says.

My head snaps back up at her defensive words. *We're ending it.* Her words sting my soul. "And what I saw today, you call that ending it?" The bitterness is my voice cuts away at us both. Carrie's sobbing gets louder. "What about Robert?"

"I haven't told him."

"You'll break him with this news. He won't be able to handle it," I say now. "He won't understand it. Damn you, Carrie."

"I know," she says. "I'm a terrible person. I'm weak, sad, and awful."

I don't say anything for a long time and the silence between us grows. There is only the sound of Carrie's crying. The rage for both of them just builds inside of me; it practically incinerates me where I stand.

"This is your last chance at happiness, Carrie," I say, barely under control as the anguish and heartbreak wash over me. "Use it wisely. Don't you *ever* cross the line with Michael again. Because if you do, I will tell Bobby and you will lose *everything.*" Her sobbing gets even louder with my words.

"Okay. Okay. I'm so sorry, Ellie. You need to come back. We need to make this right between us, between all of us."

"I'm not coming back, right now."

"What? But, you have to!"

"No, I don't. I have to figure my life out, Carrie. Please take care of my kids. I need you and Bobby to do that for me."

"Okay. I promise; we'll take care of the kids. But, Ellie, please come home.

"I can't," I say in this broken voice. "I can't. Put Bobby back on the phone." Carrie says a broken good-bye.

I hear the door open. The minutes go by and I finally hear Robert's voice in the background.

"Ellie?" He asks. "Why is Carrie crying?"

"I don't know, Bobby. I think she's upset about my missing chemo…but, I think she's really still trying to deal with Elaina. Bobby, you need to be there for her. You need to take care of her and be there for her. She won't always tell you what she needs, but you just have to be there."

"Okay," he says uncertain. "Ellie, is everything okay?"

"Almost," I say. I hold back the tears that threaten again, until after I say goodbye to him.

I turn off all the lights and open the drapes to the star-filled, night sky. The moonlight filters through the windows shining light on me and the polished urns holding Nicholas and Elaina.

I'm in an introspective place. It's as if none of the revelations from Carrie have affected me. I feel this unfamiliar serenity. Peace that I have not known or found for forty-four days.

My mind sifts through the events of the day. Carrie and Michael. Court Chandler. Dan the bartender. Elaina Miles. Ellie Shaw. Nicholas. Elaina. Mathew. Emily. Bobby Bradford. Carrie. Michael.

*Michael.* Michael lied to me. Something happened.

Something happened. Infidelity happened.

Carrie and Michael happened.

One lone tear makes it way down my face. I wipe it away with the back of my hand. Before talking to Carrie, I'd resolved to tell Michael *everything*, as in, everything about my encounter with Mr. Court Chandler, my reservations about chemotherapy, my fear about wishes, my fear about Carrie, my fear about him. *Everything.*

I had wanted to talk through it all. Now, I have nothing to say.

I glance at the clock. It is one in the morning in New York. Michael should be here any time, now. My heart pounds; my breath is uneven. I feel unsteady.

And, then it comes to me this thought, unexpected and true: *my chance to see Paris is fading.* It will probably never happen. This thought takes over my senses. I feel the last stirring of Elaina Miles looking for a different life, a different result. Elaina Miles does not want to return to Bainbridge Island and shop at Safeway or even Town & Country Market and make kids' lunches and send a surgeon off to work and wonder if she can ever trust him again. Elaina Miles wants a different life, even if it's short.

I glance at the urns of my two beloved children. Dying young is the most tragic thing of all. They haven't seen Paris. Nicholas and Elaina will *never* see Paris. This makes me sad. And, so, in that cataclysmic moment, I choose a different path—a different life because Nicholas and Elaina never got to see Paris and neither has me, myself and I. Somehow, in some way, I have to salvage that particular wish for one of us.

I look down and see my packed suitcase. I've thrown all my clothes into it, while I was thinking of Elaina Miles' life and thoughts. I pack the laptop. I sweep the make-up into the suitcase and I gently lay the urns back in as well and zip the sides of the bag together. I pause long enough to write a note on the linen stationery that the Gramercy provides for its guests.

> *Michael, I didn't think this would happen. Not to us. Bobby doesn't know. So there's one of us left who's happy. Ellen Kay*

*Ellen Kay*. I don't even know who that is anymore. Ellie is gone, too. Elaina Miles closes the door and hears the finality of the click of the lock and makes her way onto the elevator. She expresses her surprise and delight, when she discovers Mr. Court Chandler just sitting there near the concierge's desk, just waiting *for her*, it seems.

"Hey," I say.

"Hey," Court says back to me.

"I'm going to Paris," I say.

"So am I."

I look around at the empty lounge—empty as it should be at 1:30 in the morning in New York and I don't see the reason for why I shouldn't do this. Michael isn't there. He isn't standing there. He doesn't touch me anymore.

I look over at Court. He stands and comes over to me. His arm encircles my waist and we walk out to the limousine that appears to be waiting for him. My suitcase and the laptop bag are already ensconced in the trunk. "How did you know?"

"I know how much you want to see Paris," Court says.

I don't even look back, when the limousine pulls away from curb side. Court tells me we're flying out tonight on his company's private plane. When I ask why he flew commercial earlier today, he just gives me that enigmatic smile and doesn't answer. Elaina Miles just smiles over at him, now. She watches its effect on this engaging twenty-nine-year-old man as he gazes down at her.

Elaina Miles doesn't have cancer. She doesn't have kids. She doesn't have a past. She doesn't have a future. Elaina Miles has the present and she holds on to him as tightly as he holds on to her.

"We're not friends," Court says meaningfully to me now.

"I know." I'm fearless. This man can cure anything. I smile.

# Chapter Eighteen

 *Black and White*

Our journey to Paris has taken the circuitous route. We're in London for the first week. We stay at the 41 in this landmark hotel's Master Conservatory Suite with these fantastic windows serving as the roof that displays the London sky, day and night, just for us. The décor of the 41 is famous for its signature black and white look. Black and white—my life has taken such a departure from this kind of look on life that I view it as a sign of some kind. I tell Court this, at one point and he just gives me a secret smile.

All of it is beyond amazing. Mr. Court Chandler is beyond amazing. What we are together is beyond amazing, too. We've been to see Buckingham Palace on a private tour arranged by one of his handlers. We've been to the play, *Wicked,* which plays just blocks from us at London's West End Theatreland. The opulence and ease in which we do these things is beyond me. I have a wish and Court fulfills it.

We live in this little bubble of a world unencumbered by familial obligations and marriage vows. Reality is very far away, as we stay together in this black and white world at the *41*.

We both agree this is an untenable situation.

We agree we don't want it to end, just yet.

It occurs to me, many times now, that Mr. Court Chandler is *more* than he has been telling me. He has rock star status at the hotel. He has prince-like status with his entourage—the handlers, limousine drivers, image consultants and stylists—all have accepted me into this bizarre fold without question or comment, with the exception of his public relations guru, Kimberley Powers, who is a different matter entirely. Ms. Kimberley Powers is much more verbose in her displeasure over me.

She's making that point known with Mr. Court Chandler right now in our hotel suite. Neither of them realizes that I'm here. I'm supposed to be at the spa, but I've chosen not to do this today.

I am "spa"-ed out. I have grown tired of treatments for my hair, my skin, and my body. I've been pampered, massaged, and stroked. I've had makeovers and highlights and manicures. I've had mud baths and fragrant oil massages.

I consented to it all because there wasn't anything else to do that didn't involve too much evaluation of where I am and even more plausible where I'm going.

The spa treatments have taken five years of aging off my looks. I barely recognize the early-thirties sophisticate that looks back at me, now.

Court has bought me a new wardrobe of lingerie and clothes. Who knew that designer lingerie and maternity clothes even existed? I'm wearing one of these striking outfits, now. This white sheath miniskirt number that hides my baby bump with these carefully designed folds of silk across my somewhat expanding waistline. White strappy sandals adorn my feet. My toes are freshly painted with this blood red polish. My hair swings back in a ponytail pulled up in this diamond clasp that Court casually tossed my way just yesterday. He spends money on me like it is Evian water and very much in an endless supply.

I haven't had the courage to even do a Google search of him to better understand who Mr. Court Chandler really might be. *No.*

I want this bubble world between us to last as long as it can. So does Court.

The conversation between Mr. Court Chandler and his PR handler, Kimberley Powers heats up. I'm broken from my reverie at their angry exchange and stand in the shadows in the guest bedroom which is separated from the main part of the suite. I'm caught in the uncomfortable position of being the very subject they are discussing. With a queasy feeling in the pit of my stomach, I listen, unable to do anything more at the moment.

"Look! You pay me millions of dollars to give you this awesome image of philanthropy, not philanderer."

"It's *not* like that, Kimberley."

"It doesn't matter what it is or isn't. You can't afford the perception of cheating on Eve, even if you're not. God damn it, Court! We're trying to do this launch, put you in the best possible light, and you're fucking around!"

"I am *not* fucking around!"

I've never witnessed Court's temper before. Its intensity is surprising even from a distance of fifty feet. Only Kimberley Powers could withstand it. I envision her mahogany hair and flashing green eyes—she's a powerhouse all on her own.

A long silence ensues. I step closer to the doorway out of hiding, debating with myself whether to enter into the argument or not. *What exactly would I say?* Kimberley's right. It doesn't matter whether we are together or not; perception is everything. Infidelity is so easy. It has been so easy—even if our version of it is child's play and nothing more. Even though I've done no more than kiss this man, lain with him at night beneath the covers, and only stroked his body without doing anything more than touching him, it doesn't matter because I've left my husband and my children behind for him.

*Court.* The charming Mr. Court Chandler is all I see, but Kimberley Powers is right: perception is everything.

"Fine," Kimberley says with an insolent tone. "You have to go along with what I say in connection with Ellie/Elaina whatever the fuck she is calling herself these days." I blush as I hear her say this. I've been evasive about my identity. Ellie Shaw has dropped off the face of the earth for the last week or so and Elaina Miles doesn't care.

"And what *exactly* does that entail?" Court asks in a clipped angry voice.

"She stays in the hotel. She doesn't leave. You don't go out to dinner with her. You don't go to plays with her. You do your CEO thing and then we move on to Paris. You do your thing there. Then! If you do what I say, you can go off and do your own private, whatever-it-is-that-you're-doing thing in Italy in some faraway villa. I don't care, but God damn it, Court, if you fuck this up, we're through. I'll resign you as a client. I swear I will."

"You like my money too much."

"I do not!"

"You like *me* too much," Court says now.

"I do not!"

"I'll be good," Court says in this solemn voice.

"You'd better. You're on in two hours. You're wearing the black suit with the charcoal shirt. Grow up, Courtney. Give it a try and do not fuck with me," Kimberley says. I hear the anticlimactic sound of the suite door close with a single decisive click.

Now, it's completely silent. I hesitate for a few more minutes. My mind is reeling with the implications of what Kimberley Powers has just said. Eventually, I step out of the shadows and into the bedroom doorway and look out across the suite where Court stands at the window. He senses my presence and turns toward me with his charming introspective smile.

"I'm making your life complicated."

I gesture helplessly with my hands as Court walks over to me.

"You make my life *real*. You complete me and make me whole, Ellie." Court holds my face between his hands and kisses me.

The words are Michael's and remind me of him for a split second. I hesitate. Then, the fleeting thought of Michael disappears, like a rare Monarch butterfly—a thing of beauty you've seen only once, a very long time ago.

All I can see is Mr. Courtney Chandler and I kiss him back.

Paris. Paris is a spectacular place filled with the promise of romance and sentiment. Yet, all I see is endless flower bouquets from my vantage point in the hotel suite where we're staying. Court upholds the bargain he's made with Kimberley and keeps me hidden in his life.

After a week of such confinement, I yearn to be outdoors. I've grown tired of being out of sight and long to be outside and escape this imposed captivity that has brought the edge of reality into my bubble world. In reaching for that edge of reality, I've powered up my laptop and plugged into the Internet without Court's assistance, since he's gone like he has been so much of the time since we got here.

Since our arrival in Paris, Kimberley Powers has kept Mr. Court Chandler mostly occupied for the past seven days. There have been presentations, keynote speeches, interviews with various high profile publications, late dinner meetings, clothes fittings, stylist consultations, breakfast meetings, and strategy meetings. Kimberley has made sure that Mr. Court Chandler has attended them all. When he finally returns to the suite, I'm usually asleep. Sometimes, he's gone again before I'm awake. He leaves me these little notes, telling me how amazing I am. His last note simply said:

*I love you, Ellie.*

C

I click on Outlook and see that I have no less than fifty e-mails from Michael. I cannot even read them all. I cannot even read one. There are five new e-mails from Dr. Lisa Chatham each marked urgent. There are fifteen from Robert. I dully note that Michael has sent me three times as many. There are sixteen from Mathew, one for each day that I have been gone. Eight are from Carrie; these are also marked urgent, but I am sure that her reasons for this are very different than Lisa's. I'm overwhelmed by them all. I haven't communicated beyond the note I left at the Gramercy for Michael. My cell phone has been powered off. I did that as we boarded the plane to fly out of New York.

I continue to lie to Mr. Court Chandler. Well, I continue to keep secrets and withhold the truth. I don't tell Court that I've confirmed Michael's infidelity with Carrie. I don't tell Court about my cancer or chemo or my team of doctors who are most likely besides themselves about their missing patient and their treatment regimen, at this point. *We have the plan, but no Ellie.*

He knows I'm Ellie Shaw but I've only allowed him to see the persona of Elaina Miles. I am fictitious, made up, living a life of fantasy, avoiding reality as if I can stop both time and cancer.

It's been uncomplicated so far because we haven't fully consummated this relationship. I think we're both afraid that if we take our relationship to the next level, we would irrevocably untie ourselves permanently from the lives that we both need to return to. Yes, we agree this thing between us is still untenable and cannot last, but neither of us wants it to end.

Court is late. It is late. The moon hangs low in the Paris sky. It's after one in the morning and Mr. Courtney Chandler has yet to make an appearance. I haven't powered on my cell phone, while we've been in Europe, but I do it now out of some kind of desperation to connect to someone, *anyone.*

This prisoner in the luxurious hotel suite at Le Meurice in Paris has had enough. There are fifteen voice mails for me. I imagine, after a while, the communication with voice mail became impossible as the mysterious server for voice mail filled up and those callers, my family and Michael, trying to reach me just gave up. I press the speaker button and find myself looking at the list of callers as I scroll through. The majority are from Michael. It upsets me more than I thought it would to hear his broken voice, begging me to come home. He promises to do whatever I need him to do, if I will just please come home.

"I don't know where you are" he says in the next one. "I know why you left, but I don't know where you are."

Emily is next and she's pleading with me to come home. Somehow, she's overheard Mathew and Michael talking about my chemo. "Mother, you need the chemo," she says in this sassy little voice and then she starts crying.

There are three more messages from Michael. I hear the desperation in his voice as he recites his wedding vows to me. Was it just over two months ago that we got married? It seems like a lifetime away from me, now. All the new messages have played, but the next one is an old one that I'd saved.

"Mom, it's Nick. Are you coming to get me or what? Come on, Ellen Kay. It's day ninety-one. Your act is supposed to be together by now. Elaina's here, too. We're waiting for you. Okay, love you. It's Nick, by the way."

I replay the message just to hear my son's voice again. I play it again. I play it again.

I have kept the cancer at bay for more than nine weeks by refusing chemo therapy, by generally ignoring it, but the grief? I've only been successful for these past two and half weeks to close the door on that dark place that captured me for so long because of Mr. Court Chandler.

But, Court isn't here, so I can't hide from grief any longer. It finds me. And, it all comes back at the sound of Nick's voice, as I play his message over and over.

I can't get back out of the abyss. Court has carried me to bed and I just lay there with my eyes wide open staring at the white ceiling. I cannot speak. I cannot even cry. I hear the desperation in his voice as he pleads with me to talk to him, but I can't speak.

He's made a frantic call to Kimberley Powers and her arrival doesn't even faze me. I'm unable to tell them why I can't speak. I can't feel *anything*. I don't want to feel anything. I want to tell them this, but no words come out. I continue to clutch my cell phone and I will not let them take it from me.

It has been two nights. I know this because I've counted the first appearance of the moonlight twice. Somehow, the cell phone is missing from my hand. I move my head realizing this and stare at my hand, wondering, if by willing for its appearance, my cell phone will come back to me. I feel empty. I raise my hand to my stomach and feel surprise at the foreign movement.

"What day is it?" I ask in this hoarse, unrecognizable voice. Someone moves from further away. Court appears and looks into my face and then, slides up right next to me on the bed. It is semi-dark in the room, but I would recognize his face and the shape of his jaw line and his lips anywhere, now.

"Hey," he says. There is real fear in his eyes. I trace his lips with my fingers. "Ellie, are you okay?"

"I don't know." My answer makes him unsure. It is a strange sight to see from Mr. Court Chandler. He's always steadfast and certain. Tears form in his intriguing grey-blue eyes. I reach up and touch his face. "Courtney Chandler…thank you…for being here."

My words are his undoing. He starts to cry. I know this is a rare event for this twenty-nine-year-old, high tech, charming magical man from Seattle. I almost smile.

"Ellie, do you want to go home?"

"Not yet. You?"

"Not yet." He climbs beneath the covers and holds me to him, kissing my forehead, my cheeks, and my lips.

*Yet.* We acknowledge our ending. That is enough for this night.

Kimberley Powers predicted an Italian villa at the end of our Paris trip and Mr. Court Chandler does not disappoint. We are somewhere in Italy far away from the rest of the world. The entire entourage has left with the exception of one intense Ms. Kimberley Powers.

Kimberley's leave-taking will commence only after a long discourse of do's and don'ts to both of us. Do have a good time in the privacy of the villa. Do enjoy the sunsets and the sunrises from the confines of the villa. Swimming in the Olympic-size pool at the villa is acceptable, but only late at night. The don't list is very specific. Do not go into town. Do not call Eve. Do not call whoever it is that Ellie would like to call. Do not use the phone at all. Do not use the laptop for Internet access. Do not go beyond the villa. Do not wander out, during the day, through the villa grounds. Do not leave the villa.

Court makes fun of her by pretending to write everything down that she is saying. This only sends Kimberley into a further tirade and she starts her speech over again of all do's and don'ts. She is so outspoken, so outrageous, and so brilliant that I find myself laughing midway through her second round of speech. She seems surprised by this and is momentarily mesmerized by the Ellie former-UW-cheerleader-yeah-team smile. She looks at me in an appraising, almost affectionate way, now. Before she leaves, she hands me one of her business cards.

"Ellie, if you ever need anything," she says, biting her lip in vexation.

"I'm an editor from Bainbridge Island, Washington. What could I possibly need?" I ask.

"Right." She kisses each side of my face and hugs me. She repeats the same gesture with Mr. Court Chandler. "I must say, you keep it interesting, Mr. Courtney Chandler."

"We try," he says in his most charming voice.

It is eerily silent once Kimberley leaves us. We're alone. Our bubble world forms around us and is now complete. I know that we both feel this unexplainable solace from within it.

"We have three days," Court says to me now. "Let's not waste it."

I walk over to him. I take his hand and hold it in my own. We are at the precipice, together. I can feel it and I know he can, too. I see the look in his eyes. He is so sure of himself, so certain. I look back at him and realize I feel the same.

"This is untenable," I say.

"Not today, not tomorrow, not the day after that."

I smile at him now. "Untenable," I say again.

"But real enough," Court says, pulling me in his arms. He kisses me and I kiss him back.

Our passion takes us to the bedroom, where Mr. Court Chandler in his masterful wisdom and endless charisma has already lit candles for this planned seduction. He hands me a glass of champagne. "I did some research, just one glass will be okay," he says with a charming laugh.

"Uh-huh," I say.

*Yes. Chemo would be much worse.* I smile at him now, this benevolent smile. I can feel myself getting swept away, far away from the shores of grief and my real life with my remaining children and Michael.

We undress in this hurried fashion. I am farther along in disrobing than he is because I am wearing only a white cotton dress and lingerie. I prepared during our last days in Paris for this moment. He sucks in his breath when he sees my body.

Any worries I might have had about how I would look to him, pregnant and completely naked, are put at ease by the way he gazes at me now, though a part of me hesitates. The Ellie Shaw part. I'm about to make love to a man who is not Michael. Some small part of me cares about this, even when the unspeakable image of Michael and Carrie kissing flashes through my mind. Carrie's words come back to me. "It was just while we were at the hospital with Elaina. We got a hotel room. We were tired and just wanted to sleep. I just wanted her back. I just wanted what we had back. I just needed him. I needed to know if we could get it back. I'm sorry. He wanted it, too, Ellie. He was hurting and he kissed me and it just happened…we both agree it's wrong. We're ending it."

I'm broken from my reverie when Court calls my name. "Ellie," he says. "Where'd you go?"

"Nowhere," I answer.

Michael broke my heart. Michael did this to me. I'm going to be with someone. Be with Court. Have sex with him. *With someone else.*

Ellie Shaw still cares about this; Elaina Miles does not. She takes over and struts towards this young god who is hers for the next three days and never hesitates.

Infidelity is so easy, if that's what this is. It feels like my future. Court is everywhere, like the light air of Italy all around us. I can feel his touch, even when he isn't touching me, as if there is kinetic energy between us. We have extended our stay at the villa by another seven days. We are in trouble with *everybody*.

Kimberley has resorted to calling the villa twice a day. Her messages are direct and to the point.

"Court, get your ass back to Seattle, pronto. I cannot explain your absence to Eve for much longer."

Kimberley has inadvertently become my publicist, too. Apparently, in a fit of rage she had her staff pull any and all information on me. She knows about Michael. She knows about Nick and Elaina. She knows about Mathew and Emily, too. At this point, she is pulling out all the stops to get us to listen to her when she calls and leaves these tough love messages at the villa.

But her last message is for only me.

"Ellie, you need to get the *God damn chemo!* I just talked to your doctor, Lisa Chatham, and she says you are risking your life at this point. Ellen Kay Shaw, get your *ass* back to Seattle, now!" Her voice breaks as she finishes the message, probably done in, like so many, at the idea of cancer.

I don't even really know this woman and she is yelling at me through the answering machine. I stand across the room as Court plays the message; his back is to me. We have just taken a forbidden swim *in the daylight* in the spectacular pool and captured a passionate moment at the far end. I'm shaking my hair out and toweling off as Court pushes play again and the message replays.

"Is she always like that?" I ask with a little laugh, coming over to him. I reach out to stroke his arm. He turns to me then and I'm stunned by the look of fury traveling across his handsome face.

"*Chemo?*" He asks, incredulous.

Our bubble of a world bursts, just like that, just like bubbles do.

"No chemo," I say in this flat don't-fuck-with-me imitating Lisa Chatham voice. My vehemence seems to surprise him for a moment. He just stares at me, then anger crosses his features again.

"You *endanger* your life by refusing chemo?"

Court is beside himself, all at once. He starts pacing, only clad in his black swim shorts because we just spent an intimate moment by the pool together. He rakes his hands through his wet dark hair in agitation.

Then, he gets this panicked disbelieving look. He stops.

"I'm taking you back," he says in this commanding CEO kind of way. Kimberley Powers would be so impressed; I am not.

"No! I'm *not* going back. I…love it here. I love you."

He shakes his head and gets this inconsolable look. We have not used the word *love* to describe what this is between us, beyond his handwritten notes to me.

"I love you, too," Court says in a heartbroken voice.

He comes over to me and pulls me into his arms and begins stroking my face, my lips, and the tops of my breasts as if trying to memorize my features. He leans down and kisses each breast. Then, he gets this anguished look. "I love you enough to let you go," he whispers. "Ellie, you have to go back."

"I don't want…to go back." My voice breaks because I can already sense this change in him, even the way he holding me now seems different, more distant. "I don't want to go back," I say, even more resolute.

"I know. I don't either," he says, running his hand back and forth along my neck feeling my wild pulse beneath his fingers. "But Ellie…you have to get the chemo. It's breast cancer; isn't it? Those are the tiny scars I see. That's it; isn't it? God damn, *breast cancer*." I can only nod, unable to speak as I see the desolation cross his face at my answer. "God damn it, Ellie! You should have told me."

"Why?" I ask with a bitter laugh. "So you could send me back *sooner?*"

"You have to get the chemo, Ellie," he says with profound sadness. I grab his face between my hands before he can turn away from me, sensing something in his mannerism that has suddenly changed.

"What is it, Court?"

"My mother died ten years ago of breast cancer. I was nineteen," he says in a hollow voice.

I watch the devastation of that memory cross his features. His eyes sweep over me with this look of disdain as if he can protect

213

himself from feeling anything more for me by doing this alone. I make this guttural sound as if he's punched me in the stomach, when I see his face fill with unbelievable dread and this vast desolation. It suffocates me. I can't breathe.

"No," he says. I can't go through that again."

His pronouncement is so final, I gasp for air, knowing I've lost him in that single moment, just like that. He is far away from me, even though he still stands right in front of me, still holds on to me, and still touches me.

He is gone. Mr. Courtney Chandler is gone.

Elaina Miles is gone, too. And, Ellie Shaw is going home.

# CHAPTER NINETEEN

## Unclaimed Baggage

We fly from Florence, Italy to London on his private plane, then on to New York. In New York, we wait to take a first class commercial flight to Seattle. I don't even ask why the change again from private plane to commercial. My questioning look gets a three-word response from him. "Kimberley arranged it."

He spends the majority of his time in between flights making phone calls on his cell and makes a point of being at least twenty feet away from me to make them. His thoughtfulness remains. He ensures I have Evian water and enough food to eat if there's been any sort of delay. *The prisoner is well taken care of; the guard is very kind* go these errant thoughts in my head.

I watch Court as he takes another cell call just as they call for first class to board for the New York flight home.

"Eve," he says in a tired voice. "Yeah, long trip. I'll be home in about six hours. Pick me up?" There's a long pause. He looks over at me. "Can't wait," he says into the phone.

It's like having knives thrown at me, the way he says this. I'm the circus act, evading daggers when he does this to me. I turn away from him, dealing with the heartbreak of losing him in this private hell of my own. He doesn't seem to even realize what he's done to me by what he's said and not said.

We've barely spoken during the flight back to Seattle. We've been traveling for more than twenty-four hours and the closer we get to Seattle, the more indifferent he becomes. I feel this chasm between us. Gone is the charming smile and debonair ways one Mr. Court Chandler. He seems to be back reliving a memory from ten years before. He's nineteen again, reliving a history that I can only guess at. He will not talk about it with me. The only way that I know he's thinking about his mother is in the way he looks at me now; I personify his mother's ghost. He sees her, when he looks at me. I try not to show him my fear—the fear I carry, over dying, not dying, about all of it. But, I see the reflection of the ghost that he sees me as, every time I look into his eyes now.

His silence gives me time to think; something I haven't allowed myself to do for weeks now. Me, myself and I have returned: pieces of the old Ellie: Ellie Shaw, even Ellie Bradford, and this new Ellie that I haven't quite figured out yet.

I discover I still have and want my wish list. I still want these things, even though I haven't been thinking of them very often in the last month. I want Emily and Mathew, this baby, me, and even Michael.

These five things, these are all I wish for. I'm saddened that Court didn't make the list because he so soundly rejects me now. If I had another list, he would be the only thing on it besides me, myself and I. Us, together, is all I would ask for.

I try to thank him when we finally land at Sea-Tac. He gives me this contrived smile, but it doesn't reach his eyes. He leans over and kisses me. "I love you, Ellie," he says. I glimpse his charming smile for the first time in two days, since we left Italy, but then it disappears when he gets up from his seat. He grabs his carry-on and without another word, he's gone.

I'm stunned. *He's gone.*

His words mean nothing. His actions say it all. Dazed, I struggle out of my seat, retrieve my laptop bag and purse, and deplane. I walk up the jet-way, alone.

I'm undone, devastated, by the way he just said goodbye to me, as if I'm no more than a stranger. I guess that's what twenty-nine-year-old successful CEOs do. They just leave and don't look back.

I'm swallowed up into the crowd and trudge toward baggage claim at a listless pace. He's up ahead; his dark brown hair being caressed by the air circulated overhead from the ceiling duct. We make our way, separately, toward the shared destination for luggage—baggage claim.

Court doesn't even glance in my direction when a gorgeous brunette runs straight at him and puts her arms around his neck and kisses him. Eve Chandler is a rock star, too. She wears designer jeans on her endless long legs, a low-cut white silk blouse, and a black leather bomber jacket. Eve Chandler is fully aware that strappy sandals can be worn in any kind of weather. They are the beautiful couple. His final send-off to me: he has a life and I'm not in it.

"I've missed you, Court," Eve says in this alluring voice. "I can't believe Kimberley kept you an extra ten days."

"I know. You know what a taskmaster she can be," Court says back to her.

He half-smiles. Then, there's this long silence between them.

"I took off work for this, big boy, you better make good on that."

Eve traces his lips with an index finger and kisses him with obvious possession. I hold my breath as I watch this, unable to look away from the two of them, and then recoil from my covert position as if I've been physically struck in watching them interact this way together

"I'll go get the car. See you out front." Eve Chandler blows him a kiss as she leaves.

In extreme despair, I move over to the other side of the baggage carousel away from him. I've heard and seen enough.

I stare at the conveyor belt and watch a parade of endless bags go by, while all the other airline passengers move and jostle for position to retrieve their luggage. The crowd begins to disperse as the amount of bags to be claimed begins to diminish, while the unclaimed ones continue their endless journey around and around the conveyor belt. I just watch, helpless, forlorn, and abandoned; *because I have cancer, probably; most likely because I didn't get the chemo, but who cares?*

I feel him behind, before he actually says anything. The potent bond between us is still there, still alive. Everything else is now dead, but this weird connection between us remains.

"I will…never…forget you," Court says softly; he sounds so broken-hearted that tears spring to my eyes. I nod. He moves in front of me and picks up his lone suitcase and looks back at me, now. We're in this very public place, two feet apart, and he reaches for me from where he stands. "I love you, Ellie."

"Untenable, but real enough," I say. "I love you too, Courtney." I give him my best, former-UW-cheerleader-yeah-team smile, but my eyes fills with tears.

He nods and flashes me that crooked smile of his, but then it falters. Devastation crosses his face; it reflects my own. The connection fades with each step he takes away from me, until he is *really* gone.

My bag takes another turn around the conveyor belt; and then another. I let the tears fall. I can only think of my other wish list with him and me, myself and I as the only wishes I have, the only ones I want.

⁓❦⁓

Curb side. My suitcase rests against my thigh, while my laptop bag and purse straps cut into my shoulder; I welcome this pain.

The desolation in losing Court Chandler, once and for all, weighs me down just in standing here, saturated in fresh grief with the loss of another, piling on to all the loss and heartbreak I already carry.

In a haze, I power up my cell phone. The voice mail count is ten. I'm surprised at the number. Surely, everyone who knows me must realize by now I won't play them or call them back. I *do* play them in this determined kind of way, secretly hoping that my former life will somehow pull me back in.

There are a few from my mother. Apparently, she has not been brought into the loop. She's busy planning her summer trip to the beach house, our beach house. She wants to come up and be with me. She wants to know when she can come. *What?* What is going on with my mother? Then, she launches into an I-know-life-can-be-so-hard-Ellen-Kay speech. She is cut-off after two minutes in the middle of this soliloquy and I actually smile. There is a part of me cheered up by her nagging voice alone.

There are five messages from Michael. He's shortened his messages considerably. "Ellen Kay, please come home. I love you; I can't live without you. What should I tell the kids? God, Ellie, I love you, please come home."

The last message is from this morning, which is surprising, until I play it. "It's Lisa. Okay, so I get a call from Court Chandler and if I'm putting this together right…Holy shit! *Court Chandler?* He promises me that he's bringing you home. So, when you get in, *call me*. Just me. No one else. I'm not even going to tell Michael of this possibility so just *call me* when you get in. Oh, by the way, your car is at home, not the Park-N-Fly where you left it. I'll give you a ride. Call me, Ellie."

My hands tremble, just hearing Lisa utter Court's name upsets me further. I can feel something breaking inside of me.

*What should I do?* The answer is there, of course. Lisa can be a neutral party like no one else. There must be some sort of

Hippocratic Oath for secrecy that any conversation we have must fall under. She is one of my doctors. I'm her patient. *Aren't I?*

Fifteen minutes later, I'm still standing here, still debating on who to call. It's a fairly warm day for late April in Seattle. It's raining, but it isn't all that cold, so I just continue to stand there. I check my watch, but I can't figure out what time it is. I've made too many time changes in the last twenty-four hours, in the last month.

I turn to this twenty-something guy waiting curb side about five feet away from me. "Do you know what time it is, here in Seattle?" The guy's wearing an old Nirvana t-shirt, a dark leather jacket and blue jeans. I give him my most winsome smile.

"It's two in the afternoon," Mr. twenty-something says, checking his watch and returning my smile.

"Oh, okay, thank you." He turns away from me with a shrug. My former-UW-cheerleader-yeah-team smile does not have the desired effect on him. I'm a little disconcerted by this for no reason at all.

I should call Lisa. That is what I should do. But then, that just prolongs this other thing—this thing with Michael. It's two in the afternoon. It April 30th; isn't it? I set my phone to Pacific Time.

I turn back to the twenty-something guy. "It's April 30th; right? It's Thursday?"

"It's May 1st actually. It's Friday." He grins at me. "Where have you been?"

"Italy," I say.

"Nice."

"It was paradise on earth."

My answer triggers an instant memory of Court Chandler by the pool and I experience this fresh heartache. I think the bleakness must show on my face because he looks at me more closely.

"Are you okay?"

"I'm fine," I say with a defiant lift of my head.

"Just deciding what to do. I've really fucked up my life, so just trying to think things through. I…can't afford any more mistakes," I say.

"Everybody feels that way, sometimes," he says to me now.

The reassurance in his voice reminds me of Court and I hesitate. I can feel the tears coming. I try to give him another winning smile, but it is not quite as good as the last one.

"Untenable," I say to myself. "Thanks for the time and date info."

"Untenable…baseless, without sound judgment, weak, questionable, without grounds… untenable," the stranger says to me.

His words cut across me and I feel the fissure in my heart break wide open, as he emulates Mr. Court Chandler in this weird déjà vu way.

"But, real enough." I wipe the tears from my face in this distracted, I'm-just-flipping-my-hair-kind-of-way, but the stranger is not fooled.

"Are you *okay?*"

"I'm okay."

"Do you need a ride?"

"No, I can get a taxi. I'm just going down to the ferry for Bainbridge."

"Look, my girlfriend will be here soon. We can give you a ride wherever you need to go. I'm Danny, by the way."

"Ellie Shaw." I shake his hand. "I knew a Danny once, in New York, best bartender there ever was."

"Hey! I'm a bartender at the Triple Door. Come on by sometime. I'll make you a drink."

I watch the next line of cars slink by, picking up or dropping off passengers. Danny's going on about his job at the Triple Door and I'm just nodding and smiling.

A vaguely familiar silver Jaguar comes racing up the parkway, driving a little too fast with all these people around. The car stops right in front of me. The electric window is already about halfway down. I hear Lisa's familiar don't-fuck-with-me voice say, "Get in."

The passenger door swings open in my direction and I'm too surprised to refuse. I say a swift goodbye to Danny, my newly-made friend, and promise to stop by at the Triple Door some time soon. "I guess I have a ride," I say with a half-smile. Lisa gives me a questioning look as she unceremoniously drops my luggage in the trunk, relieves me of my laptop bag, and even my purse. We're moving out of the airport drive inside of two minutes from when she first pulled up.

"Who *told* you I was here?"

"Court Chandler called me about twenty-five minutes ago. I thought I might miss you; and then where would you be?" Lisa asks irritably.

"I would have figured it out," I say. "And, just so you know, I'm not talking about *him*, so if you wouldn't mind *not* mentioning his name..." My voice trails off at her fiery look.

"Whose name? Court's?" Lisa asks, incredulous. She says his name like she knows him personally and this just sends me into a new spiral of angst and turmoil. I give her a withering look, nod, and swallow hard, attempting to chase back the tears that threaten once again.

Lisa gives me this intense look and alternates back and forth between my face and negotiating the traffic ahead. "God, you look fantastic," she says with dismay, which actually makes me laugh. I sense her taking in the designer clothes Court had tailored and bought for me in Italy: the red silk blouse, the blue silk mini skirt perfectly cut at mid-thigh with a fantastic design that secretly hides my baby bump, and the Italian white leather sling back sandals and the freshly manicured red nails. I watch her sniff the air between us, taking in the expensive scent of my perfume made especially in Paris for me. "Nice trip?" Her sarcasm is hard to miss.

I give her an irritated look. "Nice enough."

"You want to tell me what's going on?"

"Didn't Michael tell you?"

I glance away from Lisa's close inspection and stare out the window, unseeing, because just saying Michael's name brings about this unbelievable pain I haven't allowed myself to feel all these weeks. It courses through me like an out of control forest fire. Amazingly enough, it's far worse than the heartache I've just experienced with Court over the past few days.

"No," she says softly, seeing my stricken face. "Oh God, Ellie, what happened? We've been out of our minds with worry for the past month."

I'm starting to pay attention to where we're going and getting more nervous as she skirts the side streets heading towards Swedish Hospital.

"Where are you taking me?"

"We're headed to the clinic. I can't let you out of my sight until we've taken a few films and at least perform an ultrasound on that baby. I take it you haven't done any of these things."

"No," I say in this small voice.

I glance away from her accusatory stare. I haven't thought about this baby, about my children, none of them often enough. Guilt overtakes me. My self-hatred runs especially high at the moment. Lisa grabs my hand.

"Sorry. Sorry. I told myself I wasn't going to do this: put pressure on you as soon as you got off the plane. Court told me it's been pretty rough. Sorry I didn't mean to say his name. Okay," she says, taking a deep breath. "We'll just do the basics, blood work, x-rays, and an ultrasound."

"Oh goody," I say sarcastically.

"Then, we'll take you home."

"I can't."

"Can't what?"

"I can't go home," I whisper.

Lisa looks over at me for a long moment. "Okay, you can stay with Stephen and me, but Ellie; you're going to have to tell me what's going on, sooner or later."

I just nod as the unwanted tears make their way down my face. The car gets incredibly quiet the last ten minutes through the city. We pull into the physicians' parking garage and I automatically glance over at Michael's parking space as we pass and discover it's empty. It's surgery day—Friday. Michael should be here. There's a part of me that cares that he's not here and another part that is secretly relieved. Seeing Michael, facing Michael, is not something I'm prepared to do quite yet.

Lisa's cell phone rings. "Hi. Yes, I've got her. Hey, thanks for calling me. We'll take it from here." Lisa glances at me. "I'll let her know. Yes, she is," Lisa says with a laugh. "Okay then. Take care."

"Who was that?" I demand as soon as she hangs up.

"Who do you think?"

"*Court?*" I ask, incredulous. "He's calling you? He basically strands me at the God damn airport, while his *wife* picks him up, and now he's calling to check up on me? Give me your phone!"

"Do you think this is a good idea?"

"Probably not." My hands shake as I press redial.

"Court Chandler." The way he says his name in that fucking charming way of his practically has me jumping out of my seat.

"Do *not* call me. Do *not* ask how I am. Do *not* call my friends. Do *not* call me ever again."

"Who is this?" Court asks with a nervous laugh. *Eve must be right there.* I end the call without answering.

"How'd that go for you?" Lisa asks, glancing over at me.

"Not well enough." I follow her up to the medical office without another word, reeling from this fury and heartbreak all at once.

❧

# Chapter Twenty

 *A Weird Combination*

I am supposed to be getting undressed. I am supposed to be changing into one of the designer patient gowns Lisa's sporty nurse provided me with that opens in the front and spills everything out, regardless of how it's been designed. I am supposed to be ready to go in five minutes, according to the militant Dr. Lisa Chatham, who has only my best interests in mind for blood work, x-rays, and an ultrasound. But I'm still dressed in my chic travel clothes, contemplating getting undressed, yet searching for a way out. I am fuming over Court and the scene with him greeting his wife at the airport and pretty much everything that has happened in the past forty-eight hours, but also lamenting over the way things are with Michael. My life is fucked up; what should I do? Get an ultrasound, give blood, and get undressed? None of these options are going to resolve things with Michael. And me. And my life. Cancer can probably wait until Monday. Seeing Michael again, seeing where things are, probably can't wait that long.

On impulse, I call Carrie. Carrie should be at work in downtown Seattle. Since I don't have access to a car, I'm hoping this is the case. I can't deal with Lisa's lecture today.

I definitely can't talk about Court Chandler with Lisa. Who will, without a doubt, ask.

"I just need to know the lay of the land," I say without preamble as soon as Carrie answers. We used to say this kind of thing to each other. It was our secret code for: tell me what's really going on. I haven't spoken to her on such a personal level in months. It feels weird to do so now.

"Jesus, Ellie. Where the hell are you?"

"Let's leave that a minute," I say. "Just tell me where everyone is." A part of me misses all of this and it's coming back to me now.

"Emily's at school," she says with a sigh. "I'm picking her up in an hour. Mathew has a baseball game. Robert and I were going to go to that. Michael…is, well, he's at *home*, Ellie. You're obviously not there."

"Why isn't he in surgery? This is his surgery day."

"He hasn't been able to do surgeries for a while. The doctors think it's stress-related. He's been pretty broken up about you being gone. Ellie, where did you go?"

"That's a long story and there's only one person who's going to hear it," I say to her now. "I would appreciate it, if you wouldn't say anything to the kids just yet. Are you downtown?"

"Yes. I was just getting ready to leave for the ferry."

"Can you pick me up? I'm at Swedish at Lisa's clinic. I'll meet you at the side entrance by the physicians' parking garage."

"Yes, of course."

"Carrie," I say. "Don't call Michael."

"I won't." I hear the contrition in her tone. I'm almost ready to accept it.

"Thanks."

"I'll be there in ten."

Call ended comes up on my phone and I stare at it for a few moments. Then write a quick note to Lisa: *I'll call you tomorrow. I have some stuff I need to deal with first. Sorry. Ellie.*

With a heavy sigh, I gather up my belongings, sneak out of Lisa's medical spa, and trudge to the side entrance of the hospital to wait for Carrie.

The irony of all of this is not lost on me. *I'm waiting for Carrie.*

⁂

I slide into the passenger seat of her white Mercedes, while she stows my luggage and laptop in the trunk. I attempt to put the scene of Carrie and Michael in this very car as far out of my mind as it will go.

"How are you?" Carrie casts me a sideways glance. "You look amazing."

Her face is incredulous as she inspects me. I can see her taking in my tanned legs, the designer outfit, and the manicure of perfection, just like Lisa did less than an hour before.

I can't even smile. *Who is the biggest sinner among us, now?* Avoiding her direct gaze, I look out the window because this woman can still read me like no other.

"I'm so sorry, Ellie," Carrie says to me now.

"Tell me all of it," I say in a demanding, do-not-fuck-with-me-in-any-way voice.

"It was this weird combination of things," she says slowly.

I glance over. She has this haunted look. I almost feel sorry for her, asking her like this, but not enough to stop.

"He was so sad. We shared that sadness. He would be on one side of her and I was on the other. Our hands touching. Robert was grieving over Nick; I couldn't really reach him. So," she says with heavy sigh. "We began to have this connection to each other, just like the one I saw him have with you on your wedding day. I remember the way he didn't hesitate to tell you he loved you in a way he never could with me. And, I wanted that."

She stops talking and wipes away a tear. I try to breathe, fascinated in some bizarre way by what she's telling me.

"I wanted the three of us together and I thought, maybe somehow, we could make it work. I needed it to work. He was despondent, vulnerable over Elaina and so was I. And, I think we began to feel this connection might somehow save her. We both wanted that so badly. So, one night when we were there late with Elaina, I talked him into staying at a hotel instead of going home to you. And, it just happened. He was so guilty about it. He cried afterward and I…I was so angry that he was thinking of you, instead of me, even then. We tried to put it behind us." Carrie pauses and looks over at me with this fresh look of remorse and guilt. "Then Elaina died; and we started up again."

I gasp when she says this. Additional pain takes hold of me now. Somehow learning their affair was more than a one-time thing completely changes my perspective. It's even more devastating and I struggle to cope and hide it from Carrie. "It happened more than once," I finally say with contrived indifference.

Carrie nods. She gets this tormented guilty look.

"It's like we were feeding off of each other's grief, both knowing we were destroying any chance we had apart with anyone else. Me with Robert. Him with you." She sighs. "But, God, we ended it, after you found out. I've barely seen him. We just exchange the kids. Then, he started having tremors with his hands and had to quit doing surgeries."

She gets this accusatory look when she looks over at me. Then glances away to negotiate the car into the ferry line and drive it onto the boat.

"You're kidding; right?" I ask. "You're not going to blame his God damn tremor problem on me because if you are, you can stop the fucking car, right now."

"We're getting on the ferry. Where are you going to go?" She asks irritably.

"Don't fuck with me, Carrie." She gets this fearful look. Carrie's never really experienced my wrath before. The old Ellie always capitulated to her; the new one doesn't.

"Then, when he wasn't able to find you," she says, shaking her head side-to-side with disapproval. "Well he's just been falling apart. Robert and I are so worried about him. He's so angry, so despondent. He sees his patients three days a week, but we don't really know what's happening with him. He doesn't answer the phone half the time when we call."

"I can't go home," I say in a broken voice.

"No, no. You have to! He needs you."

"I don't need him," I say with contempt. "He's been with you, Carrie. He still loves you."

"No, it's not like that," she says, anxious all at once. "Look, Ellie. He loves you so much. Being without you is destroying him, the best part of him. Ellie he loves you. He's always loved you. Don't fuck up your life because you're angry with me; work it out with him. You have to."

"Why? Because you need it to work out with Bobby? And, if he found out about you and Michael…" I shake my head. "Bobby wouldn't be able to handle it." I laugh with scorn. "You think I've handled things badly, just wait until you see Bobby Bradford's response."

"Please, Ellie, don't tell Robert." Carrie looks terrified.

"I'm not telling him," I say, suddenly weary. "But, it doesn't change anything, where we are." I turn back to her. "Carrie, I can't talk about this anymore with you. After today, I don't want to talk about it. I just want to try and put my life back together."

"With Michael." Her tone is firm, certain.

"Yes." My voice doesn't waver. I still lie so well.

I actually have no idea what I'm going to do, what I want, but I'm damn sure I'm not going to confide in Carrie. We leave the rest of this conversation unsaid. All the business between us regarding Michael, years of unspoken torment, is left unspoken

*There are too many sinners among us now.*

I don't tell her what I've learned about how easy infidelity really is. I remain silent on what I've learned about what can transpire and what these revelations have taught me.

"I'm just glad you're back. The kids are going to be so happy," Carrie finally says.

"I'm sure you've been mothering the hell out of them. Look what a great child you turned out in Elaina." I sigh and finally say, "Carrie thanks…thanks for taking care of my kids."

"Yeah." She looks over at me and I spy tears gathering at her lashes.

"How's Bobby?" I ask.

"He's good. We're good."

I watch her face. Her green eyes light up as she talks about him. I half-listen as she talks about an upcoming trip they've got planned to San Francisco. She and Robert are clearly more suited to each other. They like gourmet food, fine wine, traveling. Carrie goes on talking about their plans to visit the wine country, while they're there. I nod at the appropriate intervals and hear her in this intangible kind of way, while my nerve endings become more and more alert as we travel the familiar ferry route toward home.

"You better call Lisa," Carrie says.

Her directive brings me out of my reverie. She holds up her ringing cell phone where Lisa Chatham's name displays across the screen.

"Don't answer it," I say. "Lisa can wait until Monday. I doubt very much cancer is going to kill me over the weekend, although there are other distinct possibilities." I actually smile.

"God, I've missed you, Ellie," Carrie says with a nervous laugh. She reaches across the car and squeezes my hand. We could bring the kids by tomorrow afternoon, if that's okay."

"Sure, maybe we can grill out or something. Walk the beach." The uncertainty of what awaits me at home takes over completely. My smile fades along with any bravado I may have had.

Carrie drives off the ferry and takes the back roads to my beach house. My breathing becomes more labored, the closer we get to it. Carrie starts talking again about picking up Emily from school and then going to Mathew's baseball game. She assures me they're doing well.

"They've missed you. They'll be so glad that you're back," Carrie says. I nod and can only look out the window.

"I'm sure they're pissed at me," I say in dejection.

"No. They just want you back. They'll be *thrilled* you're back. Maybe, you can call them later tonight and we can firm up the plans for tomorrow."

"Okay."

We pass the intersection where our two oldest children met their untimely deaths. Someone has erected two white wooden crosses with their names painted in black on them. There are all kinds of flowers strewn around as well as a few Mylar balloons that state "We miss you." I stare at the scene.

"Nick and Elaina had a nice trip. They got to see the world."

My words cause a new round of tears with the newest Mrs. Robert Bradford. I finally reach over and pat her hand.

"Carrie, it's going to be okay. They're together. And, we're going to be okay, too. Now."

I'm not sure where this benevolence is coming from, but it brings a peace to the beautiful face of my former best friend. Carrie nods and wipes away the tears with the back of her hand.

"We're okay," my former best friend finally echoes back to me.

"We are."

Carrie negotiates the gravel drive and keeps the car running while she lifts my luggage out and stands there for a minute.

"See you tomorrow, Ellie," she says, uncertain.

We hug each other. Another surreal moment. Then, she gets back into her car.

I stand at her rolled down driver's window. *Stalling.*

"Thanks for the ride," I say. We both share this weird sense of humor at the double entendre of what I've just said and laugh a little.

"What else? Right? It's done. Everything's been fucked up for a while now." I sober up at this disparaging thought. "But it's over. Done and over," I say.

I'm left standing in the gravel drive and just watch her leave, awaiting the answers to my life.

# CHAPTER TWENTY-ONE

## *He Brought Me Back*

*T*repidation grows within me as I turn back from watching Carrie's car navigate the drive and contemplate the front door. With every passing second, I feel myself moving back toward my life. There's no going back, no turning back. I have four wishes I know for sure; Mathew, Emily; me, and the unborn child I carry.

Only one wish remains unanswered and suddenly he's standing right there in the doorway. I do an Eve Chandler move and run straight into his open arms and put mine around his neck and kiss him. "Michael," I say. "I'm home."

"Ellie." It's all he can say. He's kissing me back and crushing me to him.

Late afternoon. I've put the cremated remains of our children back on the mantel, while Michael carries my suitcase upstairs. I plug in the laptop and put my cell phone on the charger.

Once settled, I decide to take a bath. Minutes later, I'm mesmerized for some reason by the drip drip drip sound of the leaking faucet, I take needed refuge in the privacy of the locked master bath and surrender to the extraordinary silence. I try to relax, resting my head against the tub. I cup the warm water in one hand and watch it flow over my swelling stomach. I feel strange, outside of myself, but sense this bizarre communion to this house, to this place. I am Ellie Shaw, but somehow different, transformed in some way.

I can hear Michael milling about in the master bedroom. His muted footsteps move in a regular rhythm across the carpet. *Is he pacing?* After a while, he stops. There's no sound of him.

Then, in another few minutes, his shadow is evident at the lighted slit of the doorway. I sense his hesitation in standing there. Trepidation combines with this weird sense of anticipation in what his next move will be. The door is locked. *What will he do when he discovers that? What will he think about that?* Our earlier embrace and welcome back kiss has disintegrated into uncomfortable awkward silence between us. We've gone our separate ways in this house in the past hour.

He tries the door. There's a long pause after the handle is jiggled.

"Sorry," I say in a trembling voice. "It's locked." I swing out of the tub, trailing water everywhere, unlock the door, and open it in a matter of twenty seconds. He's standing there with a cup of tea in one hand, looking disconcerted, found out.

"I brought you tea," he says, looking surprised at my nudity.

For a moment, I've forgotten about my normal shyness. The new Ellie Shaw is not as shy, not as reserved about her body. I boldly lift my eyes and return his gaze, while his eyes audaciously appraise my nakedness.

He gets this defiant look, as his hand reaches out of its own accord to trace my protruding stomach. I practically vibrate at his touch, but step back from him. He looks surprised and then disappointed by my reaction. He hands me the tea cup and quietly closes the door again.

*Oh God. I shouldn't have done that. What am I doing? Why did I reject him like that? Why am I here?*

The idea of a bath seems foolish now. The water's cold, when I stir it. I drain the tub and watch the water swirl and disappear.

I wrap a towel around myself, sip the tea for a minute, and try to determine my next course of action. I'm also undone, by what just took place between us. It just adds to the turmoil and foreboding, fully aware that a confrontation of some sort lies ahead. With reluctance, I dress in fresh lingerie and walk into the master bedroom. Michael sits in one of the chairs by the fireplace, looking forlorn.

I walk past him toward the master closet and begin unpacking my suitcase. I have all these beautiful clothes from Court. I touch them, one by one, as I hang them up in the closet, while Michael just watches me. I know he has many questions, although he has not asked a single one. I pull on this light pink mini-skirt sheath number. From behind me, Michael draws in his breath. I turn around and give him a questioning look.

"He must have loved you very much to buy you so many beautiful clothes, see you in them, and still let you go." His voice is at the breaking point as he says this.

*There will be no lying tonight.* There will be no sidestepping the issues right in front of us that separate us now.

"He did. But, we knew it was untenable, real enough, but untenable." I give him this defiant look, knowing my words hurt him just by the devastated look on his face. "How did you find out about him?"

"Dan at the Gramercy Park hotel in New York was able to fill me in," Michael says in this harsh tone. "He saw you leave with *him.*"

I move past Michael. I'm already tired of this conversation. I'm not as fully prepared as I thought to talk about Mr. Courtney Chandler with Dr. Michael Shaw. Michael reaches out and grabs my hand.

"I'm not leaving you, Ellie. I probably deserve what you've done, but I'm not leaving you because of it."

"It wasn't like that. That's not why…It wasn't like that."

"What was it *like*, Ellie?" I hear the devastation in his voice now. "What's Court Chandler like?"

"How do you know his name?" I ask in dismay. After all the hiding out in Europe, I'm shocked to hear Michael utter Mr. Court Chandler's name so easily. The game's up. Everything's come undone.

"I told you. Dan was able to fill me in."

I pull away from him and go and curl up in the chair next to the fireplace in our bedroom. Michael comes and kneels in front of me. "Who else knows?" I ask, defeated.

"No one."

I nod into the silence. "He called Lisa this morning and told her he was bringing me home."

"Why? Why did he bring you back?"

"He found out about the cancer, about me needing chemo. His mother died from breast cancer, ten years ago, so he…he's pretty adamant about chemo therapy and he brought me back." I look away from Michael.

"Brought you back?" Michael asks, uncertain.

I shrug into the silence, still not looking at him. "He said he couldn't go through that again." Just saying this cuts across my heartbreak and I know Michael can hear it. I look away.

"God damn you, Ellie." Michael gets up from his kneeling position and stalks from the room.

"God already has," I say to the empty room.

I've never seen Michael like this—this sullen, undone, angry man. I've seen him completely broken over Elaina's death, when he didn't talk to me for days at a time, but this coldness and this kind of seething rage is all new. I've done this to him. I don't really know what I was thinking in coming back here.

The love between us seems so far away. We're two strangers

simply occupying space in the same place. Our life together is shattered into inconsolable broken pieces.

I make dinner and set the table for two. He comes over and eats in complete silence. I clear the table after he's finished and go do the dishes.

I look out into the setting twilight. It's been raining all day, but the sun has made a last desperate attempt to shine. As the sun begins its descent, the water sparkles with the last rays of blue and gold light. It's a beautiful sight and I breathe in deep, just taking it all in.

It's so strange to be back in this house—this house that I love so much. It's almost spiritual and in some way uplifting. I take it as sign that I'm in the right place. Little pieces of myself and my life come back together the longer I'm here.

I grab my cell phone and head out to the beach to watch the sun's last effort for the day. In the silence, with only the lapping waves as background, I play Nick's last message to me.

"Mom, it's Nick. Are you coming to get me or what? Come on Ellen Kay, it's day ninety-one. Your act is supposed to be together by now. Elaina's here, too. We're waiting for you. Okay, love you. It's Nick, by the way."

I push replay and put it on speaker and listen to it again. I settle down in the Adirondack chair and play it again.

"Nicky, I miss you so much," I say. "Give Elaina a kiss for me."

I re-save the message, set the phone down, and put my head down in my hands. Just listening to the lapping waves and the end-less silence and thinking of them causes me to cry.

"He was a great kid," Michael says, sliding down into the chair next to mine. I lift my head and look over at him.

"They both were."

I wipe away the tears with the back of my hand and lean back in the chair next to him.

We stare out at the water. The majestic sunset beholden to the dancing blues, whites, yellows and oranges of the coming night sky meets up with the water. He reaches for my hand and holds it just as the sun dips below the horizon.

"I took them all over Europe," I finally say, looking over at him. In some way, I'm compelled to tell him my part in all of this.

"Where did you go?" Pain crosses Michael's features when he asks me this.

"London, Paris, Rome," I say in this quiet, faraway voice. "Paris was hard. I played Nick's message for the first time there. I kind of broke down. He helped me through that. I was a wreck for a while." I pause for a moment, trying to keep my breathing steady. The memories of Court are painful now and I try to hide this from Michael. "It's hard to explain."

"Try." I hear desperation in his plea. His need to understand, to know the truth, is so obvious.

"We didn't do anything physical for a long time. We both agreed the situation was untenable."

"But real enough," Michael says sarcastically, now.

I can feel his heart breaking because in some way it is connected to mine. "Then, we got to Italy."

"I *hate* that country." The way he says this almost makes me laugh, but I catch myself in time and give him a twisted smile in the fading light.

"Yeah, I don't ever want to go there, again." I give him my best former-UW-cheerleader-yeah-team smile.

"Please don't do that. It's hard to stay pissed off at you when you smile like that."

*This I know.* My smile deepens.

"I've discovered something, Michael."

"What?" He turns toward me.

"I want to live. I want to live for you, Mathew, Emily, and me, and this…"

I take his hand and put it on my stomach where his unborn child moves across me in a regular rhythm.

"What about Court Chandler?" Michael asks.

"He brought me back." I bite my lower lip to keep it from trembling, failing to hide the painful heartbreak of the past few days, and shrug my shoulders. In my mind, I've just bared my soul to this man. I've spoken the truth, but I'm done sharing my memories of Mr. Court Chandler with Dr. Michael Shaw. I think my face tells him this. I stand up awkwardly and pick up my cell phone. "I'm sorry I hurt you, Michael."

I race toward the house as fast as my with-child state lets me. I'm still not fast enough because Michael is already there, pulling the door open.

"I'm sorry, Ellie. I should be saying I'm sorry to you. I lied to you." He's out of breath. I can see what the words he's said are costing him. "I...did...I was with Carrie. There was one night when we were with Elaina and then, we got a hotel room. It just happened."

"It just happened? You *lied* to me! You broke my heart. You did that, Michael. Now, you want to *judge* me?" My anger takes over. I yank the door away from him and go inside.

"Ellie! I'm sorry. It...we knew it was a mistake. It's just. We were trying to capture something of Elaina. I'm sorry. I still love you."

I stare at him from across the room. His words cut across my very soul.

"Just one time, Michael?" I watch him carefully, awaiting his answer, deliberately setting the trap with the truth. He nods and knowing that he's lying to me unleashes this unforeseeable rage.

"I loved you. I needed you, Michael," I whisper. "My son was dead! And, you were never here. *Never* here! Elaina was still alive and I hated you both for it, you and Carrie." I shake my head.

"All that babble about her waking up. She was never going to wake up! *Ever!*" I'm screaming now and I cannot stop the words from spewing forth.

"So, I told her, Michael, I told her that Nick was dead. *I told her!* And, then…she died. She was waiting for him, waiting to hear his voice. When I told her he was dead, she *died*."

My crying reaches a hysterical pitch. The tears keep coming and the fury just takes over.

"You slept with Carrie while Elaina was still living! You hadn't even lost her yet. And then, you went back to Carrie after Elaina died, again and again. Carrie told me how you started up again after Elaina died. I needed you, but you were with her. And, now you lie to me? You stand there and you lie about it."

"I'm sorry," he whispers. "I didn't mean to. I don't want to lose you."

"You already *have*," I say. "Over and over, you lied. How many times did you write nothing happened in your e-mails to me? How many *times*, Michael?" I'm shaking. My whole body quakes with anger. I look over and see his hands tremble. The surgeon no more; it seems. "I don't even know why I came back."

I swipe my cell phone from the counter, grab at the railing, and climb the stairs two at a time. I slam the door to the guest room and lock it.

Michael soon pounds on the door. "Ellie! Don't do this. I'm sorry. Let's talk about this." It tears at my very soul, but his lying does even more damage.

"No! I'm done talking to you, Michael. No more."

I go to the farthest corner of the room and sink down to the floor and cover my ears so I can barely hear his voice. After another interminable fifteen minutes of knocking and pleading with me, he finally goes away.

My breath is uneven and jagged. I cannot stop crying. I rub my fists into my eyes to try and stop the tears. My cell phone makes a chirping sound. I pick it up and look at the text.

*"Eve knows."*

I text Court back. *"Michael too. Dan the bartender filled him in. Better call Kimberley."*

*"ILU"*

I text back. *"Is that what I think it means? Untenable, but real enough, huh?"*

He texts back. *"Very."*

I'm making more mistakes. I just keep making more. I undress, crawl into bed, and hold my cell phone—the only lifeline I have. I've gone to my other wish list. I only want Court Chandler and me, myself and I.

I wake up in the middle of night still on European time. My biological clock is completely messed up. I had no problem sleeping for the last thirty-odd days, but tonight, I'm wide awake. I review the major events of the day and get stuck on a few of them, starting with Michael's own confession that he slept with Carrie. It is nothing new. I already knew this, but his admission and subsequent lie about how many times sends me into a new round of despair. I can't get past it. And, then he lied to me about it over and over in at least fifty e-mail messages to me over the last month. I find myself wondering how many times he actually wrote "nothing happened" in his e-mails to me. Somehow, I need to know the exact count. I pull on a robe from the guest bathroom door and slip out.

The house is quiet. It's feels strange when Mathew and Emily are not here in this house, still uncanny without Nick and Elaina. Melancholy takes over. I stop in front of the mantel and touch each urn. This greeting is something I've been doing this past month. Sometimes, I talk to them as if they were in the room with me.

I remember the lonely days of Paris. It wasn't the most perfect memorable time. I spent so much of it alone. Mr. Court Chandler does have a few of his priorities mixed up. He's a workaholic in the extreme, which is probably why he is so damn successful; and he and Eve haven't had children.

I sit down at the desk in the home office and stare at my laptop and finally open up Outlook. All my e-mail messages are still there unopened. I open all those from Michael. They start to look the same after awhile.

> *Ellie,*
>
> *I'm sorry. I don't deserve you. I never meant to hurt you. Nothing happened.*
>
> *Please come home. I love you. Michael*

He never meant to hurt me, but he had no problem lying about what he'd done. The "Ellie, nothing happened" declaration appears in fifty-six e-mails by my count. Fifty-six of them where he lied, over and over. Then, his attempt earlier to deny doing it more than once, fucking her more than once, causes this incredible rage to return. I can't get past it.

I wander around downstairs for a few more minutes, then, slowly climb the stairs. After closing and locking the guest room door, I lie in the bed and stare at nothing. I reach for my cell phone, but it isn't there and I don't have to wonder who has it.

I yank open the door and stalk down the hall to the master bedroom. Michael is awake, sitting up in bed, bare-chested. The physicality of him messes with my pulse rate, enraging me still further. The only light emitted is from the cell phone that he holds in his left hand, *my cell phone.*

"So, he's texting you already. And, his wife, Eve, knows the score. Untenable, but real enough, huh? How nice for you, Ellen Kay." His tone is bitter and full of betrayal.

"You *did* this, Michael. You broke us first. Live with that."

I march over to his side of the bed and make a reach for my cell phone, but he holds it out and away from me.

"I plan to live with it. I plan to live with you and make you forget him." He forcefully pulls me to him, while tossing the cell phone onto the night stand. He kisses me with this fierce passion that I'm unfamiliar with and I struggle to hold back from his allure. I can feel his anger and I know he can feel mine, but soon enough, this fire storm is unleashed between us.

"Damn you, Michael." This only makes him laugh and he kisses me more ardently.

"I love you, Ellie. Come back to me."

Before long, I'm kissing him back. His fingers work their magic, traveling over my body; he traces the outline of our unborn child and dangles them between my legs. I cry out at his brazen touch as he takes full possession of my mind, body, and soul.

His commanding presence insists I see only him and it's true; he's all I see. I whisper his name again and again. While this strange liberation overtakes me and unchains me from all the pain and heartbreak of the past few months. At one point, he holds me away from him and just gazes into my eyes. "Ellen Kay, God, I've missed you so much. Come back to me."

He kisses the inside of my palm and I shudder at his exquisite touch. The anger for him seeps away from me, like spilled water from an open bottle, gushing forth into the parched earth of me; it disappears just like that. His love fills me up as he trails his tongue over my baby bump and further still.

"I'm back. I've missed you, Michael," I say with sadness.

He undresses me. It's evident he's turned on by the spa laser service that's left my vajayjay smooth. Surprise, jealousy, desire—all of these—cross his features, mirroring mine as we traverse this latest journey with one another, knowing of the others we've shared.

I arch up at him as he slides his fingers inside, while he takes in this new wonder of me and then rushes forward, leaving no part of me unexplored by his thrilling touch. I return the favor in kind.

"Tenable, Ellie, capable of being defended, maintained, held; and more than real—soul mates, Ellen Kay," Michael says.

Our sensuality with each other is somehow different, somehow changed, demanding exploration. This intoxicating experience captures us both. It takes a firm hold of our senses. There's this crescendo to our lovemaking, as if at the same time we both fully realize that we can never untie ourselves from each other. He is still a part of my soul and I am still a part of his, no matter how far away we are or who tries to come between us. He is mine and I am his.

An hour later, there's a chirp from my cell phone, again. Michael reaches over and simply powers it off. All I can do is watch in this state of disbelief and inexplicable wonder.

"I'm back, Michael." He takes my hand and holds it next to his beating heart.

"I'm back too, Ellen Kay."

After traversing this inexplicable desire between us, we lay naked side-by-side and luxuriate in this sanctuary sans children who would have invariably walked in on us by now. There's this sense of extraordinary freedom in knowing that we can walk around nude throughout the house for hours without interruption. Testing this theory, we do this very thing upon awaking in the pre-dawn hours after only a few hours of sleep. We make love in every room, except Nick and Elaina's, behaving like two newlyweds who've been kept apart for far too long, intent on making up for lost time.

He opens a bottle of champagne from our wedding night and we toast one another. I only slightly hesitate when he says, "I don't think one glass is going to hurt you."

I turn away a moment, chasing away the fleeting memory of Court's exact words to me. Guilt and anguish takes turns with me.

"Are you all right?" Michael asks, intuitive to my reaction within seconds.

"Never better." I shiver in the chilly air of morning. He pulls an afghan from the sofa and drapes it around my shoulders. Then, he kneels before me, naked, spent, and repentant.

"Ellen Kay." Contrition leaches from his very bone marrow.

"Don't. Michael. Don't. Don't say it."

He gets this vexed look, as if he'll combust right in front of me if doesn't say he's sorry one more time. I fight my own battles with this overwhelming guilt. *What have we done to each other? To our marriage?* These multitude of sins we've both committed seem almost insurmountable.

"Show me, Michael," I say.

He stands up, his naked god-like self, and sweeps me up in his arms and carries me back upstairs. He shows me how sorry he is and I try to do the same.

It feels like we've come home, but then again it feels unlike home: better, worse. It appears to be a new beginning, since our earliest days of marriage were filled with this inconsolable grief and despondency.

These past few hours we've manage to eradicate those memories and majestically replace them with all these new ones as if it's a religious experience, we must capture and atone for. We're naïve enough to think we can pave over the irreparable damage that wreaks havoc at a soul level within us both, unaware of the challenges that lie ahead for our renewed connection.

# CHAPTER TWENTY-TWO

## *Reconciliation*

Saturday is spent with Robert and Carrie and the kids. There is this strange tenuous truce between Carrie and me. I actually find myself gravitating towards her for emotional support in all of this. It's surreal. Both, Robert and Carrie seem to sense that there is some strange undercurrent running between Michael and me, but none of us openly talk about it.

"Is everything okay?" Carrie finally asks, giving me a sideways knowing look. We're taking a stroll by ourselves along the beach because there is a break in the rain.

"Yes, we're working it out," I say.

Carrie nods into silence and intertwines my arm with hers. "I'm pregnant," she says after a few more minutes.

"What?" I practically choke on the word.

Her green eyes sparkle with tears. "I just found out. Lisa called this morning with the results."

I feel incapacitated, like I'm going to pass out. I can't even look at her. "How far along?" I look out at the water and do the calculations.

"About six weeks," she says with a laugh. "Lisa's got it down to a science. I'm due at Christmas time."

She stops walking for a moment when she sees the tormented look on my face.

"It's Robert's. She did a paternity test. I wanted to know, to make sure, before I tell him." I nod but still feel uncertain, outside of myself. "It's a miracle, Ellie, just like your baby with Michael. Weird how things turn out; huh?" She smiles. "I'm telling Robert tonight."

This sickening sensation roils through me. I still don't know the results of my own paternity test Lisa did before I took off. In my haste to escape yesterday, I neglected to ask her about it.

Emily starts calling my name and I pick up the pace, suddenly desperate to return to my family and get away from Carrie and her news which in some way eclipses my own.

I catch Michael's eye as I return. He and Robert look a little tense and I wonder what's been discussed while I've been walking the beach with Carrie. I can't quite hide my own irritation with Carrie, with Michael, with everybody, all at once. The perfection of our reunion from earlier seems a distant memory in this moment.

"Momma," Emily says impatiently from the edge of lawn. "Come back to me." I try to smile at my six-year-old as she runs straight into my arms, but I look at Michael over her head and I know he senses my discontent.

After a few minutes, I make a point of going back in the house for more coffee. With a few minutes to myself, I grab my cell phone and call Lisa. "I need to know something," I say without preamble.

"Nice to hear from you," she says with a bitter laugh. "You fucking sneak out of my office and now I'm what? I'm supposed to take your call? Because you got your *stuff* done and now you *need* me?"

"Don't Lisa," I say in agitation. "The paternity test. The result. What was it?"

"*See?* This is what I'm talking about. If you would read your email, you wouldn't have to make these frantic phone calls and beg me for this kind of news. If you would just stay in one place long enough for me to tell you these things." She sighs heavily.

"*Some friend.* I pick you up. I invite you to stay with us. Then, you ditch me. I'm just trying to *save* your life; this is the thanks I get."

"You're killin' me," I say.

"Well, ditto sweetheart. You've been gone for weeks. You had us worried sick." Her voice rises. "And now you take a moment to call to ask for the *results*? Thanks so much." Lisa's wrath reaches at me through the phone.

"Can you…please…just be my one true friend for a fucking minute and not be pissed at me?" I stem the tears trying to make their way down my face by pressing my fingers to my eyes. The stress of it all catches up to me. I lean over the kitchen sink, allowing the tears to spill directly into it. "Please. I'm begging you."

"Sorry," Lisa says, contrite at once when she hears my crying. "Is Carrie there, by chance?"

"Uh-huh."

Michael comes into the kitchen. I turn away from him, making a point of filling the coffee maker with ground coffee, but spilling half of it as I go. I try to juggle the phone. "God damn it," I say for a multitude of reasons.

"It's Michael's," Lisa says softly. "It's Michael's. Your due date is early July. The 2nd of July, I believe. I want to see you *tomorrow*."

I take a shuddering breath, attempting to move air in and out of my lungs. "It's Sunday," I say with sudden exhaustion. "It's Lisa," I say to Michael avoiding his direct gaze, but see his questioning look.

"So what? Sunday's as good a day as any to start chemo."

I close my eyes. Some things never change including my fears about chemotherapy. "No chemo," I say emphatically.

I open my eyes. Michael is about a foot away from me. He moves in closer and traces the recent evidence of tears on my face.

He looks anxious and unhappy.

"We'll talk tomorrow," Lisa says in her best don't-fuck-with-my-plans voice. "Put Michael on."

Wordlessly, I hand the phone to Michael. At the same time, he pulls me closer by putting his arm around me as if barring my escape before I can think about doing this.

"Lisa? What's going on?" Michael asks. There's a long pause. He scrutinizes me closely and traces the blotches that must be on my face with his thumb. "Yes. Really," he says flatly. He gets this worried look a few seconds later; then, it disappears. "Okay," he says with sigh. "Well, thanks for letting me know. Yeah, I can see that," he says grimly. "All right; we'll see you both tomorrow. One in the afternoon sounds good. Thanks." He ends the call and looks at me for a long minute.

"Carrie's pregnant," Michael says, uneasy. I silently nod. "It's not mine. It has nothing to do with us," he says to me now. "It has *nothing* to do with us, Ellie."

"I never thought this would happen, any of this, not to us." I know he can hear the desolation in my voice. Grief, loss, and this incredible sadness have found their way back to me.

He holds me closer. I can feel his fast heart rate. Yet, he says, "Everything's going to be okay, Ellie."

I frown at the incongruence of his words in comparison to his racing pulse. There's this place deep inside that seems set up for self-preservation that isn't quite ready to believe him.

"You don't believe me, yet, do you?" Michael lifts up my chin and kisses me again. "That's okay. I believe it enough for both of us. Everything is going to be all right."

His steadfastness renews my spirits a little bit. It's enough to tell him what Lisa has just told me that he still doesn't know. "Michael," I say, taking his hand and putting it on my stomach where our child moves in an almost musical rhythm right now. "He's ours."

There's a joyful moment when I tell him this that I bear witness to in the elation that crosses his face. It's remarkable. His blue eyes light up, while his smile becomes more definite and unbound from the strain and trauma of the past few months.

I stand on my tiptoes to reach him to feel his joy. I kiss him.

"Let's tell the kids our news," he says.

"Okay," I say.

Revealing that Michael and I are going to have a baby is met with bewilderment, not exactly the reaction I thought we would get from my offspring. Mathew gets this indignant look as if this all a bit too much. He shakes his head and moves away from me for the first time this afternoon. Finally, he says, "Aren't you a little *old* to be having a baby, Mom?"

"Probably," I say with an insecure smile.

*I am old.* I feel old right this very minute. Mathew's right. This is all wrong. I glance away from my teenage son and try to deal with the truth in what he's saying and find solace in what I know to be real, but nothing really bubbles to the surface in terms of profound wisdom or understanding because I am a little old, kind of, but definitely with child.

"Sorry, I shouldn't have said it like that," Mathew says. "It's just...it's a lot to take in with everything that's happened to us." I nod at him, too upset by his reaction to say more. Mathew steals a glance at Michael, then back at me. "I kind of figured something was up, when I first saw you." He grins, and then nods. "I'm glad you told us."

"Mathew, this doesn't change anything," Michael says. "We're going to be a family. All of us. It'll be different, but it's going to be great."

There's this profound silence among the four of us. This is the moment when Nick would normally jump in with one of his witty remarks and say something like, "Nice going, Ellen Kay" and make us all laugh. We all seem to feel his absence at the same time.

Then, Emily breaks the moment. "Well," she says with a decided humph. "I'm *glad* because I'm won't be the baby anymore around here; and you won't be able to boss me around so much." She looks directly at Mathew and gives him a dismissive wave of her little hand.

"Don't be so sure," Mathew says with a weary smile. He gets up, comes over to me, and kisses the top of my head. "Nice going, Ellen Kay, Michael," he says with a sly grin.

He and his little sister effectively break the subtlety of grief trying to steal its way back into all of us, just as Robert and Carrie walk in. They've been outside, giving us a little private time with the kids.

"We're going to have a baby," Emily says to them and then twirls around a few times.

"Oh," I say with a laugh. "I almost forgot. It's a boy. Lisa and Stephen ran the tests for that." Michael comes over. He puts his arms around my baby bump and hugs me from behind.

"I get to name him!" Emily says.

Michael, Mathew, and I say all at the same time, "No!" Everyone laughs.

My children stay near me the rest of the afternoon. I'm encircled in their love somehow insulated from Carrie and her news. Emily plays with her dolls near my feet, glancing up every so often to make sure that I'm still there. Mathew covertly watches me from the lawn chair right next to mine, his lanky long legs draped over it, staying close by and just listening, even in the midst of all the adult conversation.

I'm pleased by the camaraderie I witness between my children and Robert and Carrie. My absence may have served a singular purpose, bringing them closer together as a family. This is a positive thing to come about in such a disquieting desperate time. Michael stays close by as well, but my earlier jovial spirit begins to wane due to general exhaustion, time change, too little sleep from the night before, and the emotional turmoil of this afternoon. The conversation between the four of us becomes a little more forced once dinner is finished.

It isn't too long before Robert gets up and says, "I'm tired. I imagine you are, too, Ellie." He gives me a sympathetic smile, then looks over at Carrie. "Let's go home."

Carrie returns his gaze, but seems lost in her own little world of bliss for her secret: their baby. I almost feel sorry for Robert and what lies ahead in their evening together when Carrie announces she's pregnant. Robert doesn't enjoy surprises any more than I do He likes to plan things out and surely this is an unplanned event.

Michael gets up as if on cue and goes to help Robert load up the car and help the kids pack up their stuff, again. My children look as surprised as Robert that they're going back with him and Carrie.

"Your mom's tired. She needs to get some rest," Michael says by way of explanation to the kids and Robert. "We'll see you guys later in the week after she sees Lisa. Okay?"

My children give me this imploring look as if to say, *do something mother*, but I don't say anything. I'm unsure what Michael is up to, but I feel this need to be alone with him without any distractions and Emily and Mathew would most certainly be a distraction.

Our foray from the night before is vivid and fresh in my mind. I want to further explore the newest physical part of our relationship, uninterrupted, as much as he does.

I need to try and understand it; I have this desire to *feel* it. I cannot explain what has come over me.

As soon as Robert and Carrie's car disappears up the driveway, I'm walking over to Michael and kissing him. He carries me up the stairs and we start again where we left off this morning.

"I know what this is," I say in this sated voice, as we intertwine with one another in the dark of the night. "This is day five of our marriage. We never got this far."

"We never got a honeymoon, either."

"True," I say quietly.

"So, I've been thinking about that. I thought we could run a few tests tomorrow with the Chatham's. See how things are with your bodacious tah tahs and then make some plans."

"I thought you would have me scheduled for a double mas and complete reconstruction on Monday, regardless of Stephen and Lisa's grand plan, essentially over-ruling them."

"No. I've studied your films. The margins looked good. Granted, we are way out of protocol, but if we can wait another nine weeks…"

"Michael, what are you saying?"

"I'm saying chemo should be a last option. I know how much you like your hair." He pulls on a long strand of it now, twines it between his fingertips, and kisses it.

"Me or you?" I'm floored by his response. He's a surgeon with a surgeon's mind and he is taking a more passive, let's-wait-and-see role than I've ever witnessed from him. "Have you talked to Lisa and Stephen about this?"

"Yes. They don't agree."

"They want me to do chemo."

"Yes."

"And, you don't. Why?"

"I want all our wishes too, Ellie. I want you to get everything you want." He buries his head between my breasts and the growing swell of my stomach. I stroke his golden head and trail my fingers down his bare back with the other.

"Michael, I…I love you," I say, almost breathless as emotion overtakes me. He pulls me closer to him and kisses my chest. I'm sure he can feel my beating heart beneath his lips.

"I love you so much, Ellen Kay," he says against my skin.

"Tenable, Michael, capable of being defended, maintained, held; and more than real—soul mates, Michael Thomas."

Sunday. At precisely one in the afternoon, we meet up with Lisa and Stephen at their medical spa office to an ultrasound, a mammogram, and blood work. Apparently, the doctors Chatham have all the equipment as well as the agreeable personnel willing to come in on a Sunday.

Our unborn son is still doing well. I see arms and legs where they are supposed to be. According to Melanie and Lisa, his head is a good size and his other measurements are right in line with growth predictions. I breathe a secret sigh of relief. I'm starting to believe it's real; that my baby is okay. I can tell that Michael is, too.

He is right beside me instead of over by the sixty-inch monitor this time. He's holding my hand and stroking my face, while Melanie talks with us.

"Ellie, you know it's a boy, right?" Melanie asks. She's looking at the screen. "Oh, what do we have here? Hmmm…Lisa, take a look."

"Take a measurement right there. I don't believe it. Wow, you both ready for this?" Lisa asks.

"What?" I ask anxious now.

"There's two heart beats, Ellie. We couldn't see this little one last time, but there are two babies. This one's smaller."

"How much smaller?" Michael asks.

I hear the anxiety in his voice. I give him a squeeze of my hand and he looks down at me, suddenly anxious.

"It's in the twenty-five percentile range," Lisa says with concern. "The bigger baby is about eighty percent."

"That's a pretty wide margin," Michael says.

"Yes. Let's not get too excited," Lisa says. She waves her hand in agitation. "We can do an amniocentesis on this one. I'll be careful, Ellie. We just have to check out what's happening with this second baby. It's just a precaution."

Michael lets go of my hand and follows Lisa out the door. Their raised voices carry on in the hallway. Melanie does her best to distract me by pointing out features of the second baby, but I can still hear Michael asking how come we didn't know this before. Lisa's own answer is indistinguishable.

"Can you tell if it's a boy?" I ask.

"No. This one's not in a position to let us know that. The amniocentesis will test for that."

"Okay, Melanie, how come we didn't see this baby before?" I ask with a nervous laugh.

"It was nineteen weeks a little more, right? Well, sometimes, the bigger baby's position is just so and it will hide the second one. I wasn't looking for it. Everything's okay, Ellie, you know that right?"

"I know that." I wish for just one second I could enjoy the impending birth and possibly these two babies without having to worry so much. I sigh audibly now, just as Lisa and Michael walk back into the room. Lisa is carrying a metal tray with a large needle on it. "I guess we're doing the amnio now," I say with irritation.

"Yeah, I never know when you're going to take off to Europe." I give Lisa a withering look and she just glares back at me. Michael slides a chair in next to me and holds my hand.

"Well, I'm not going back to Italy," I say now. I give Michael my most seductive smile. He smiles and then leans down to kiss me, while Lisa swabs my stomach with some brown liquid to sterilize the area and then drapes the area with a blue sterilized cloth with a hole in the middle.

"Could you two stop making out for one second?" Lisa asks in exasperation.

"How can I help?" Asks Stephen. He enters the room, before Lisa starts the procedure.

"Calm your wife down. She's testy today," Michael says with an edge to his voice. I knew the Europe comment would catch up to him. I feel a little deflated myself by it as well.

"We've got twins, Stephen," Lisa says with a meaningful look.

"That's fantastic!" Stephen is always the cheerleader among the duo. Lisa rolls her eyes at him. "Let's see what we've got here." Melanie holds the wand over my abdomen trying to get a reading on the smaller baby. I'm just watching Michael's face, trying not to think about what an amniocentesis involves for me or the baby.

"I love you," I whisper only to Michael as he bends down by my face.

"I love you, too."

I've been through the proverbial ringer. I have had multiple x-rays done as well as ultrasounds done of my bodacious tah tahs. I am now dressed again and sitting next to Michael with the Doctors Chatham on the other side. The gigantic screen is filled with more than life-size films of my breasts. I'm left alone while all three jump up to get as close to the screen as possible.

There are no words spoken by any of them. I'm looking at the films at a distance through amateur eyes. I don't see anything. Still, they don't speak. They go through the deck of films three times, spending two to five minutes on each one.

A half hour later, there is still nothing said by any of them with the exception of the phrase "next one" to Lisa who controls the remote that advances the slide.

Finally, I've had enough. I stand up and walk over to them. "What do you see?" I demand. "Tell me! I can't take it anymore. What do you see?"

"We can have Ben look at the films tomorrow, and Josh, too, of course, it's his handiwork," Michael says.

"What are you saying, Michael?" The stress in my own voice is evident to all three of them. This stress that has been wearing me down for months. I wave a dismissive hand in the air, imitating Emily from the night before.

"What are you saying? Just tell me."

"The margins are still clear. There's no spots, no tumors. There's nothing there," he says to me gently.

I finally smile. I finally hear him.

"Does this mean we get a honeymoon?" I'm subjecting him to my best yeah team smile and remembering his promise from the night before.

"Yes, I think it does." He smiles back to me and his blue eyes sparkle with this desire that I can feel just standing next to him.

"What honeymoon?" Lisa asks irritably.

"A week away isn't going to kill her, Lisa," Michael says, still looking at me.

"Interesting choices of words, Michael." Lisa gives him a withering look when he looks up at her. It just makes him laugh.

"Lisa, you're getting all worked up, unnecessarily," Stephen says with a loving glance at his wife. He reaches over and takes her hand. "I agree with Michael. A week away is fine."

"We're out of here for a week. Show the films to Josh and Ben. We'll check in with you from the road," Michael says.

"What about *chemo*? What about following some kind of fucking protocol here?" Lisa gives Melanie an apologetic look for swearing. "Where are you going anyway?"

"It's a surprise for Ellie. I can't say, right now." Michael winks at her. His arm encircles my waist as we head towards the door.

"I'd like to *talk* to my patient," Lisa commands.

Michael gives Lisa a quizzical look and lets go of me. The three of them leave the room, while Lisa starts pacing the room.

"First you run off to God knows *where*…and only God knows *why*. Then, I don't hear from you other than a sappy, thanks-for-everything-see-you-later e-mail. Then, weeks later, I get a strange call from a billionaire high tech guy, named Court Chandler, who tells me he's bringing you back and now you are off on a honeymoon with Michael?" She studies my face closely. "From what I've been able to put together you just had one with *someone else*. Do you have anything to say for yourself?"

"Are you asking me what the fuck is going on?" I ask.

"Yes! That's *it*, exactly. I'm fielding calls from Court Chandler by the *hour*, asking for your health status, which I *can't* legally provide to him.

"He's been calling? Asking about me?" I ask, stunned by this news.

*Okay*, that's what I'm trying to *tell* you. God damn it Ellie, you can't have both of them!"

"I know."

"You're having twins with Michael. Let that *register* with you. *Twins. Michael.* Oh, and your thirty-eight years old and your high tech boyfriend isn't even thirty!"

"Of course, you would have to bring that up. That's a really bitchy thing to say."

"Bitchy, but true," Lisa quips back at me.

"Tell me something," I say looking at her closely. "You would never sleep with Michael; right?"

"No!" Lisa says, incredulous. "What are you *asking* me?"

"I'm just checking." I try to shrug in this nonchalant kind of way. There's a long pause.

"I cannot make the same promise for Court Chandler," Lisa says.

We both laugh. "Thank you for being honest," I say.

I power up my cell phone and look at the texts that have been sent in the last two days. I haven't looked at them since Saturday night.

*ILU Where are you? Why won't you answer me? I'm leaving Eve.*

*Kimberley says I can't, but I'm going to. Is this too untenable and not real enough? Ellie?*

I type a text back to him.

*Courtney Chandler you are amazing. Thank you. Michael and I are having twins. I'm cancer free. No chemo for a while. We're going on the honeymoon that we never got to take. It's untenable; yes. Okay I write too much for text. Lisa said to tell you hello. She thinks you are too wise for me. Ellen Kay Shaw.*

I let Lisa read what I've typed and sent.

"I did *not* say he was too wise!"

"I've got to let him down easy. If I say he's too young for me, he'll be crushed," I say.

"Well, we wouldn't want *that*," Lisa says sarcastically. "He wasn't too young for you?"

"No. He was amazing."

"Jesus…and you get Michael, too?"

"Not perfect; far from perfect, but Michael's my soul mate. Tenable and real." I blush, take the phone back, and type another .

*You should buy my house on Bainbridge Island; good things happen there. Love, Ellie.*

And, press send. My phone chirps when I get a text back.

*I WALU*

"Okay, what does that mean?" Asks the doctor with two advanced degrees as she reads the text over my shoulder.

"I will always love you," I say unevenly.

"Oh my God," Lisa says.

I power off the phone completely.

# CHAPTER TWENTY-THREE

 *Questions and Answers*

We've spent the week on the Oregon coast in some of the most pristine ocean beach front in the world. It has been just the two of us. It has never been just the two of us—not in the twenty years that we have known or been aware of each other.

We have asked the hard questions. We have asked the easy ones. We have asked the fun ones and the not so fun ones. By the end of the week we are out of questions. We have answers.

Michael has told me that he loved me when he first met me at college. He thought the thing with Robert Bradford would blow over. Then, before he could declare himself for me, Bobby and I got married. He admitted his own culpability in marrying Carrie on the rebound and trying to make something work that was doomed from the start. He admitted that he went along with the whole sperm donor thing because he thought maybe a baby would make a difference and, of course, Elaina was the best thing that ever happened between Carrie and Michael. Elaina did make a difference.

Since I was pregnant with Nicholas, he knew it was less likely I would ever leave Robert. He admitted that he had thought about leaving Carrie a dozen times over their marriage.

When I asked him what stopped him from doing that? He replied, "*You*, Ellie," Michael said. His explanation was he didn't want to leave his life and me behind. He figured having me so close would be enough.

"You must be going crazy now," I teased him.

"Pretty much," he said with a laugh.

I told him that Robert and I had been growing apart for a long time. I, of course, refused to see my marriage as less than perfect. I think that is why it was so easy to overlook Bobby's affair with Carrie, which, on some level, I think I knew was going on before I actually discovered them together at the Four Seasons all those months ago.

Today, we walk along the beach with the mist coming in all around us. It's a partly sunny, partly cloudy day. I hold on to Michael's hand.

"So," I say. "What are we going to do with twins?"

"I've been waiting for you to bring that up. How do you feel about that?"

"Well, baby, I'm a little freaked out. I'm not a super-mom."

"We'll get a nanny."

"I don't know Michael. Can we afford that? I want to be here for everything."

"Are you excited or scared?"

"Can I be both?" I look over at him uncertain, seeking his reassurance.

"Yes. Ellen Kay, I'm right here. I'll always be here standing close enough, so I can touch you whenever I want. Is that going to be enough for you?" Michael stops walking. He's looking for an answer. His blue eyes look at me expectantly now. I reach my hands out to his chest and pull him to me. I look up into his face and he bends it towards me. Our kiss is sweet; and then turns fiery.

"Dr. Michael Shaw, do you still have doubts? Insecurities? Really? Does a soul mate really have to ask?"

He doesn't smile. "I saw your texts. I know what IWALU means, Ellen Kay."

I hold up the palms of my hands imitating a balancing scale. "Tenable and very real." I lift my left hand. "Untenable." I lift my right hand. "*Who* to choose?" I do the balance demonstration a couple more times and I see him watching me. I push against him. "No contest. Come on Michael. It's you. It's always been you."

"I don't believe you." His voice is that of a sullen little boy. It makes me laugh.

"Okay, let me show you." I take his hand and lead him back to our oceanfront home. "What are you going to be like when we have four kids running around?"

"I'll need lots of reassurance and attention from you," he says in this wounded voice.

"Well, let's get to work on that right now. I have a little time for you, Dr. Shaw. Let me help you out."

"Ellie, I don't want to share you with Court Chandler."

"I'm aware of that. I don't want to share you with Carrie Bradford."

"Well, I guess we're on the same page."

"Let me show you what page we're on." I take off his jacket and then, slip off mine. I light the gas fireplace and then, pull him down to the rug with me. "Now, what seems to be the problem, Dr. Shaw? Show me where it hurts. I'll kiss it and make it go away."

Our week in Oregon has renewed our love, our spirit and our life together. We arrive home to the beach house in a better place. It is still difficult. Grief over Nicholas and Elaina steals into our home and into our hearts at unexpected times, but instead of hiding from it, Michael and I reach out to the other to make it through.

It is the third week in May. I'm at the end of week thirty-four of my pregnancy.

Mathew and Emily are in a state of constant wonder over the news that they're going to have a brother *and* a sister. These are amniocentesis results on the smaller baby come back with.

So far, the genetic testing on baby two is all good news, just like baby one. The good.

The Doctors Chatham are still guarded about the "no chemo" directive from me. The bad. Michael hesitates too. I sense his reluctance with my decision, but he continues to support my choice.

We are way out of protocol, at this point. Everyone on our team is on edge with us.

Everything is out of process, out of protocol, at this juncture. I should have had a double mastectomy with complete reconstruction by now. That is what all the research tells me. I should never have had the radiation, since I was probably pregnant by then. We are talking days plus or minus based on these calculations. I shouldn't have had the MRI, but then, we may not have seen the right breast tumor on Ultrasound. Should have. Could have. Would have. All these uncertainties weigh down on everyone, including me.

I brush my hair and then pull it up in a ponytail like Elaina used to wear hers. My long blonde hair shines in the mirror from the overhead lighting in our master bathroom and I stop and look at myself in the mirror. Am I really so vain that I would rather keep my hair, then have the chemo? Am I so deluded to think that I can beat odds that other people have succumbed to? And, am I willing to risk my life by not getting chemo therapy against the Doctors Chatham wishes because…I don't want to be here in two years? Is that the path I'm choosing? These wayward thoughts come out of nowhere. I pick up my cell phone with trembling hands and stare at it for a long time. Finally, I press the familiar number.

"I need to talk to you," I say.

"God, it is *about* time," Lisa says. "I'll be there in an hour."

I'm out at the beach walking the shoreline. We've been blessed with a perfect day. The sun is shining and the water is this intense vivid blue with these pure white caps floating on top. The breeze is gentle and blows at my clothes and hair like a caress.

Michael and Robert have taken the kids sailing. This is new. We purchased a sailboat with Robert and Carrie about a week ago. The gorgeous thirty-five foot schooner is now moored at the Bainbridge Island Yacht Club, when they aren't out sailing her. I'm not comfortable on a sailboat, right now, so I beg off on the trip. And, because I don't go; Carrie doesn't go either. We have this unwritten, unspoken agreement going on between us. Carrie does not attend functions with Michael, if I'm not there. We've never talked about it again, about her and Michael, since our shared car trip that brought me back home, but knowing Carrie as I do, I know she's very afraid of her life with Robert Bradford completely unraveling. She's willing to do whatever it takes to ensure that doesn't happen.

I've accepted the loss of a close friendship with Carrie. The trust and love that we had for each other is far away from us. I feel sorry for her, but not enough to risk having her insecurities and her twisted moral code around Michael and me. So, we're distant. She's doing more and more things with Marjorie Bingham. This doesn't surprise me. It doesn't amuse me. It makes me sad. She chose this course for us. I can live with it.

"Well, I guess I can see why you came back from Italy, after all," Lisa drawls. She stands with her arms crossed in front of her from the edge of the lawn, watching me.

I take leisurely strides towards her. My sandals fill with the warm sand and I smile at her.

"It's a form of paradise." I hug her. "Thanks for coming."

"Been waiting for your call for a while now," Lisa says.

She goes over to the far chair and sits down. "You want to tell me what's going on?" I sense her frustration. The miracle worker is way out of her element and definitely not in control.

"Why did you go into a practice for both gynecology and cancer?" I ask. She gives me a wary look. I realize that as close as Lisa and I have become in these past months, I don't know the answer to this question. She looks over and studies me, measuring my ability for secrecy, I think. "I won't tell anyone."

"I'm not worried about that." She hesitates. "I don't want to *scare* you more than you already are."

"I'm not scared." I can still lie like a tarot card reader.

"Sure you are," Lisa says with an edge to her voice. "And, you *should be*. Cancer is a wicked...a wicked thing."

She gives me an appraising look and doesn't say anything for a few minutes. She just stares out at the water. Finally, she sighs. "My mother died from cancer. I was fifteen. She was six months pregnant and discovered...a lump in her breast."

My head whips up at this revelation. I stare at her, open-mouthed, in shock.

"Well, this was twenty years ago." Her face contorts with unforeseen pain. "So, a pregnant woman with breast cancer was virtually unheard of and they followed the protocol of the time. Cut her up like a filleted fish—took her breasts and her lymph nodes, but they didn't catch it. It had already spread to her bones."

She stops. Then, she looks at me for a moment, studies my reaction. "I watched her die a little bit each day. The baby died, of course. They didn't exactly perform an abortion, but they basically killed that baby. They dumped so many drugs into her system, trying to kill cancer that they almost killed them both. And...she died anyway. She was thirty eight. *Thirty-eight.* Two years older than I am now. Your age, Ellie."

"I'm sorry. I'm so sorry, Lisa." My heart pounds wildly in my chest. *Am I hearing the story of my own fate?*

"Me, too," she says back to me. I see the sorrow and pain in her golden brown eyes. "So, I'm driven to go into medicine to become a specialist in fighting cancer and helping pregnant women keep their babies, while fighting this wicked, awful disease because of my mother. But…" I see regret in her expression, as if, she has said too much.

"But what?" I grab her hand, imploring her to tell me.

"I don't know if we're winning," Lisa says with a sad smile.

I drop her hand, get up, and begin pacing the lawn back and forth in front of her. "I don't know what to do anymore. I don't know if what I'm doing is the right thing for anyone." I look over Lisa and stop pacing. "I miss Nick and Elaina. Sometimes. Sometimes, I wonder if I'm supposed to be with them."

"God damn it, Ellie! Don't ever say that!" Lisa is on her feet and towering over me in this frightening fury. "Ellie, you have everything to live for. You have two beautiful children and two more on the way. You have Michael. You could have Court Chandler if you want; you just have to say the word. He still calls me every other day to ask how you're doing."

"He does?" I ask in this faraway voice.

I have ignored his texts on my cell phone for weeks, not that I didn't still think about him and wonder what could have happened between us if…if I didn't have cancer, if I wasn't married to Michael, if he wasn't under thirty, if I wasn't pregnant with twins. Twins just seemed to make it completely impossible to be with Court Chandler. As soon as I learned I was carrying twins, it seemed to kill the last of the connection between us. Of course, not seeing Court has helped out with that as well, but now, hearing Lisa say his name brings it all back. *Untenable, but real enough,* I think now.

"Have you heard a single word I've said?" Lisa asks in exasperation.

"No," I say with this twisted smile. "I lost you when you mentioned Court's name and said he's still checking up on me."

"Come inside, Ellie," Lisa says gently, now. "Let's get some iced tea and talk this through." I nod, while Lisa leads the way inside my home. *Home*, the one I share with Michael and Mathew and Emily, not Court Chandler.

Guilt courses through me because, today, I feel like making a trade in wish lists. I *want* to choose Court Chandler. Lisa fills two glasses with ice and pours the tea over them. The house is quiet, as I sit there with my friend, Dr. Lisa Chatham, my oncologist, my gynecologist, my truth-seeker.

"Lisa," I say. "What is wrong with me? Why can't I move past this? Past *him*?"

"I know more than I should about what went down this spring," Lisa says to me now.

I lift my head from my fascination with the iced tea in my glass that I've been absently swirling and look at her. I flinch at her words.

"I think Court represents the purity of what love can be. I'm not saying I condone getting back together with him," she adds. "But you are going to have to decide if you *trust* Michael."

"I thought I'd already dealt with this."

*I did.* I thought we'd made it through this intense truthful discussion at the Oregon coast. Lisa's right. I have to decide if I trust Michael as well as myself.

"Ellie, what do you want?" Lisa asks me now.

"I want all of my wishes. I want Nick and Elaina back."

Lisa grabs both my hands. "I'm sorry they died. I can't imagine what it's like to lose a child, but, Ellie, you have to look at your future and decide what you want it to be."

"Do I have a future?" I ask with a trace of hostility—a permanent side effect of grief and cancer.

"Ah, so that's what this is. You're afraid of dying as much as you are afraid of living. It's okay to experience joy again, Ellie, to go on without Nick and Elaina," she says.

I let the silence drift between us for a while. I sip the iced tea. Finally, I look at her.

"Yes. I feel guilty that I'm here, *living*, without them. It's why I…it's why I took them to Paris. Truly, I felt like I needed to go with Court to Europe for both of them." Lisa nods in understanding, I think. I see this look of sympathy and anguish cross her face.

"Okay. Let's start with your future. I want you to come to the office tomorrow

"We'll run through the tests again and see where we're at. It's been weeks, since we looked at the films. We'll look again and go from there. If they're clear, we can stay with the no chemo regimen. We're just a little more than six weeks from the twins' births."

I experience pure panic as she reminds me of this. "I'm not ready," I say in alarm.

"You will be," Lisa predicts.

We talk a few minutes about the babies' arrival. I show her the nursery where Michael and I have begun setting things up. There is double of everything—cribs, changing tables and baby clothes, most of it is ready. The only thing I haven't dealt with is lining up some extra help, a nanny or someone like this. For some reason, I'm hesitant to find one. I am already behind in doing this and still, I cannot bring myself to hire someone to come into our home. Deep down, I realize that I am going to have to clear out one of the bedrooms that still serve as a shrine to Nick and Elaina and I cannot bring myself to do it. I haven't even told Michael about this fear.

Lisa is watching me closely now. She asks me if I'm okay. I adopt nonchalance and smile. Inside though, I'm starting to get this disquieting feeling, but Lisa nods, satisfied with my answer. She smiles as we traverse back down the stairs again.

"Okay, I have to jet," she says, making a face. "My wonderful husband has committed us to a backyard barbecue at the neighbors. I'll see you in the morning at my office."

"Okay," I say.

I hug her and try to put on a brave face for her, but the revelations of our discussion weigh upon me. I'm still in a daze when she leaves a few minutes later to catch the ferry back to Seattle, while I leave to go pick up the kids from school and try to crush this uneasiness that our deep discussion has stirred up inside of me.

# CHAPTER TWENTY-FOUR

## Risking Everything

Mathew is quiet in the backseat of my SUV. I look at him via the rear-view mirror. "What's up?" I look directly at him before shifting my eyes back to the traffic ahead.

"Nothing," he says. He fidgets with his notebook without looking back at me.

"Mattie, come on. What's wrong?"

"Are you and Michael okay?" Mathew asks. His tone is wistful and uncertain. I think my son, like me, is barely hanging in there. I try to smile at him in the mirror.

"We're doing just fine. Why?" Now, I'm wary. *Why would Mathew ask me this?*

"I don't know. There was this lady at school. She was asking about you...and Michael. She talked about this guy named Court Chandler."

"What?" I slam on the brakes and pull the car over to the side of the road. I turn and look at Mathew. "What? Tell me who this woman was."

"I don't know who she was," Mathew says. "She said she was a reporter for one of the magazines for celebrities. She said she was just doing a background check on facts," Mathew's voice trails off.

I think he's taken aback by the look on my face. My pulse sky-rockets. I dig through my purse and dial Kimberley Powers' cell phone.

"No. No. No" I keep repeating over and over. My hands shake by the time she answers on the third ring. "Kimberley, it's Ellie." I fight for my composure as my thirteen-year-old son looks on.

"Fuck! Are they already there? I was just about to call you," Kimberley says. "They've got the story, Ellie. They have a photo with you and Court from Italy and they're running it."

"What kind of photo?" I ask.

"One of you and Court, it must have been taken with a tele-photo lens, but it's damaging, Ellie. They're running with it. I tried to stop them from printing it, but once they had the photograph and figured out who you were, well, it's a great story in their view."

"Some reporter was at my son's school, Kimberley."

"Okay. I'm on my way. I'm just boarding the plane in New York. I'll be landing in Seattle in the next five hours. I want you to gather your family. Go home and wait for my call. Do you understand? I don't want you to use the landline or your cell or answer the door—same goes with your family."

"Does Court know?" My heart starts pounding faster in just saying his name.

"Yeah," Kimberley says with a hint of sympathy. "He's already been told *not* to call you. I wonder how long he'll actually follow that directive." I hear the sarcasm in her tone along with a little laugh. "I'm sorry, Ellie. I'm sorry this has happened to you. It's... I'm sorry. Court said to tell you that as well."

"How bad can it get?" I ask with a trembling laugh.

"Oh, Ellie." Kimberley groans. "I wish I didn't know the answer to that. Just hang tough, until I get there. We'll check in to a hotel tonight and I'll be in touch with you soon."

"Okay." I hesitate. "I have a doctor's appointment in the morn-ing. We're re-running all the tests—"

Kimberley is swearing. "Ellie, they'll have the hospital staked out. Your husband works at one of them; right?"

"Yes. Oh, God. I should call Michael."

"Yes. Call him now. He'll need to lie low like the rest of us for a couple of days, until we come up with our response."

"Okay."

"Gotta go. The flight attendant is giving me the evil eye," Kimberley says. "Hang in there. I'm on my way. I'll work on strategy on the flight and call you after I land. Gotta go."

Call ended flashes on my phone. I can't even talk. I just sit there in a stunned silence. Frozen. I begin trembling all over and then hear Mathew say something to me from the backseat. "Mom, we need to get Em."

I can only nod as I start the car again and pull back onto the road. I pick up my cell again, stare at it a few minutes, and slowly dial Michael's cell phone. It goes straight to voice mail and I leave a message that he needs to come home right away and to call me as soon as he gets my message. I hesitate wanting to give him the gist about the media story and the connection being made about me to Court Chandler because Mathew is right here.

I can feel my life falling apart even as I pull up to Emily's school. I put the car in park, stalk towards my child, and pull her to me just as the flash goes off from some photographer's camera. I awkwardly pick up Emily and hide her in my coat and stagger to the car with her. It takes another five minutes to get past the two reporters that are busy taking pictures of me and my children as we leave Wilkes Elementary.

I take a back route to our beach house. My paranoia runs at an all-time high. I tell the kids that they are not to answer the phone or their cell phones or use the computer or watch television.

"So, exactly, what are we doing, mother?" Emily asks.

"You're watching *Enchanted* in the family room," I say.

"Awesome!" Emily responds with a giggle.

Mathew actually laughs at his sister's excitement. I smile at him and mouth "Thank you."

I park the car in the garage and we make our way into the house. The message light is flashing on the answering machine. I press play. There are three calls from a reporter and a call from Michael as well as Robert all within the last half hour. I call Robert first because it is the easiest call to make as my apprehension with Michael grows.

"Robert," I say, subdued when he answers.

"Ellen Kay, what's going on? I'm leaving court today and a reporter is asking me all kinds of questions about you…and this guy Court Chandler."

"Uh-huh," I say, ensuring the kids can't hear my conversation. "Look, it's a long, complicated story. Michael already knows about this. I just need you to not say anything to the media. Can you do that?"

"Yes, but, Ellie…are you in…*involved* with this guy?"

"There's a lot you don't know about, Bobby," I say sharply, too sharply, reacting to his judging tone. "Look. I'm sorry. I don't want you to have to get involved in this anymore than you already are. The less you know the better."

There's a long pause on his end of the phone and knowing Bobby as I do, I'm sure he's sifting through arguments on how to approach this situation with me. "Okay," he finally says with a heavy sigh. "Let me know if I can do anything."

"Okay. It might be best for you to take the kids this weekend."

"All right. Ellie…are you going to be okay?" Robert asks.

"Yes, we're all going to be okay," I say back to him.

The surety in my voice is for both of us. Even I want to believe the sincerity in which I tell this lie, though uncertainty has already started to creep in on me. "Look. I need to go. I need to reach Michael. Can you get the kids from school tomorrow?"

"Sure," Robert says, and then hesitates. "Ellie, whatever you did;

I'm sure Michael will understand. The one thing you are is loyal."

I end the call with Bobby and let the tears run freely down my face. Eventually, I wipe them away as the shame courses through me. I'm a liar and a cheat and somehow, Bobby Bradford never sees me this way. Exactly, where and when did I get off track? Was it twenty years ago when I was secretly hoping Michael would ask me out again even after Bobby proposed? *What is wrong with me?* I brush at my tears, awash in self-hatred.

I race through the house deciding to start some sort of dinner, while I try Michael's cell phone again. He answers on the first ring.

"I'm on the ferry." I can tell by the tone of his voice that he's already been touched in some way by this disaster.

"Tell me."

"A reporter caught me in the hospital parking lot and started asking all kinds of questions about you and Court Chandler. He showed me a picture of you and Chandler…and wanted to know if I had a comment about my *wife's* affair."

"I'm…sorry, Michael. I didn't intend to…hurt you this way."

"Well, I guess that's what happens when you fuck around with someone famous," he says back to me with a bitter laugh. His flippancy barely contains the fury I can easily detect beneath his words. His breath is staggered as if he's gasping for air. We are right back to where we started, a few months ago. The image of Michael with Carrie in her white Mercedes assails me now. I involuntarily cry out, remembering the desolation of that life-changing moment.

"Let's just remember who fucked around first," I say without thinking.

There's this stunned silence between us. I hear his unsteady breath. Then he says, "I'm sorry." His remorse reaches for me through the phone line. "I'll be there as soon as I can." We say our goodbyes and I stare at 'call ended' on my phone, until it disappears from the screen. Call ended, just like that.

*Life ended, just like that, too.*

With growing fear, I busy myself with getting dinner for the kids, looking around for plates and serving up re-heated leftover lasagna for Mathew and Emily. I have this sudden overwhelming sense of loss of Nick. I miss his smile and his teasing. I miss my sixteen-year-old son so much. I wipe away tears with the back of my hand and carry the heaping plates of food into the family room and set them down in front of Emily and Mathew and try to act normal. I tell them I'll be upstairs and leave before they can get a good look at my tear-streaked face.

Minutes late, I'm staring at my undressed self in the bathroom mirror where I stand in only a lacy white bra and panties. I scrutinize my breasts and my rounded basketball of a stomach and feel the babies move. "How did I get here?" I ask the woman in the mirror. She doesn't answer.

The fact is, whatever this media explosion might be, it is nothing compared to what we've been through over the loss of Nick and Elaina and the loss of each other.

In a daze, I put on a robe and walk down the hallway, open the door to Nick's room, and close it quickly behind me. Standing in the center of his room, I note it's just the way he left it. There are his Seven Jeans thrown haphazardly across the bed. His laptop is still open. As I move the mouse trying to capture the essence of him as he must have sat at this very desk. His computer screen lights up. An e-mail that he started to Elaina is in full view.

> Elaina,
>
> I guess the newly-married Shaw's want us to go bowling. I can deal with that, if you can. Look, I know I didn't say it right the other night, just know I love you and I can wait. I will wait for you, Elaina. You mean

Nick left it unfinished.

I remember stopping in his room after the wedding to check on him and recall him at this very laptop typing away, probably, this e-mail. He loved her so much. I wrap my arms tightly around myself and try to capture my son in my arms. The grief I feel is overwhelming. I stagger to his bed and lie down on top of the covers and close my eyes.

"Nicky," I whisper. "I love you so much." I give into the grief and feel it steal over my body like a black mist. I'm so sad. Yet, I can hear his voice so clear, saying it's going to be okay. "Do you think so, Nick? How do you know?" I whisper to the empty room, now.

I awaken up to the pitch black of Nick's room and the incessant ringing of my cell phone and answer automatically.

"Ellie," Court whispers. The sound of his voice brings back memories of his incredible smile. It serves like a lifeline from the sadness I've been battling the past hour. "Kimberley told me that she told you *not* to call me," I say, sitting up in the dark.

"Well, she's on a plane, so there's not much she can do about it. Ellie, are you okay?

"I'm okay," I say with a sigh. "This whole thing…it's surreal; isn't it? Are you okay?"

My emotions surface all at once, just hearing Court's voice causes these dormant feelings for him to come to life inside. *But I love Michael.*

"I'm okay. Kind of," he says, uncertain. "I'm just sorry you got pulled into this mess, sorry about everything."

"I haven't seen anything come out yet. How bad is it?"

"That depends on what you told Michael," he says in that charming way of his. I haven't heard his voice in so long, part of me gives way upon hearing it.

"I told him everything," I say quickly. But fear begins to take hold because this isn't true. I didn't tell Michael everything about

Court Chandler. I flush in the darkness unable to control the heat that begins to pulsate inside of me, just thinking of our intimate moments in Italy.

"So you told him about Italy, at the pool?" Court says slowly.

"Nooooooo. Oh God. That's the photo they're running?"

My pulse mind races, working through who would have seen us. Somehow, I thought it would be something from the places we saw in London. I didn't think anyone saw us while we were in Italy.

"Yes, that's what they're running. It was one of the most memorable moments of our time together, Ellie, but, it was private, not for the public."

"Oh God," I say, helpless now. "You've seen it?"

"Yeah, they've already run it in Europe. Eve's seen it. If she wasn't going to divorce me before, she's ready to now."

I begin to wonder if Michael has seen the photo. Or, if there's some way I can prevent that from happening.

"Ellie, are you *listening* to me? I want to see you, be with you. Maybe, all of this is happening for a reason. Maybe, we're supposed to be together."

"Courtney Chandler, this is an untenable situation and we both know it."

"No! Even if I lose everything—"

"You're not going to lose *everything*," I say with a sigh.

It's impossible to explain to a guy under thirty what losing a child is like. How it in no way can be compared to the devaluation of the high tech stock of a company or the loss of a job even as CEO or the loss of someone's integrity or stature.

*Everything* to Court means something entirely different to him than it does to me. Sadness takes over as I think of Nick and Elaina and even Michael when he sees this photograph.

"I've got to find Michael before he sees that photo." My breath gets uneven as the panic surges, knowing what it will mean if Michael were to see that intimate scene of Court and me pool side.

"It means nothing without you in my life. I have to see you. I'm sorry Ellie about the way things ended between us," Court says. "I shouldn't have reacted the way I did. I shouldn't have brought you back."

"Court," I say with a heavy sigh. "This is untenable."

"But, real enough," he says back to me. "I think of you all the time. I want to be with you. Ellie, tell me you've thought about me, too. You have; haven't you?"

"Yes, but Court this is untenable. We both agreed."

"I love you, Ellie. Tell me you feel the same way."

I don't answer, all at once, I'm confused and afraid. I sit up further on Nick's bed, just as Michael turns on the lamp next to the chair, where unbeknownst to me he's been sitting in the dark the entire time. Rage emanates from him. His handsome face contorts with inconsolable sorrow and betrayal.

"I have to go." I end the call with Court in mid-sentence and stare at Michael, quickly running through my head how my side of the conversation with Court would sound to him. "Michael...I..."

"Untenable, but real enough with Court Chandler," Michael says harshly.

"No, it's not. He was just calling...to say he was sorry."

"So that wasn't him saying we can make this work; I want to see you? Come on, Ellie, I heard what he said and I heard what you said. He thinks about you all the time and you've been thinking about *him*."

"I didn't mean it," I say, but my face flushes and he sees it.

"I don't believe you," Michael says with cold indifference. His words slice through me, but then, he takes me into his arms. He kisses me in desperation. It's as if he's torn between believing me or not and in search of a way to trust me. Misinterpreting what he's doing, I kiss him back just as passionately and give way, when his hand slips inside my robe and reaches further down. He stops.

"You're *hot* for him," Michael says in disbelief. "I guess it's *real enough* with him." He staggers back from me.

"No!" I say in a panic. "It's you. It's only you." I tremble, knowing my body has just betrayed me. All my lies have come undone.

"You're lying to me even now. I *heard* you on the phone with him, Ellen Kay. All that intimate talk about Italy. How memorable it was. You still *want* him. You still think about him." The sadness in his voice reaches at me.

Without another word, my surgeon goes to the bathroom sink, washes his hands, while I slip to the floor, hanging my head in shame. *What have I done? Why have I done this?*

My lies dangle between us like downed power wires, still live, sparking with electricity, too hot to touch, lying in wait to electrocute us both if we dare reach out to one another.

Reality comes swiftly. I've risked everything with Michael in being with Court Chandler. *Everything.* I watch our relationship end right in front of me with the look on his face

"I don't know who you are, anymore. I don't think *you* even know who you are."

"Michael, I *do* know who I am and what I want. I love you. *I came back!* Don't do this to us." My breathing gets more erratic; I'm frightened by his fury and his sudden distrust.

"I didn't do this to us, Ellen Kay, *you did.* I take ownership for my part, but you need to own up to yours. You don't seem to know what you want." His eyes glint with anger. "And, I'm not going to serve as your second choice because he couldn't deal with your *cancer.*"

I look up at him in surprise; this ominous feeling courses through me. "Don't do this. You've got to believe me."

"I don't anymore," he says. "Something you said that first night keeps coming back to me. You said he brought you back. I didn't want to believe what you meant by that at the time. I didn't even want to ask, too afraid of the answer, but deep down I *knew.*"

Michael takes an unsteady breath and looks at me closely.

He shakes his head and gets this bitter smile. "But he said it. I *heard* him. He brought you back because he couldn't deal with *cancer*. His mom died of it ten years ago; right? *He* brought you back, Ellie." Michael looks at me with true heartbreak. "But you weren't coming back; were you?"

I'm too shocked by his accusation and its close proximity to the truth at the time. I reach for him again, but he easily breaks my hold and stalks from the room.

I follow him to our bedroom. His anger is palpable between us. I can only watch as he haphazardly throws his clothes into a suitcase.

"Don't do this, Michael. Please. You've got to believe me."

It's as if I'm in the center of seesaw traversing either side, trying to find the middle ground and steady the scale, desperate to restore a semblance of truth between us.

"Michael, there's a picture of Court and me at the pool in Italy. It's—"

"I've seen it! It's all over the news. CNBC, CNN, every six o'clock news channel on the West Coast ran the salacious story, Ellen Kay. You're famous, almost as famous as your fucking lover, Court Chandler."

I close my eyes and sink to the floor. "Please don't leave me."

"I have to. I feel like I'm dying right along with you. I want to be with you, Ellie. I love you, but I don't want to be your second choice and if you don't want to be here and have a life with me..."

"You're not my second choice. I want to be with you, Michael. I want to live because of *you*."

"I don't believe you," he says sadly.

He grabs his bags and leaves without another backward glance. In desperation, I race after him down the stairs and almost fall. He looks anxious, reaches out, and steadies me, then abruptly lets go of me as if he's been burned by the contact.

"How can I convince you that I love you, Michael, only you?"

"I'm not sure you can," Michael says unevenly. He moves towards the door, then hesitates, and finally looks at me. "Get Court Chandler out of your life, once and for all."

I watch Michael drive away. My body sags against the doorway for support and it feels as if he's taken my life away with him.

# CHAPTER TWENTY-FIVE

## The Only Wish

Fame, a short-lived thing, it comes swiftly and leaves in much the same way. After two weeks of sensational headlines that have reached all the way to the secluded upscale community of Bainbridge Island, Court Chandler and I are no longer front page news on every tabloid newspaper or magazine. The stock in Court Chandler's now public company has made up much of the thirty percent loss it sustained. The interest in his infidelity with his much older love interest, me, in deference to his much younger wife, Eve Chandler, that's been paraded across every entertainment channel and news media outlet throughout Europe and the United States, has ended. Mr. Courtney Chandler's life seems to have righted itself. Mrs. Eve Chandler has agreed to stay with her husband, decreed that they belong together, during a very public news conference.

I haven't made any public announcements. I've been out of the public eye for much of the time dealing with my own private hell.

The night Michael left, I told Kimberley that she would have to handle Court's problems without me. I have my own problems I assured her. I think Kimberley admired my tenacity for standing up to Court and telling him in no uncertain terms that we were over, which I did in a separate phone call the night Michael left me. I'm willing to do whatever it takes to bring him back to me. I started with Court. This media fire storm that Court considered an all consuming problem; I saw it for what it really was: a blip on an imaginary radar screen, nothing more. It wasn't real life. It wasn't dead children or broken hearts or even betrayed soul mates.

Michael and I have been through far worse, losing our two children, now that was complete devastation and heartbreakingly permanent. In comparison to Court's media problem, losing each other through all of this is more devastating; and, I can only hope, temporary.

The day after Michael left, I showed up in Lisa's medical office in spite of the media barrage that greeted me from every newsstand and every television set tuned into the major networks. Seattle was under siege by the national news. The city seemed to be set afire by the local sensation that their local golden boy of the high tech world had done wrong and his *cougar girlfriend* lived on Bainbridge Island.

The media had no qualms about digging up the recent head-lines about the tragic deaths of Nicholas Bradford and Elaina Shaw. Those stories ran side-by-side with all the others. There were pictures of me picking up Emily from school and unflattering stories questioning the paternity of the babies I carry. There were talk shows covering the gambit of exploitable topics about older women and younger men relationships. *Feast or famine?* The headline asked. I set off whole new topics of discussion on all the major channels about sex at forty, babies at forty, and the younger lover under thirty for the older woman at forty.

It was debated and dissected just about everywhere. Court came out looking great; I came out looking like the modern-day whore wearing the famous red letter A as if painted directly across my bare chest. Once the media got a hold of the story about my bout with breast cancer, a whole new media round ensued, but I weathered it all from this faraway place of the emotionally detached, carrying a perspective for apathy. I didn't care about Court Chandler and his problems. I had enough of my own.

Mammograms of both breasts revealed something new. The cancer was back in my left one. I saw it as fit punishment. Lisa saw it as a no chemo regimen gone horribly wrong. I didn't want Michael to know that the cancer was back. Lisa was dismayed at my request for secrecy, beside herself in fact, but her Hippocratic Oath prevented her from telling him.

Two weeks. I haven't seen Michael for two weeks. *Two weeks.* Lisa and Stephen want to do a chemotherapy regimen for another two weeks and then I'm too close to my due date when the rate of infection is too high and the complications with uncontrollable bleeding would be too great.

So, I've had chemotherapy treatments and the side effects are very real. Cyclophosphamide, commonly known as Cytoxan, is this little innocent white table that I take and this alone caused me to vomit within hours of the first dose. While the Doxorubicin, commonly known as Adriamycin is administered intravenously in the spa offices of Lisa and Stephen's practice and wreaked even worse havoc.

The AC treatment was the course of action immediately taken, after I went back to surgery with Josh to have more cancer removed. This surgery was done on that very Sunday following Michael's departure, so Dr. Michael Shaw remains unaware that it has taken place. Lisa *manned up* and was even better than I would have been at announcing this edict—that Michael was not to be told of my newly developed status requiring more surgery or the chemotherapy regimen.

People on our team were encouraged to go along with this part of the program or they would be unceremoniously off the team.

No one dared cross Lisa or me, at this point, so the secret of my recurring cancer remained among the team and the latest surgical procedure with the removal of both my breasts was done in secret and only known by Josh, Ben, Tom, Lisa and Stephen. My team was a little freaked out that cancer had returned so soon and since radiation was out of the question, a mastectomy was the best option and, at this point, a double mastectomy was the preventative choice for the right one.

I was done with being sad and protective of my bodacious tah tahs because I'd lost all of my wishes, except Emily and Mathew and the babies I carry.

My team, especially Josh, Ben and Tom, struggled with keeping the secret of my *double mas* with complete reconstruction and chemotherapy regimen from Michael. I saw it in their eyes every time they came into the hospital room where I stayed for the first three days after surgery. Tom outdid himself by preserving the outer skin and nipples of both breasts and I know his promise of near perfection is pretty close.

Lisa is worried. I can see it on her face and she tells me she regrets her insistence that we start the chemotherapy right away. The nausea and the constant vomiting are almost more than I can handle and just the beginning of my problems. I have already prepared myself for the day that I will wake up and begin to lose my hair. Lisa hasn't held anything back and she's told me to expect this.

I've broken down; I called my mother and asked her to come and stay with me. I wasn't sure that she could really help me, but I'm so sick after the first two weeks of the chemo that I've asked her to come. I asked Carrie to go and pick her up.

I've pulled out all the stops. I've begun asking everyone, who I have never wanted to owe anything to, for favors. Marjorie Bingham has been ferrying my children to and from school each day.

It's impossible for me to drive anywhere because of the surgery and constant nausea. Lisa is more than worried. She would like to put me back in the hospital, but so far I've convinced her not to. I've literally begged her not to.

The pain from the double mas and breast reconstruction stays with me. It's fitting punishment for all the mistakes I've made with Michael. There is still no word from him, not one. I'm crushed by his silence. It's more painful than anything else.

Lisa's made a point of coming to the house every other day as if a ferry trip to Bainbridge Island is on her way home to her fabulous house in West Seattle. "Court called," she says now.

"Don't talk about him." I think the fierce look on my face gives her a moment's pause.

"He just wants to know how you are."

"All you need to tell him is that I'm just fine and to quit calling. Tell him I said so."

"He cares about you." I get up from the sofa and get busy refilling our glasses with iced tea. Lisa follows me into the kitchen. "You're going to have twins in little more than a month. You need some help. He seems willing."

"He's back with his wife. Eve."

"Oh, I hadn't heard that." Lisa takes the glass of iced tea I offer her and looks over at me in concern. "What are you going to do? I could talk to Michael."

"No! Please. No," I say more gently. "I don't know what to do about Michael, anymore. I don't know what else I can do, but I don't want him to see me like this. Right now, I'm just staying focused on Mathew and Emily, and getting better."

"Okay, but you'll tell me if you change your mind about contacting Michael."

"When I feel better, I'll think about it," I promise her now.

My ability to lie with the best of them has not left me and the sincerity in my voice is convincing even to me. Lisa nods, satisfied, I think, with my answer. She doesn't even suspect that I'm breaking inside. I'm fractured into a million tiny pieces inside. She doesn't know that I spend my nights lying awake in the dark, fighting nausea, and suffering with the mental anguish of losing Michael, practically twenty-four hours a day. I've kept this private hell from everyone, including Mathew, Emily, and my mother.

"You need a nanny," Lisa says now.

"Yes," I say. "I'm working on that." This isn't true either, but I give her one of my yeah-team smiles anyway.

Stephen and Lisa decide to take me off the AC treatment after another week because we can't get the nausea under control. I don't argue; the side effects are still with me two days after the last one. My mother looks at me as I lay on the bathroom floor, *resting*.

"Ellie," she says tentatively. I lift my head up off the floor and try to focus on her.

"What Mom?" I've just vomited up every part what little breakfast I just ate an hour ago. I've already cried three times today. It is day twenty-three, since Michael left me.

"I think you should talk to Michael and tell him what's going on here."

"No."

I've tried to explain to my mother the details of our separation. I showed her the tabloid pictures that show the intimate details of my affair with Mr. Court Chandler. She's seen the television shows that covered this particular aspect of my indiscretions for herself. Yet, every day, we have this same conversation about Michael.

"Ellie, you can't go on like this. You're wasting away. You're going to have two babies in a few weeks or less and I'd like to know who is going to be able to take care of them."

"I'll…get a nanny." I can barely speak and as if to emphasize the point, I throw up in the toilet basin, again. A few minutes later, when I look over at the doorway, she's still standing there.

"I love you, Mom," I say with a weak smile. The tears stream down her face. "Don't cry. Truly, I can't take it."

"I'm not crying," she insists. My mother with her perfectly cut silver bob, her Arizona tan, her high-waist mom jeans and her western ladies shirt continues this vigilance over me as the tears stream down her cheeks.

"Why don't you take Emily to the zoo or something? Take Mathew, too," I say in this contrived cheery voice. "I'll be fine. It's not like I'm fit to go anywhere. I'll be right here or downstairs when you get back." She starts shaking her head. "Mom, *please*. Take the kids out. They need to get out and do something fun. Take them for ice cream, at least. *Please*."

"Fine. I'll take them out for a few hours. Maybe you can take a nap or something."

"That sounds great, Mom." I summon a yeah-team smile. "I'm feeling much better." My ability to lie remains with me; it knows no bounds. I force myself to a stand and move over to the sink to wash my face and brush my teeth.

I keep up the pretense of being okay for another fifteen minutes, while my mother herds my two children in general protest out the front door. Helen Katherine Miles is an even match for Emily, who is unable to convince grandma that she's better off staying home. I wave at them from the upstairs bedroom window. Both Mathew and Emily give me forlorn looks. I watch them drive away and almost smile, but the effort is too much for me as the last of my manufactured energy fades away at their leaving. Just putting the façade up for my mother the last couple of minutes takes the last vestiges of my hard-fought strength out of me.

As soon as I see the taillights disappear down the drive, I give into despair and lean against the window pane for support. The coolness of the glass feels good upon my face. "Yeah team," I say into the silence that engulfs me.

I move steadily over to the shower and strip out of my clothes and step under the warm water. It's easier to give in to the tears, when I'm in the shower. I let myself cry for a long list of reasons—my long list of lost wishes: Nick, Elaina, Michael, and me, myself and I, my bodacious tah tahs.

My wish list now consists of Emily, Mathew and these two babies. I delicately touch my new breasts. According to my team of doctors, I'm healing nicely. The scars are fading. Tom did an excellent job of making them look real and I chastise myself for being so attached to the old ones for so long and endangering my life by not getting chemotherapy sooner. My list of sins is long, too.

I let the tears fall and absently grab the shampoo and begin to wash my hair. Then, I discover long strands of blonde hair in my hands and I cry harder. I thought I might have escaped that bullet and might not lose my hair. But now, I hold the clumps in my shaking hands. "No!" I scream. My voice reverberates against the walls. "Oh my God."

I quickly rinse out the rest of my hair and discover more hair gathering at the drain. In anguish, I step out of the shower and wrap up in a giant bath towel, bend down to clear the drain of my hair, and cry the entire time. "Fuck!"

Someone's running down the hallway. I stop screaming to listen, filled with fear.

"Ellie! What is it? What's wrong?" Michael asks in alarm from the doorway.

It has been three weeks and four days, since I've seen him. He looks tired and out of sorts, standing there in blue jeans and a grey University of Washington sweatshirt. To me, he's still this golden god and causes my heart to pound wildly. I can only imagine how I look to him, clutching my strands of blonde hair. Childishly, I put my hands behind my back, so he can't see what I'm holding.

"Michael, what are you doing here?" I ask. "You scared me!"

"I'm sorry," Michael says. "I didn't mean to. I heard you and I thought..." He looks uncertain and rakes his hand through his hair. "I'm looking for the kids. Emily called me a few hours ago and begged me to come by and take her for ice cream." He looks at me, intently, now.

"My mother just took them for ice cream," I say in a tired voice. "I wasn't aware of your plans." I transfer the hair in my left hand to my right still behind my back and try to casually wipe the tears from my face with that now free hand.

"Your mom's here?" Michael asks in surprise. He is fully aware that Helen Katherine Miles is better taken in small doses. One visit a year is about all I can normally handle and she has already been here twice this year.

"Yes. She wanted to visit before the babies arrived," I say this so convincingly; I almost believe it myself. I see Michael nodding. "So...I guess you could try Mathew's cell phone and catch up to them."

Michael stares at me while I stand here, hiding my clumps of hair behind my back. I'm not exactly sure how my head looks. I have a lot of hair in my hand, but convince myself that what remains on my head looks normal; however, keeping up this façade of nonchalance is wearing on me.

I'm feeling vulnerable and exposed with only a bath towel around me. I stare back at him with defiance. My body betrays me further as the nausea rises, too.

"I need to get dressed." I give him this imploring look, but he still he stands there. "I need to get dressed *alone*."

"Sorry. I'll leave you," he says and gets this wounded look.

He turns toward the door. I take a shallow breath.

"Okay. Call Mathew. I'm sure they would love to see you," I say in a kinder tone.

I watch him go.

Then, I immediately run over and lock the door behind him. I stare down at the hair in my right hand for a long moment, then drop it in the sink, unsure what to do with it just yet. Overwhelmed, I lean against the vanity and start to cry. I say fuck, over and over, at least a few dozen times. It makes me feel slightly better.

Once dressed in maternity jeans and the red blouse Lisa picked up for me, I finally face the mirror and take a good look at my hair. No bald spots are prominent. I gingerly comb through it and part it slightly different.

I'm sure I'll have a few more days of normalcy. Then, I'll have to deal with this latest issue. I leave it down and let it dry naturally. I'm afraid to do any blow-drying; fearful that may cause it to fall out even faster.

I don't even contemplate rational thought at this point. I'm too uneasy at seeing Michael again and losing my hair all in the same day. It's too much for me.

I'll admit it. I'm vain about my hair. I considered it my second best asset right behind my bodacious tah tahs and look where that got me.

I make up my face and stare at the woman looking back at me. I guess my cheekbones are an acceptable asset and my lips are a natural rose color. My blue eyes are kind of pretty, this kind of glacial aquamarine. I apply a little blush and a light beige eye shadow and pencil in a light brown across my eyebrows. Lisa already warned me that my eyebrows will go by the wayside, just like my head of hair. With make-up, I feel slightly better and due to being pregnant, I'm somewhat glowing, despite chemo. I finish up by brushing my teeth, again.

I've almost convinced myself I'll be okay, if I can keep the nausea at bay for a little longer.

With reverence, I grab my hair from the other sink, intent on keeping it, until I can figure out what I want to do with it. Can you donate stuff like this? Or, is chemo hair the wrong kind of thing to donate? I move cautiously down the stairs, grabbing the railing with one hand as I descend. I'm so tired. It's hard to keep going, even at this glacial pace. I move even slower towards the kitchen intent on finding a Ziploc bag, now. I'm still holding my hair in one hand, when I turn around and discover Michael coming from the direction of the family room. I thought he'd gone.

"What are you doing?" Michael asks in bewilderment.

"Nothing."

I have nothing left to say. I have nothing left to give.

It has all been taken from me. I have paid the price.

I frantically search the cupboards looking for the Ziploc gallon-sized bags, no longer caring that Michael is watching me. I put my hair in the bag and zip it up.

"Are you doing *chemo*?" Michael asks, incredulous.

"Yes."

"Why?"

I look over at him and just shake my head without answering. Nausea comes back full force at this action and I race back up the stairs at a frantic painful pace and head for the first bathroom. I barely make it to the toilet before I'm dry-heaving again.

I sink to the floor and wait, knowing another session of this will follow within five minutes or less. Michael watches me from the doorway with this renewed intensity. He seems desperate to try and put this all together for himself.

"Tell me *why* you're doing chemo, *now*, after all this time."

"No," I say with as much dignity as I can manage.

Michael stands there, with his hands on his hips, contemplating me. He has this bewildered look. I turn away from his scrutiny and finally vomit once more before pulling myself up from the floor. I wash my hands and grab a new toothbrush from the drawer and begin brushing my teeth and continue to ignore him.

"What's the regimen? What did Lisa and Stephen put you on?" Michael finally asks.

"Adriamycin and Cytoxan," I say too easily.

I move past him, while he's still taking in what I've just told him. Intent on escaping these close quarters as I realize my mistake in telling him the regiment for AC too late.

I go to the master bedroom determined to make the bed, since I can't stand crawling into an unmade one. Of course, he follows me.

"I thought you were going to call Mathew and catch up to the kids," I say irritably. I'm at the breaking point. I don't want him to see it.

"Adriamycin and Cytoxan would only be appropriate if you had another reoccurrence," Michael says slowly. "AC is a good combination chemotherapy. Lisa and Stephen only talked about using one of those drugs, not both. And, why wasn't I *told?*"

"You're *off* the team." I see him wince.

With false bravado, fighting through the pain pulsating through the middle of my torso, I pull up the sheets and start to make the bed. I'm so tired. My whole body seems to ache. *What's wrong with me today?* Then, I remember I haven't taken any pain medication this morning. And, my hair is falling out. And, now, Michael is here asking me too many questions, when all I want to do is crawl into the bed and really, at this point, die. Truly, I do.

"Ellen Kay," Michael says unevenly.

I look up at him. Apparently, he's been helping me make the king-size bed, while I've been lost in my own feel-sorry-for-Ellie-soliloquy.

"It came back," I finally say.

The last of his resolve crumbles away. His shoulders sag and his eyes fill with tears. I'm reminded of the day with the big burly movers. I step back away from him.

"I can't take it anymore, Michael. Your *sadness. Mine.* I can't take any of it anymore!"

I move out of the room away from him. He catches up to me, of course, because I can't move that fast between being this pregnant with twins and this pain that's become unbearable by the minute. He grabs me by the arms and I cry out.

"What is wrong with you? Why are you in pain like that?" He unbuttons my blouse. "They went back in, again?" He examines the incisions as he talks to me. "A *double mas* with reconstruction? And, no one *told* me."

"*The team* was told not to say anything to you."

"By who?" Michael demands.

"By me!" My voice trembles. "Lisa. Stephen. Josh did the surgery and Tom did the reconstruction."

Michael is looking at me in utter astonishment. "When?"

"The day after you left."

I try to give him a nonchalant shrug, but the movement causes me to recoil in pain. My hands shake as I try to button my blouse, but it hurts too much to raise my arms. Michael begins buttoning it for me.

"I can't do this. I can't talk to you, not today."

"Pain level?" Michael asks.

His persistence about my pain level pisses me off.

"A fucking ten! How about that? I forgot to take my meds this morning, not that it would have mattered, since I've thrown up five times this morning already." I pull away from him "I'm too tired to fight with you."

I race down the stairs, intent on getting away from him before he sees me completely breakdown. With shaking hands, I grab a glass of water from the tap and take two pain pills. I lean against kitchen sink, wipe at my face with the back of my hand, and stare unseeing out the window.

In the stillness, I acknowledge that Michael's presence is wreaking this incredible havoc on my senses. I shake my head. It's a heady experience to have him here, even if my circumstances seem beyond dire. I wearily smile, silently admitting to the irony of all of this. I stare out at the blue-grey water on this rainy day, while the nausea still threatens. I grab a cracker from the drawer and eat it quickly, hoping to quell it a little longer. Michael comes into the kitchen. He opens the cupboard, grabs a coffee cup and fills it with hot water from the steamer. I look over at him somewhat dismayed, but curious.

"How about a cup of tea? Maybe some soup? Go sit down in the family room. I'll bring it to you." His gentle tone brings fresh tears. I turn away before he can see them.

"Fine," I say with disquiet.

In the family room, I sit down and pull an afghan around my shoulders and close my eyes for a moment and try not to think of him just thirty feet away from me. We are four months and a whole lifetime away from where we were when we said *I do* to each other.

Hearing him come into the room, I open my eyes. He carries a wooden tray laden with a steaming cup of tea, a bowl of cottage cheese, sliced apples, cubed cheddar cheese, and a bowl of hot broth. It is more food than I've been able to eat in the last three weeks and keep down, but I don't tell him this.

I just try to smile one of my yeah-team smiles, but it fails me as I stare up at him. *Michael.*

He hands me the cup of tea and sits down next to me.

"Thank you." I take a few tentative sips, just hoping I can keep it down. "It's good."

"It's tea, Ellen Kay. It isn't the cure for cancer. It doesn't excuse what I've done. How I've hurt you." Michael gets this tormented look. "It doesn't take away your pain. It's a simple combination of hot water and a tea bag, nothing more."

"It's good. Thank you." I take another sip before I set it down. "It's not going to bring back my hair," I say.

I look over at .him again, uncertain.

"Your hair will grow back."

"It won't be the same."

296

He smiles upon hearing my imitation of our six-year-old's tone. "No, it won't be the same. But…you'll be here and that's all I ever wished for."

We share this long silence between us. This sense of peace seems to steal into the room and overpower both of us at the same time.

"I'm your only wish?" I ask.

"You're the only wish I ever had." He takes my hand and brings it to his lips.

I'm the editor. I'm the one who has worked with words my entire adult life and this is the man who brings me to tears with his every time. "You're my wish, too," I say. "With our two wishes, everything else will be okay."

"I just need to be able to touch you any time I want." He reaches out and traces my lips and the racing pulse at my neck and finally smiles. He trails his fingers down the curve of my new breasts, until they come to rest on my protruding stomach. It's as if he is igniting fire along my skin; everywhere he touches comes to life. He gets this remorseful look as his hand rests against me.

"I wish for you. I choose you. All I want is you, Michael."

He tries to smile, but looks at me, all at once, powerless, I think. I have trumped him with my words. I lean over and kiss him. I slowly smile beneath his lips, knowing I've finally won the words contest.

# CHAPTER TWENTY-SIX

## Coming Together

Five days later, my hair is all gone. The Drs. Chatham have a special area of the medical spa for their chemotherapy patients facing hair loss. My head is completely shaved now. Hair loss is not an exact science. It comes out in clumps, uneven. The only real alternative is to shave it all off. The Drs. Chatham have a hair stylist on staff, who works with chemotherapy patients and fits them with scarves, wigs or simply just helps the process along by removing all their hair.

I look in the mirror with a contrived lack of interest, masking the horror I feel inside as best I can. Gianna, the hair stylist, I swear Lisa probably hired her for her exotic name, does my make-up. I stare at my face as the anxiety builds inside of me. I'm missing eyebrows, too. I can't pretend to accept this aspect of chemo. My hair meant a lot to me. It wasn't everything, but it was right up there in the list of good assets about Ellie Shaw along with the bodacious tah tahs. I stare down in anguish at my silicone replicas peeking out from my lacy white top. *This sucks.* It's something Nick would have said. Thinking of him almost makes me smile.

I should be grateful. I'm alive. I should be thankful. I have Michael. Emily and Mathew. Two babies in my future. I shouldn't cry.

I steal a glance at this bald-headed girl in the mirror and angrily wipe away the tears. Gianna leaves the room.

I take advantage of the much-wished-for privacy. I move out of the chair closer to the mirror and touch my shiny bald head. I look like a completely different person. Between being almost thirty-seven weeks pregnant and baldness, I'm officially not myself.

"Fuck," I say now to the girl in the mirror. In my reverie and disdain for what I see in the mirror, I don't realize Michael has come into the room until I look up.

"Hi," he says as he strides over to me with purpose.

"Please don't tell me that you like me better this way. I don't think I could take it."

"Okay, I won't," Michael promises. He takes me into his arms and leans down and kisses me. "I just thought we should just get this over with, right away, so you don't start going into this serious doubting process about how I feel about you, even without your hair." He kisses me again, even more passionate than the last time and I kiss him back with reluctance. "Ellen Kay, you're not trying very hard," he lifts his head from my face, inspecting me. *Waiting.*

"Sorry, I just got shorn like a dog and I don't feel very sexy. So fucking sorry about that," I snap at him and move away out of his reach.

"How much more do you have to do here?" Michael gives me this wide grin as if he has a secret that he is just about ready to tell.

"I don't know. She wants to show me how to fit the wig, apply eyebrows of some sort. Tie scarves around my head. Another hour, I guess."

"All right. I'll be back in forty-five minutes. It's a date."

Michael starts to leave. At the open doorway, he blows me a kiss. I wave him off and refuse to smile. These insecurities about my appearance still get the best of me, despite Michael's love and reassurance.

The last five days together have been amazing, but today I struggle to hold on to any of that happiness. Today, happiness eludes me as I stare at my bald self in the mirror.

A few minutes later, Gianna returns, carrying a long honey-blonde wig to replicate the head of hair I have just lost. She fits the wig on my head and begins cutting the hair into the style of the picture of me that I have shown her. The wig comes in one long length and within a half hour she has replicated my longish style with some subtle layering. With each passing minute, I look a little bit more like my former self.

I'm surprised and intrigued, when she applies replacement eyebrows in a golden-blonde shade and am amazed at how natural they look. She shows me how to do this for myself as well. These will apparently last for up to four months, if I'm careful about showering and avoid swimming pools. Each touch she adds brings me closer to my former self, to Ellie Shaw.

Begrudgingly, I'm pleased with the eyebrows and the wig. I'm not one of those selfless, humble women that can walk around proud of my bald status, this much I do know about myself. And, even though I might be married to the most understanding man in the entire universe, I'm grateful for the semblance of normalcy that eyebrows and the wig provide. I stare at a closer version of myself in the mirror. It's been days since I've seen her. I finally smile.

"Just thought I'd check in." Lisa sails through the door. "Looking good, Ellie Shaw." She gives me a wide smile and I give her one of my better yeah-team ones.

"Gianna is a miracle worker, I must say."

"She's the best." Lisa winks over at Gianna and comes to stand next to me. "It looks great! How do you feel?"

"Better. Had long moments of sadness, but I feel better with the eyebrows and the wig. It's going to be okay," I pronounce with a slight laugh.

"Gianna, are you done with our best client? I'd like to borrow her for a few minutes."

"Yes, Dr. Chatham, Mrs. Shaw is ready to go."

I thank Gianna with a grateful smile. Then, follow Lisa out the door and walk along the hallway, consciously fingering my fake hair. We enter one of the spa exam rooms. I look over at Lisa in surprise.

"What's up?" I was just in three days ago for the gynecological visit with her.

"Well, based on what I think your husband has planned for you this afternoon, I thought I would check up on my patient." Lisa gives me a strange look.

"What?"

"Michael has plans, Ellie. He's taking you away for the night to some romantic place downtown."

"And you're spoiling this surprise because—?"

"I'd like to keep these babies inside your uterus as long as possible."

"You're a real killjoy, you know that?"

"Disrobe. I'll be back in five," Lisa commands.

I strip out of my clothes and put the examination gown on, fuming all the while. Dr. Lisa Chatham could be really impossible some days and today was one of those. I'm excited at the prospect of spending the afternoon with Michael and Lisa has just unceremoniously destroyed the surprise.

With a quick knock, Lisa steals back into the room. "How do you feel, baby-wise?"

"Pregnant. Very." I sigh and lay back on the examination table.

"Besides that. Any back pain? Cramping? Anything unusual?"

"Not really. I mean my back has been killing me for a while. It's hard to find a comfortable position to sleep in at night, since I'm as big as house now." I stop talking and hold my breath, while Lisa examines me.

"That's what I thought. You're fifty percent effaced and two centimeters dilated."

"Okay, remind me about what that means? Exactly?"

"It means your romantic rendezvous just got cancelled. I'm putting you on full-time bed rest. And, Ellie, you better start picking out some names."

"What? It's June 19ᵗʰ. I've got another two weeks."

"No. You don't." She's shaking her head now. "You're not going to go full-term. If we can buy another week with full bed rest; I'll take it. But, I doubt we get that much time. My preference would be to have you close by. What are the chances of that?"

"I don't know." A new kind of terror takes hold. I'm really not prepared to have these babies. We haven't spent enough time getting ready. "Let me think," I murmur to Lisa.

"Why don't you get dressed and we'll wait and talk to Michael." Lisa tries to give me her version of a yeah-team smile. I roll my eyes at her as she leaves.

I dress in record time and adjust my wig in the mirror. In all this time, during this whole pregnancy, I haven't taken more than a moment to think about the ramifications of having a baby, to say nothing of the fact, that we're having twins. Drained, I sit down in the chair next to the bed and rest my head at the back of the chair and close my eyes trying to quell the rising panic inside of me.

The door swings open. "Michael," I whisper.

He's over to me in a matter of seconds. "Ellie, what is it?"

"I have to go on full bed rest," I say in this forlorn voice. "Lisa thinks we have a week, if we're lucky, before we have twins. *Twins*, Michael. Oh my God."

"Babe, it's going to be okay. You're hair looks great, by the way." He laces a few stands between his fingers, as he kneels in front of me. He pulls me forward and kisses me.

"Sex is out of the question, Dr. Shaw," Lisa says in this nun-like voice, as she enters the room, spying Michael and me.

"So I hear," Michael says, as he smiles only at me. "We'll just have to find something else to do." His adoring look comforts me in this mysterious way. I reach out to trace his face.

"She's two centimeters dilated and fifty percent effaced. She is on full-time bed rest, as of now. So, you can cancel your hotel room and take her home. Or, you can check her into the hotel room, which I hope is nearby the hospital and we wait."

"Bed-rest in a hotel room?" Michael asks, looking over at Lisa with a quizzical glance.

"I'm not a fan of the ferry system and am not interested in de-livering these babies anywhere else, but here."

"Okay. Can she at least go home for tonight and say goodbye to the kids and her mother?"

"It's not my favorite option, but I guess for one night I'm okay with that, as long as I have your word that she is back within the vicinity of the hospital beginning tomorrow.

"Okay. Ellie, are you good with that plan?" He refocuses on me. I nod, grab Michael's hand and try to smile.

"I guess I don't understand why you have to go away," Emily says to us, now.

Everyone is gathered in the confines of our master bedroom. It seems Michael is intent on full bed rest being exactly that. All five of us, including my mother, have enjoyed pizza on top of the king-size bed.

I'm propped up on pillows and being treated like an invalid, which I haven't allowed throughout the past eight months in any form whatsoever. I'm in awe. A combination of things seems to be going on here. We seem to be reforming as a family and given the turmoil of the last month and the cataclysmic loss of Nick and Elaina four months before; it is the witnessing of some kind of miracle. We're finally coming together again with a different make-up, but a family, nonetheless. I don't even think my latest foray with chemo and cancer has any impact on what is going on this master bedroom tonight. Something new is taking place. Something different has happened. The birth of the twins is something wonderful. Its sudden reality transforms my little family right here in this very room. The excitement and the anticipation of these new babies emanates from every person here.

I hold out my arms for Emily and she gratefully tucks herself into them. I look over her head at Michael and smile. Mathew stands at the foot of the bed, unsure of what to do. I know there's a secret part of him that would like to join his sister and be right next to me, but teenage pride prevents him from doing this.

"Mattie, can you get me a glass of ice water?" I ask. I reach out and grab his hand and he grins back.

My mother hovers, but begins clearing paper plates and the pizza box. I think she is still in a state of shock that we shared pizza on top of my duvet.

"Mom," I say. "You don't have to do that."

"Ellen Kay, you're on bed rest. I will do whatever I want," she says with a slight sniff. She picks up the last remnants of dinner and follows Mathew out the bedroom door.

"I don't see why Michael gets to go to the hotel and stay with you. Yet, we have to stay with grandma."

"Well, Em, you and Mathew still have another week of school before summer break. Michael and I are married. This is what married couples do to prepare for their babies. We wait together, until the babies get here. Michael is working at the hospital, so he'll work during the day and then come to the hotel and be with me at night. The twins are his babies too, so it's only fair that he's there with me and gets to see them first."

I look over at Michael, who is beaming and has been, since we left Lisa's. Like so many things I've missed, I've never stopped to take note of how happy and excited Michael is to become a father, in the most profound, biological sense. These babies mean so much to him. It shows in every gesture and every facial expression that crosses his handsome face right now.

I'm still fighting the edges of panic. I know what the arrival of a newborn entails and I am having two. Somehow, this has only resonated with me within the past couple of hours. And, when I should be rushing around and getting all the last minute preparations done, I'm now on full bed rest and married to a doctor who is following Lisa's decree to the letter.

"Emily, why don't you go put your pajamas on and bring back a book I can read to you? I need to talk to Michael for a few minutes alone." My six-year-old slides off the bed with reluctant compliance and heads down the hallway with a slight protest, not wanting to leave me.

Michael moves across to be right next to me on top of the covers. "What's up, Mrs. Shaw?"

"Don't tease me, if you can't follow through." I give him a demure smile, but it fades a moment later as I give in to the incessant worry about having two babies. "I need to get a list going of what we still need for the babies' nursery. I didn't get everything done and now, I don't see how it's going to get done."

"You're worrying about the nursery?" Michael asks in surprise.

"Yes," I say in a defensive tone. "I haven't even washed their little onesie things or their pajamas. We're going to come home and it's going to be utter chaos and I'm going to be exhausted and feeding them all the time and I won't feel like doing the laundry and washing up all the onesie things, then. And you have to use special detergent and I haven't purchased that, yet."

"Now, you're freaking me out," Michael says. He kisses my forehead. "It's going to be okay, Ellie, I promise.

"You promise," I say. "And you know this because you're a brilliant surgeon?"

"No. Because I love you and I feel better knowing I can touch you any time I want." With that, he traces my face with his finger and then kisses my left temple. "I'll go to the store and buy the onesie things and the detergent, tomorrow. I promise."

I close my eyes and savor his touch. I wrap my arms around him and pull him to me. Our kissing would lead to more; I'm sure of it, but then there's my mother's voice echoing from the hallway.

"A hotel might be a great idea," Michael says in my ear. He pulls away from me with reluctance and slides off the other side of the bed, just as my mother enters the room.

It's late that evening when we're getting ready for bed when Michael's looking at me in this remarkable way as I remove the wig from my head and set it on the vanity. Self-conscious, I climb into bed, wearing one of his old t-shirts, carrying one of my manuscripts, intent on getting it finished.

"What?" I ask, shy all at once by the look on his face.

He doesn't say anything. He just comes over, sits down on the edge of the bed, takes the blue pencil and document from my hands and sets them on the night stand. I lay back and he begins to trace my jaw line, my lips, and my bald head.

"You're turned on by this; aren't you?" I ask, incredulous.

He just nods and pulls my hand to where I can feel him. "You're amazingly beautiful," Michael says in awe. "I've always known this, but now? I don't know. Your eyes sparkle like a glacier hit by the sun and your mouth is this sensual wonder and your head is this ideal shape; I just want to touch you all the time. It's all very moving, amazing really." He kisses me and then groans. "God, Ellie, I can't take it."

I smile beneath his lips and kiss him more fervently. He slides into the covers right next to me.

We move into each other, like synchronized swimmers performing a familiar dance that feels almost spiritual. We only pause for a moment.

"You know this is going to get us in trouble with Lisa. She'll know exactly what we did."

"We don't have to if you don't want to," he says without much conviction.

I stare into his amazing blue eyes and feel overwhelmed by the love I see there. I slowly smile.

"Oh I want to. I most definitely want you."

# CHAPTER TWENTY-SEVEN

 New Wishes

abies arrive in the world in their own way, despite the best of plans. I awaken ten minutes after three in the morning to the steady build-up of pain in a familiar area of my body as contractions come on just like that. And, I vaguely remember going fast with Emily six years before and tell Michael this as we climb out of bed. Michael's on the phone within the next two minutes to the hospital, to the Chatham's. After that, he openly curses the ferry system and displays an unbelievable run of panic that I've never seen from him before.

I'm the calm one. I'm packing the suitcase with his clothes and mine, baby pajamas, diapers and bottles. I'm serenity, itself, as we awaken Emily and Mathew and my mother and remind them of their schedule for the day and promise to call as soon as we have news. We catch the first ferry to Seattle at 4:45 a.m. after last good-byes and kisses to my two sleepy children and my hand-wringing mother.

I'm epitome of tranquility, itself, as the pain seems to coordinate with the building waves of Puget Sound as we cross to the other side to downtown Seattle. Michael races through the empty streets at the ready to run red lights. I'm the one who says in the most soothing voice, "It's going to be okay. Everything's fine. We're almost there, baby."

The next twenty-four hours are a whirlwind. There's the crescendo of excruciating pain I'd forgotten from six years before. Then, the deliverance of an epidural which I audaciously bless, and the endless anticipation while we wait. The grand finale for all of this—this inexplicable joy—overrides all the roller coaster emotions that have come before, when baby boy Shaw and baby girl Shaw enter our world.

We've had weeks to come up with names. *Weeks*. Our babies are here, sleeping in their little bassinets right by my hospital bed; *nameless*. It is the middle of the next night. They are twelve hours old and nameless. I stare over at them in awe. Our babies are beautiful with their wisps of golden blonde hair so much like Michael's. Their little hands and fingers twitch with deep sleep. I watch each steady breath. I can't quite believe they're here. I can't quite believe they're perfect. I can't quite believe they're ours. Michael's and mine. With all the heartbreak and loss of these past months, I can't believe the elation I experience in just looking at them now. They're here. Our nameless babies are here.

"You're supposed to be sleeping," Michael admonishes as he comes into the room and slides in beside me in the bed. His finger trails along my face and he wipes away a stray tear from my left cheek.

"I can't sleep." I see his head nodding in the dark above mine.

"Too much excitement for one day, isn't it?" Michael leans down and kisses me gently. "Six weeks is going to be a long time." I hear the impatience in his voice.

"We'll just have to stay busy," I confide, smiling in the dark at him. "Are you going to tell me what names you've come up with?"

"Ellen Kay, I told you; it's up to you."

"Michael, I need you to tell me what you're thinking of in the way of names. These are our children. We have a son and a daughter. What do you want to name them?"

I watch Michael's face in the semi-darkness. He seems uncertain. "What's wrong?"

"I keep thinking of Elaina and Nick. I'm happy and sad at the same time. Everything is just so surreal, right now." He lays his head down next to mine.

"I know," I whisper back. My whole body aches with this dull throbbing pain from my upper torso to my inner thighs. I shift my body slightly and let out a little moan.

"Pain level?" Michael asks, raising his head; he stares at me.

"About an eight." He moves off the hospital bed and disappears through the door. A few minutes later, he returns with the night nurse, who hands me a glass of water and drop two white tablets in my hand.

"Mrs. Shaw, if there is anything else, just turn on your light." I give the nurse a grateful smile. She smiles, first at me, a little sheepish, I think, and then at Michael and bids us both good night. Michael gives me a guilty grin, as he removes his shoes and climbs back into bed with me. Somehow, I know that he has intimidated the nursing staff, just by being the great Dr. Michael Shaw.

"Let's get some sleep. The babies aren't going to even know if they're not named by the time we take them home. I'll try and think of some names some time tomorrow," Michael says with a yawn. I snuggle into him closer. The pain medication begins to take effect and brings some relief. I kiss the top of his golden head.

"Tomorrow," I say.

With enough pain medication, I can hold one of the babies and its bottle at the same time. It is a thrilling experience. I'm holding Baby Boy Shaw. The nurses have begun calling him that, since as his parents, we're still inept at naming children.

I stare down at my newborn son in wonder. He is amazing to watch, so keenly aware. Is this even possible for a newborn? He has these beautiful tufts of golden hair and these beautiful eyes that seem to look straight through me, as he sucks the bottle of formula. I have this moment of regret that I cannot breast-feed this baby and, as if to reassure me, he reaches up with his delicate fingers and touches mine where I hold his bottle.

This child is a wonder. I'm transfixed. He is so beautiful.

"What about Beau?" I look over at Michael. He's feeding Baby Girl Shaw also named by the nursing staff. "Beaumont Michael Shaw?"

Michael looks over at me in surprise and then grins. "Okay, I wasn't ever going to tell you this, but I always wanted a son named Beau. Can you imagine a sportscaster announcing the name Beaumont Shaw across the loudspeaker? It'd be awesome."

Michael has this look of elation that is hard to describe. I've never seen him quite like this before.

"Okay, Beaumont Michael Shaw it is. That's one. One more name to go." I give him a former-UW-cheerleader-yeah-team smile.

"Ellen Kay, you've got to stop smiling at me like that. It's already hard enough," Michael looks over at me with this longing; I just laugh and try to concentrate on Beau.

The naming of baby girl Shaw has taken on a new urgency. Emily has been to visit and already announced that if we can't come up with a name, she likes the name Giselle. I cannot name my second baby girl Giselle after a Disney film. The reasons add up to many.

We are waiting for Lisa to come by and pronounce us all fit to go home. The pediatrician has already been by and authorized the release of the babies. I'm anxious to go. I want to sleep in my own bed. With Michael. Start our life. I want to put my babies down to sleep in their nursery and just watch them in endless wonder. Michael is amazingly calm. He seems like a man of many secrets as he stares at me now. We're trying to entertain ourselves by watching some old classic movie on the television in the corner, but we're both restless.

The babies are both asleep. Beau is holding one hand up in mid-air. His little fingers curl around. He weighs eight pounds; a giant compared to his little twin sister weighing in at just five pounds, but they're both healthy and just fine. Baby girl Shaw just needs a name.

"Ava, A-V-A," Michael says softly. "Ava Katherine Shaw."

I glance over at him. "I love the name Ava. When did you get so good at this?"

"I think you're an inspiration," Michael says with a meaningful glance. I laugh.

"So, what's the verdict?" Lisa asks as she walks into the hospital room.

"Meet Beaumont Michael Shaw and Ava Katherine Shaw," I say.

"Wow! Beaumont and Ava, those are beautiful names."

"Well, Michael is the man of the hour in naming our children," I say now. Lisa glances over at Michael, all the while, shaking her head.

"Well, Dr. Shaw, you really are a charmer. I almost feel sorry for you having to wait for the next six weeks." Lisa looks at him deliberately as she signs off the paperwork that allows us to go home.

I'm in shock just loading the car because Michael has replaced his black Lexus SUV with something bigger. I'm not sure I will even be able to drive this white boat of a car and I tell him this now. He tells me proudly that it seats up to eight passengers.

"I guess I'm glad it's not a van," I say with hesitation.

I covertly watch Michael, while he puts Beau in one of the car seats. Next, he takes Ava from me and buckles her in as well naturally tucking in the baby blankets that somehow were miraculously sitting on the seat. Pure joy lights up his face; he's thrilled to be taking all of us home. I get caught up in his excitement and quell my uncertainty about the car.

"I love you so much." Michael brushes my forehead with his lips and leans down to kiss me. I snake my arms up around his shoulders and bring him even closer, ignoring the pain in my chest that this action causes.

"Michael, you're my only wish," I say against his lips. I can feel him smile beneath mine.

"You're mine," he says back to me with a wide grin.

He makes his way through downtown Seattle and gets in line for the Bainbridge Island ferry. I've already called home to let my mother and the kids know that we are on our way. There's a lot of noise in the background when I call and I'm surprised at this. Michael just gives me one of his angelic smiles, when I ask what's going on at the house.

During the ferry ride, the twins nap and I move over from the passenger side to rest in Michael's arms. We talk briefly about getting a nanny and Michael asserts he has some ideas around this already. I nod, but I can barely stay awake as the lull of the waves of Puget Sound and my sleepless night catch up to me. Plus, my husband is stroking my face with his fingers and the rhythm is taking me under.

"Get some sleep, Ellie."

His voice is the last thing I hear as I drift off, lulled by the quiet interlude and sound of the waves lapping the ferry boat.

I wake up as Michael starts the car. For a moment, I'm unsure where I'm at. I sit up and slide over to my side of the car and buckle my seat belt. I pull the mirror down and fix the wig, which has become slightly askew with my nap. I glance over at Michael, while he drives off the ferry and onto our road toward home.

"What?" I ask with a sheepish grin.

"Let's just say, I'm glad we're finally going home."

"Me too." I turn towards the twins and see they are still asleep. We may be able to make it all the way to home without a crying baby. I don't really have new mom status. I have borne three other children, but I'm a bit rusty and slightly intimidated at almost thirty-nine-years of age. "Um…Lisa mentioned discussing birth control in the next month or so. I guess the pill is out because of the cancer and a relation to hormones? I don't know."

"And, we're having this discussion, now, because?" Michael asks with a laugh.

"We're alone. We may not have a single moment alone for the next month or so," I say with a grin.

"We'll use the car as a refuge, then."

"I like the sound of that." I flash him one of my winning smiles and watch a look of consternation cross his face while he navigates the road toward home.

"Babe, we just had twins. I'm not ready to talk about birth control."

"Why not? I mean Michael; we're going to have our hands full."

"Maybe, we'll have more kids."

"You *can't* be serious."

"I think a big family with you would be great." He gives me this devilish grin.

"You haven't seen me with a big family, yet," I say in sudden alarm. "Four kids, Michael. *Four.*"

"I've seen you with four kids before," he says quietly. "At Nick's basketball game."

I'm transported back to January just like that. I have to look away from him so he won't see my tears. I feel him reach for me and I take his hand without looking at him.

"Ellie, I miss them, too."

I can only nod, but I still won't look at him.

"It's so hard. I want them here. I want them here with us," I finally say.

"I know. Me, too. I want them here, too, Ellie."

We share silence, as Michael drives the new SUV down the long drive toward the beach house. The house is all lit up and somehow I know that the luxury of taking an afternoon nap just evaporated. There are numerous cars in the circular drive in front of the house. We have a welcoming committee. I recognize Robert and Carrie's car and a few others. I look over at Michael and he gives me a studied look.

"I figure we should give them what they want for the first hour or so and then we can settle in by ourselves."

"You think they'll actually leave?" I ask.

"I hope so," Michael says with a hesitant laugh.

I finger my wig with sudden self consciousness. The only ones I've seen lately are Emily and Mathew and my mother and my doctors. Everyone will get to see the transformed Ellie Shaw.

"You look great," Michael says.

The man can read my mind like no other. Yet, uncertainty plagues me.

# CHAPTER TWENTY-EIGHT

## In The Matter of Trust

*T*am unprepared for what awaits us inside as we each transport a bundled up Baby inside the beach house. There are people everywhere. Who authorized this? I try to smile as I'm hugged by Carrie, then Robert, Marjorie Bingham, Mr. and Mrs. Avery our neighbors to the south of us, my mother, Michael's parents, who normally don't make the ferry ride from North Seattle to Bainbridge. I spy a few friends of Mathew's, even Emily has a friend over. I'm disconcerted by the scene that greets us as soon as we walk through the door.

Beau and Ava are now awake, unceremoniously awakened, with all the cries of joy and greetings of our guests, as we step into our living room. Carrie's walking around with Ava, holding her up in the air and gushing over her. I experience uncertainty, even distrust of her, just watching as she carries my baby daughter all around. Marjorie Bingham picks up little Beau and oohs and aahs over him and I try not to cringe. *Ungrateful. Undone. That's me.* Michael's arm comes around my shoulders and I look up in dismay.

"Let's get changed upstairs," Michael says to me. He pulls me along towards the stairs. I go with reluctance, feeling this surge of helplessness and this ridiculous anger course through me.

I force myself to smile. We traverse the stairs and the hallway toward our bedroom, away from the frenetic activity below in our living room, away from my older children, away from my babies for the first time since they were born and sadness follows. Once in our bedroom, he closes and locks the door and leans against it. He studies me as I stalk across the room away from him.

There is nowhere inside of me to put these competing emotions of rage and jealousy and sadness. I look over at Michael as I strive for some form of control, but I feel powerless to contain it.

"I'm sorry, Ellie. They wanted to help and I thought that it would be…I didn't know it would be so chaotic. I'm sorry."

Exhaustion overtakes me. Tears well up on my lashes and I know I am about to cry for a multitude of reasons that Michael will not understand. I know all of this.

I turn away from him and head to the closet to find clothes to change into. Can I wear something besides maternity clothes, now? The errant thought gives me enough pause to prevent a crying jag.

Michael comes up behind me and gently puts his arms around me. "I'm sorry," he says again. "I didn't think it would be so… overwhelming. I didn't mean to upset you. They wanted to help, to be here."

"I know. I'm sorry for being such a baby. I'm sorry for being unreasonable. I know that all those people down there are just thrilled to be a part of all of this as you and I are. I know that." I turn into Michael's open arms and feel them gather around me. "I love you, Michael." I bury my face in his shirt and listen for his heart beat striving to feel his assurance.

"Let's just have them help out for an hour or so. Let them do their thing and then they'll leave. I was thinking Robert and Carrie can take Mathew and Emily with them and that would give us a day to acclimate with the twins. Are you okay with that?"

"I don't know. Are we excluding them too much? Maybe, we should leave it up to them. If they want to stay and help, that would be great, too. I don't know…maybe I'm over thinking it. Maybe, it would be best for them to be with Robert."

"I think, you're exhausted and I think we should take up any offer of help that we can get. Mathew and Emily will have plenty of time to be with the twins and us, but . . . Ellie, you really need to get your rest. I know you didn't sleep most of last night."

I look up at Michael and nod. "I am exhausted." The tears stream down my face. "I'm so tired I can barely stand." He carries me over to the bed and sets me down, takes off my shoes and helps me shimmy out of my jeans. He brings over a pair of pajamas and begins putting them on. "What about all those people?"

"I'll take care of it. I'll be back in a few minutes with a cup of tea. Just close your eyes and rest until I get back."

Michael kisses my forehead and disappears through the doorway. I close my eyes and long for sleep, but all I can see is Nick's handsome face.

I cannot explain why, today of all days, grief transports me back to despair. If I'm not seeing Nick's face, I'm seeing Elaina's. Sleep eludes me as this overwhelming sorrow takes hold. Fifteen minutes later, I'm back out of bed, dressing in an old pair of jeans, and pulling on a sweater and slipping into sandals. I fix my make-up and apply lipstick and ensure my wig's in place and head downstairs.

I take the tea off the tray that Michael's been busy preparing. He looks over at me in consternation. "I thought you were going to take a nap?"

"Later," I say with a yeah-team smile. It's not one of my best and I think he knows this, but he walks over to me and kisses me, apparently unconcerned with the audience that watches us from everywhere.

"You and I will take a nap a little later," he whispers.

I hug him back, then move out of his arms intent on finding Robert. I want to solidify the plans with Emily and Mathew first.

Surprisingly, Robert is just as intent on finding me as I am him.

He pulls me into the office off of the family room. His face is serious and troubled.

"What's up?" I ask. He's looking at me strangely as if afraid of how to begin. This is alarming. The man is rarely at a loss for words.

"We've had an offer on the house," Robert says to me now.

He studies my face as I respond with, "That's great news."

"Four hundred thousand more than the asking price."

"*What?* Why would someone offer so much above the asking price for our house?"

"I don't know. It's an all cash deal. I've done some checking and the transaction is being done through a law firm downtown. The client has requested anonymity."

"Okay. Do we care? I mean four hundred thousand more is a lot of money, Robert. I know that Michael has been taking care of all the medical bills, but I'm sure we could really use the money."

"Yeah, Michael and I have talked about that. I don't want you to worry about the loan. He can pay me back whenever it's convenient."

"What *loan?*"

"Oh. Oh God, I thought he told you. Oh, Ellie, okay this is...I told him to talk to you about this. I don't understand why he would keep this from you. You always took on the finances with us. Well..." he says with a sigh. "You should really talk to Michael."

"I intend to," I say cutting him off. "But, right now, I'm talking to *you*. What loan? For how much?" My tone is all business and I know Bobby knows this.

"I loaned him two hundred thousand, a few months ago...while you were...away. It was, well, he got into trouble between buying the house, the medical bills, and not being able to perform surgery. He was completely stressed out about all of it, whether you were coming back or not. I can't believe he didn't tell you."

I sway on my feet from exhaustion. I try to make sense of what Bobby's saying to me, reeling with the news that Michael hasn't said anything about a loan. "Okay, so we sell the house to this anonymous buyer. We need to do this. Michael and I owe you money."

"I don't want you to worry about that…" Robert begins.

"No. I appreciate what you've done. You know that. It's just, well; we need to retire our debts, obviously. This house didn't come cheap. We need the money to right our finances. God knows neither one of us needs the other house. You don't want it; do you?"

"Not enough to walk away from an extra four hundred thousand." Robert smiles at me now. "We'll clear most of the $1.8 million. I mean it's enough money to do a lot of things with."

I nod. "Fine. Let's sell it, then."

"Do you want to talk to Michael, first?"

"No. This is our house. Our deal. I'll tell him, when I can hand him the check."

"It won't take that long. I've got a friend of mine, who handles real estate transactions that can work with this law firm. We can wrap this up in a matter of days. I'll call you when it's done."

"Okay."

"What did you want to talk to me about?" Robert asks with a curious smile.

"Can you take Mathew and Emily with you and Carrie? Michael and I have a few things to work out and we'd like to concentrate on getting the twins settled."

"Sure." I watch my ex-husband hesitate for a moment. "Ellie? I just want you to know how glad Carrie and I are that you're doing okay." He looks worried. "You're okay now; right?"

"I'm doing great. I'm fine." I walk over and hug him and he hugs me back. "Thank you." I hear his sigh of relief. "Bobby, you worry too much," I say in the awkward silence between us. He smiles again as he hesitates at the doorway.

"You're quite something, Ellie," he says to me now.

I try to smile, but just shake my head.

"Not really," I say.

The distant cry of a newborn adds to the muted crowd noise. I follow Robert back out to the family room, where the majority of our visitors are gathered, only to find a flustered Michael trying to prepare bottles for Beau and Ava. I retrieve the formula from Michael's unsteady hands, fill the bottles, and add the spring water that we picked up earlier. He watches me, as if trying to memorize the steps, as I heat the bottles one at a time in the microwave.

"We should probably be steaming these in a pan of water on the stove, but no sense in making Beau wait," I say to Michael. He nods at me and I try to smile back. Carrie brings Beau over to me.

"I thought you'd want to do his first feeding at home," Carrie says. I take my baby from her.

"You thought right," I say with a slight edge.

Carrie is a complication that I'm really unprepared for in person. We've done all our communicating via cell phone or e-mail. Seeing her brings back all this hurt, anger, and profound feeling of betrayal. I glance over at Michael, who's intently watching me in this little exchange with Carrie. He gives me a measured look; I turn away.

"I'll get Ava," he says.

I hand him the bottle and head off to the living room. Within a few minutes, Michael joins me and sits with Ava in the chair opposite of mine.

I concentrate on Beau for a few moments taking in his beautiful features. Beau rests his little wrinkled hand over mine. He's a charmer already; it reminds me of Nick. I kiss his forehead.

"I talked to Robert. He and Carrie will take Mathew and Emily. It's all settled." I try to keep my voice even and my tone light, but even I can hear the anger there. Michael looks over at me in surprise.

Beau finishes his bottle and I set it down and put him over my shoulder and ignore the ache in my chest as I do so and head upstairs, knowing Michael will soon follow. Within a few minutes, both the twins are changed and already sleeping in their baby cribs. Michael and I stand over them for a while in silence. Then, I slip away with Michael close behind me now.

"You're pissed at me, about what, exactly?" Michael asks defensive all at once.

I just nod and say, "I can't talk to you, right now. We have twenty-five guests, but yeah, as soon as they're gone, you and I are going to chat."

I leave him standing there in utter astonishment; his mouth half open. I can see that he has no idea that I know about the loan from Robert. It makes me wonder what else he is keeping from me. The distrust seeps back in between us, just like that.

Mathew and Emily are both disappointed they're going back with Carrie and Robert. My two oldest children protest loudly as they gather up their overnight bags with a change of school clothes and pajamas. I almost give in to keep them here, but the prevailing thought that Michael and I really need to have this night to ourselves wins out.

Fatigue begins to take over, but I steel myself against it.

My mother is also a bit reticent about leaving us, but I already arranged earlier in the week for her to catch a flight back to Arizona and I'm insistent that we keep to those plans. I convince her that she'll have plenty of time over the summer to stay with us and enjoy all the children. I can tell that she is worn out and so am I. Her visit of a month was longer that we both anticipated. I know she's anxious to return to her life and her friends in Arizona. Michael's parents have volunteered to take her to the airport. With teary goodbyes, the three proud grandparents leave the beach house with a promise to return in the next few weeks. Most of the well-wishers have gone, leaving behind baby gifts and promises to visit again soon. I fix a smile on my face as some of them leave.

Carrie gives me an imploring look and I know she wants to have a deeper discussion about us, our friendship or lack thereof. I cannot deal with Carrie tonight and I think my weariness conveys this. She promises to call me in the next couple of days and I absently nod, knowing she will hold me to this.

Covertly, I watch the stilted interaction between her and Michael, judging every action between them and looking for some hidden attraction or message. *Infidelity wreaks damage long after it ends.* I frown at the irony of this thought and turn away from all of them and call out a final goodbye.

Michael makes a point of avoiding our upcoming discussion and heads in the direction of the garage with some excuse about getting something in his car. I shrug indifferently and just watch him go.

Neither one of us seems willing to get into a heated discussion tonight. We should be happy and excited to have the twins here with us; and yet, distrust seeps in between us again.

I move through the house at a listless pace popping a couple of pain pills as I go. Sad, all at once.

Within fifteen minutes of perusing our home office, I've added up our mounting debt and all outstanding medical bills. It isn't just my multiple surgeries. It's the chemotherapy, the various medications, and the never ending doctor visits.

It appears that my team has given us a substantial discount on everything, but bodacious tah tahs and saving my life and trying to save Elaina's has been expensive. The hospital has no forgiveness for money owed, even when the patients die, the numbers add up quickly to over three hundred thousand dollars. It looks like insurance will cover most of it, but there's some confusion in what Robert's insurance is paying for when we were married and what Michael's will cover, since his insurance company considers my condition pre-existing when he put me on his medical plan.

It appears that my little editor's job with its insurance coverage may cover more of the costs than Michael's. I smile bitterly to myself. My little editor's job has never really resonated with anyone, never with Bobby and not even Michael.

All said and done, we'll still be paying out almost seventy-five thousand dollars. My mind flashes to the new white SUV and the sailboat. I hate being in debt. Bobby always understood this; Michael, obviously, doesn't.

In the family room, I stare at their silver urns on the mantel, then, carry one under each arm even though my chest aches with pain. Sitting in the darkened living room, I have this whispered conversation with both of them, as if they're still with us.

I tell Nick and Elaina about the twins; how we struggled to come up with names, but Beau and Ava seem so right. I talk about Mathew and Emily and confess my worries about their possible struggle with all the changes that's been brought in our lives without them. "It's hard," I say to the answering stillness. "We miss you both so much. I'm just glad you're together. It makes me happy to know that you two are together. It makes it bearable." I start to cry.

I sense Michael. When I open my eyes, he's coming to kneel in front of me. He lays his head down in my lap. I stroke his golden head. After a few minutes, he takes the urns from me and sets them down on the coffee table. Then, he comes to sit beside me and holds my hand.

"Are you going to tell me what's going on?"

"I know about the loan from Robert," I say in a low voice.

He sighs heavily. "I didn't...want to worry you."

"I know. But, you should have told me. We need to be a partnership. I took care of all the financial stuff with Robert and it's my fault for not paying any attention to it, what with Nick and Elaina. Then with you and Carrie and my leaving, well, everything got messed up. I'm sorry that you had to carry the financial burden for all of this by yourself."

"It's okay. You've had everything else to deal with."

"It's not okay." I turn to him and take his face in my hands. "Michael, we have to work on things together. We have to talk about things. You can't go out and buy a sailboat with Robert or buy a new car without telling me. We have to work together, discuss these things."

"What? I have to ask your permission?"

"It's not like that. It's just we can't afford a new car, right now. We have debt. *Tons* of it."

"I'll take care of it. I'll do more surgery, take on more patients."

"Michael." I grab his arm. "That's not the answer. We have to live within our means. Plan for things. We have two more children, more expenses. We just have to work together and plan it out." I hesitate at the look of determination in his eyes. "I'll talk to Bobby."

"Why would you involve him? This is our business. I can provide for you."

"Michael. This is a partnership. *Us. Together.*" I'm just about to tell him about selling the old house, knowing this will solve most of our financial issues when he gets up abruptly.

"This is about *Carrie*." He gets this wounded look and paces the floor. "I know you don't trust me."

"That's not it." Though what he's saying starts to resonate with me. Distrust of him returns full force, especially since he's the one bringing up Carrie.

"Yes it is. I saw the look you gave us when she said goodbye to me. I know I have to earn your trust back. I *know*."

"I don't want to have this conversation."

"We *need* to have this conversation. When would you like to have it? When Mathew and Emily are here? You feel it; don't you?

It's still as if it could all fall apart tomorrow. You think I don't wonder if Court Chandler will just show up one day and take you away from all of this. You think I *trust* you, Ellen Kay? Think again!" Michael moves away from me to the far end of the room.

"Michael, why would you bring up Court Chandler? Why now?"

"Because he haunts me. Every day. Every day, I wonder if this is the day that he'll come back into your life and take you away. He loves you. I *know* that. I can't do anything about it because, on some insane level, I understand it. I love you, too."

"It's crazy to love me? Is that it? I don't even *think* about Court Chandler." My face betrays me with a sudden flush even as I say this. Michael winces.

"Don't lie to me, Ellen Kay. Don't lie!" I hear his heavy breathing and feel the panic rise in me with his anger. "So, you don't answer his texts?" He grasps my forearms, compelling me to tell him.

"Noooooo." Just my tone gives me away. I pull away from his grasp, even as it causes me pain with the sudden movement.

"Don't lie to me," he says.

I lash out, feeling exposed by his accusations, assailed by the flashback of him and Carrie—the action that started all of this. "You broke us, Michael. Damn you."

"Yeah, damn me. It always comes back to me and what I did. I've told you, I'm sorry, a thousand times. And, I am. But, Ellie, are *you*?"

"Of course."

"You're lying. That's the thing, Ellen Kay, I'm *sorry* for what I've done, but *you*? You would go back to him in a heartbeat if he asked."

"That's not true." The tears steam down my face. "It's not true, Michael."

But, even as I say this, it's clear that neither one of us believes it. We turn away from each other.

"I don't want to have this conversation anymore."

"Fine. There's nothing left to say anyway." The bitterness in Michael's tone is like a knife twisting deep inside my very soul. It feels as if he's cut me loose. I feel adrift and alone, as I walk away from him.

Weary, I climb the stairs leaving Michael to close down the house. I get ready for bed, slipping on an old grey t-shirt and check on my sleeping babies, relieved that they'll be asleep for a few more hours. I look at our master bed and contemplate if I should sleep there or sleep in one of the kids' rooms down the hall.

I keep making the same mistakes. I just keep making them. I check my cell phone and see the number three by the text message symbol.

They'll be from Court. He's been texting me on a regular basis. For the most part, I've ignored them, but now I slide my thumb over the symbol.

*E, congrats on the twins. C*

*I know ur busy. I was just TOY.*

*E, I need to talk to u. When can we meet? C*

How does the man know about the twins already? *Lisa.*

Dr. Lisa Chatham confuses me. She's supportive of my relationship with Michael and then there is this other part where she champions Court Chandler in this innocent-third-party-sharing-information-about-Ellie kind of way.

*"About what; exactly?"* I text to Court now.

*"Ur there?"* He texts back.

*"For a min."*

*"I need to talk to u."*

*"So you said. About what; exactly?"* I text back.

*"Us."*

His answer causes my heart to race. My hand shakes as I put the cell down on the night stand. After a minute, I pick it back up again.

*"Where? When?"*

*"Fri. 10 am. BI Ferry. pk me up."*

*"Ok. But, untenable."* I write back.

*"But real enough."* He texts back to me.

I should text back and cancel this whole thing, but I don't. No. I lock my cell phone and put it on the charger and guiltily climb into bed and turn out the light.

A few minutes later, Michael comes in and slides into the covers beside me. I pretend to be asleep, even when he kisses me good-night. I shift and turn away from him, so he can't sense my pound-ing heart, which beats with equal measures of excitement and guilt at making plans to meet Court.

*What am I doing? Why am I doing it?*

# Chapter Twenty-nine

 *Keeping Secrets*

Many forces are at play all beyond my control. After twenty-one days of being a mother to two newborns, again, I realize this. I've forgotten how sleep deprivation works. It's a slow decay of the senses. I'd forgotten that. I stand at the washer, trying to determine if I ran the load or not. The clothes are somewhat damp, but they don't smell of fabric softener, so I program the load to be washed, perhaps, again. I paste a post-it note over the detergent dispenser and scribble: "Ellie, put in the dryer."

It's Wednesday. I know this because Michael went back to work today. I'm on my own.

Mathew and Emily are at summer camp. Carrie will be dropping them off later today. I'm looking forward to it, if only because it will fill in the awkward silence between Michael and me.

I keep making mistakes. I just keep making them.

I'm still scheduled to meet up with Court this Friday morning, more than two weeks beyond our original planned liaison. Two more days from now. I feel anguish and excitement at the same time, just thinking of him.

I just keep making mistakes. I seem to embrace the mistakes. Follow them around and make bigger ones than the ones I've already made. *What is wrong with me? What is wrong with Ellie Shaw?* Why does she try to recapture the fictitious life of Elaina Miles? *Why?*

The old house has sold. I've already deposited the check into my savings account, mine, not our joint one. But, do I tell Michael? No. And, I ask Robert not to tell him, either. I've already transferred the two hundred thousand that Michael borrowed from Robert back into my ex-husband's account, but I don't tell Michael about that either.

I'm waiting for something. I'm not sure what, but I'm busy making plans. I book a trip for two to Italy. I find a villa similar to the one that Court and I stayed in and make a reservation for two weeks around Valentine's Day to be there. I'm extravagant with these plans, buying first class tickets from Seattle to Rome, leaving on the 5th of February and staying at villa that is private and decadent for two whole weeks. But, even I don't know who I'm going to take with me. I do all of this without telling Michael. Keeping secrets, making plans, making mistakes over and over. This is what I do, when I'm not caring for the twins and Mathew and Emily.

By mid-morning, I finally have the babies down for a nap. Already exhausted, I pull off my wig and stand in front of the bathroom mirror. My hair is slowly coming back in. I look like a boy with this quarter inch blonde crew cut. That's me. There are new dark circles under my eyes and I trace them with my index finger.

The crimson scars at my breasts are healing, but they're still there and I trace them, too. I turn away from the mirror with a feeling of disgust and disappointment.

I'm Ellie. The woman, who keeps secrets and makes mistakes over and over.

I should cancel my plans with Court. I should cancel my plans with Court. *If I keep thinking this over and over, will I do this? Cancel my plans with Court?* I sink into the bath water and slide all the way under, sloshing water over the sides of the tub. I only come up for air, when I can no longer hold my breath. The hot water feels good on my body, as if, it is cleansing me all the way to my soul. My mind drifts. I think about Court. This is what happens when I let my mind wander. *Why do I do this?* I love Michael. I love Michael. I love Michael. Why do I think about Court, when I love Michael? *Why do I do this? Why?*

I'm fighting some kind of depression. That's what this is. I think about Court because I have happy memories with him, not so with Michael. There's been too much grief, too much devastation, too much sadness with Michael. The happy moments have been too few. It's not enough. It's not. *I love Michael; don't I?*

I finish my bath and tell myself to think of nothing. Nothing. Nothing.

With shaking hands, I get dressed in black slacks and a white blouse. I pick up my cell.

*"I can't see u."* I text to Court.

*"Why?"*

*"Just can't."* I text.

*"Can't or won't?"* His petulance makes me smile. The man is used to getting what he wants when he wants it.

*"Both."* I text back.

Our communiqué is interrupted by a cell phone call from Lisa. "Dr. Chatham," I say with irritation.

"Hi. Am I interrupting something?" Lisa asks. I detect the hint of sarcasm in her contrived cheeriness. I don't trust that voice. The woman is clairvoyant at times.

"No, of course not," I say. Too quickly.

"Yeah, sure." I hear her sigh. "Look. You were supposed to be here at ten this morning. It's Wednesday. I guess you forgot."

"I did," I say in this small voice.

"Are you okay?" Lisa asks in her best clinical searching tone.

"I'm...I'm fucking tired."

"You need a nanny. Why are you being so stubborn about that?"

"I don't know."

"Look, Ellie, you cannot take on the whole world. You're recovering from having twins and from fighting cancer. You can't do everything."

"Did Michael put you up to this?"

"Noooooo," Lisa doesn't lie as well as me, not that my finesse with lying has been stellar lately.

My ego still smarts from the heated exchange with Michael, three weeks before.

She sighs. "He's worried about you. I'm worried about you. You need to keep your stress levels low. You need a nanny!"

I give in to the argument that Michael and I have been having for days about getting help. "Fine," I say with a heavy sigh.

The truth is I can't fight Michael and Lisa, too. The immensity of my life weighs me down.

Lisa doesn't miss a beat. "Fine," she says. "She'll be there this afternoon. I've re-scheduled your appointment for ten on Friday."

"Friday?" My upcoming liaison with Court evaporates at her words.

"Is there something wrong with Friday?" Lisa asks with an edge to her voice.

"No. Friday's great."

"Great. Ellie, have some tea, drink some water, eat something, and go take a nap. We'll be there at one this afternoon."

"You will? Lisa, you're a great friend," I say.

"Not as great as I should be," she says to me now.

Her gentle tone unleashes tears I've been holding back for weeks now. They stream down my face as I end the call.

I can only stare at Rachael Williams. She is twenty-five, having graduated from Seattle University five years before. She just finished serving in the Peace Corps. She loves children. She loves

Bainbridge Island. Her husband of three years is serving his last tour of duty in Afghanistan. She is intent on working for the next year as a nanny while she waits for his return. She is intrigued about a family with four children. She has no problem living in a smaller home. She doesn't mind getting up at night with babies. She did this in the Peace Corps, quite often, she assures me at one point.

She's perfect. I'm in awe of her. Rachael Williams is amazing. At twenty-five, she has done more living than I could ever have hoped to have done, I tell her. She looks at me in surprise when I say this. Her grey-blue eyes search my face. She swings her long, braided dark hair behind her back and smiles at me. She is pretty in a Peace-Corps-saving-the-world kind of way. Her beauty comes through with her easy smile and the sparkle of her incredible eyes. Rachael has the kind of beauty that doesn't need to be made up every day. I feel this stab of envy and find myself unable to look away. There's something about her that's so familiar and I just can't place it.

"You just gave birth to twins and survived breast cancer," she says to me now. "I think you underestimate yourself, Mrs. Shaw."

"If you're going to take the job, I insist that you call me Ellie," I say with a laugh. I give her my best yeah-team smile. I watch its immediate impact on her as she smiles back at me.

"Okay," Rachael says with a laugh. "I'll take it."

I glance over at Lisa. "How did you find her?" I ask when Rachael leaves the room for a few minutes.

"I didn't."

"Then, who did?"

Lisa gives me a twisted smile. "Court Chandler."

I take in air and am unable to let it out. I get up and look out the window. Slowly, I allow myself to breathe again. "Damn it, Lisa. You're not helping me out here," I say, uncertain.

"He insisted. He said you would love her."

"I do." I look over at Lisa. I helplessly lift my arms and wince at the pain it causes at my chest. "I'm drowning here."

"I know." Lisa gives me this measured look. "I took the liberty of prescribing something for you. I think you're combating depression. The list is long as to why, but I think for now, we should just deal with it. I'm recommending a therapist, too."

"I don't need a therapist!"

"No? You think most people can go through what you've been through this past year and not have any repercussions from it? Your marriage is going swimmingly, right now, huh?" I avoid meeting her gaze. "I'm fielding phone calls from *everybody*."

"Like who?"

"Carrie. Robert. Michael. Court. Stephen thinks I'm over-reacting, but I don't think so. I'm worried about you, Ellie. Court told me about the episode in Paris. You never told me about that."

"It wasn't that big of deal." I stare back at her.

"It *is* a big deal. Ellie, I want to help you." Lisa stands too, and towers over me. "I want to see you…happy."

"I'm happy." Tears gather at my lashes. Lisa hands me the pills.

"There's a sixty-day supply. Take one a day and let's see where we're at in a couple of months."

"Fine." I finger the pill packet, take a deep breath, and finally ask the question I need help in answering. "Should I see him?"

I stare at her, willing her to answer. "Yes," Lisa finally says.

"What made you change your mind?" Court asks. He absently twirls the stem of his wine glass as we sit at the corner table of *The Pink Door*, drinking chardonnay in the middle of the afternoon.

Lisa's answer released some sort of hold on me. I left the house inside of an hour to go meet Court in downtown Seattle, leaving my babies behind in the capable hands of Rachel Williams and a dismayed Lisa Chatham.

"Not sure," I say with hesitant smile. "I wanted to say...thank you."

Court gives me an uncertain look. "Ellie, I just left in the middle of a major meeting with the board to be here with you. I didn't do it so you could *thank me*."

His irritability makes me laugh. He looks angry with me for a moment, then that charming crooked grin spreads across his face.

"I can think of a number of ways that you *could* thank me though," he says with a laugh.

I nod in answer. "I just want to say thank you for being so amazing, for taking care of me in Paris when the world was so dark. Thank you for being *you*, Court."

He's looking at me in that special way of his, the one that makes me want to breathe him in forever. Court personifies the finest Cabernet, the finest cognac, the best drug—all addicting, but too much for the mind, body and soul, all at once. I experience this longing for him, while at the same time I realize I'll never see him again. I return his gaze and betray my sadness at this discovery.

"Ellie," he groans with clairvoyance. "We can make this work." I hear the desperation in his tone and steal myself against feeling anything more for him.

"We could. And, it would be wonderful." I take a deep breath and try to smile. "But, there are too many people we we'd hurt in the process." I look at him more closely. "Eve," I say and watch him shudder. I nod and take another breath. "And, I love Michael."

I watch the truth of my words cut across his handsome face, chasing a variety of emotions. First he's incredulous, then stunned, and finally resigned. I covertly ride the wave of emotions with him.

"On a secret list, you're my only wish, Court. But, I have Michael and Mathew and Emily and now, Ava and Beau to think of. All these other wishes on another list I'm choosing," I say.

"Ellie."

Court finishes his wine glass and flashes me his crooked smile filled with pain. "We can't be friends," he finally says.

"I know."

I lean over the table and he meets me halfway. Our kiss is devoid of promise and filled with this incalculable heartbreak. I close my eyes and savor this last moment with him. Then, he pulls away me.

I hear his chair scrape the wood floor and open my eyes. He towers above me. The flash of his crooked smile is the last thing I see of him as he leaves.

Now, there are even more secrets from Michael: my secret rendezvous with Court, Court's goodbye kiss, the feelings that I acknowledge for Court as the secret wish I can never have. The whole afternoon, I secretly indulge in the last moments with Court; of being with him as if experiencing my very last high and all the guilt that arrives with it, in feeling this way about him.

By the end of the afternoon, I'm worn out. Yet, I hide behind a mask of nonchalance with Lisa. Her scrutiny upon my return was bad enough and keeping up the detachment about my meeting with Court is draining me now.

Her constant question all afternoon: "Are you okay?"

"I'm fine." My answer comes with a smile every time she asks.

I let go of the breath I've held all afternoon when I watch Lisa leave. I just wave at her last call out from the car, promising to call me first thing in the morning.

Upstairs, I stash the medication Lisa gave me in our master bathroom after taking one of the pills, chasing it down with a fresh glass of red wine, even as I read the label stating no alcohol.

*Fuck it. Fuck it. Fuck all of it.*

Rachael is busy fixing dinner. She's already finished the laundry. With every task she completes, I feel a little bit of this heavy burden lift from me, although I'm being assailed by all the others: guilt, remorse, and loss. I've shown her around the house and outlined some of the routines, as if there's been any semblance of routines over the last year.

I've put her in Elaina's old room for now and briefly explain the tragedy of Nick and Elaina. Apparently, I've explained it well enough so that when I am through telling this heartbreaking story, Rachael cries and I comfort her as much as myself.

Fresh from summer camp, Emily is already in love with Rachael. My six-year-old pulls Rachael into her world. The joy is evident on Emily's face as she describes her favorite movie, her most loved book, and most treasured stuffed animal. Rachael listens intently. Later, she easily converses with Mathew and Emily, while preparing dinner as the kids sit chatting with her at the kitchen table. There's a sense of peace settling over all of us that has been absent for months. Rachael Williams is magical; she touches all of us in some way.

I keep vigilance for Michael. When the headlights of the silver Mercedes finally light up the drive, I go out to the garage to meet him. *So many secrets.* I feel the weight of them as I watch Michael alight from my SUV. He's been leaving the new one for me, although I've been too tired and too intimidated by its size to take it anywhere. I borrowed Lisa's car for my secret rendezvous earlier.

*Secrets. Secrets. I keep too many.*

"Hi," I say. Shy now; overcome with guilt and misery all at the same time. I basically tremble in Michael's presence.

"Hi," he says, uncertain.

Our fight from three weeks before has spilled over into a détente kind of existence. He's wary of me, now. And, I have so much to be sorry for. I've made so many mistakes and it seems I'm intent on making them still. I take a deep breath.

"We...have a nanny."

"We do?" Michaels ask in surprise.

"Lisa brought her over. She's amazing. She's..."

My words die on my lips, as I realize who Rachael is. I know why she's so familiar to me. Her mannerisms, her easygoing nature, her enthusiasm for life—she's Courtney Chandler in the female form—and his sister. The story of his kid sister comes rushing back. I turn away from Michael.

"Ellie, what is it?"

"You should meet her," I say in defeat. "She's an angel, but she can't stay."

"Why not?"

I don't answer him. I just retreat to the house. My steps are heavy with this crushing sadness. From faraway, I watch Rachael as she takes care of my children. She carries Ava while she checks on dinner and then stops to play with Beau in the baby swing. Rachel seems to be in four places at once with all of my children. The smile upon her face is so much like Court's. I'm momentarily mesmerized by it.

Rachael introduces herself to Michael. I listen in this absent way as she tells him about the Peace Corps and her husband, Thomas. I look at Michael, while he carries on this easy conversation with Rachael about Afghanistan. Michael knows all about Afghanistan and I'm taken aback that I've never known this about him before.

"You look familiar to me," Michael says with a shake of his head. "Have we met before?"

"I don't think so," Rachael says. "I probably remind you of my brother. He's been all over the news." She gets this vague look. Her eyes widen as she studies my face and I can see her putting together the puzzle pieces of the news stories about her brother's affair with an older woman. She gets this uncertain look.

"Your brother?" Michael asks.

I shudder. Here we go. I should have told him, even though I didn't officially know, I should have told him. It wasn't my secret.

It wasn't intentional, but I should have told him. I watch Michael, now, as Rachael says his name.

"Yes," Rachel says in confusion. "Court Chandler. He's my brother." She looks at me. "Ellie, do you know him?"

"I see," Michael says.

All the enthusiasm for this girl leaves his face all at once. He looks over at me and gives me a bitter smile.

"Well, Ellen Kay, I see you have it all worked out."

"It's not like that," I say in a low voice.

I'm instantly filled with guilt, shame, and foreboding, knowing what this latest mistake will cost me now as Michael abruptly gets up and leaves. Fear courses through me at his look of disappointment and something else, the acceptance of defeat.

"Did I say something wrong?" Rachael asks of me now.

"No," I say. "Let me talk to him."

There are too many secrets and they catch up to me. I climb the stairs two at a time. My chest aches with the rapid movement. I run down the hall to our closed bedroom door, rush at it, close and lock it behind me, as if, somehow, by doing so, I can keep him here.

"Michael." The closet light is on and my heart starts pounding fast. "Don't do this."

"Don't do what?" His voice is muffled.

I race to the closet. He's going through his clothes, jamming them into a suitcase.

"Don't…leave…me."

He shakes his head. "I keep breaking my promise to you. I keep saying I'll stay that I'll never leave you again, but I always do." His speech is slow, sad, and heartbreaking. "The thing is…I don't want this anymore, not like this. This constant fighting. All the secrets you keep, Ellen Kay. I don't want any of that anymore."

"I don't either." I wipe away sudden tears, desperate now.

"I don't want that either. I don't know why I've kept things from you," I say with anguish. "Michael…you have to believe me, when I tell you that I didn't know who she was. I didn't figure it out, until I told you about her and when I described her, only then, did I realize who she reminded me of. He talked about her once and I remembered he said she was a saint and served in the Peace Corps, while her husband served in Afghanistan. I'm sorry. I should have told you. I just wanted you to meet her, to get a moment of happiness with her, before I tell her she can't stay."

His continued silence crushes me. I feel the weight of it as if it is a physical thing. I stagger towards him, trying to keep my balance and grab on to him even as he tries to push me away. I gasp in pain as we both fall to the floor. He stops fighting me, lies still beneath me, and takes a deep breath as if it is his last.

"Ellie, I want you to be happy," Michael says. "And, if I can't make you happy…if it's Court Chandler." He sighs. "So be it."

"I have to tell you everything, Michael."

I grasp his face with my hands, imploring him to look at me. There's another long silence between us. He takes another deep breath.

"Okay, then tell me," he finally says to me. "Tell me everything, Ellen Kay."

"Bobby and I sold the house. Some all cash deal. I paid him back the loan of two hundred and put the rest of it in the bank in my account. I wanted to tell you, but after our fight about Carrie and your insecurities about Court…" I sigh. "I didn't tell you. I *should* have told you. We should decide what to do with the money. Pay off the house, invest some of it? I don't know. We should decide…" He's looking at me with even more distrust, not the reaction I was hoping for. "I have a trip for Italy planned around our anniversary. Two weeks, just you and me. I know it will be sad, but I think we should go. I think Nick and Elaina would want us to go." I take a deep breath and intently focus on Michael's face. "Court texted me last week. He wanted to meet with me. I said no, then, I said yes, then, I said no."

My words begin to register; jealousy traverses his features. I start to waver on my commitment to tell him everything.

"You should see him," Michael says, stunned. "You need to figure out what you want."

With a jagged breath, I let go of one of my last secrets. "I went and saw him today. To say good-bye. To end it. Forever." Michael's body shudders beneath mine. I sense his doubt. He holds his breath, just waiting. "We said goodbye. I kissed him goodbye. It's over." I look at him with guilt and newfound terror as the idea of him leaving me again takes hold. "It's *over*."

Michael sighs and shakes his head. "I don't know what you want from me."

"I want you. Only you. And, that's what I told him, Michael. I told Court I love you. I choose you and now he understands that and so do I." My fierceness surprises him. It surprises me, too.

I give away my last secret, an easy one. "I talked to Lisa. She thinks I'm suffering from depression. She prescribed something for it and wants me to see a therapist."

I see the intensity in his blue eyes as he stares at me. "I need you, Michael. I can't do this by myself. I can't do this without you. That's it. No more secrets. Now, you know everything I know," I say.

*Silence.* It pervades this enclosed space and the two of us.

I feel his heartbeat beneath my hands. Its steady rhythm is so fast and true. *Like Michael.* He has always been there for me.

*And I? I have to go way back to remember when I've really been there for him.*

The remorse in realizing this is instantaneous and painful. I bite my lip to keep it from trembling as fresh tears slide down my face onto his.

Anguish and uncertainty parade across his features. Finally, I see acceptance and maybe even the beginning of trust come over him. I caress his clenched jaw and finally feel it relax beneath my fingertips. He begins to smile that gorgeous white smile of his and soon his physical desire betrays him.

I smile through my own tears and shift my weight, moving in closer. My intentions clear.

"I love you, Michael. I've always loved you. I choose you. Only you."

His body moves beneath mine. "I love you, Ellen Kay. You're my only wish."

And, I finally believe him. I feel his love and my love for him down to my very soul. My own truth bursts forth. "You're mine," I say in wonder.

The truth is simple.

It's always been Michael and me.

# EPILOGUE

## Celebrations

*T*enable, capable of being defended, maintained, held, and more than real—this is Michael and me. We've been married for more than a year and have survived the first anniversaries that mark tragic losses of Nick and Elaina and almost each other. We're a new family—renewed, transformed, and happy again. Beau and Ava are eight months old; Mathew is fourteen and Emily just turned seven.

A big summer celebration is being planned for the twins' first birthday and, somehow, the survival of me with my new bodacious tah tahs as well as my fortieth birthday are being included in these party plans. Carrie and Lisa are working out the details, while Michael and I are in Europe. A trip completely planned by Michael.

Today, we lounge by the amazing pool at our private villa that overlooks the vast blue of the Mediterranean Sea in Napoli. In two days, we'll return home after spending three weeks in Paris and the last week here in Italy.

I miss my children, but they're in good hands with Rachael Williams and her husband Thomas, who has finally returned from Afghanistan for good. Thomas and Rachael are busy moving into our old house on Bainbridge Island that her brother Court mysteriously bought for them. As soon as I put this together, I told Michael. He'd just laughed, shook his head side-to-side and said, "Ellen Kay, your charm knows no bounds."

Court is busy with his wife, Eve, awaiting the birth of their first child or so I've heard. Rachael knows that her brother is a touchy subject at the Shaw household.

My depression is gone; cancer, too. I take only vitamins, now. My hair has grown back. I wear it in the latest short chic style, a Victoria Beckham kind of thing that Gianna assures me is all the rage. It's a nice honey-blonde, a shade or two darker than my former long blonde locks, but Michael likes it this way. As, do I.

My therapist has encouraged me to write down my feelings about loss, love, and life. This has transcended into the semblance of a story that Harriet wants to publish. I'm going to call it, *Wishes*. I've already written the dedication to Michael and the kids, all of them.

Here's what I know to be true: relationships are tested in all kinds of ways and it is the endings we are unprepared for, so I no longer take anyone or anything for granted. I no longer strive for perfection in myself or others or my life because I've learned to embrace and trust everything good: true friends, family, and Michael.

Michael.

Our time away together has been well spent. We've put away the past, addressed our insecurities, and shared all our secrets. Our trust is this impenetrable bond, a force within us both that grows stronger each day. There are no questions between us any longer. There is no one else, but us.

I glance over at Michael and smile. My golden god is deliriously happy, too, and gives me a knowing look as I stand up and stretch in my new white swimsuit he bought for me in town a few days ago.

"Babe," I say to him. "What do you want to do today?"

Michael sits up from the lounge chair with this evocative look.

"I was thinking along the lines of something to remember Italy by, kind of like the private tour of the Eiffel Tower in Paris," he says with a secret smile.

I strut over to him, blocking the sun's rays from his handsome face as I stand above him. My tanned legs touch each side of his long body where he lies beneath me.

"You're in luck, Dr. Shaw. I have plenty of time to work on something to remember Italy by."

I settle myself down on top of him. We intertwine our fingers and gaze at each other with this recognizable trust.

"I've got time," I say.

"Tenable—capable of being defended, maintained, held; and more than real, Ellen Kay," he says.

I smile in answer.

This is Michael and me.

# *Acknowledgements*

Writing is something that I have been doing my entire life. It is only the last few years that the timing has been just right to focus upon it full-time. I've been encouraged by so many: family, friends, colleagues, teachers and readers, of course. *Thank you, all of you, for your encouragement, support, and love.* I know I'm not easy to live with or love, when it comes down to it, especially when I'm in the throes of writing and often appear disengaged when you try to talk to me. Just know, somewhere in there, I'm listening or, at the very least, stealing your story, your ideas, your words, your phrasing, your expressions, your name, and/or aspects of your life for my next novel. *Deal with it.* It's just fiction after all. Again, thank you *so much* for reading my work.

Katherine Clare Owen

# Q & A Discussion of Not To Us

Hello readers,

I have received many questions and/or comments about *Not To Us*. It is one of those stories that contains so many thought-provoking elements that it leads to all kinds of discussion. I've provided a question and answer from an author's perspective, *mine*, on some of the finer points below.

## Is this a memoir or fiction?

This is fiction. All of these characters were made up by me and in no way reflect real people. Ellie's strive for perfection and her feeling of inadequacy in never quite measuring up were universal traits I've observed that I wanted to explore. I wondered: What happens in a relationship that seems to have everything? What happens when one is betrayed? By a husband? By a best friend? What happens to a person when they're confronted with a life-threatening illness? Does he or she strive to change their course? Choose a different path?

I considered these to be thought provoking, at the very least, and wanted to write a story where these volatile, life-altering situations take place and explore how characters might handle them. Also, the idea of being married to someone else, while being in love with another, intrigued me. There's no hidden meaning; I just wondered what a person would do if given an alternative path. Would they take it?

I wanted to explore how a friendship influences the choices one makes over a lifetime and also how a best friend's betrayal affects that. There's also the fragility of relationships one has over a lifetime. I wanted to consider other character traits such as the strive for perfection and how it governs what people act upon and don't act upon. These were all intriguing to me. In *Not To Us*, both Michael and Ellie strive to do the right thing most of the time, but they both respond to grief in the same kind of way, seeking consolation from others, not trusting each other or themselves, until the very end. I wanted to write about how tragedy can change or alter a person's life and even, perhaps, change their life choices.

## What made you want to write a book about breast cancer?

I would argue this book is never really about breast cancer. Cancer is a side issue, while the rest of Ellie's life falls apart. I don't want to be too specific because some of you read the last pages first, but this is about one woman's journey in discovering who she really is and what she really wants, when her life tragically falls apart and she has to make choices. A subset of this theme is the impact that grief and loss have on all of the characters in this story, though the main focus resides with Michael and Ellie.

Obviously, it's mostly Ellie's story, told from her point of view, but readers get a sense of all the other characters that touch her life in some way. Keep in mind the first two lines of the book: *There are all kinds of ways for a relationship to be tested, even broken, irrevocably. It's the endings that we're unprepared for.*

*Not To Us* deals with a lot of different relationships throughout the story that are broken or end, some irrevocably.

## Can you talk about Carrie?

Carrie was such an intriguing character to write. Many can relate to having a friend like this—the most attractive, the most popular, the most sought after—a taker, in the extreme. The friendship Ellie has with Carrie exemplifies the stamp of longevity, even permanence. On the surface, they seem to be friends for all the right reasons. Yet, Ellie doesn't realize what's really happening beneath, until she discovers that Carrie has committed the ultimate best friend betrayal. I think readers can relate to a friendship like this. It's someone one gravitates toward, someone who isn't necessarily good for them and never has their best interests in mind, yet the friendship is pursued.

I wanted to further explore the idea of two women who have been friends since college and subtly bring to light how this friendship has influenced their lives and their choices. I wanted to examine the other side of the relationship when something happens that tears them apart. In this story, betrayal was consequential and devastating. And then, it happens more than once! Ah, but the pattern is set in Carrie; isn't it?

Check out the passage of Ellie's inner dialog in the elevator (Chapter 16):

*Am I Carrie, now? I sway with the movement of the elevator. I close my eyes and try to think. I could never be Carrie. No one can. That's the thing. Always. I could never be Carrie. I could never be Carrie. I could never be Carrie. I can feel the tears sting behind my eyes. I can never be Carrie. Now, I can't even be Ellie.*

This is the epitome of Ellie. She could never be Carrie; this is her biggest insecurity and began at the beginning of their relationship and set the pattern for the choices Ellie made for her adult life early on. Yet, what does Carrie reveal to her before Ellie's about to marry Michael? Carrie felt she could never be Ellie. Carrie always knew Michael loved Ellie even while she was married to him.

$\wp$

### Why did you approach the opening the way you did?

Some readers wanted me to change the beginning to better emphasize the confrontation of Ellie seeing Robert and Carrie together three weeks earlier when she first learned of their affair, but I think seeing how Ellie (silently) deals with this blow is more telling of her character. Her strive for perfection, her denial of reality, and even her guilt over her attraction to Michael are all revealed in that first chapter.

There's something Michael says in the very beginning of the book that is all telling, too: *"Because, now, you need someone more than ever. Someone who loves you more."* This reveals Ellie and Michael exceptionally well. There's always been this secret attraction between them and now they are finally acting upon it, a big step for both of them. Yet, neither one of them would have taken it, if not for Robert and Carrie becoming involved first.

### What about when Ellie leaves?

The story is from Ellie's point of view and I really tried to show the mental breakdown that was taking place within her, while still writing in her point of view. Her thinking when she leaves Michael is not sound. She's desperate, despondent, and spinning out of control. In her mind, she's just lost Michael and feels she's lost all of her wishes, except Emily and Mathew and, at this point, she doesn't know how to hold on to the two of them anymore either. This is why she leaves.

Before long, she also reveals her feelings of inadequacy about Carrie which affects so many aspects of her life, including her relationship with Michael and her feelings for him. She's running away from her life, grief, and cancer—all of her remaining fears. In Ellie's mind, she's lost everything, including herself.

### *Tell us about Court Chandler.*

Court was a minor character in the early drafts. I didn't even take their relationship all that far in the early versions of this story. But, he kept coming back to me with more to say. Court is young and successful, yet he yearns for something he doesn't have and seems to find it in Ellie.

Ellie isn't caught up in his status, power, or money. Court is attracted to her early on because of her naiveté; she doesn't even know who he is. Then, when he finds out she's heartbroken and pregnant, he has to help her because a family is something Court wants. Yet, it's missing from his own life.

Court's engaging and charming, personifying an older version of the young sixteen-year-old Nick Bradford. This wasn't intentional. It just worked out that way, once the story came together. It effectively explains Ellie's attraction to him. Court served as a way for Ellie to deal with her grief and loss of Nick. On a subconscious level, he fulfills a void in her life for a while she never even fully realizes. There's something innocent about their love for each other; it's just like the first love between Nick and Elaina that Ellie recognizes early on.

The pivotal moment for Ellie with Court Chandler is his reaction to her when he finds out she has cancer. It is the complete opposite to Michael's first response. It clearly shows the distinctions between these two men. Michael's impassioned desire to save her is so evident from the very beginning in comparison to Court's response, "I can't go through that again." This was a defining moment for Ellie. It just took the rest of the story for her to recognize who loves her more and who she loves the most.

### *What's your favorite scene?*

The scene between Michael and Ellie at the basketball game was fun to write. Everyone's watching the two of them. Ellie hasn't seen him for three months and her life has completely changed and fallen apart. Michael is this amazing man and the reader can already sense how he feels about Ellie from just this scene alone. I also loved when Michael showed her the beach house where he reveals he has bought the house for her and their blended family—Michael, the caretaker, as always.

## *What was most difficult to write about?*

Chapter fourteen came out of nowhere and I couldn't get it out of my mind. It ended up being the turning point for the story. I kept asking myself: what happens when someone is focused on something threatening like breast cancer, but then loses something else? Writing this scene was so profound and heartbreaking; it changes the course of the story. It showed how tragedy can break up a family or affect someone so deeply that they experience a lapse in judgment or lose faith and trust in the ones they care about the most. It happens to Michael, and then, Ellie.

Next, all the scenes with Michael and Ellie fighting with each other or displaying their distrust were difficult to get just right. These are all from Ellie's point of view and yet the reader has to understand what is going on with Michael as well. A lot of Michael's personality comes through in his actions and what he does and doesn't say; and then, there's the whole Court Chandler angle. I didn't want it to be the old cliché about being jealous of somebody else's money and youth and it's not that simple for Michael, even though he says this at one point. Ultimately, it is about who loves her most and Michael know this. He loves her enough to let her go, but Ellie has to see this and believe it first.

The overriding theme to the story is about Ellie and her ability to trust and love another person. She has to make a personal journey in self-introspection and learn to trust herself first, something she's never allowed herself to do.

Then, she needs to put her trust into Michael and their relationship. That's the turning point at the end of the book after she says her final goodbye to Court and finally admits to Michael she needs his help and tells him she's chosen him. It's more than words when she finally admits this. Ellie discovers the truth within herself in realizing Michael has always been there for her. It's very powerful.

## *How about Kimberley Powers?*

Kimberley Powers is one of my favorite characters. She has a minor role in *Not To Us*, but plays a major role in another novel of mine called *Seeing Julia*. My favorite characteristic of Kimberley is the way she handles Court and even Ellie. In a way, she serves as a mentor for them both, clearly demonstrating how to stand up for what she believes in. Kimberley serves as a catalyst in calling out the relationship between Court and Ellie. She brings them straight back to reality when she finds out Ellie's been missing her chemotherapy treatments and this revelation reveals Court's insensitivity and his own character flaws.

## *What about Dr. Lisa Chatham?*

Lisa serves as a loyal friend and a different point of view from a medical standpoint from Dr. Michael Shaw, the extraordinary surgeon. Lisa is not afraid of disagreeing with Michael or Carrie or even Ellie's talented, but traditional medical team comprised of: Josh, Ben, and Tom. She's honest and forthright and this helps Ellie in a way become her own person and decide what she wants.

I love the scene between the two of them on the phone when Ellie is trying to find out about the paternity results and Lisa is shredding her about ditching her at the office the day before.

*Ellie says, "Can you...please...just be my one true friend...?"* This dialog begins to reveal the changes taking place in Ellie in recognizing who she can really trust. All her adult life, Ellie has had Carrie as her best friend. Yet, here is her newly-formed friendship with Lisa where Ellie already recognizes Lisa is her one true friend.

### *What's next?*

I'm hard at work writing other projects. I'm very excited about these stories as well and hope to provide updates as to their release on my website/blog (See below).

### *How can we reach you?*

My website/blog is at: www.katherineclareowen.com. Please stop by and leave a comment or two. *Thank you* for reading my work.

9 780983 570707